Thomas Belsham

Memoirs of the Late Reverend Theophilus Lindsey

Thomas Belsham

Memoirs of the Late Reverend Theophilus Lindsey

ISBN/EAN: 9783337016227

Printed in Europe, USA, Canada, Australia, Japan

Cover: Foto ©Raphael Reischuk / pixelio.de

More available books at **www.hansebooks.com**

MEMOIRS

OF THE LATE REVEREND

THEOPHILUS LINDSEY, M.A.

INCLUDING

A BRIEF ANALYSIS OF HIS WORKS;

TOGETHER WITH

ANECDOTES AND LETTERS OF EMINENT PERSONS,

HIS FRIENDS AND CORRESPONDENTS:

ALSO

A GENERAL VIEW OF THE PROGRESS OF THE UNITARIAN
DOCTRINE IN ENGLAND AND AMERICA.

By THOMAS BELSHAM,

MINISTER OF THE CHAPEL IN ESSEX STREET.

Simulacra vultus, imbecilla ac mortalia; forma mentis, æterna,
quam tenere et exprimere tuis ipse moribus possis.   *Tacitus.*
Care . . . . Vale. At veniet felicius ævum
Quando iterum tecum, sim modo dignus, ero.   *Lowth.*

THE CENTENARY VOLUME.

LONDON:
WILLIAMS AND NORGATE,
14, HENRIETTA STREET, COVENT GARDEN;
AND
20, SOUTH FREDERICK STREET, EDINBURGH.
1873.

LONDON :
PRINTED BY WOODFALL AND KINDER,
MILFORD LANE, STRAND, W.C.

PREFACE TO THE CENTENARY VOLUME.

It was in November, 1773, that this venerable man, Theophilus Lindsey, when over fifty years of age, and in the enjoyment of a rich living in the Church of England, surrounded also by many friends, and with the certain prospect of a bishopric, resigned all the comforts of an elegant home, and all chances of preferment, for the sake of what he esteemed to be Christ's truth and a good conscience. He became a Dissenter when dissent was very much despised, and Dissenters generally shunned. He also openly avowed his Unitarian views when these sentiments were nearly everywhere abhorred. From a commanding sense of duty he left the Church when he knew not where to find a home for himself and wife; and sold his library and some other effects to supply for a time the necessaries of life. In 1774 he came from the North to London, and founded Essex-street Chapel—probably the first distinctly named Unitarian congregation in England. And now, after the lapse of one hundred years, we confidently affirm that Lindsey's theological views are becoming daily more widely known and honoured; and we are inclined to believe they will remain as a pyramid for ever on the landscape of religious truth, to guide into all truth; while his integrity, like a star, will lead onward the theological inquirer to be sincere, not to palter with words in a double sense, or to tamper with conscience. It is surely better to suffer affliction for what we esteem to be truth, than to enjoy the emoluments or positions of dishonesty. This reprint is now published to advance the highest moral and religious interests of society at the suggestion of Mr. Samuel Sharpe, of Highbury, London, whose zeal for the Unitarian Christian faith is only surpassed by his admiration of the sincere and upright of all denominations. It is possible that this volume may induce other members of the Unitarian Church to republish, in a cheap form, some valuable religious works which are little known to the present generation. The best monument that any one can leave behind—next to the memory of a good life—is a good book that may reach the homes of all our people.

ROBERT SPEARS.

73, Angell Road, London,
November, 1873.

PREFACE.

THE publication of this tribute of respect to the memory of a highly venerated friend has been delayed beyond expectation, partly by a necessary attention to other publications, but chiefly by the time which was occupied in the perusal of letters and other documents, which far exceeded what was antecedently supposed to be requisite.

The events which occur in the life of a scholar and a pastor seldom possess novelty and variety sufficient to excite public attention. Those of Mr. Lindsey's life, indeed, were of no common complexion. But the chief design of publishing this Memoir is to exhibit the picture of an eminently virtuous, pious, and disinterested mind in circumstances of great difficulty and perplexity, as an example to others who may find themselves in similar difficulties, and as an encouragement to sacrifice every secular consideration in the cause of religious truth, and to prefer the performance of duty and the approbation of conscience to all the honours and emoluments which the world can offer. It was also the author's design to mark the progress of that glorious cause which lay nearest to the heart of this venerable man, that of a long-lost and almost-forgotten truth, the proper Unity of God, and the supreme unrivalled undivided homage which is due to the Father alone : a cause for which he voluntarily sacrificed all his secular possessions and expectations, to the promotion of which he devoted all his labours, and in testimony to which he would, if needful, have cheerfully laid down his life. Happily, he lived in an age which was enlightened and liberal beyond all that preceded it : and though some alarm was excited, and some risk incurred, when he first opened a chapel for Unitarian worship, he met with no real impediment or molestation in the discharge of his official duties : and he lived to see the time, when, in consequence of the increasing knowledge and liberality of the age, owing in great measure to his unwearied and successful exertions, the profession of Unitarianism ceased to be regarded either as singular or hazardous.

It was also the design of the author to communicate some information relative to other generous advocates of the same righteous cause, some of whom were also sufferers for truth. Among these are Dr. William Robertson, Mr. Tayleur of Shrewsbury, and, above all, Dr. Priestley, whose letters cannot be perused by any feeling and intelligent reader without great interest and sympathy with the venerable exile: and it cannot but excite astonishment in every serious and reflecting mind, that such a person should not have been allowed to end his days in peace in his native country. But Providence had wise and good ends to answer by permitting this afflicting event, some of which are sufficiently apparent; so that Dr. Priestley might justly say to his enemies and persecutors, as Joseph said to his brethren, "It was not you that sent me hither, but God."

· The author very much regrets that the respectable relict of Mr. Lindsey did not live to see this work complete, and to give her sanction to the narrative. But it may be some satisfaction to the reader to know that the first eight chapters were written some time ago, and were read over as they were finished to Mrs. Lindsey, who expressed her kind approbation of them, and her decided attestation to the truth of the facts stated in them. And the author flatters himself that no circumstances will be found in the remainder of the narrative which are not supported by sufficient testimony.

By far the greater part of the materials from which this Memoir is composed were supplied to the author by Mrs. Lindsey, for the express purpose of selecting from them what might be interesting and useful. To other friends and correspondents of Mr. Lindsey he is indebted for the rest; and on this account he acknowledges his particular obligations to the Rev. William Turner, of Newcastle, and the Rev. Dr. Toulmin, of Birmingham. Of these materials, he trusts, it will appear that he has not made an indiscreet use. There is no living friend of Mr. Lindsey, from whose correspondence he has made more copious extracts than from the letters of the Rev. Dr. Freeman, of Boston, in New England ; but these are of a public nature, relating wholly to the state and progress of the Unitarian doctrine in America; and they do great credit to the ability and the piety of the writer, who, it is hoped, if he should chance to hear of this Memoir, will pardon the liberty which the author has taken with the letters which he addressed to his venerable friend.

This Memoir will be of little interest to any but those to whom a calm impartial inquiry into the sacred Scriptures is a consideration of supreme importance, and by whom the firm undaunted profession of Christian truth is regarded as among the first of duties. To these the author hopes it will not be unacceptable; to their candour he commends it; and if they derive any portion of that satisfaction and advantage from the perusal, which he has done from the composition of the Memoir, they will not have read, nor he written, in vain.

Essex House,
July 16th, 1812.

POSTSCRIPT TO THE SECOND EDITION.

THE Author has republished the Memoirs of Mr. Lindsey without any material alteration, excepting the addition of an Appendix to the Ninth Chapter. This Chapter having been republished separately in America, gave rise to a warm controversy at Boston and in its vicinity; which, though it does not make it necessary to introduce any considerable change in the state of facts, has rendered it expedient for the Author, in his own vindication, to show that he has not used his terms in any new or unusual sense; and much less that he has affected to set himself up as the head of a religious party.

Essex House,
March 23d, 1820.

CONTENTS.

CHAPTER III.

From Mr. Lindsey's resignation of Catterick, to his opening the Chapel in Essex-street.

CHAPTER IV.

From the first opening of the Chapel, to the purchase of the premises, and the erection of the present building in Essex-street.

CHAPTER V.

From the erection of the building in Essex-street, to the appointment of Dr. Disney to be the colleague of Mr. Lindsey in 1783.

CHAPTER VI.

Mr. Lindsey publishes the Historical View. Some account of Dr. William Robertson. Society for promoting the knowledge of the Scriptures.

CHAPTER VII.

Controversy with Robert Robinson.   Analysis of the Vindiciæ Priestleianæ.   Misunderstanding and reconciliation with Dr. Price.

CHAPTER VIII.

Analysis of Mr. Lindsey's second Address.   Dr. Watts an Unitarian.
Mr. Lindsey's alarm at Dr. Priestley's bold assertions, and ultimate
conversion to his doctrines.

CHAPTER IX.

Unitarian Liturgy adopted by the congregation at the King's Chapel, at Boston, in New England. Mr. Lindsey corresponds with Dr. Freeman, Mr. Vanderkemp, &c. Progress and present state of the Unitarian churches in America.

CHAPTER X.

Account of the New College at Hackney. The Author's introduction to and intimacy with Mr. Lindsey and Dr. Priestley. London Unitarian Society. Western Unitarian Society. Reverend Timothy Kenrick. Unitarian Fund Society.

CHAPTER XI.

Analysis of the Conversations upon Christian Idolatry. The Duke of Grafton corresponds with and visits Mr. Lindsey, and attends Unitarian worship. A brief account of the progress of the Duke's opinions, and of his reasons for seceding from the Established Church. Reflections.

CHAPTER XII.

Mr. Lindsey publishes a new and reformed edition of his Liturgy; resigns his office in Essex-street Chapel. His Farewell Sermon printed, but not preached. Interests himself for those who suffered by unjust prosecutions. Cases of Fyshe Palmer, Muir, and Winterbotham.

CHAPTER XIII.

Dr. Priestley emigrates to America. His reasons for this measure. Mr. Lindsey's judgment in the case. Dr. Priestley's Farewell Sermon at Hackney. Letters to Mr. Lindsey from Gravesend, Deal, and Falmouth. Arrives at New York. Reception in America.

CHAPTER XIV.

Dr. Priestley's Reply to Paine's Age of Reason; reprinted in England
by Mr. Lindsey, with a Preface in vindication of Dr. Priestley's
character.   Mr. Lindsey republishes another work of Dr. Priestley's,
with a short preface.   Dr. Priestley's acknowledgment of Mr. Lindsey's kindness.   Analysis of Mr. Lindsey's last publication, entitled
Conversations upon the Divine Government.

CHAPTER XV.

Mr. Lindsey suffers a paralytic seizure, but recovers. Dr. Priestley's reflections upon the situation of his friend, and upon Mr. Lindsey's last work. Mr Lindsey interests himself in the appointment of the author to the chapel in Essex-street. Encourages and assists the Improved Version. His gradual decline and death. Conclusion of the Work.

APPENDIX.

MEMOIRS

OF THE LATE

REVEREND THEOPHILUS LINDSEY.

CHAPTER I.

ACCOUNT OF MR. LINDSEY FROM THE TIME OF HIS BIRTH TO
HIS SETTLEMENT AT CATTERICK, IN YORKSHIRE.

THE Reverend Theophilus Lindsey was born at Middlewich, in
Cheshire, June 20, 1723, O.S.   His father, Robert Lindsey, descended from an ancient family in Scotland, was a mercer in that
town, and also possessed a lucrative concern in the salt works in
that neighbourhood.   He was a man of excellent character, and
originally in easy circumstances; but through the imprudence of
an elder son by his first wife, whom he had admitted into partnership, his property was considerably reduced.   His second wife,
the mother of the subject of this Memoir, was a lady of exemplary
character.   Her maiden name was Spencer; she was distantly
related to the Marlborough family, and previously to her marriage
had lived upwards of twenty years in the family of Frances,
Countess of Huntingdon.   By Mr. Robert Lindsey this lady had
three children, the youngest of whom was named after his god-
father Theophilus, Earl of Huntingdon, the son of the above-
mentioned lady, and the husband of Selina, Countess of Hunting-

B

don, so well known as the zealous and liberal patroness of Mr. Whitfield and the Calvinistic Methodists.*

Lady Betty and Lady Ann Hastings, the kind friends of Mrs. Lindsey, who had lived with them from their childhood, soon remarked the ingenuous temper, the promising talents, the love of learning, and the serious spirit of her youngest son, and took him under their own immediate patronage. From a school in the neighbourhood of Middlewich, at which he had made considerable proficiency in proportion to the advantages which he enjoyed, they removed him to Leeds, and placed him under the care of the Reverend Mr. Barnard, master of the free grammar-school in that town; a gentlemen of great eminence both for learning and piety, who devoted himself wholly to the honourable and arduous duties of his profession; and to whose superior talents and exemplary assiduity his grateful pupil was wont to ascribe, under Divine Providence, not only all his literary attainments, but almost all

* With this very respectable lady Mr. Lindsey lived many years in habits of friendship. And though after his secession from the established church, and the public avowal of his theological principles, all personal intercourse was for many years suspended, yet when Mr. and Mrs. Lindsey, in the summer of 1786, called upon Lady Huntingdon at Talgarth, in Wales, they were received, as he expresses it in a letter to a friend, "most graciously, as usual." Not only did she direct that every possible attention should be shown them in their visit to her Academical Institution in the neighbourhood, but she earnestly pressed them to prolong their stay. With her old and much respected friend she had much serious conversation; and seemed particularly impressed with a hint which Mr. Lindsey threw out, in reference to a dear and only surviving son, of the safety of whose final state her ladyship entertained the most painful apprehensions, that possibly the state of future punishment might be only a process of severe discipline, and that the greatest sinners might ultimately find mercy. And when they parted, she took a most affectionate leave of them, and gave them her kind maternal benediction, expressing at the same time her hope of meeting them in a better world. "Some good I hope is done," says Mr. L. to his correspondent above referred to, "where much is intended, by this praiseworthy lady, who has, for full forty years, devoted her fortunes, time, and labours to promote what she believes to be the truth: though I cannot but hope it will be a place for more rational inquirers after she drops into her grave." This venerable lady was at that time "turned eighty, but hale and sensible for that age." And though she might for a moment be soothed by a glimpse of hope of the ultimate restoration of a darling child, it was not to be expected that Mr. Lindsey's conversation would make any permanent impression upon her mind. He afterwards speaks of his aged friend as " still in the depths of mysticism and methodism, though she was become more moderate towards those who held different opinions." Nor does it appear that any material change ever took place in Lady Huntingdon's religious views, though the abuse of her generosity by some persons in whom she had placed a confidence which they did not deserve, made it necessary for her, in some measure to restrain her munificence, and gave rise to a report that she had deserted the Methodist connection.

that was honourable and right in his personal character. To the edifying instructions of Mr. Barnard, in concurrence with the impressions of his earlier domestic education, Mr. Lindsey was indebted for that ardent love of truth, that firm integrity, that purity of spirit, that early and deeply-rooted principle of piety, by which he was so eminently distinguished.

His vacations were usually spent at the mansion of his noble patronesses, in the vicinity of Leeds, during the life of Lady Betty Hastings, and, after her decease, at Ashby Place, near Ashby de la Zouch, in Leicestershire, where Lady Ann then fixed her residence. To this house, likewise, Mrs. Lindsey removed, together with her only daughter, at the invitation of Lady Ann Hastings, after the decease of her husband in the year 1742, where she continued to reside with her noble and pious friend till her death, which took place A.D. 1747, after having been gratified by the accomplishment of the first wish of her heart, that of seeing her son in the pulpit. Over the remains of this exemplary lady a neat monument was erected in Ashby churchyard, with an inscription, purporting that "while a child she had been the play-fellow, and a widow the friend, of Lady Ann Hastings, who erected that monument to her memory, and was a sincere and affectionate mourner for her death."

With these advantages, public and domestic, for improvement both in learning and piety, in concurrence with a temperament cast in the happiest mould, "having," as he expresses it in the modest account of himself annexed to his Apology on resigning the vicarage of Catterick, "been impressed from early youth with a love of truth and virtue, a fear of God and desire to approve himself to him, which never left him;" and having been well instructed in classical literature, Mr. Lindsey was well qualified for the university, and was admitted as a student at St. John's College, in Cambridge, May 21, 1741, in the eighteenth year of his age. Here his literary attainments and exemplary conduct soon attracted general notice and admiration. And when the late learned and pious Dr. Reynolds, Bishop of Lincoln, being desirous of sending his grandson, a promising youth of fifteen, to the university, inquired after some senior student under whose care he might place him, to assist his studies and to protect his morals at that early age, Mr. Lindsey was the person recommended for the office. This circumstance laid the foundation for a firm and tender friendship, founded upon a thorough knowledge of each other's character, and a consequent mutual affection and esteem, which continued without interruption to the end of Mr. Lindsey's life; and the recollection of which is cherished by the venerable and grateful survivor as one of the best blessings which Heaven bestowed upon him. Mr. Reynolds, after having finished his education at the university, was taken by the late Lord Sandwich as his private secretary to Aix-la-Chapelle, where he remained during the negotiation of the celebrated treaty which takes its name from that city. After his return to England, declining the engagements of public life, he retired to his estate at Little Paxton, in Huntingdonshire. There he still resides (1812); and amidst the high estimation in which he is universally and deservedly held, both for his public and his private virtues, he justly regards it as not the least of his honours to be known as one of the earliest friends and warmest admirers of the venerable Theophilus Lindsey.*

Having passed through his academical course and taken his degrees with high reputation, Mr. Lindsey was elected a Fellow of St. John's College in April, 1747; and had he chosen to devote himself to literary pursuits, he was well qualified to have attained considerable distinction; but his chief ambition was to be a minister of the gospel. Accordingly, he relates of himself that, "after the usual time spent at school and in the university, he entered into the ministry of the gospel, out of a free and deliberate choice, and with an earnest desire to promote the great ends of it.

---

* "I recollect," says this gentleman in a letter with which he favoured the writer of this Memoir, "that Mr. Lindsey excelled in college exercises; that he was singularly pious; that he attended the chapel prayers, and monthly received the sacrament. His manners were mild and gentle, and his conversation was of a serious turn, but agreeable, and sought by his fellow-students. I have reason to believe that he obtained the highest honours on taking his degree, I mean Wranglership, but this I cannot positively assert." Mr. Reynolds died in 1814.

And having been educated in the established church, he did rot at that time feel any scruples either concerning the use of the liturgy, or subscription to the articles."

Having been ordained by Dr. Gibson, the learned and exem-. plary Bishop of London, he was in the twenty-third year of his age presented to a chapel in Spital Square by Sir George Wheeler of Otterden Place, in Kent, at the recommendation of his noble sister-in-law, the unwearied friend and benefactress of Mr. Lindsey, Lady Ann Hastings.

In a short time after his settlement in London, Algernon, Duke of Somerset, being in want of a discreet and pious clergyman to officiate as his domestic chaplain, received such a character of Mr. Lindsey from Francis, Earl of Huntingdon, the nephew of Lady Ann Hastings, that he immediately invited him into his house. To this amiable nobleman and his accomplished lady, better known as the Countess of Hertford, the honoured patroness of genius and virtue, he recommended himself to such a degree, by his prudent and exemplary conduct, and by the suavity of his manners, that he soon acquired the affection and confidence of his illustrious patrons; and during the short remainder of the Duke's life, who expired in his arms, he was treated not with the distance and coldness of a dependant, but with the liberality and affection of a friend.

After the decease of the Duke of Somerset, Mr. Lindsey continued for some time in the family of the Duchess. And at her particular and earnest request, he accompanied her grandson, the late Duke of Northumberland, then about nine years of age, and in a delicate state of health, to the continent, where he continued two years; at the expiration of which term he brought his noble pupil back, restored in health and improved in learning.

Of the kind and successful attention of Mr. Lindsey to Lord Warkworth, his illustrious parents entertained a just and grateful sense, and from that time they were set upon advancing his interest in the church.* Nor was his faithful superintendence lost

* See Appendix, No. I. How anxiously these noble personages were bent upon making a comfortable provision in the church for their highly esteemed friend, appears

upon the mind of his noble pupil, who, to the latest hour of Mr. Lindsey's life, entertained the highest esteem for his character, and manifested his regard for his venerable preceptor by more than empty professions.

Immediately after Mr. Lindsey's return from the continent, he was presented by the Earl of Northumberland to the valuable rectory of Kirkby Whiske, in the North-riding of Yorkshire, at first under condition to resign it when the person for whom it was intended came of age; but this young man dying a short time afterwards, it was given to Mr. Lindsey unconditionally in the usual form. And Mr. Lindsey, declining the proposal of his noble patrons to accompany Lord Warkworth to Eton as his private tutor, hastened down into the north to take possession of his living, and to enter upon the office of a parochial minister, which was the highest object of his ambition; this being, in his judg-

---

from the following extract of a letter from the late Duchess, then Countess of Northumberland, to Mr. Lindsey, when he resided at Piddletown, in Dorsetshire:—

"I dare not give you another invitation to come to us, though both my lord and I wish much for the pleasure of seeing you, as you say it may be inconvenient to your affairs. I am truly sorry that it is so, and shall be sincerely glad to do anything in my power to make it otherwise, and find myself really obliged to you for believing I would do so. You say, dear sir, that if any small matter fell in my way for your service, you are persuaded I would think of you. Of this you may be assured. At the same time, I could wish you would be so good as to hint to me of what kind; whether in the church, or a domestic chaplainship, or a private tutor, would be most agreeable to you. At the same I must tell you that I some years ago told my lord that I desired he would give me the next presentation of Hasilbury Bryan, as I hoped its vicinity to Piddletown might make it agreeable to you; and upon this you may depend whenever it shall become vacant: but, in the meanwhile, I beg you will let me know if any of these above would suit you. And if I can be of any service to you in these, or any other things, it will give me great pleasure. I will not trouble you now any longer than to assure you of the sincere and affectionate friendship with which I am, dear sir,
"Your most faithful humble servant,
"E. NORTHUMBERLAND."

It may be proper to mention here, that during his residence at the Duchess of Somerset's, Mr. Lindsey so recommended himself by his discreet and exemplary behaviour, that a worthy and pious lady, Mrs. Pearce, a friend of the Duchess, bequeathed to him without his knowledge the next presentation to the rectory of Chew Magna, near Bristol. The living became vacant after Mr. Lindsey had left the church and was settled in Essex Street. And, honourably resisting all the proposals which were made to him to dispose of it to great advantage, he presented it to a worthy clergyman, Mr. Hall, the brother-in-law of Mrs. Lindsey, who married Archdeacon Blackburne's youngest daughter, and who is now (1812) the respectable incumbent.

ment, " the way in which he could best serve God and be useful to man ;" and which, therefore, he engaged in, " with an earnest desire that he might promote these great ends of the ministry of the gospel." *

In this very retired situation Mr. Lindsey continued about three years: and during his residence in Yorkshire he was introduced to the acquaintance, and became a visitor in the family, of the celebrated Archdeacon Blackburne, at Richmond, a circumstance to which he was afterwards indebted, under Divine Providence, for the most valuable blessing of his life.

At the request of the Huntingdon family, who considered themselves as having a prior claim, which they were unwilling to relinquish, to the honour of providing for Mr. Lindsey, he resigned the living of Kirkby Whiske, in the year 1756, in order to succeed Dr. Dawney in the living of Piddletown, in Dorsetshire, which was in the gift of the Earl of Huntingdon. In this place he lived and laboured in his parochial and official duties with high reputation for seven years. While he was minister of this parish, Mr. Lindsey was married, Sept. 29, 1760, to Miss Hannah Elsworth, the stepdaughter of Archdeacon Blackburne, † a lady whose principles and views were congenial to his own; whose superior understanding and exalted virtues were eminently calculated (as her excellent consort most cheerfully acknowledged) to aid and second him in all his schemes for the temporal and spiritual benefit of his parishioners, and especially of the poor and ignorant; to go hand in hand with him in his researches after divine truth; to encourage him in every labour, in every

* Apology, p. 217.

† Archdeacon Blackburne, noticing this event in the Memoirs of his own life, prefixed to a new edition of his Works, published by his son, the Reverend Francis Blackburne, A.D. 1804, says, " The friendship between Mr. Lindsey and Mr. Blackburne was not nearly so much cemented by this family connection, as by a similarity of sentiment in the cause of Christian liberty, and their aversion to ecclesiastical imposition in matters of conscience. In the warfare on these subjects they went hand in hand." The Archdeacon, who did not, for reasons which were afterwards published, approve of the magnanimous sacrifice which his relation had made, coldly adds, that "when Mr. Lindsey left Yorkshire and settled in London, Mr. Blackburne used to say he had lost his right arm." See Blackburne's Works, vol. i. p. 48. Upon the subject of Mr. Lindsey's marriage with Miss Elsworth, see an entertaining letter of the Countess, afterwards Duchess, of Northumberland, Appendix, No. II.

profession, and in every sacrifice, to which he might be prompted
by a sense of duty; and to fortify and console his mind under
trials and privations of no common sort, and which it required no
ordinary share of fortitude and magnanimity to support with dignity and to encounter with success. *

It was while Mr. Lindsey resided at Piddletown that he first
began to entertain serious scruples concerning the Scripture war-
rant for Trinitarian worship, and the lawfulness of his continuing
to officiate in the established church.   His susceptible and inquisitive mind had, indeed, from early youth disapproved of some
things in the thirty-nine articles; and even while he was at the
university, it struck him as a strange unnecessary entanglement,
to put young men upon declaring and subscribing their approbation of such a large heterogeneous mass of positions and doctrines,
as are contained in the liturgy, articles, and homilies.   "But," he
adds, " I was not under any scruples or great uneasiness on this
account.   I had hitherto no doubt, or rather I had never much
thought of or examined into the doctrine of the Trinity, but supposed all was right there." †

Some years afterwards, many doubts concerning the truth of
this doctrine sprang up in his mind, which induced him to study
the Scriptures with very close attention, in order to settle his
judgment and to relieve himself from a painful state of suspense
upon a question of such high importance.   The result of his
learned, calm, and diligent inquiries shall be stated in his own
words : " The more I searched, the more I saw the little foundation there was for the doctrine commonly received, and interwoven
with all the public devotions of the church, and could not but
be disturbed at a discovery so ill suiting my situation.   For in the
end I became fully persuaded, to use St. Paul's express words,

* Mr. Lindsey, who was deeply sensible of the high value of the inestimable treasure he possessed, in a letter to a friend, when he had it in contemplation to resign his
benefice in the church, speaks of Mrs. Lindsey as one who was ready to run any
hazard or loss to promote the cause of truth, and that in every step which he took in
this business he had the full concurrence of his wife, "quæ quoque currentem incitat."
See Memoirs of the Reverend T. Lindsey, published in the Monthly Magazine for Dec.,
1808, drawn up by a friend from original papers in his possession.
† Apology, p. 217.

1 Cor. viii. 6, 'that there is but one God, the Father, and He alone to be worshipped.' This appeared to be the uniform unvaried language and practice of the Bible throughout : and I found the sentiments and practice of Christians, in the first and best ages, corresponding with it." *

The scruples excited in Mr. Lindsey's mind from the result of his inquiries, gradually rose to such a height as to induce him, while he lived in Dorsetshire, to take some previous steps with a design to relieve himself by quitting his preferment in the church. The considerations which chiefly weighed with him to relinquish this design at that time will be stated hereafter. It may be sufficient for the present to observe, that self-interest and worldly considerations were not the motives; for by these, as he truly observes, and as all who knew him and the whole tenor of his life will testify, " he was never much influenced." Besides which, " he had at that time a prospect of not being left entirely desti-tute of support if he had gone out of the church." †

In the year 1762, upon the resignation of the Whig adminis-tration, the late Duke of Northumberland was appointed to suc-ceed the Earl of Halifax as Lord Lieutenant of Ireland. Upon this occasion his illustrious consort, eager to testify her regard to distinguished worth, at the Duke's desire wrote immediately to Mr. Lindsey to offer him the place of chaplain to the Lord Lieutenant, accompanied with a request that he and Mrs. Lindsey would reside with them in the vice-regal palace till some prefer-ment should offer worthy of his acceptance ; " at the same time assuring him that the Duke and herself should consider his acquiescence as a favour conferred on themselves ; that they should want the society of so kind and faithful a friend in a situation so new and untried." ‡ That the acceptance of this

* Apology, p. 218.　　　　　　　† Ibid. p. 221.
‡ See the Memoir of the late Rev. Theophilus Lindsey, in the Monthy Repository for December, 1808, by Mrs. Cappe. This lady, the daughter of Mr. Lindsey's worthy predecessor at Catterick, and the widow of the late learned, pious, and eloquent New-combe Cappe, of York, who is also herself well known to the public by various works which equally display the superiority of her intellect and the ardour of her piety and benevolence, was the early and faithful friend of Mr. and Mrs. Lindsey : and to her great honour be it known, that this lady was one of the very few who remained firmly

offer would have been a prelude to some exalted station in the church of Ireland cannot admit a doubt.*   But ambition of high ecclesiastical dignity formed no part of Mr. Lindsey's character. Eminently qualified as he was by learning and piety, by prudence of conduct, and politeness of manners, to have filled and adorned the most conspicuous station in the church, his humility aspired to no higher preferment than that of a parochial minister.   With much gratitude, therefore, but with equal firmness and decision, he declined the splendid offer of his noble friends, and contented himself with remaining for the present in his beautiful retirement in Dorsetshire.

Not, indeed, that Mr. Lindsey felt any particular predilection for the situation in which he was now placed, however agreeable or advantageous.   It was the secret wish both of him and of Mrs. Lindsey to return to the north, and to fix their residence in the vicinity of Richmond, where they might enjoy the society of many valuable friends, and particularly of the venerable Archdeacon Blackburne.   An opportunity for effecting this purpose occurred in the year following, by the vacancy of the vicarage of Catterick, in Yorkshire, occasioned by the decease of the Rev. Jeremiah Harrison, in July, 1763.   With the consent and by the interest of Lord Huntingdon, Mr. Lindsey was permitted to exchange his living in Dorsetshire for the vicarage of Catterick; a benefice in every respect inferior to that of Piddletown, excepting that of its proximity to those learned and virtuous friends whose society he was most anxious to cultivate. †

It may appear singular that Mr. Lindsey, who, while he resided in Dorsetshire, had, in consequence of his more diligent study of the Holy Scriptures, discarded the doctrine of the Trinity, and other doctrines of the established church which are

and affectionately attached to them in the season of severe trial, and who, upon all occasions, came forward as their generous and intrepid advocate, when many who had formerly made great professions stood aloof, and not a few were disposed to cavil and condemn.

* Dr. Dodgson, who accepted the appointment which Mr. Lindsey declined, was soon advanced to the Bishopric of Ossory, from which he was afterwards translated to that of Elphin, where he died a few years ago.

† See Mrs. Cappe's Memoir in the Monthly Repository, ibid.

connected with it; who had even proceeded so far as to have formed a design of resigning his preferment in the church, and had taken some steps towards the accomplishment of this purpose, could by any means reconcile his ingenuous mind to that renewed subscription to the articles and declaration of his assent, which were necessary upon his induction into his new living. And the case appears the more extraordinary, as many clergymen, who in consequence of a revolution in their opinions had become dissatisfied with the articles, would never, for the sake of obtaining the most valuable preferment, subscribe them again, though, while they were permitted to remain unmolested, they did not perceive it to be their duty to retire from the church. * With the frankness natural to his liberal mind, Mr. Lindsey himself gives the following solution of this difficulty. After having stated the considerations which at that time overruled his scruples of remaining in the church, he adds, " My great difficulty was the point of worship. In comparison with this, subscription to the articles, however momentous in itself, gave me *then* but little concern. For as the devotions of the church are framed in strict agreement with the articles, and correspond with them more especially in what relates to religious worship, I looked

* In the foremost rank of these worthy confessors is the venerable Archdeacon Blackburne, who, though he has opposed the Unitarian doctrine with much more of acrimony than of argument, in a small tract which he left for publication after his decease, entitled, An Answer to the Question, Why are you not a Socinian ? has, in the same tract, advanced reasons for the continued conformity of those who disapprove of many things in the doctrine and discipline of the established church, which, if not completely satisfactory, will at least induce a candid reader, who can make allowance for human frailty, to pause before he passes a sentence of unqualified condemnation upon those serious and inquisitive persons, who retain their official situations in the church so long as they continue unmolested in making those alterations which they judge to be necessary in the unscriptural phraseology of the public liturgy. Upon these principles, Archdeacon Blackburne continued to the end of life an officiating minister of the established church, while at the same time, though the whole emolument which he derived from his profession amounted to little more than the scanty pittance of a hundred and fifty pounds a year, he peremptorily and repeatedly refused to accept of better preferment, which required renewed subscription to the thirty-nine articles. On the other hand, he declined an offer of more than double that income from the numerous and respectable congregation of the Old Jewry, in London, who were desirous of inviting him to be their pastor, in succession to the learned Dr. Chandler.—See Memoir of Archdeacon Blackburne's Life prefixed to his Works, pp. 74, 75, and 120. See Appendix, No. III.

upon my continuing to officiate in them as a constant *virtual* repetition of my subscription : and therefore I needed not nor did decline the *actual* repetition of it when occasion served; though I was not forward in seeking such occasions." * It cannot be denied that Mr. Lindsey's conduct in this instance has the merit of consistency ; for it seems hard to assign a satisfactory reason why they who do not hesitate to use the liturgy should decline subscribing the articles of the church. It would, however, be the extreme of uncharitableness to pass a severe censure upon those who approve their integrity by rejecting preferment, when it could not be obtained but at the price of a renewed subscription to articles, even though (inconsistently as we may think) they may continue to retain their stations in the church, and to officiate in its devotions. Every man has not the firmness of a Luther or a Lindsey, and to his own master must every one stand or fall.

It may now therefore be proper to state those considerations which reconciled this venerable confessor's own mind to remaining in the church, and to the regular performance of his official duties, for so many years after that by his own acknowledgment he had abandoned its main doctrines, and regarded its forms of worship as erroneous and unscriptural. Upon this subject, we are happily not left to vague conjecture ; for Mr. Lindsey himself, with all his native modesty and candour, has clearly stated, in the last chapter of his Apology on resigning the vicarage of Catterick, the interesting process of his mind upon this trying occasion. I transcribe his own words. †

" 1. Destined early and educated for the ministry, and my heart engaged in the service, when the moment of determination came, I felt a reluctance at casting myself out of my profession and way of usefulness that quite discouraged me. This was probably heightened by my being alone at the time, having no intimate friend to consult or converse with, and my imagination might be shocked by the strangeness and singularity of what I

* Apology, p. 225.   † Apology, p. 220.

was then going to do; for such subjects, then upwards of fifteen years ago, were not so much canvassed or become so familiarized as they have been since. *

"But I did not enough reflect, that when unlawful compliances of any sort are required, the first dictates of conscience, which are generally the rightest, are to be attended to; and that the plain road of duty and uprightness will always be found to lead to the truest good in the end, because it is that which is chalked out by God himself.

"2. Many worthy persons whose opinions varied little from mine, could nevertheless satisfy themselves so as to remain in the church and officiate in it. Why then, it often occurred to me, and others did not spare to remonstrate, why must I alone be so singularly nice and scrupulous, as not to comply with what wiser and better men could accommodate themselves to, but disturb others and distress myself by enthusiastic fancies purely my own, bred in gloomy solitude, which by time, and the free communication and unfolding of them to others, might be dispersed and removed, and give way to a more cheerful and enlarged way of thinking? It was worth the while at least to try such a method, and not rashly to take a step of which I might long repent.

"3. It was suggested that I was not author or contriver of the things imposed and complained of. All I did was ministerial only, in submission to civil authority, which is within certain

---

* The time alluded to must have been about the year 1758. This was previous to the resignation of the Reverend and learned Dr. William Robertson, who, in January, 1760, for the sake of a good conscience, gave up a valuable living in Ireland. So that at the time when Mr. Lindsey first thought of relinquishing his station in the church, he had scarcely any example, for nearly a century back, of a similar act of self-denial to encourage and fortify his mind. Those eminent divines of the established church who, at the commencement of the eighteenth century, thought and wrote with great freedom upon theological subjects, contented themselves, for the most part, with declining to renew their subscription to the articles in order to obtain further preferment, but did not feel themselves obliged to resign the stations which they held. And though, as the century advanced, much had been said and written in recommendation of greater liberality and latitude in the terms of conformity, the lawfulness of clerical conformity had been but little canvassed. It is not therefore surprising that Mr. Lindsey should have been at first shocked, and in some degree intimidated, at the prospect of the *strange singularity* of the measure which he had in contemplation. After the resignation of Dr. Robertson, he was much affected and encouraged by the example of that venerable confessor.

limitations the authority of God, and which had imposed these things only for peace and public good. . That I ought not only to leave my benefice, but to go out of the world, if I expected a perfect state of things in which there was no flaw or hardship. That if there was a general tendency in what was established to serve the interest of virtue and true religion, I ought to rest satisfied, and wait for a change in other incidental matters that were grievous to me, but not generally felt by others. That in the mean time I had it in my power to forward the desired work, by preparing men's minds for it, whenever there should be a disposition in the state to rectify what was amiss. Therefore, if I could in *any way of interpretation* reconcile the prescribed forms with the scripture in my own mind, and make myself easy, I was not only justified, but to be commended."

Being influenced by these considerations to regard it as a duty to retain his station in the church, the great difficulty now was, to devise some *way of interpretation* by which to reconcile the prescribed form of Trinitarian worship with his own just and scriptural view of the proper unity of God, and that the Father alone is to be worshipped. In comparison with this, the objection against subscription to the articles appeared to Mr. Lindsey to be of trivial account, or rather as a less intricate case under the same problem. And the method which he took to satisfy his mind upon this subject he thus describes :—

" I brought myself to consider the Trinitarian forms in the liturgy, and the invocations at the entrance of the litany, as a threefold representation of the one God, the Father, governing all things by himself and by his Son and Spirit ; and as a threefold way of addressing him as a Creator and original benevolent cause of all things, as Redeemer of mankind by his Son, and their Sanctifier by his Holy Spirit. *

* This, which is usually called the Sabellian hypothesis, and which differs only in words from the proper Unitarian doctrine, was advanced by the learned Dr. Wallis, Savilian professor of mathematics at Oxford, and well received by the university, in opposition to the hypothesis of three infinite minds, maintained by the celebrated Dr. Sherlock, which underwent a public censure.

" This reasoning," says Dr. Wallis, alluding to the objections of the Unitarians, " is

"I took all opportunities, both in public and privately, to bear my testimony to this great truth of Holy Scripture, that *there is but one God, the Father,* with great plainness and without any reserve. And I hoped I was laying a good foundation to build on for those that come after me, when the time of a further reformation should come; and that I might thus innocently continue in a church where there were many things I disapproved, and wished to have amended, as I knew not where I might be in any degree alike useful."

These were the considerations which, as Mr. Lindsey expresses it, were of weight to divert him *then* from the thought of quitting his station in the church, and which brought him in time to remain *tolerably quiet and easy* in it. But however plausible these arguments might be, and whatever real weight some of these considerations might possess, they were not likely to maintain a permanent ascendancy over the honourable, ingenuous, and inquiring mind of this excellent man ; and in his Apology he frankly and with great humility acknowledges their invalidity, and his own infirmity in yielding to them.

"Not," says he, p. 225, "that I now justify myself therein. Yea, rather I condemn myself. But as I have humble hope of the divine forgiveness, let not men be too rigid in their censures. Let those only blame and condemn who know what it is to doubt,—to be in perplexity about things of the highest importance,—to be in fear of causelessly abandoning a station assigned

grounded on this *silly* mistake, that a divine person is as much as to say a Divinity or a God, when indeed a divine person is only a *mode,* or *respect,* or relation of God to his creatures. He beareth to his creatures these three relations, modes, or respects, that he is their Creator, their Redeemer, their Sanctifier : this is what we mean, and ALL that we mean, when we say God is three persons. He hath those three relations to his creatures, and is thereby no more three Gods than he was three Gods to the Jews because he calleth himself the God of Abraham, the God of Isaac, and the God of Jacob. See Considerations on the Explications of the Doctrine of the Trinity, p. 7, 1693, apud Lindsey's Apology, p. 227. The learned professor might have spared his supercilious reflection upon the understandings of his *Unitarian brethren,* whose only error consisted in taking common words in their common acceptation. Is Dr. Wallis's doctrine that which still prevails in the learned university? If so, the pure Unitarian doctrine is much more extensively diffused than many of its most zealous advocates imagine. Happy would it be for the cause of truth if, when error is detected and discarded, the language of error were discarded with it.

by Providence, and being found idle and unprofitable when the Great Master came to call for the account of the talent received." He must be a very severe moralist whom such a concession does not satisfy.

These reflections, however, occurred at a subsequent period. For the present, Mr. Lindsey had made up his mind to continue as an officiating minister in the established church; and with those views and in this posture of mind, in the month of November, 1763, he took possession of his vicarage of Catterick, fully determined to seek out and accept of no other preferment, and expecting "here quietly to have ended his days,"* though it pleased God in his providence to order it otherwise.

No sooner was Mr. Lindsey settled in his new situation than he applied himself with great assiduity, in his extensive and populous parish, to perform the duties of a parochial minister. He regularly officiated twice on the Sunday in his parish church, and in the interval between the services he catechized young people. He visited the sick, he relieved the poor, he established and supported charity-schools for the children, he spent considerable sums of money in feeding the hungry, in clothing the naked, in providing medicines for the diseased, and in purchasing and distributing books for the instruction of the ignorant. In his domestic arrangements the greatest economy was observed, that he and his excellent lady might have the greater surplus to expend in liberality and charity : for it was a rule with him to lay up nothing from the income of his living. "It is a great satis-faction," says he, in his Farewell Address, p. 7, "at this, my departure from you, that I can truly say I have coveted no man's silver, nor gold, nor apparel. In nothing have I made a gain of you, or sought to enrich myself; nor am I enriched by you at all; but what was over and above the supply of necessary wants has been freely expended in what was thought might be most useful for your present benefit and future happiness. I have not sought yours, but you."

* See Farewell Address to the Parishioners at Catterick, p. 1.

His instructions, public and private, were judiciously adapted
to the state of his hearers. " I have endeavoured," says he, p. 8,
" to teach you the truth which Christ our Lord taught, as far as
I was able to learn it by an impartial and diligent search of the
Holy Scriptures. And I often reminded you that you were not
to believe anything because spoken by me, but to examine and
compare how far it was agreeable to Holy Scripture, our only rule
and guide."

His discourses were scriptural and practical, consisting, as he
says, " altogther of expositions of large portions of the New Testament, with such inferences as naturally and plainly flowed from
them." " In these discourses," he adds, " I was led continually
to point out to you that religion lay not in outward forms and
ordinances, even of God's own appointment, though they be helps
to it ; but in an entire conversion and devotedness of the heart to
God, influencing to sobriety, chastity, brotherly love, kindness,
integrity, in all your conversation; to do everything out of a sense
of duty to God, ever present with and supporting us in life; and
chiefly for his infinite love to us in Christ Jesus our Lord, by whom
he hath called us to his eternal glory."

Mr. Lindsey often pressed upon his village hearers the duty of
family religion : " That every house should be a little church, as
it were, wherein all the members of it were carefully instructed in
the things of God ; and once at least at the close of each day called
together to join in a short prayer to God." This he represented
as a constant check upon parents in their daily conduct; as a
means of inducing them to hasten home with pleasure after their
labours were over ; of making their families orderly and happy;
of preventing early depravity and corruption in the youth of both
sexes ; and of training them up in habits of piety and virtue.

He still more inculcated upon them the necessity of keeping
the Lord's-day holy. " As many of each family as can be allowed,
to attend the public worship of the great Creator and Heavenly
Father, and to be mindful afterwards of a suitable employment
of time at home. For the spending one part of this sacred day
in unnecessary worldly cares, or in sports and diversions, tends
c

to efface every serious impression made on the mind on the other part; and by degrees leads to spend the whole of it in the same ungodly sort. Not that the service of God is to make us morose, or sad and uncheerful at this or at any time. There are ways of passing this holy day in walking out and contemplating the works of God, in pleasing charitable offices to our neighbours, and in innocent useful conversation, which will cheer and refresh both mind and body far beyond all those noisy and riotous games, always accompanied with profane oaths, and generally ending in the alehouse or worse."—Ibid.

Thus did this truly apostolic man, at the conclusion of his ten years' ministerial labours in the parish of Catterick, modestly yet firmly appeal to those who had been the constant witnesses of his life and doctrine, to bear their testimony to the simplicity, fidelity, and zeal with which he had instructed them in the truths of divine revelation, and to the unblameableness and the uniform disinterestedness of his conduct. He laments that he had not seen so much of the fruits of his labours among them as he desired. But, he adds, " I would not now complain. Let us all make haste to repent and amend, for the time is short. I would hope that more good may have been done than I know of; and that there are more truly pious than the few that appear to be so; and that some seed of the word which has been sown may hereafter spring up and bear good fruit."—Ibid. p. 11.

To the exemplary conduct of this venerable man in the discharge of his official duties, and in particular to his interesting and con-descending manner of communicating instruction to the young and the ignorant, I willingly transcribe the eloquent testimony of an early and attentive hearer and witness, who was also a frequent visitor at his house, and through life an ardent and grateful admirer, to whose narrative I have before alluded.

" Young at the time," says Mrs. Cappe in her elegant Memoir of Mr. Lindsey in the Monthly Repository, " uninformed, and accustomed to the society of those among my general acquaint-ance who form their estimate of right and wrong in the scale of commonly-received opinion, I was little qualified to comprehend, or duly to appreciate, the full excellence of such a character; yet I was exceedingly interested by the amiable, unassuming disposition of my new friend; by the patience with which he endeavoured to set right every mistake or prejudice; by his total disregard of every personal indulgence; and by his unwearied solicitude to make all around him good and happy. It was the constant subject of his thoughts in what way he could most effectually benefit the people committed to his care, whether in their temporal or eternal interests. And to this end a plan of great frugality was adopted by himself and Mrs. Lindsey, who perfectly acceded to his views, that they might have the power of distributing books, in aid of personal instruction; of giving medicines to the sick, and food to those who were ready to perish with hunger. But it was on a Sunday evening chiefly, when the labours of the day were over, a day devoted to the public and private instruction of the congregation at large, of the children of those who composed it, of servants and others who attended in his own study, that the irradiations of a mind so heavenly were the most striking. Never shall I forget, as he walked across the room with cheerful and animated step, unmindful of weariness or fatigue, discoursing, perhaps, on the beauties of creation, the goodness of God everywhere manifested, the perfect example of Christ, or on the heroism and virtue of martyrs and confessors gone to their reward, how his eyes would sparkle with delight. When, he would say, will the happy time arrive, that all men will be virtuous and happy? "

In this pleasing manner, and with these promising prospects, did Mr. Lindsey commence his career at Catterick. Surrounded with parishioners who idolized him; in the neighbourhood of friends who loved him, and whose society charmed and edified him; and engaged in offices most delightful to himself and useful to others, he devoted himself wholly to the duties of his ministry, and aspired to no other preferment.

CHAPTER II.

BUT this sunshine of felicity did not continue long without interruption : Mr. Lindsey's ingenuous mind could not satisfy itself in a compromise with sincerity. A dangerous fit of sickness roused his conscience, and he became secretly but firmly resolved to seek an opportunity to relinquish a situation which was no longer supportable. The further process of his mind upon this interesting occasion I shall state in his own words.*

"I could not now satisfy myself with Dr. Wallis's and the like softenings and qualifications of the Trinitarian forms in the liturgy. I wondered how I had been able to bring myself to imagine that I was worshipping the Father in spirit and in truth, whilst I was addressing two other persons, God the Son and God the Holy Ghost, and imploring favours severally of them in terms that implied their personality, and distinct agency and deity, as much as that of the Father.†

---

* Apology, p. 230.

† This miserable casuistry, for such it now appeared to the venerable man who had formerly been entangled in its web, silenced the scruples of many of the learned Unitarians at the close of the 17th century, and induced them to acquiesce in conformity to the established form of worship; while, contrary to the obvious meaning of the words, they interpreted the language of the liturgy in a Unitarian sense, upon the principles of Dr. Wallis's explanation of the Trinity, and of the Oxford Decree. Amongst others, the celebrated Thomas Firmin, the friend of Tillotson and the patron of the poor, who made no secret of his Unitarian principles, from which, at the particular request of Queen Mary, the pious Archbishop in vain laboured to reclaim him, was influenced by these considerations to adhere to the communion of the established church, and to dissuade others from separating from it. His friend John Biddle appears to have seen the question in a juster light; and rather chose to suffer imprisonment and banishment than to join in worship, the language of which, however he might interpret it to his own satisfaction, must necessarily convey an erroneous sense to the majority of those who use it.—See the Life of Firmin, p. 14, ed. 1791.

" If invocations so particular, language so express and personal, might be sifted and explained away into prayer to one God only, I might, by the like supposals and interpretation, bring myself to deify and pray to the Virgin Mary, and maintain that I was still only praying to the one God, who was thus invoked in his creature that was so nearly united to him.

" It appeared to me a blameable duplicity, that whilst I was praying to the one God the Father, the people that heard me were led, by the language I used, to address themselves to two other persons or distinct intelligent agents : for they would never subtilize so far as to fancy the Son and Holy Spirit to be merely two modes, or respects, or relations of God to them.

" As one great design of our Saviour's mission was to promote the knowledge and worship of the Father, the *only true God*, as he himself tells us, I could not think it allowable or lawful for me, on any imagined prospect of doing good, to be instrumental in carrying on a worship which I believed directly contrary to the mind of Christ, and condemned by him.

" If it be a rule in morals, *quod dubitas ne feceris*, it is still more evident that we are not to do anything that we know to be evil; no, not to procure the greatest good. For God does not want my sinful act. It would be impious to suppose that he cannot carry on his government, and promote the felicity of his creatures without it. And although in his providence he may bring good out of any evil, he will not let the doer of it go unpunished. And if anything be evil and odious in his sight, prevarication and falsehood is such; and most of all an habitual course thereof in the most solemn act a creature can be engaged in,—the worship of him, the holy, all-seeing God."

While these thoughts were passing through Mr. Lindsey's mind, and probably before he had formed an absolute and final determination upon the subject, he had the happiness to be introduced to the acquaintance of two persons, like-minded with himself, whom he ever afterwards numbered amongst his most intimate and confidential friends, and whose friendship he with reason

regarded as among the greatest consolations and blessings of his
life. These were the Rev. William Turner, the learned, liberal,
and pious minister of the Presbyterian congregation at Wakefield,
in Yorkshire, and the celebrated Dr. Priestley, then a Dissenting
minister at Leeds. Early in the summer of the year 1769, these
gentlemen met Mr. and Mrs. Lindsey by appointment at the
house of Archdeacon Blackburne at Richmond, where they passed
some days together in that unreserved and delightful interchange
of sentiments, and in those free and amicable discussions which
would naturally take place among persons of high intellectual
attainments, in whose estimation the discoveries of divine revelation held the most honourable place, and who were all equally
animated with the same ardent love of truth, and with the same
generous zeal for civil and religious liberty.

This memorable interview made a favourable and lasting impression upon the minds of all the parties, and was followed with
very important consequences. It gave birth to friendships between
the strangers who were then first introduced to each other, which
improved rapidly upon further acquaintance, which were ever
afterwards a source of the highest mutual satisfaction and improvement, which continued unimpaired to the end of life, and
will no doubt be resumed under happier auspices in a better and
immortal state.

In a letter from the Archdeacon to Mr. Turner, which is now
before me, and which was written soon afterwards, he says: "I have
had Mr. Lindsey's thanks in form, for bringing him acquainted with
two valuable men. The company of such worthies as Mr. Turner
and Dr. Priestley is one of my luxuries; and the last small taste I
had of it will make me long till another opportunity affords me a
second course. And I had the less relish for the dessert (1 mean
the rambles), as it was a kind of interruption of that conversation
for which I am always sharp set. Friend Lindsey can talk and
even dispute on horseback. In that situation I am sure to fall
into reveries, and often forget both myself and my company; and
for something of that sort which might look like ill manners, I

believe I ought to make an apology in our pilgrimage to Master Buncle's cave."*

Dr. Priestley, in the interesting Memoir of himself, mentions this introduction to Mr. Lindsey as one of the greatest blessings of his life. Speaking of the connections he formed during his residence at Leeds, he adds :—

" Here it was that, in consequence of a visit which, in company with Mr. Turner, I made to Archdeacon Blackburne at Richmond, I first met with Mr. Lindsey, then of Catterick, and a correspondence and intimacy commenced, which have been the source of more real satisfaction to me than any other circumstance in my whole life. He soon discovered to me that he was uneasy in his situation, and had thoughts of quitting it. At first I was not forward to encourage him in it, but rather advised him to make what alteration he thought proper in the offices of the church, and leave it to his superiors to dismiss him if they chose. But his better judgment and greater fortitude led him to give up all connection with the established church of his own accord."†

Mr. Turner was not less sensible than Dr. Priestley of the value of Mr. Lindsey's friendship; and to these two excellent men, of spirits congenial with his own, did this venerable confessor first communicate his intention of resigning his preferment in the church. And that, not to ask their advice upon the subject, for his resolution was already fixed, but to consult with them concerning the proper time and manner of accomplishing this extraordinary design, and to derive that support and

---

* Mr. Turner was as eminent for prudence as he was for learning, piety, and liberality of sentiment. An intimate friendship was formed between this gentleman and Mr. Lindsey soon after the interview at Richmond, and an interesting and confidential correspondence took place, which only terminated by disability on the part of Mr. Turner from age and infirmity. It was then taken up by his son, the present highly respected minister of the Unitarian congregation at Newcastle-upon-Tyne, and continued till Mr. Lindsey himself became disabled by the infirmities of age. To the kindness of this gentleman the author is indebted for a sight of Mr. Lindsey's letters; of which it will be perceived that a liberal, though it is hoped not an improper, use has been made in the course of the narrative. It will easily be conceived that Mr. Lindsey was not deficient in expressions of affection and esteem. How high a value he set upon the friendship of these excellent men, will be seen from various extracts of letters to Mr. Turner, which will be introduced in the sequel of this Memoir.

† Dr. Priestley's Memoirs, p. 61, London edition.

'comfort which a virtuous mind, in trying circumstances, needs and seeks from the sympathy and kind suggestions of enlightened and generous friends, who, having adopted similar principles, enter cordially into all its views, feelings, and difficulties, and by seasonable counsel, and tender expressions of encouragement and approbation, soothe and tranquillise the emotions of an anxious and disquieted spirit.

Mr. Lindsey was now in a situation to need all the comfort which his friends could administer. This venerable man was no professed ascetic : he was no enthusiast or visionary. He had ever lived in a station of ease and affluence, and comparatively high consideration. His company had been sought after by the opulent, the learned, and the great. Nor was he insensible to the advantages and the comforts of an eminent and respectable station. He had not been at all accustomed to struggle with difficulties, or to endure the privations and the obscurity of indigence. His delight had been to employ his affluence in doing good, and he had even made conscience of saving nothing for his own use from the revenues of his living.

He was fully apprised that, if he carried his present virtuous resolution into effect, the scene would soon be changed. "To leave a station of ease and affluence" (he observes in his Farewell Address to his Parishoners at Catterick), "and to have to combat with various straits and hardships of an uncertain world, affords but a dark prospect." Instead of opulence and high estimation in the world, he clearly foresaw that the step he was about to take would entail poverty, contempt, neglect, and calumny. He could not but be sensible that by the majority of those who either knew him or who might hear of his withdrawing from the church, and who could not or would not duly appreciate his motives, his conduct would be severely censured as rash, fanatical, and absurd. He expected that his means of usefulness, whether in the way of instruction or beneficence, would be exceedingly reduced, if not entirely annihilated. Among the dissenters his connections were very limited, and he had little prospect of encouragement. By the great majority of them his principles and his person would be

regarded with horror.* Not many even of those societies which
call themselves rational and liberal would endure to hear the pure
Unitarian doctrine; and very few indeed would justly appreciate
the sublime principles and the exemplary character of this faithful
servant of Christ. And, as he observes with great feeling, it was

> * They now are deem'd the faithful and are prais'd,
> Who, constant only in rejecting Thee,
> Deny thy Godhead with a martyr's zeal,
> And quit their office for their error's sake.
> Blind, and in love with darkness !—COWPER.

Such is the language of our admired poet, whose gloomy system of theology cast a
deeper shade upon the natural morbid tendency of his constitution, and involved his
innocent and tender spirit in the darkest clouds of religious melancholy, under which
he sunk in sad despondency to the grave. Peace to his hallowed ashes! When the
last trumpet shall summon the sleeping sufferer from the tomb, free from the oppressive
chain of ignorance and infirmity, he will rejoice to find the parent of the human race
infinitely more kind and merciful to his erring offspring than his rigid system, so much
at war with his gentle temper, led him to believe; and will greet with delight on their
thrones of glory, those whom his rash and misguided zeal had formerly consigned to
regions of woe.—Let the reader forgive the above almost involuntary effusion of respect to departed genius, combined with high moral worth, but oppressed with melancholy, and entangled in a system the most sombre and terrific of all that have ever
been grafted upon the mild and benevolent doctrine of Jesus. As to the rest, the
sentiment expressed in the above quotation was certainly that of the great body of
Dissenters at the time when it was written. It is so still; but not to the same extent.
Happily, within the last thirty years, owing under God to the labours and sacrifices of
Mr. Lindsey and others his worthy coadjutors or followers, " the gospel light of the knowledge of the one true God, and the worship to be paid to him only, as taught by Jesus
Christ, has been spreading *its beautiful ray* through the British nation : so that many
of all ranks begin to see with concern the striking opposition betwixt our public forms
of worship and those laid down in the word of God." (Apology, p. 236.) And
among the dissenting churches in particular, where there were formerly only one or
two solitary individuals who received the proper Unitarian doctrine, and who were
almost afraid of avowing their belief, lest they should be hunted out of society like
wild beasts, flourishing congregations of professed Unitarian Christians have of late
sprung up, whose conduct is an ornament to their profession, and whose enlightened
zeal is diffusing the salutary odour of pure evangelical truth with a rapidity and success
almost unprecedented.

Nevertheless, that all the Dissenters who were Mr. Lindsey's contemporaries, though
differing from him in doctrinal principles, were not insensible to his great moral worth,
is evident from the correspondence of the late Reverend Job Orton, the able assistant
and confidential friend of the late pious and celebrated Dr. Doddridge ; who in one of
his letters published by and addressed to the Reverend S. Palmer, of Hackney, expresses himself in these words : " Were I to publish an account of silenced and ejected
ministers, I should be strongly tempted to insert Mr. Lindsey in the list which he
mentions in his Apology with so much veneration. He certainly deserves as much
respect and honour as any one of them for the part he has acted. Perhaps few of
them exceeded him in learning and piety. I venerate him as I would any of your
confessors. As to his particular sentiments, they are nothing to me. An honest, pious
man, who makes such a sacrifice to truth and conscience as he has done, is a glorious
character, and deserves the respect, esteem, and veneration of every true Christian."
—Orton's Letters, vol. ii. p. 159.

a severe aggravation of his distress, in the prospect of straits and difficulties, that he was *not alone* involved in them.   The person who was most justly the dearest in the world to him must share in his privations and sufferings.   And though that excellent person, as soon as his pious and honourable resolution was communicated, expressed the highest approbation of it, animated and encouraged him to pursue it, and urged him on with a zeal almost superior to his own, testifying the utmost readiness to forego ease and comfort, and, what was the most dear of all, the many opportunities of active benevolence, and to accompany him into the shades of solitude and poverty ; yet Mr. Lindsey did not on that account feel less sensibly the hardships and miseries to which his beloved and worthy consort would inevitably be exposed.   But none of these things moved him.   He fixed his eye upon the line of duty, and determined to adhere closely to it, and to leave the event to God.

These were the difficulties which Mr. Lindsey foresaw, and which he made up his mind to encounter.   But though the conflict of his feelings must have been inexpressibly great, the delicacy of his spirit would not permit him to disclose them at large even to his most confidential friends, that he might not give them unnecessary pain ; and, chiefly, lest, if they were acquainted with all the circumstances of the case, they should endeavour to dissuade him from that measure which was now become the fixed purpose of his heart.   " It was not till long after this," says Dr. Priestley (Memoir, p. 61), " that I was apprised of all the difficulties he had to struggle with before he could accomplish his purpose."

It had occurred to himself, and had been suggested by Dr. Priestley and some other friends who knew the embarrassment he was under, that " he might change the public service of the church, and make it such as he could conscientiously officiate in," leaving it to his superiors to dismiss him if they disapproved his conduct.   And there was no ground to suspect that he would ever have met with any molestation from them ; but, as Dr. Priestley observes, " Mr. Lindsey's better judgment and greater fortitude led him to determine the contrary." The foundation of this determination he has explained in his Apology, p. 237.

" I could not," says he, " reconcile myself to change the public service of the church, because I looked upon the declaration of conformity and subscription at institution to be such solemnities, that I could not be easy under so great a violation of them. For I must have adopted all Dr. Clarke's amendments, or even more ; which would have been making almost a new service of it.*

" But, could I have brought my own mind to it, there were some things in my situation in so large a parish, with three chapels in it, which would have made such a change impracticable. Not to mention, also, that when incapacitated by sickness or re- moved by death, the people in all probability must have returned back to their old forms again. In short, such an attempt would have been likely, in my place, to have produced much confusion and perplexity, to say the least : and I could not see any adequate religious improvement or edification among my people likely to arise from it ; the only justifiable end of making such a change, and staying with them."

The venerable writer adds : " Upon the most calm and serious deliberation, therefore, and weighing of every circumstance, I am obliged to give up my benefice, whatever I suffer by it, unless I would lose all inward peace and hope of God's favour and accept- ance in the end."

Mr. Lindsey was encouraged and fortified in his virtuous resolu- tion † by the example of those pious and conscientious clergymen,

---

* The following is the form of the engagement to conformity at institution to a living before a bishop :—

" I do declare that I will conform to the liturgy of the Church of England as it is now by law established. A. B."

" This declaration was made and subscribed before me by the said A. B. to be admitted and instituted into the rectory or vicarage, &c., in the year of our Lord —— and in the —— year of our consecration."

† Mr. Lindsey was particularly struck with the following pious and affecting soliloquy of Mr. Oldfield, an ejected minister of Carsington, in Derbyshire, whose pri- vate papers fell into Dr. Calamy's hands :—

" When thou canst no longer continue in thy work without dishonour to God, dis- credit to religion, foregoing thy integrity, wounding conscience, spoiling thy peace, and hazarding the loss of thy salvation ; in a word, when the conditions upon which thou

who, in the year 1662, on the 24th of August, the too memorable
Bartholomew-day, being the day on which the Act of Uniformity
was carried into effect, to the number of *two thousand*, suffered
themselves to be ejected and silenced, rather than submit to the
new impositions, and subscribe and conform to the liturgy and
articles against their consciences; "a *long list*," continues Mr.
Lindsey, "that does honour to human nature, and to our own
country in particular, which has hitherto taken the lead in the
restoration of God's true religion."

But the example which, if possible, pressed with still greater
weight upon his thoughts, and which urged, and, if I may so
express it, even stung his tender and upright mind to a decisive
resolution upon the subject, was the recent and affecting but
little noticed case of the Reverend Dr. William Robertson, who, in
the year 1760, having embraced Unitarian principles, though he
had a large family and very slender means of subsistence, for the
sake of preserving his integrity inviolate, resigned a valuable preferment and the offer of much better in the diocese of Ferns in
Ireland. This venerable confessor, in his affecting epistle to his
worthy diocesan, Dr. Robinson, afterwards the celebrated Primate
of Ireland, who was anxious to retain him in the church, expresses
himself thus :—

"In debating this matter with myself, besides the arguments
directly to the purpose, several strong collateral considerations
came in upon the positive side of the question. The streightness
of my circumstances pressed me close; a numerous family quite

---

must continue (if thou wilt continue) in thy employments are sinful and unwarranted
by the word of God, thou mayest, yea thou must, believe that God will turn thy very
silence, suspension, deprivation, and laying aside, to his glory and the advancement
of the gospel's interest. When God will not use thee in one kind, yet he will in
another. A soul that desires to serve and honour him shall never want opportunity
to do it; nor must thou so limit the Holy One of Israel, as to think he hath but
one way in which he can glorify himself by thee. He can do it by thy silence as well
as by thy preaching: thy laying aside as well as thy continuance in thy work. ——
It is not pretence of doing God the greatest service, or performing the weightiest duty,
that will excuse the least sin, though that sin capacitated or gave us the opportunity
for the doing that duty. Thou wilt have little thanks, O my soul, if when thou art
charged with corrupting God's worship, falsifying thy vows, &c., thou pretendest a
necessity for it in order to a continuance in the ministry."—Calamy's Account of
ejected Ministers, vol. ii. p. 175.

unprovided for, pleaded with the most pathetic and moving eloquence. And the infirmities and wants of age, now coming fast upon me, were urged feelingly. But one single consideration prevailed over all these—that the Creator and Governor of the universe, whom it is my first duty to worship and adore, being the God of truth, it must be disagreeable to him to profess, subscribe, or declare, in any matter relating to his worship and service, what is not believed strictly and simply to be true."*

" The example of this worthy person," says Mr. Lindsey, Apology, p. 239, " has been a secret reproach to me ever since I heard of it. For I thought, and perhaps justly, that he might not have all those reasons of dislike to our established forms of worship that I had : and though myself not without unknown straits and difficulties to struggle with, and not alone involved in them, yet have I not all those dissuasives and discouragements that he paints forth in his affecting letter to the Bishop of Ferns, subjoined to his instructive and learned work."

Mr. Lindsey's purpose being now irrevocably fixed quietly to retire from the established church, he only waited for a favourable opportunity of carrying his honourable design into effect.

In the mean time an event occurred which induced Mr. Lindsey for the present to postpone his intended resignation. This was an Association formed in the year 1771, by some of the clergy of the established church and a few of the laity, for the purpose of making an application to parliament to obtain relief in the matter of subscription; that a declaration of assent to the sufficiency of the Holy Scriptures might be substituted in lieu of subscription to the thirty-nine articles and the book of Common Prayer. Mr. Lindsey from the beginning "entertained very slender hopes of success. Least of all did he expect that reformation in the liturgy, would be carried to such an extent as to make it practicable for him, with a safe conscience, to retain his situation in the church. But he was anxious to avoid the charge of precipitancy. He

---

* This epistle is annexed to a small publication of Dr. Robertson's, entitled, An Attempt to explain the Words, Reason, Substance, &c. Of this excellent man some further account will be given in the sequel of this narrative

would not leave room for cavillers to allege that he had deserted his post before he knew that such a step would be necessary. And he thought that after having waited the issue of this important measure, his resignation would be more justifiable in the sight of the world, and would produce a better effect."*

This application to parliament originated in the great impression which was made upon the public mind, and especially upon the minds of many of the learned, liberal, and serious clergy, by the celebrated work of Archdeacon Blackburne, entitled The Confessional. At the desire of some of his brethren, the Archdeacon published, in the beginning of the year 1771, " Proposals for an Application to Parliament for Relief in the matter of Subscription, &c., humbly submitted to the consideration of the learned and conscientious Clergy." In consequence of these proposals, a meeting of the clergy residing in or near the metropolis was advertised for the 17th of July, when it was unanimously agreed to form an Asssociation for the purpose of applying to the legislature for relief. This, from the place of meeting, was called The Feathers' Tavern Association; and an excellent petition having been drawn up by the Archdeacon, was adopted by the Association and circulated through the country with great industry, in order to obtain signatures previous to the meeting of parliament.

It is almost needless to add that, in a cause so right and honourable in itself, and so congenial to his principles and feelings, Mr. Lindsey exerted himself with more than his usual activity and ardour. He undertook to solicit signatures in the extensive district where he resided; and for the purpose of adding names to this venerable list, he spared neither labour nor expense.† For

* " From the first that I engaged," says Mr. Lindsey, Apology, p. 235, " with the associated clergy for procuring the removal of subscription to formularies of faith and doctrine drawn up by fallible men, I forsaw that if no relief was obtained, nor any prospect opened of a reformation of the liturgy with regard to the great object of worship, or of a disposition to indulge a latitude to private persons to make discretionary alterations in it for themselves by the *express* rule of Holy Scripture, it would certainly terminate, as to myself, in resignation of my office in the church ; and I thought this would be a fitting season for it."

† In a letter upon this subject to his confidential friend Mr., afterwards Dr., Jebb, Mr. Lindsey says, " I own to you, sir, I cannot but be greatly interested in a cause in which I bless God that I have an opportunity to engage and declare myself ; and

this end, he travelled upwards of two thousand miles at the worst season of the year, and often through roads which were almost impassable. But his success did not correspond with his labours and his hopes. The majority, as usual, saw no reason for any alteration; the violent and bigoted expressed their abhorrence of the undertaking, and calumniated the motives of the petitioners; the cautious and timid were unwilling to commit themselves, and thought it more prudent to defer the application;* and some, of whom better hopes were entertained, and who were known to be in their judgment friendly to the objects, unexpectedly hesitated and drew back at the critical moment, and instead of their signatures they could only proffer their good wishes.

"These well-disposed and good sort of men," says Mr. Lindsey, in a letter dated November 19, 1771, written just after his return from one of these fruitless circuits, "have done the cause more harm than they intended. They may wait long before the season of reformation comes, and their brethren of the clergy and the governing powers be more inclined to promote it than they are at present. May they have no regrets in reflecting that Providence put it in their power to bring on the desired season, and propagate the requisite dispositions and zeal for relieving the oppressed truth of God by their much-wanted example! I really never expected success in this our undertaking; and still less, since I have had cause to observe the desertion of many from whom one might have expected better. And yet I do not give it up for gone; nor will those worthy persons who have taken an active part in promoting it."

In another letter to the same friend, dated December 21, 1771, and written soon after his return from a general meeting of the Association in London on the 11th, in which it was finally deter-

for which I do not know, with the help of God, the pains or sufferings that I would refuse. ———I have offered, and if health be permitted will carry the petition to Kendal in Westmoreland, to Newcastle in Northumberland, to York and Wakefield; all places at a very great distance from me, and in which labours I am alone without any assistance whatever."—See Mr. Joyce's excellent Memoir of Mr. Lindsey in the Monthly Magazine for December, 1808.

* It has been observed by an elegant writer, that the verb *reform* wants the *present tense*.

mined to present the petition to parliament during the present session, after stating the violent opposition which was expected from the University of Oxford, from Lord North, from the Methodists and others, Mr. Lindsey adds,—

" Be the event, however, what it may, still good, much good, I am sure, has arisen, and more will rise from this shaking of the stagnant waters, and stirring up of better principles. Political statesmen without any principle are afraid of disturbances which may hurt the enjoyment of their ease and emoluments. Political divines, and reverend unbelievers and half-believers, are still more haunted with fears of the like kind. Bigots are enraged at the thought of a free, rational examination of the Holy Scriptures. Whilst serious and honest men, for such there are in all places, rejoice at the Christian and Protestant undertaking."

The petitioners, though comparatively few in number, not amounting to two hundred and fifty, were of high consideration in point of talents, of learning, and of moral worth. The names of Lindsey, of Blackburne, of Wyvill, of Jebb, of Law, of Disney, of Chambers, and many others, are such as would do honour to any cause. The majority were clergymen ; the rest were gentlemen of the professions of law and medicine, who thus entered their protest against the yoke of subscription imposed upon students at the universities who had no view to the clerical office.

It being determined by the Association not to defer the petition to another session, the petitioners and their friends were very active in soliciting the support of those members of the House of Commons who might be disposed to listen to their arguments. Their reception in general was civil, but not very encouraging. Many regarded the object of the petition as frivolous ; and many believed, or pretended to believe, that it would be hazardous to meddle with the articles. The prevailing opinion was, that the application was ill-timed, and that it was best to let religion alone. Some, however, who were in the foremost rank for talents, integrity, and eloquence, took up the cause with great ardour, and promised their most zealous support. The state of the business is thus represented in a letter from John Lee, Esq., who was afterwards

Solicitor-General, to a friend in the country, dated January 31, 1772 :—

"It will surprise you who live in the country, and consequently have not been informed of the discoveries of the metropolis, to hear that the Christian religion is thought to be an object unworthy of the least attention ; and that it is not only the most prudent, but the most virtuous and benevolent thing in the world to divert men's minds from such foolish subjects with all the dexterity that can be. This is no exaggeration, I assure you : on the contrary, it seems to be the opinion (and their conduct will show it) of nine-tenths of both houses of parliament. On Thursday, a committee of petitioners waited upon Lord North to apprise him of the nature of their application, and to inform themselves of his inten-tion concerning this matter. He received them with great cour-tesy, commended the decency of the petition itself ; but before he parted with them, he told them that all with whom he had con-versed were of opinion that innovations would be very improper. Mr. Pitt, the nephew of Lord Chatham, has undertaken to second the motion, and I am sure he will acquit himself ably. I spoke with him on the subject, and he understands it very well. Lord George Germaine is hearty in the cause, has studied the contro-versy, and speaks admirably. Mr. Dunning has promised me to attend it ; and as his abilities are unequalled by any man's I ever knew, I hope he will do honour to the cause and to himself. Some others there are of less note who will enter into the debate ; yet such a general confederacy is there against the measure, that I do not believe we shall divide forty members, perhaps not twenty ; yet the debate will do honour to the petitioners, though at present no good to the cause. Perhaps it may excite an attention to the subject ; and who knows what time may do ? This may cure Dr. Priestley of writing divinity, which, to be sure, hardly anybody minds. Yet I do not think our sons are more honest, our daugh-ters more chaste, our liberties more sacred, or our property more secure, than in the days when it was thought no dishonour to read or to believe the Scripture."

This able advocate, whose powers were equalled by few, and

D

whose integrity was surpassed by none, the worthy and confidential friend of Mr. Lindsey, and Dr. Priestley, and Mr. Turner, was engaged to exert his superior abilities and energetic eloquence in pleading the cause which he so well understood, and which he had so much at heart, if the petitioners had been permitted to be heard by counsel at the bar of the House of Commons. "If I attend at the bar," says he, "I will do my utmost to serve the petitioners; but I fear counsel will not be permitted."

On the 6th of February, 1772, agreeably to the resolution of the general meeting, the petition was presented to the House of Commons. It was introduced with a very neat and appropriate speech by Sir William Meredith, the member for Liverpool; Lord John Cavendish and Sir George Savile having declined the office, not from any want of zeal for the cause, but because they did not consider themselves as sufficiently masters of the subject. It was intended by the Minister that the petition should be treated civilly, be laid upon the table, and the consideration of it adjourned for six months. It was Lord North's policy, if possible, to preclude debate upon so delicate a subject. But the intemperate zeal or the secret instructions of Sir Roger Newdigate, one of the members for the University of Oxford, a gentleman of mild dispositions and exemplary character in private life, happily defeated the artful policy of the noble Lord, and gave rise to one of the most interesting and animated debates that was ever heard in that house; "a debate," as Mr. Lindsey expresses it in a letter to a friend, "which entered gloriously into the whole merits of our cause, and which was well worth going two hundred and forty miles to hear." It lasted for eight hours. Of this debate I will take the liberty to introduce a brief account, extracted from a letter of the learned gentleman above mentioned to his friend in the country :—

"Sir William Meredith in a few words informed the House that he had in his hands a petition of a number of respectable clergy and others, praying relief in the matter of subscription; and therefore he moved that it might be brought up. Mr. T. Pitt seconded the motion. On this, Sir Roger Newdigate rose up in great anger, and demanded to know what the contents of the petition were, and what the number and names of the men who had subscribed it. Sir William then read the petition in his place, and a few of the names, adding, that the number was about two hundred and fifty. Sir Roger Newdigate then began the debate, and opposed with great vehemence the bringing up of this petition. In his opinion it aimed at the destruction of the church, whose existence depended upon the continuance of the articles. Sir Roger spoke contemptuously of the number and quality of the petitioners, and sustained with great fortitude the character of member for Oxford. He was followed by Mr. Hans Stanley, who opposed the bringing up of the petition, as it tended to disturb the peace of the country, which, in his opinion, ought to be the subject of a fortieth article, which would be worth all the thirty-nine.*   He was succeeded by Mr. Fitzmaurice, who is brother to Lord Shelburne, and spoke on the same side, throwing out some very indecent reflections on . The Confessional and its author, and endeavouring to prove the petitioners to be a parcel of canting hypocrites, who, under pretence of reformation, meant the ruin of our civil and ecclesiastical government. This conduct roused the resentment of Mr. Pitt, who with great dignity and good sense observed upon the indecency of calumniating any persons appearing in the character of petitioners for redress of grievances, more especially the persons then applying for relief in a matter that highly concerned the purity of religion, the integrity of their own minds, and even the morality of the people. He stated very well the principles of the Reformation, and fairly inferred from them the propriety of the petition.

" The motion for bringing up the petition was also supported by Lord George Germaine, Mr. Sawbridge, Mr. Thomas Townshend, Lord John Cavendish, Mr. Dunning, Sir Henry Hoghton, Mr. Solicitor-General Wedderburne,† and Sir George Savile. I believe

---

* Upon this subject see a very curious letter of Mr. Hans Stanley to Mr. Lindsey, Appendix, No. IV.
† The author of this Biographical Memoir is neither inclined nor called upon to vindicate Mr. Wedderburne, afterwards Earl of Rosslyn, and Lord High Chancellor

Sir George Savile's speech was one of the best that was ever delivered in that house. I can give you no idea of its excellence, unless by repeating some parts of it when I have the pleasure of seeing you. I cannot help saying, however, that I never was so affected with, or so sensible of the power of, pious eloquence as while he was speaking. It was not only an honour to him, but to his age and country.* Mr. Solicitor-General spoke

of Great Britain, in the whole of his political conduct. But let it be remembered to Lord Rosslyn's praise, that he was always the enlightened advocate of a liberal toleration; and that he was the steady zealous friend and disinterested patron of the late learned Edward Evanson, A.M., vicar of Tewkesbury, whom he carried triumphantly through a mean and savage persecution instituted against him by a few of his parishioners, in opposition to the sense of a decided majority of the inhabitants of the town, under pretence of heresy, and because of a few verbal alterations or omissions in reading the Liturgy.

* The speeches of Sir William Meredith and of Sir George Savile were afterwards written down from memory by Dr. Furneaux, and corrected by Sir W. Meredith himself. Of these speeches, so corrected, I am in possession of a copy, from which I will trespass upon the indulgence of the reader by presenting him with a few extracts of the admirable speech of Sir George Savile, which he will easily perceive was well entitled to the high eulogium of Mr. Lee. The earnestness and fervour with which it was delivered manifested how deeply the honourable speaker was impressed with his subject, and the house listened from beginning to end with silent astonishment.

The honourable speaker, after a few preliminary remarks, in which he distinguishes between the church of England and the church of God and Christ (with which Sir Roger Newdigate had confounded it), after having stated that adherence to the Scriptures only, in opposition to human inventions, was the grand principle of Protestantism, and having made some judicious and pointed observations upon some of the doctrines which are contained in the articles, proceeds to vindicate the character of the petitioners, and to reply to the objections which had been started in the course of the debate. It may be proper to premise that the zealous member for the University of Oxford had in his speech used words to this effect: "Some, perhaps, may ask what is the use of requiring subscription to the thirty-nine articles? All blind as they are, cannot they see that the articles are barriers for the protection of the church?" It was also fully understood at the time that the beautiful allegory, in reply to this allegation, though mentioned as a quotation, was in fact the extemporaneous suggestion of the eloquent orator's own vivid imagination.

"I must now, sir, express my very great concern at the manner in which the petition, and they who signed it, have been treated. They have been treated in a manner very unparliamentary, in a manner that none should be treated who come to the bar of this house to represent grievances and to solicit redress. Their characters have been aspersed: injurious suspicions have been thrown out against their designs and intentions. I wish many things not to have been said which have been said. The petitioners, sir, are clergymen; men of respectable characters; I verily believe good and conscientious men. We may treat their situation with indifference, because we are strangers to it and feel not their difficulty. But let us for a moment put ourselves in the place of these petitioners, who are required to bring themselves under a solemn obligation on the one hand to preach according to Scripture (which, if it means anything, must mean according to what they apprehend to be the sense of Scripture), and on the other, are required to declare their belief of articles which in their

very well, and gave a very handsome testimony to the character of Mr. Blackburne as a learned, pious, virtuous, and venerable man,

consciences they think contrary to the Scripture, and which few will pretend to believe or to understand. . . . . . This sir, is a debate in which the honour of God, the interests of religion and virtue, our own consciences, and the consciences of others, are deeply concerned. Let us, then, hear no more of private characters, of confessionals, and Feathers' Tavern. I have always thought that the *persons* of men who petition this house were under our protection. Their *characters* ought to be still more so. I therefore beseech you—I become a humble and earnest supplicant to you, by the benevolent spirit of the Gospel, by all that is serious, I beseech you by the bowels of Christ, that this affair be treated, not as a matter of policy, not as a matter of levity, not as a matter of censoriousness, but as a matter of religion.

"Some gentlemen seem to apprehend that we are to make the doors of the church as narrow and to exclude as many as possible. I think we should make them as wide as we can to take in as many as possible. Others are apprehensive that, in case the Scriptures are substituted in the room of the articles, it will be the means of admitting into the church a great number of sectaries. Sectaries! sir : had it not been for sectaries, this cause had been tried at Rome. Thank God, it is tried here.

" Some gentlemen fear that if we lay aside the articles and place the Scriptures in their stead, by throwing down all distinctions, we shall admit Papists, and together with them their religion too. But they forget that Papists are excluded by the oath of supremacy, and by the declaration against transubstantiation, against the invocation of the Virgin Mary and other saints, and against the sacrifice of the mass. And if any other test be needful, let them be made to acknowledge liberty of conscience and the right of private judgment ; let them abjure persecution—that were a truly Protestant test. But can any one seriously think that encouraging free inquiry and the study of the Scriptures will issue in the Romish religion ? When I see a rivulet flow to the top of a high rock, and requiring a strong engine to force it back again, then shall I think that freedom of inquiry will be prejudicial to truth— then shall I think that liberty of judgment will be prejudicial to the Protestant religion—then shall I think that adhering to the Scriptures only will lead to Rome.

" Some gentlemen talk of 'raising barriers about the church of God, and protecting his honour.' Language that is astonishing, that is shocking, that almost approaches to blasphemy. What ! man ! a poor, vile, contemptible reptile, talk of raising barriers about the church of God ! He might as well talk of protecting Omnipotence, and raising barriers about his throne. Barriers about the church of God, sir ! about that church, which, if there be any veracity in Scripture, shall continue for ever, and against which the gates of hell shall not prevail ? If I may be allowed on so serious an occasion to recollect a fable, it puts me in mind of one which I have met with, of a stately, magnificent, impregnable castle built on a rock, the basis of which was the centre of the earth, the top of it pierced the clouds, the thickness of the walls could not be measured by cubits. At the bottom of it a few moles were one day very busy in raising up a little quantity of earth, which when some mice saw, What are you doing, said they, to disturb the tranquillity of the lord of this castle ? We are not disturbing his tranquillity, replied the moles ; *all blind as you are*, you may see that we are only throwing up a rampart to protect his castle.

" The church of God, sir, can protect itself. Truth needs not be afraid of not obtaining the victory on a fair trial. The lovers of truth will love all sincere inquirers after it, though they may differ from them in various religious sentiments. For it is to impartial and free inquiry only that error owes its ruin and truth its success. Those who are penetrated with the benevolent spirit of the gospel will not condemn as heretics, will not reject as unworthy of their affection, any who believe the Christian

and vindicated his book as an excellent and entertaining performance. The speakers on the opposite side were Sir Roger
Newdigate, Mr. Fitzmaurice, Lord Folkstone, Mr. Byrne, Lord
North, Mr. Charles Fox, Mr. Burke, Mr. Dyson, Mr. Jenkinson,
Mr. Stanley, Dr. Hay, and Mr. Cooper. Nobody but Sir Roger
Newdigate attempted to defend the articles. And all the house
explicitly declared it was foolish to require subscription at the
university, and expressed a wish that it might be laid aside
there.

"After a very fine debate the house divided; the numbers
for not receiving the petition were two hundred and seventeen—
for receiving it, seventy-one—which, considering the influence of
the bishops and ministry, and the character and weight of the
minority, was thought a very great affair. The clergy petitioners
were delighted with the debate, all of them that were in town
being admitted to hear it. Dr. Hallifax, of Cambridge, was
in the gallery, and seemed disappointed that his violent nonsense
had produced so little effect on the house. This scene was acted
yesterday, beginning at three and ending at eleven o'clock."

"The XXXIX. Articles," says Mr. Lindsey, in a letter of nearly
the same date to the same friend, "underwent such a scrutiny, and
had such a just exposition, that the civil power must soon be
ashamed of imposing what not one of our adversaries defended, except Sir Roger ; and many of them gave them up.

religion, who search and endeavour to understand the Scriptures, though they may be
unable to comply with creeds and articles.

"Some gentlemen suppose that the Scriptures are not plain enough to be a rule and
centre of union to the church. They must have articles and creeds to supply its
defects. But if the things which are necessary to salvation are not plainly revealed, there
is no way of salvation revealed to the bulk of mankind at all. Whatever is obscurely
revealed will be always obscure, notwithstanding our decisions. It can never be
authoritatively determined by men. The only authority which can explain it, and
make the explanation a test of faith, is the authority of God. As to what he has
plainly revealed, it needs no articles to ascertain its meaning. We should not then
adopt views and measures which are contracted and narrow. We should not set bars in
the way of those who are willing to enter and labour in the church of God. When the
d'sc'ples came to Christ and complained that there were some who cast out devils in
his name, and said, We forbad them because they followed not us—what did our
Saviour do? Did he send them tests and articles to be subscribed? Did he ask them
whether they believed this, or that, or the other doctrine? whether they were Athanasians, or Arians, or Arminians? No. He delivered that comprehensive maxim—He
that is not against me is for me. Go ye, and say likewise."

" Burke declaimed most violently against us in a long speech, but entirely like a Jesuit, and full of popish ideas; the multifarious strange compound of the book called the Scriptures; the uncertainty what were the Scriptures; the necessity of a priesthood; of men in society, religious as well as other, giving up their right of private judgment, &c., &c.

"Can it be true?" continued Mr. Lindsey; "I hope not; but it is said, and suspected, that this man spoke the sentiments of his patron, Lord Rockingham. The persuasion, however, does my Lord Marquis no good in the esteem of judicious men.

"Though defeated," adds he, "we sing a victory; as truth and reason were all for us, and overpowered only by power; and we are not disheartened, but in high spirits, with thankfulness to the good providence of God so happily disposing things; and shall certainly not give up the cause, though what steps next are to be taken we cannot say."

So little interest did the Dissenters take in this application of the clergy, that only two of the General Body of Dissenting ministers happened to be present at this memorable debate. These were, indeed, gentlemen of the first eminence and respectability among their brethren; the late Reverend Edward Pickard,* minister of the congregation at Carter Lane, a gentle-

* Let it be permitted to one who, after an interval of more than thirty years, entertains a grateful and unabated sense of many and important obligations, to bear a humble testimony to the distinguished, but retiring and unobtrusive, merit of the friend of his youth. The Reverend Edward Pickard was born at Alcester, in Warwickshire, A.D. 1714, of reputable and pious parents. He was educated in high Calvinistic principles, and after he had finished his studies under the Reverend and learned J. Eames, F.R.S., he settled with a congregation at Stratford-upon-Avon. The excellence of his understanding and the benevolence of his heart, combined with a serious and diligent study of the Scriptures, soon led him to discard the gloomy system in which he had been brought up, and to embrace the more rational hypothesis of Arianism, which was then in the zenith of its glory, being supported by the great abilities, learning, and reputation of Dr. Clarke, Mr. Whiston, Dr. Daniel Scott, and others. To this opinion Mr. Pickard ever afterwards adhered. His deviation from the orthodox creed having created uneasiness in his situation at Stratford, he removed to London and was at first settled with a small congregation in the borough. But his eminent talents were not destined to remain long in obscurity. And in 1746, upon the accession of Mr. Newman to the pastoral office in the flourishing congregation at Carter Lane, in the room of Dr. Wright, Mr. Pickard was chosen afternoon preacher; and, upon the death of Mr. Newman, A.D. 1759, he was appointed sole pastor, and continued in that connection, happy, useful, and beloved, beyond the common lot, till his own decease in February, 1778. Mr. Pickard

man distinguished by benevolence of heart and urbanity of manners, who was afterwards Chairman of the Committee for conducting

had great pulpit talents. He was, indeed, no professed orator; and perhaps he entertained too great a prejudice ag inst the artificial helps of public elocution. But his
voice was clear and strong, his matter was judicious, well composed, interesting, and
practical. He spoke as one who deeply felt the power of religious truth. In prayer,
he chiefly excelled. In variety of thought, in copiousness of language, in simplicity,
in propriety and pertinence to the occasion, in pathos, and in fervour of devotion, he
was unequalled. No one could hesitate in preferring free prayer to written or public
forms, if all could pray like Mr. Pickard. He rivetted the attention and captivated the
heart. And it was the same in the more private and family circle as in public. His
public services did not indeed attract the crowd, but they delighted the intelligent, the
judicious, and the devout, and have been honoured more than once by the attendance
of dignitaries of the highest order in the established church.

Mr. Pickard possessed talents which qualified him eminently for conducting business.
What he planned with calm and cool deliberation and advice, he executed with promp-
titude, with vigour, and with perseverance. And his kindness of heart and conciliatory
manners made it a pleasure to every one to transact business with him. He was a
leading and active member in many important trusts. He was chairman of the committee for that application to parliament which originated with him, for the relief of
Protestant Dissenting ministers, tutors, and schoolmasters; and in this office he conducted himself with a degree of prudence and activity which commanded universal
approbation. His conduct in this affair was, indeed, severely, not to say rudely,
attacked, in an anonymous pamphlet, by an author who did not at that time fully
appreciate his worth. But at the next general meeting of the three denominations,
which was most numerously attended, Mr. Pickard, as chairman, delivered a most excellent
speech, which he was strongly solicited to publish, stating and defending his own conduct and that of his brethren of the committee, and repelling the attack which had been
made upon him and them, with a spirit, truth and energy, which gave complete satisfaction to the audience, and even to the accuser himself, who was present, and who was
ready frankly to acknowledge that he had not formed a just estimate of Mr. Pickard's
character and talents.*

In the American war, and in the party politics of the time, Mr. Pickard took a side
opposite to that of Dr. Price and most of his Dissenting brethren. This he did honestly
and conscientiously, and without any improper or interested bias of mind. He was a
man of a truly independent spirit, and disdained to be the tool of a party. And when
the Minister of the Crown, knowing his character, his political principles and his weight
among the Dissenters, offered him the whole management of the Regium Donum. he absolutely declined having any concern in it at all, that he might not give the shadow of
pretence for the allegation that he was warped in his political principles by court
favour.

Mr. Pickard died after a short illness, in February, 1778, in the sixty-seventh year
of his age. And very few in a similar situation have been more justly, more generally,
or more deeply lamented. It is much to be regretted that his great humility and
modesty, together with his numerous avocations, did not permit him to instruct and
edify the Christian world from the press as well as from the pulpit. But he has left

---

* The anonymous assailant was Dr. Priestley, who has, to the author himself,
acknowledged his error with respect to the qualifications and merits of Mr. Pickard;
and the gentleman who requested that the speech might be published was Mr. Turner,
of Wakefield.

the application of the Dissenting ministers to Parliament for relief; and the learned Philip Furneaux, D.D., minister of the congregation at Clapham, well known to the public by his Letters to Mr. Justice Blackstone upon the subject of Toleration, and whose memory was so correct and tenacious, that having taken down from recollection the celebrated speech of Lord Mansfield in the House of Peers, in the great Dissenting cause, concerning the liability of Dissenters to serve the office of sheriff, and having shown it to the noble and learned Lord for his correction, it was returned by Lord Mansfield with very few alterations, and with his express consent to publish it as his genuine speech : which Dr. Furneaux has accordingly done in the Appendix to the second edition of his Letters to the learned Judge. In the course of the debate, many of the speakers who opposed the petition of the clergy, and particularly Lord North, who, having with his usual good-humour observed, that he saw no ground to complain of intolerance in times when every one was permitted to go to heaven in their own way, remarked, that had a similar application been made by the Dissenting clergy, who derived no emoluments from the church whose articles they were compelled to subscribe, he could see no reasonable objection to it. These two reverend gentlemen, talking the matter over with each other after the debate was closed, and consulting with some others of their brethren, summoned the General Body of Dissenting ministers of the Three Denominations, who concurred in an application to parliament the next year, for relief from the obligation to subscribe the articles of the established church, in order to secure the benefits of the Toleration Act. And though they were for a time vehemently opposed by bigots, both of their own body and of the establishment, and though the bill for their relief, having twice passed the House of Commons, was twice rejected by the Lords; yet a few years afterwards, A.D. 1778, the times becoming

one splendid and lasting monument of his philanthropy and piety, the Dissenters' Orphan School, in the City Road; of which noble and useful institution I believe that I am correct in saying that the idea originated with him; at least, it will be allowed that he was one of its first founders, and of its most able, most unwearied, and most successful managers and advocates.

more favourable, the bill for their relief passed both Houses almost unanimously, and received the Royal assent. So that at present Dissenting ministers, tutors, and schoolmasters, are entitled to all the benefits of the Toleration Act, by making a declaration, in addition to the oaths usually required, that they receive the Scriptures of the Old and New Testament as containing a divine revelation.

The associated clergy having resolved, notwithstanding their late defeat, to renew their application for relief the next session of parliament, Mr. Lindsey, though his hopes of success were less than ever, did not deem it expedient at this juncture to carry into effect his resolution of resignation. This, however, he plainly foresaw must soon happen; and in the mean time he fortified his mind by reading Calamy's Account of the Ministers who were ejected for nonconformity in the year 1662, and by collecting materials for a history of persons who had suffered for their profession of Unitarian principles. Upon the former subject he thus expresses himself, in a letter to a friend, dated April 12, 1772:—

" I never was more affected with any book than with Calamy's History of those worthy confessors that gave up all in the cause of Christ, and for a good conscience, at the Restoration. No time or country ever did furnish at once such a list of Christian heroes; and I fear our own country now would fall far short of furnishing so large a number upon a like trying occasion. But it was the effect of their Puritan education. They had learned to fear God from their youth, and to fear nothing else."

He further adds to the same correspondent, in reference to the plan which he was himself pursuing, of collecting materials for a similar history,—

" As it was your own obliging offer, I need not ask you, as it falls in your way, to inquire out, and to note down for me, any such good *witnesses* of our own days. And I will endeavour that their names and example may not be wholly lost."

In another letter, dated May 10, 1772, he observes,—

" If I did not sufficiently in my last, I ought to acknowledge

myself highly indebted to you for the pains you have taken, and
are taking, in the inquiry first started to me by you, though
thought of by me, and to which you so willingly lend your aid.
Their names have gone up for a memorial before God, who have
suffered for the testimony of Jesus, and nobly refused to worship
the beast and his image. But surely their memory should live,
and be preserved upon earth for the benefit of the present and
succeeding times. But such materials are slowly collected, and
hardly to be come at by us of the church; and, to our shame be
it said, fall more in your way. Therefore I will beg you, at your
utmost leisure, to go on as you have begun."

Mr. Lindsey, though his own mind was fully made up as to the
step which he would take if the application of the associated
clergy did not succeed, was very cautious of dropping any hint
of his intention, even to his most intimate friends, till the time
approached when it would be necessary for him to take public and
decisive measures. The first allusion which he makes to his own
secret purpose, in his correspondence with Mr. Turner, is in a
letter dated June 2, 1772.

" What will further be attempted in our affair," says he, " I
know not; but I trust we shall agree still to do something. For
my own particular, if no disposition to reformation appear, and
nothing be done, I do not know where things will end."

The associated clergy judging it expedient not to renew their
application to parliament at the ensuing session in the spring of
1773, Mr. Lindsey, who never expected any reformation to be
introduced which would relieve his scruples with respect to conformity, conceiving that he had now protracted his resignation to
the utmost limit that the most cautious prudence could require,
and having now an open course before him, determined forthwith
to relinquish his preferment at the close of the current year.
And in the mean time he employed himself in preparation for this,
to him, very important event—not, indeed, by hoarding up a
purse of money for the support of himself and Mrs. Lindsey
while he continued out of office, and unprovided with the means
of subsistence : for this was not his chief concern. True to the last

to the generous principle that the income arising from a parish should be employed for the benefit of the parishioners, both he and Mrs. Lindsey, as we are informed by his amiable biographer, who was eye-witness to the fact, continued their accustomed charities, and had this year the additional expense of inoculating all the poor children in the parish, the small-pox being then very fatal in the neighbourhood. Mrs. Lindsey attended them in person, gave them all their medicines, and was so successful in her attendance, that she did not lose a single patient.* Mr. Lindsey, in the mean time, employed himself in drawing up and printing a copious and learned Apology to the public, which in its original state contained a large and comprehensive view of the arguments for the Unitarian doctrine. But, upon reconsideration and by advice of his friends, he considerably reduced the size of the volume, comprising what was most material, and what related to himself personally, in a smaller work, which was to be ready for publication immediately upon his resignation; and judiciously reserving the more elaborate portion of the argument to be published afterwards, at a more convenient season, as a Sequel to the Apology. In the mean time, as opportunity offered, he communicated his purpose without reserve to his confidential friends.

In the beginning of the year 1773, some letters in a newspaper appeared under the signature Lælius, which discussed the question concerning the conformity of clergymen who in their judgment and conscience disapproved of the doctrine and worship of the established church. Upon this subject Mr. Lindsey thus feelingly expresses himself, in a letter to a friend dated March 2:—"The subject of Lælius's last letter may give one many a pang. I cannot say that I have been, for many years, a day free from uneasiness about it."†

The interesting posture of his mind, as the crisis approached, he thus pathetically describes to his friend Mr. Turner, who seems to have been almost the only person admitted to his entire confidence. The letter is dated June 13, 1773. "It is not possible

* Mrs. Cappe's Memoir of Mr. Lindsey, Month. Rep. vol. iii. p. 641.
† Monthly Mag. December, 1808, p. 448.

to describe to you the straits and anxieties of mind which *one person* daily passeth through—not through any doubts of the thing itself, but lest he should have deserved to be laid by, lest there should be anything to reproach himself with hereafter, lest he should suffer unprofitably as to himself; for a man may give all his goods to the poor, and his body to be burned, and yet want charity; may make the greatest sacrifices, and yet want the proper disposition to make them acceptable. What need has one daily to cry with the psalmist, 'Make me a clean heart, O God, and renew a right spirit within me!' You will hence observe, it was not lightly that the last word said at K. at parting, was 'Ora, Orate pro nobis;' and you gave me comfort in the assurance of this your way of remembrance. And I would beg *another person* not to be forgotten, who has indeed the true spirit of a Christian, and has been more than ready to do everything; but who must be exposed to one knows not what, and there must be a great change from what is at present. These things are hinted darkly to you, for which there is a reason. But there is a relief in it, and the more, as it is to no one else whatsoever, now Dr. P. is gone."

To the same friend, at the same time, he sent his Apology and its Appendix, now finished and ready for the press, requesting at the same time his free and impartial strictures. "You will find it run out," says he, "longer than you would think. But one thing drew on another. And it seemed to me necessary to complete my plan. I will not be ashamed to own to you that it has cost me some pains. And some things seem to be set in a stronger light than I have seen them; and some I had not seen observed before. When I have borrowed, I have fairly owned it. You know what severity of judgment, perhaps unkind, it is to pass through; and therefore I beg you will be severe beforehand, and also suggest any improvements which may occur to you." And in his next letter, dated June 21, he says, "I beg you will particularly mark any expression or sentiment that savoureth of pride or obstinacy, or contempt of others' opinions, or that is deficient in a proper and humble sense of myself." So solicitous was this excellent man that he might be influenced by none but the purest and most disinterested motives in all he did, or suffered, or wrote, through the whole of this arduous concern.

At the latter end of July, Mr. Lindsey was invited to preach the Assize sermon at York; of which opportunity he availed himself to bear his testimony to the cause of the petitioning clergy. This discourse gave great satisfaction to a liberal and enlightened audience, and the preacher was much solicited to print it. But as the bulk of it had been composed only for his country parishioners, to which a few additions had been made for the purpose of adapting it to the occasion, Mr. Lindsey did not think it worthy the public eye. Had it occurred to him that he might possibly be requested to publish, he would have been better prepared. And he expresses his regret to his friend, that "an opportunity of bearing a more public and useful testimony had been lost by him."

Soon after his return from York he made a visit to Alnwick Castle, "the noble owners of it having invited him in such a way, that *in this juncture* he thought it wrong to decline it, however inconvenient." He regarded it as proper upon this occasion to drop a hint to his illustrious friends of the important measure which he had in contemplation, not without some faint hope that, in some shape or other, some little effort might have been made to serve him, some temporary relief might have been offered. Happily, no such idea entered into the minds of the noble inhabitants of that princely mansion. On the contrary, "his words seemed to them as idle tales." Nor did it fall within the comprehension of persons of their high rank and dignity, that it was possible for a person of Mr. Lindsey's good understanding, for the sake of a few trifling scruples, to quit a situation of respectability and affluence, and expose himself and the person in the world who was the dearest to him to all the miseries of poverty and dependence. The disappointment of his expectations from the Duke and Duchess of Northumberland does not appear to have given Mr. Lindsey one moment's uneasiness. Before he set out for Alnwick he had written to his friend, " If God be with us and go along with us in all we do, and wherever we go, we shall prosper. I trust, I desire to do his will more ardently than ever." And after his return, August 10, he briefly states:— " My late journey was undertaken in view of my approaching affair, and to try something towards procuring a viaticum for the pilgrims. But I cannot say it has answered. Nobody will believe any one can be in earnest to take such a step."*

Mr. Lindsey was no fanatic who fancied merit in voluntary poverty. He had enjoyed and had duly valued and improved the blessings of affluence. Nor could anything but an imperious sense of duty have induced him to forego them. He is not, therefore, to be blamed for using any prudent and honourable means of saving himself and Mrs. Lindsey from falling at once into an abyss of poverty, in which they would be left to struggle with difficulties unaccustomed . and unknown. It could be no offence to say, " Father, if it be possible, let this cup pass away from me ;" provided that it was added, as in this case it certainly was, with the most entire resignation of spirit, " nevertheless, not our will, but thine, be done." And it was the wise and merciful design of Providence that this venerable confessor's faith and principle should be tried to the utmost. Nor indeed would it have been possible for Mr. Lindsey's character to have appeared with equal brilliancy and effect, nor could the purity of his own motives have been so evident, even to himself, if immediately upon his resignation of the vicarage of Catterick he had found a

* This disappointment was not owing to any personal dislike, or to any indifference in his noble patrons to the concerns of their venerable friend. On the contrary, they took a very lively interest in his future fortunes. And after he came to reside in London, on the very day in which he opened the chapel in Essex Street, when there was some apprehension that Mr. Lindsey might incur personal danger, the Duchess herself called at his humble apartments, after the morning service, to inquire after the safety of the revered confessor. But these illustrious persons, having offered him the highest preferment which it was in their power to confer, when Mr. Lindsey resigned his connection with the established church, probably considered him as having placed himself without the sphere of their patronage. Nor did it occur to them, nor would Mr. Lindsey's delicacy permit him to insinuate the most distant hint, to what a state of depression and dependence he had reduced himself by his magnanimous conduct. Afterwards, when his situation came to be better understood, a liberal present was made to his venerated preceptor by the late illustrious possessor of the title, which was continued annually till Mr. Lindsey's decease.

safe and splendid asylum in Northumberland House. It was therefore expedient for him, and for the cause which he had at heart, that he should be taught not only to be ready, but actually to suffer the loss of all things for the sake of truth and of a good conscience.

The disappointment at Alnwick Castle produced a very slight and momentary impression. A far severer conflict awaited Mr. Lindsey when he came to reveal his purpose to Mrs. Lindsey's relations, to Archdeacon Blackburne, her stepfather, who loved her as his own daughter, who from principle utterly disapproved the measure of leaving the church, and who could express his disapprobation with a strength and energy of language, which, though it could not shake Mr. Lindsey's purpose, might greatly agitate his feelings; and to Mrs. Blackburne, who, if she did not disapprove the principle of Mr. Lindsey's conduct, would feel most bitterly the inevitable consequence—that of tearing from her arms a beloved daughter who was the chief solace and support of her advancing years. This disclosure, so much dreaded, was indeed deferred by Mr. Lindsey perhaps beyond the time which strict propriety would justify, of which his friend at Wakefield appears to have given him a gentle hint. In reply to which, upon his return from Alnwick, he writes, "In my next I shall perhaps be able to tell you how the notification is received by one to whom you wished it to be made." This communication was made in the month of September; and the result of it, and the impression it made upon his mind, he thus concisely but feelingly describes in a letter dated September 17 :—

"What I said to you then (alluding to his last letter) I can ill recollect; for I had been then, and was some time after, under such agitations of mind in disclosing a certain important matter to some friends, that I was hardly master of myself to do any-thing properly. Something of this kind I could not avoid even at York. But *all such trials are now over.* Affliction, great, you will readily believe on the side of a loving mother and justly beloved daughter, on the prospect of so sudden a removal to such a distance ! But it gives place to better sentiments, and trust in

Providence. I cannot say the matter is so kindly taken by *others.* But such things are to be expected; and they may be of service to prepare for coldness, neglect, misrepresentation, and unkindness from the world, and to lead to depend only on Him who never faileth those who in well-doing put their trust in Him."

It was about the same time that he communicated his intention and his motives in a letter to another respectable correspondent :*—
" I think," says he, " you must have perceived in my letters, perhaps in my conversation, a dissatisfiedness with our ecclesiastical impositions, and a tendency to relieve myself from them. This indeed had taken place long before our association was formed, and the execution only suspended and retarded by it, though some pleasing expectation was formed, that Providence might unexpectedly give such a turn to our endeavours as might make me easy, or give me liberty to make myself easy. But as my chief dissatisfaction is with those Trinitarian forms which pervade the whole liturgy, all hope of that kind is entirely cut off. The resolution I have formed of retiring has been absolutely fixed

* See the Memoir in the Monthly Magazine, ibid. p. 448. This correspondent was the celebrated Dr. John Jebb, so well known and so honourably distinguished by the learned and instructive Critical and Theological Lectures which he delivered at Cambridge; by his zealous, active, and in part successful exertions to improve the system of education in the university, and to excite a laudable spirit of emulation among the students by frequent examinations and honorary premiums; and to abolish or to mitigate the yoke of subscription to the thirty-nine articles. This gentleman, however, finding his efforts for reformation in a great measure fruitless, resigned his preferment in the church, and afterwards took his degree in medicine, and entered upon practice in the metropolis with great reputation and success; but he died a few years afterwards, in the meridian of life, at the age of fifty-three.—See Dr. Disney's interesting Memoir of Dr. Jebb, prefixed to the collection of his works. Dr. Jebb did not actually quit his situation in the church till some time after the resignation of his friend Mr. Lindsey. But it is remarkable that the letters of the two friends, communicating to each other their respective resolutions to that effect, crossed upon the road. Dr. Jebb, as he was the active and energetic coadjutor of Mr. Lindsey in the business of the clerical association, so he was, with Mr. Turner, his confidential friend and adviser in all his subsequent proceedings and difficulties, particularly concerning the opening of the chapel in Essex Street, and the alterations in the Liturgy. Mr. Lindsey also submitted his various publications to the revisal of Dr. Jebb, and derived much benefit from his critical remarks upon difficult and disputed texts. It was the earnest desire of Mr. Lindsey that his pious and learned friend should have been associated with him as his colleague in Essex Street. But this Dr. Jebb declined; though afterwards when he was settled in London, he was a constant worshipper in Mr. Lindsey's chapel, and a most zealous and decided advocate for Unitarian principles, and supporter of the sole worship and unrivalled supremacy of the One God, the Father of our Lord Jesus Christ.

E

for some time, and will take place in a few months. It was absolutely necessary for my own peace with God, which is to be preferred above all considerations. But I have found great difficulties and opposition already, and expect to find more. My greatest comfort and support, under God, is my wife, who is a Christian indeed, and worthy of a better fate in worldly things than we have a prospect of; for we leave a station of ease and abundance, attended with many other agreeable circumstances. But, thanks be to God, we have not given way to ease and indulgence, and can be content with little."

In the month of October, Mr. Lindsey writes to his friend, "that their courage and trust in God did not relax, though difficulties and discouragements increased; and that, if these produced the effect of bringing them nearer to God, and to more entire reliance upon him, whatever might befall them they would have reason to be thankful."

. On the 12th of November, Mr. Lindsey wrote to his diocesan, Dr. Markham, then Bishop of Chester, afterwards Archbishop of York, to inform him of his intention to resign his vicarage, and that in a few days he should wait upon his Lordship with the legal instrument of his resignation. On the same day he wrote a long letter to Dr. Jebb, in which he says, "I have never had the least doubt, from the first moment I resolved on the step I am now about to take, but that it was right, and my duty. I have had some subsequent hope, too, that it might serve our cause, and the cause of God's truth. I bless the God of heaven for myself, and my wife, who is destined to bear a great part of the burden, that as difficulties increase (and they must increase the nearer the time approaches), our resolution and courage increase. And I have no doubt but the promises made to the faithful servants will be fulfilled to us; that we shall have strength proportioned to our trial and want of it."*

---

* In another letter to the same friend, dated December 5, 1773, Mr. Lindsey writes: " I have always had great satisfaction and information in your letters, and in your later ones much comfort and encouragement. If I had been opposed and condemned by all my friends, by all the world, in what I have been long meditating and have now accomplished, I must have done it. The track of duty was so plain and straight,

On the same day he wrote a letter to his friend Mr. Turner, who had proposed to recommend him to a congregation of liberal Dissenters at the Octagon Chapel, Liverpool, which was then in want of a minister. In this letter he expresses his deep sense of his friend's kindness, and his own further views and purposes, in the following terms :—

"I must ever say that I have had no such consolation from any one as from you, during the conflict and trial which the providence of God has cast upon me. You have ever been leading to the right point of view in which to consider it, and suggesting the most animating motives for encouragement under it. And not satisfied with doing this, your last convinces me of your earnest desire to contribute your endeavours to procure me an establishment when I quit this, which may preserve some degree of usefulness which I anxiously wish, and serve for that worldly support which we shall want. But with regard to what you kindly suggest, I believe it will be best to wait, and not lay out for anything of this kind at present, though no less obliged to you than if you procured me success in it. My reason is, that my design, which I specify very particularly in my tract, is to try to gather a church of Unitarian Christians out of the established church. My hope is, that it may please Providence to excite some *Philadelphians* in our church to favour such a design. And when I go to town, which will be in the beginning of the winter, I shall do all I can to forward it; with hope, I said before, not very sanguine however, for serious religion is not the tone and temper of the times. But attempts must be made in such matters oftentimes when there are even greater improbabilities of

I must have been abandoned to every moral principle not to have gone in it. I have no doubt I shall have increasing joy in what I have done, to the latest day of my life. And I feel myself delivered from a load which has long lain heavy upon me, and at times nearly overwhelmed me. I shall be still more happy if what I thought myself called upon to speak to the public in my own behalf, but more in the cause of oppressed truth, may but serve its interests. The Bishop of Chester, my diocesan, has behaved with great friendliness, and kindly wished and sought to have prevented my taking such a step. And the same has been endeavoured by other great friends lately, and various expedients proposed. But I now only wonder I did not sooner make my retreat; and I am persuaded that will be the general cry of many when they see my book."

E 2

accomplishing them. I could wish, and I think it my duty, to be instrumental in bringing those who are now in the darkness in which I was bred up to the acknowledgment and worship of the One true God, through the mediation and according to the true doctrine of our Saviour Christ, rather than attach myself to those who are already emancipated from that darkness. And we are willing to expend what little we have for that end for a year or two in town, and make the trial. Should it fail, I should be glad to be useful in any congregation where the worship of the true God is allowed and professed. As to future provision, though gloomy thoughts for a moment have sometimes come across the mind, we have no doubt but our own industry and the friends that Providence will raise will furnish everything needful for it.

"On Sunday last I took my leave of two of the chapels in my parish, that lie at a good distance off, near the moors, a poor simple-minded people, who much affected me by the concern they showed and expressed in words at my telling them that I should never more speak to them from that place; and all desired to have the little tract which I mentioned I should distribute amongst them, and which would give them an account of the reasons why I left them."*

* This excellent and affecting little tract, from which large extracts have been made in the preceding part of this Memoir, was originally intended for private circulation only among Mr. Lindsey's parishioners, but by the desire of many judicious friends it was afterwards published. Mr. Turner, in a letter to a friend (Mr. Astley, of Chester-field) to whom he sent a copy of this Farewell Address, says, "I think you will be pleased with the simplicity of the composition, as well as with the integrity and good-ness of heart manifested in it. In short, it bears the very spirit and character of the man." Of the effect produced by it in the district where it was first circulated, Mr. Lindsey thus expresses himself in a letter to Dr. Jebb, dated December 5, 1773 : " I may not omit to mention, though I ought not perhaps to do it, but you will be glad to know that my resignation has excited a spirit of serious inquiry not only in this parish but in this neighbourhood to a pretty wide extent. The little sheet I gave away is much sought for, and all seem to think it a *sore* thing that we should not be ruled by the Bible alone, and that their ministers should be put on praying to any but the true God whom the holy prophets prayed to, and our Saviour Christ not only prayed to himself, but ordered us to pray to the Heavenly Father and no other." He adds : " To my great surprise I have found, at this trial of them, all my large parish, even the honest and serious day labourers, not only petitioners, but Unitarians." It may per-haps be doubted whether this excellent man was not somewhat too sanguine in the credit he gave to the effect produced by his doctrine and example upon the mass of his

"With such deliberate and cheerful resolution," says his worthy correspondent, in a letter to a friend dated a few days afterwards, " does this confessor to what he conceives to be the truth of the gospel resign a certain establishment for dependence and poverty. The glorious triumvirate, Robertson, Chambers,*

parishioners. At any rate, it is to be feared that the valuable impression is now almost, if not altogether, effaced. The good seed fell by the wayside, and the fowls of the air devoured it; or among thorns, which grew up and choked it; or on stony ground, where it soon withered. Haply some may have fallen on good ground, where, in the shade of obscurity, unknown and unnoticed by the world, but not unobserved by that eye to which all things are open, it may still diffuse a refreshing fragrance and bring forth abundant fruit.

How much the parishioners were affected by their separation from their beloved and venerated pastor, may be learned from the following testimony of one who was present at his valedictory discourse. " Indeed," says the writer, " I think no one could hear that sermon without being struck and affected. The whole congregation was dissolved in tears; even children caught the infection; and the old men crowded about the church door when the preacher passed along, as if the peace of their few remaining days depended on a farewell benediction." " His life," says one of his near neighbours, a man of sense and education, in reply to some foolish and anonymous calumnies in the *York Chronicle*, "and conversation have been uniform and consistent, without spot or blemish, and his active and devout disposition of mind has rendered him no less eminently great than useful. Those who knew him best admired him most. He did not, like too many of his profession, merely preach, but he practised virtue. His example was as worthy imitation as his precepts. Most assiduous and attentive in every department of his holy function, he was an ornament to the church, and the most rare example of disinterested integrity which this age or perhaps this country has produced. Far unlike our modern churchmen, whose views are all directed on preferments, the kingdom that he sought was not of this world. He yearly expended in acts of noble benevolence the whole revenue of his vicarage, which he reluctantly resigned because he could not reconcile himself to the glaring inconsistencies of a liturgy to which, while he continued in the church, he found himself obliged to conform."—See a letter in the *York Chronicle* for February, 1774, signed " A Layman," written by Mr. Metcalfe, notary public, of Richmond, who received Mr. Lindsey's resignation. In a letter to a friend at York, dated December 3, 1773, Mr. Lindsey, with his usual humility and kindness of heart, expresses himself thus: " Great are their lamentations at our leaving them, far more than we expected. But I attribute it chiefly to the great loss they will have in my wife, who will not soon be replaced."

* William Chambers, D.D., rector of Achurch, near Oundle, in Northamptonshire, formerly of St. John's College, in the University of Cambridge, where Mr. Lindsey commenced a friendship with him which continued through life. Dr. C. is described by his friend as having a mind above all sordid love of gain, who knew no other use of his fortune than to make others happy. He was remarkable for a constant cheerfulness and innocent pleasantry which much enlivened conversation. His mind was always open to conviction; he had a thirst after all useful knowledge, and spared no pains nor cost to attain it. Yet still he was most concerned about what related to God, how best to serve and make him known. He was deeply impressed with a sense of the truth and importance of the doctrine of the Divine Unity; and was zealous to diffuse and impart his light and knowledge to others. He had long determined never to renew his subscription to the articles, and upon this ground had declined considerable preferment in London, which had been offered him by a noble Earl, his relation. He did not,

and Lindsey, do honour to Christianity and the present age. You will be surprised and grieved at the following particulars which Mr. —— of —— lately gave me in a letter. Archdeacon Blackburne thinks Mr. Lindsey wrong; that his resignation will not benefit the common cause; that he should have made it sooner; that the public has nothing to do with his reasons and apologies; and says, that when he has quitted Catterick he and his wife will have no more than twenty pounds a-year, and the interest of a very small sum of money."

This is a noble testimony from the best authority to the disinterestedness of Mr. and Mrs. Lindsey, and to the difficulties which they had to struggle with; but for a good conscience they left all, and for the sake of Christ and his word they forsook father and mother. And happily the learned Archdeacon himself, who now so much disapproved their conduct, afterwards saw reason to retract his judgment, and, if he could not altogether approve, at least he ceased to condemn and learned to acquiesce.

The venerable diocesan received the intelligence of Mr. Lindsey's intended resignation with much regret, and endeavoured, by every argument and motive which zeal and friendship could suggest, to retain in the church so bright an ornament to the established priesthood. But his efforts, though well intended,

however, think it necessary to follow his venerable friend's example of resigning his living; but he altered the liturgy in accommodation to his own views of scriptural worship, and he made it so perfectly Unitarian that Mr. Lindsey professes that the only time that he visited his friend after his own settlement in London, he attended public worship in his church with great satisfaction. If these innovations had been officially noticed, Dr. Chambers was fully prepared to have given up his living rather than have violated his conscience. But such were the popularity of his character and the moderation of his worthy diocesan, Dr. Hinchcliffe, that he met with no molestation. This excellent man died of an apoplexy, September 4, 1777. He left a widow, who survived him upwards of thirty years, and three children, two sons and a daughter, who inherit his virtues. Dr. Chambers had a near relation who was a merchant in London, who had a country house at Morden, in Surrey, where he lived with two unmarried sisters, ladies possessed of uncommon intellectual attainments, and whose characters were most exemplary. In this family Mr. and Mrs. Lindsey were accustomed to pass the greater part of the summer; and to these ladies Mr. Lindsey dedicated his last work, "Conversations upon the Divine Government," " in gratitude," as he expresses it, " for unwearied offices of the most disinterested friendship for near thirty years to himself and Mrs. Lindsey, and in testimony for their enlightened zeal for the worship of the One true God, and a constant unostentatious readiness to do good."—See Mr. Lindsey's Historical View, p. 486.

were unavailing. Mr. Lindsey's resolution had been formed upon deliberation too mature, and upon principles too sacred and too firmly rivetted, to be in the least degree shaken by the arguments or expostulations of the worthy prelate; who frankly and honourably acknowledged, when the deed of resignation was at last delivered in at the end of the month, that he had lost the most exemplary parochial minister in his diocese.*

Thus did Mr. and Mrs. Lindsey, in obedience to the voice of enlightened conscience, resign their beloved residence at Catterick, with all its secular advantages and comforts, and with their little pittance of private property set out, in the bleak month of December, in search of a resting-place where they might be able to maintain themselves by honourable industry, and might best promote the great doctrine of the Divine Unity and the sole unrivalled supremacy of the Father.

> The world was all before them, where to choose
> Their place of rest, and Providence their guide.

CHAPTER III.

FROM MR. LINDSEY'S RESIGNATION OF CATTERICK, TO THE
OPENING OF THE CHAPEL IN ESSEX STREET.

INDEED they soon found that the diminution of income was not the only difficulty with which they had to contend. In the days of their prosperity, and while they continued in connection with the established church, they had many warm friends who gladly received them at all times into their houses, and entertained them hospitably, and many of whom concurred with Mr. Lindsey in the application to parliament for relief from subscription. But

---

* N.B.—For the interesting correspondence between Mr. Lindsey and his worthy diocesan, see Appendix, No. IV.

now the case was quite altered. Former friends looked coldly upon them; and some, of whom better things might have been expected, whose conduct was silently reproved by the magnanimous example of Mr. Lindsey, were not sparing in loud and strong expressions of disapprobation of what they were pleased to term the precipitancy and imprudence of his conduct in abandoning a situation of respectability and usefulness in the church; and not a few were willing to leave them to their fate. Some, indeed, of Mrs. Lindsey's more opulent relations offered to provide for her an asylum and competence, if she would abandon the society and the fortunes of her husband. It is needless to say that such a proposal was rejected with the indignation it deserved.

From Catterick " the pilgrims " first went to Bedale, to Mrs. Harrison's, and the next day to Wakefield, accompanied by their accomplished friend who had drank deeply into the same spirit, Miss Harrison, now Mrs. Cappe, to pass a day or two in the society of the venerable Mr. Turner, to enjoy the benefit of his sympathy, his counsels, his consolations, and his prayers. Of this delightful and instructive visit this excellent man gives the following account in a letter to an intimate friend :—

" Since I wrote to you last I had the pleasure of Mr. and Mrs. Lindsey's company one whole day and part of another. They both appeared very cheerful, considering that they were launching into untried scenes of an uncertain world, with hopes far from sanguine of the success of the scheme they had proposed, and consequently of obtaining the very means of subsistence. But confiding in the care of him who promised, ' Whosover shall confess me before men, him will I also confess,' &c., they both, and particularly Mrs. Lindsey, seemed to exult in having broke loose from ecclesiastical thraldom and gained mental liberty, and expressed much indignation against those who, having been educated in liberty of inquiry, and instructed in the value of. it, have for the sordid considerations of this world submitted to shackles and to servitude."

From their hospitable friends at Wakefield, where they took an affectionate leave of their amiable fellow-traveller, Mr. and Mrs. Lindsey proceeded to Aston, near York, the residence of the Rev. William Mason, the celebrated poet, the friend and biographer of Gray, who entertained them for a week at his house with great cordiality;—though the conduct of Mr. Lindsey in resigning his living was much canvassed at York, where Mr. Mason was precentor of the cathedral, and was much condemned by some who were in repute for wisdom, who spoke of him as " a well-meaning person, who would have done much less harm to society if he had never gone into the church at all."*

To York Mr. Lindsey had sent his library, which he consigned

* Whatever might be the language of these wise judges in their select parties concerning Mr. Lindsey, none of them were so indiscreet as to publish their censures of his character and conduct excepting one, Dr. William Cooper, a dignitary of the cathedral at York, and brother to Grey Cooper, Esq., M.P., who had also been a college friend of Mr. Lindsey. This Dr. Cooper, amongst others, made great interest to obtain the vicarage of Catterick upon Mr. Lindsey's resignation. But not being successful in his suit, the living being given to Dr. Chaytor, the brother-in-law of Mr. Robinson, Lord North's private secretary, this worthy dignitary grew very angry that the living was resigned at all: and in the *York Chronicle* of January 28, 1774, under the signature of Erasmus, he published a most foolish and furious invective against Mr. Lindsey. It begins thus:—" Before you attempt to amend the liturgy, amend the articles, or amend anything else—you would do well, in the judgment of all rational beings, to amend your mode of writing, and, what is of more consequence, to amend your mode of thinking. But I cry your mercy. You cannot err, illuminated sir; you have had a Divine impulse," &c. And again,—" If you had either the courage, or the goodness of heart, to let us know what your real sentiments are, 'tis more than probable that we should deservedly hold you in extreme contempt," &c.

Such despicable and outrageous rant merited nothing but " extreme contempt." However it had its use. It brought forward a host of advocates in defence of the fair fame of the absent and calumniated confessor. In the foremost rank of these were the Reverend N. Cappe, of York, and the Reverend W. Turner, of Wakefield. To the credit of the order, and the still greater credit of Mr. Lindsey's unimpeachable and spotless character, not one of the clergy of the established church, how much soever they might be offended with Mr. Lindsey's doctrine or his secession, stood forward to join in the attack, or to assist a distressed brother. They prudently and silently left him to his fate. And the miserable assailant, having in vain attempted under different signatures to maintain his ground and to defend his charge, after being detected, defeated, and exposed in every shape that he assumed, was in the end compelled to retire from the field, humbled, confounded, and disgraced. Nor does it appear that this officious and malignant zeal for the church was at that time thought worthy of additional preferment.

.That everybody did not entertain the same opinion of Mr. Lindsey's conduct as Dr. Cooper and. his associates at York, appears from some letters written to Mr. Lindsey upon this interesting occasion, which are inserted in the Appendix; one of which is from Mr. Grey Cooper himself, the brother of Dr. C. and the friend of Lord North. Appendix, No. V.

to the care of his friend Mr. Cappe, to be sold in order to raise a temporary supply for the support of himself and Mrs. Lindsey; having reserved for himself a small number of books only for immediate use.*

From Aston, Mr. and Mrs. Lindsey went to Swinderby, near Newark, where they made a transient visit to Mr., afterwards Dr., Disney, a clergyman of great learning and respectability, who was an active member of the Association at the Feathers' Tavern. He shortly afterwards married Miss Blackburne, the daughter of the learned Archdeacon of Cleveland, and half-sister to Mrs. Lindsey, who, much to her honour, expressed upon all occasions her high approbation of the step which Mr. Lindsey had taken; and with the generosity and ardour which belonged to her character, she defended the principles and the conduct of her calumniated friends. Dr. Disney himself was at that time much dissatisfied with many things in the established liturgy; but he contented himself with making the alterations which he thought necessary, leaving it to his ecclesiastical superiors to animadvert upon him as they might think fit. This conduct, however, did not prove ultimately satisfactory to his ingenuous mind, and a few years afterwards he bore his faithful testimony to Christian truth by following the shining example of Mr. Lindsey, in resigning his preferments and prospects in the established church. Of the process of mind which led to this honourable conclusion, Dr. Disney has given an interesting narrative in a small tract which he published upon the occasion.†

While Mr. Lindsey continued at Swinderby, he met with and transcribed the alterations proposed by Dr. Clarke in the established liturgy, which he at that time intended to print, but which he afterwards made the foundation of the improvements in the reformed liturgy which he introduced at Essex Street.

From Swinderby the travellers directed their steps to Achurch, in Northamptonshire, the rectory and residence of their highly

---

* This, no doubt, select and valuable collection at that time produced no more than the scanty pittance of £38.

† This tract is in the catalogue of those which are circulated by the London Unitarian Society.

valued friend Dr. Chambers. In their road, they passed one day with Mr. Lindsey's sister, who was married to Mr. Harrison, an eminent grazier in Leicestershire. This venerable lady, three years older than her brother, and the exact model of him in piety and benevolence, is still living (A.D. 1810), meekly and with humble resignation bending under the infirmities of ninety years.

From Achurch, he writes to Dr. Jebb, in a letter dated January 1, 1774, " I cannot but rejoice in your full approbation of my conduct hitherto, and future plan, and feel myself continually encouraged by it. I have from the first entertained a feeble imagination that perhaps I might have an honourable coadjutor in the friend I am writing to for an Unitarian chapel, if it should meet with the patronage which some promise it." He adds : " Our common friend and present host is most heartily with us in everything." The patronage to which Mr. Lindsey alludes was probably that of which he received intelligence from Dr. Priestley, who was then in London with Lord Shelburne, and indefatigable in his exertions to serve his friend, and to promote his design of opening a chapel in London, and whose sanguine spirit led him, perhaps, to rely rather too much upon the promises of the great. In a letter to Mr. Turner he writes : " All my friends are very sanguine in favour of Mr. Lindsey's Unitarian chapel. Dr. Franklin says he knows several persons of distinction who will wish to encourage it, and several have proposed to subscribe to it. His Farewell Address I have just read, and was much affected with it : and so was Lord Shelburne, to whom I showed it. He is very desirous to see him as soon as he comes to London." This, no doubt, was encouraging. But it will appear in the sequel that the persons to whom Dr. Priestley alludes were not those to whose exertions and support Mr. Lindsey was most indebted for the execution of the scheme which he had so much at heart.

At Achurch, Mr. Lindsey finished the revisal of the last sheet of his Apology, which was published the beginning of January, notwithstanding the remonstrances of Archdeacon Blackburne, who was apprehensive that it might be of disservice to the cause of the petitioning clergy. To this objection Mr. Lindsey paid no attention, justly remarking, that if the Apology was to produce any effect, its publication must be immediate, while the occasion of it was fresh in memory. "To suspend it now," says he, in a letter to a friend, "would be to sink it for ever." And as he conceived that such a work was necessary for his own vindication, and, what in his estimation was of far greater moment, that it would be of use for the promulgation of truth, he also hoped that it would contribute to promote, rather than obstruct, the object of the associated clergy.

The design of this excellent treatise, as set forth in the preface, "was not barely to offer a vindication of the motives, conduct, and sentiments of a private person upon the subject of it, however important to him, but to promote that charity without which a faith that can remove mountains is nothing, and to excite some to piety, virtue, and integrity."

It begins with some strictures upon the origin of the doctrine of the Trinity, and the opposition it met with to the time of the Reformation. It then treats of the state of the Unitarian doctrine, in our own country more especially, from the era of the Reformation, with an account of those Christians who have professed it; and proceeds to prove that there is but One God, the Father, and that religious worship is to be offered to this One God, the Father, only. In the next chapter it states the causes of this unhappy defection among Christians from the simplicity of religious worship prescribed in the scriptures of the New Testament. It then shows how union in God's true worship is to be attained, and concludes with a modest and concise but affecting detail of the writer's particular case and difficulties. The work, the first in which the venerable author publicly adventured to defend his unpopular tenets, is drawn up with great care, and with much simplicity and candour. It breathes throughout an excellent spirit of piety and benevolence. It was revised with great attention by Mr. Turner; and in the judgment of every serious and impartial person, whether agreeing or disagreeing with the writer in his peculiar principles, it contains a complete and masterly vindication of his conduct in withdrawing from his situation in the established church. This Apology, in less than ten years, passed through four editions.

On the 10th of January, 1774, Mr. and Mrs. Lindsey arrived at London, having spent a day or two in their way at Paxton, with Mr. Lindsey's old college friend, Richard Reynolds, Esq., who, having imbibed the principles and the spirit of the virtuous protector of his youth, and his esteem and affection for his venerable friend having been if possible increased by his late noble act of disinterested virtue, received him and his fellow-traveller and fellow-sufferer upon the present occasion with redoubled satisfaction.*

Upon their arrival at London they proceeded by particular invitation to Dr. Ramsden's, then in an inferior situation, afterwards the worthy Master of the Charter-house, a gentleman of great learning and probity, and of the most liberal principles; who rose to the honourable office which he occupied by no other interest than that of personal merit, and who was not afraid of hazarding his reputation and his preferment by affording an asylum to his ex-beneficed friend. Here they were very hospitably entertained for ten days or a fortnight, till they had provided themselves with decent but humble lodgings, being two rooms on a ground-floor, in Featherstone Buildings, Holborn, where they now fixed their abode, and sold the plate which they had brought with them to London to purchase necessaries for present subsistence.

But the scene soon began to brighten. Though few com-

* While he was at Paxton, Mr. Lindsey received intelligence of the sudden decease of Thomas Hollis, Esq., the celebrated and zealous friend to liberty, civil and religious. Of this gentleman Archdeacon Blackburne published an interesting Memoir in two volumes in quarto. He was the friend and confidential correspondent of Mr. Lindsey, under the assumed title of Pierce Delver. He was the ready and liberal patron of all who were in distress, and particularly of those who suffered in the cause of civil and religious liberty, or for the sake of truth and a good conscience. It cannot be doubted that, had his life been continued, he would have extended a liberable patronage to Mr. Lindsey. Happily the venerable confessor did not stand in need of it. Some curious extracts from the correspondence of this virtuous and honourable man are cited in the notes to this work, and a specimen or two in the Appendix, No. VI.

paratively of Mr. Lindsey's former friends visited or noticed him
in his voluntary retirement ; though some, whose principles nearly
coincided with his own, but whose timidity and half-measures
were condemned, not by his language, for he was the humblest
and most candid of mankind, and very far indeed from making
his own conduct a law to others, but by his bright and edifying
example, not only gave no encouragement to the plan he had
in contemplation, but openly and without reserve expressed
their disapprobation of it ; he nevertheless met with great approbation and support from quarters where it was least expected.
Many persons, both of the establishment and among the dissenters,
perfect strangers to Mr. Lindsey, deeply impressed with veneration
for his character, and admiration of the noble sacrifice which
he had made for the sake of truth and conscience, visited him
in his humble lodgings to testify their regard to him, and to
offer their services in any way in which they might be of use.
And when they heard of Mr. Lindsey's design of opening a
chapel for the worship of the One God, the Father of Jesus Christ,
many expressed their warm approbation and their active hearty
concurrence in the execution of the design. Some promised to
indemnify Mr. Lindsey in making the experiment. Others,
and chiefly among the rational Dissenters, subscribed liberally
towards the design. Dr. Priestley and Dr. Price were active
and zealous friends. Samuel Shore, Esq., then of Norton Hall,
now of Meersbrook, in Yorkshire, whose name ranks high among
the advocates for civil and religious liberty, the patrons of
truth and science, and the friends of pure and practical Christianity,
called upon Mr. Lindsey with a present of a hundred pounds from
a friend whose name was then concealed, but since known to have
been Robert Newton, Esq., of Norton House,* whose delight was

---

* Robert Newton, Esq., of Norton House. Of the character of this eminently
benevolent man, the following interesting sketch is given by his intimate acquaintance,
the Reverend W. Turner, of Wakefield, to Mr. Lindsey, in a letter dated June 14,
1777 :—

  "Robert Newton, Esq., is a near neighbour to Mr. Shore in the same village,
aged about sixty-six or sixty-seven, and a bachelor of large fortune. I have known
him since the year 1732, when, and for two or three years afterwards, we were
fellow-pupils under Dr. Latham, at Findern, near Derby. His mother lost her husband

to spend the income of a large estate in doing good in the most private manner possible, and from the shade of retirement to scatter blessings upon his fellow-creatures. To this princely donation of Mr. Newton, Mr. Shore generously added a very liberal present of his own ; and to the end of Mr. Linsey's life he continued the warm personal friend, and the firm and liberal supporter of him and his cause. In this way a sum was very soon subscribed adequate to every purpose which Mr. Lindsey had in view. And by the exertions of the late Mr. Joseph Johnson, of St. Paul's Churchyard, a room was soon found and taken in Essex House, Essex Street, which having before been used as an auction-room might, at a moderate expense be fitted up as

when she was pregnant of this son, and gave so much way to grief for that event as was supposed to have an ill effect on the constitution of her child. He has always had very weak nerves and uneven spirits, but generally a prevailing hypochondria. For many years past he has been telling his friends that he should soon give them the slip : but in the mean time he has looked well and grown bulky. When any extraordinary case, particularly for the service of his friends, called for it, he could exert as much vigour, activity, and resolution as any man. To an exertion of this kind the two Miss —— owed their fortunes. They had an unhappy brother, of either defective understanding or capricious or bad temper, or both, who being past his majority, and a student at Edinburgh, died there. Immediately an episcopal clergyman, in whose house he had boarded, pretended that Mr. —— had married his daughter, and made a will by which he had bequeathed all his fortune to her absolutely. When the family was informed of this, Mr. Newton, having furnished himself with proper power, and being also a guardian and trustee, set off express, met the corpse on the road, which they were bringing to be deposited in the family burying-place, arrested and secured it ; went forward to Edinburgh, made diligent inquiry, discovered many suspicious circumstances, and partly by remonstrances, and partly by threats of a legal discussion at the expense of his own whole fortune, prevailed upon the Scotch pretenders, in consideration of a few ready thousands, to relinquish their whole claim. He then returned with great satisfaction and honour, and ordered the corpse to proceed to the family burial-place. For such a service, all the connections of the family owe and pay him great esteem and gratitude. Mr. S. says, Nature formed him for a soldier ; and that as a commander, and especially as a partisan, he would certainly have distinguished himself. When younger, he made little of riding from his own house to Scarborough in one day ; supping, and perhaps dancing there till midnight with a party of his friends, and would then remount and return next day. Like sudden excursions and returns, to and from London, Bath, Bristol, and even abroad, were common with him,—and all the while he was *dying*. From all the above circumstances you will easily conclude he must have had some humours, and even whims ; but they have always been very innocent, and only laughable. He has always been very steady in his friendships, of which Mr. H., a Dissenting minister at Mansfield, who for many years has been his most familiar friend and companion, both when at home and in many of his excursions, has had, I doubt not, ample experience.— So much for your generous back-friend Mr. Newton, who, as a friend of mine said of another person, delights to do such extraordinary good deeds and nobody must know! I need not caution you not to draw the curtain behind which he chooses to conceal himself."

a temporary chapel. In a letter to Mr. Turner, dated February 9, 1774, Mr. Lindsey thus expresses himself :—

"Dr. Priestley is indefatigable in his endeavours ; and to him, Dr. Price, and other friends of theirs, it will be owing that the matter is brought to bear at last, as they kindly offer by subscription of their friends to indemnify me on the first outset. If it be of God, as I trust it is, it will succeed. But should it fail, some good I still persuade myself will result, and others will easier take it up and proceed better. I desire the help of your prayers for illumination and direction now and always." In another letter, dated March 17, to the same friend, in reference to his Apology, he writes, "Your earnest prayers are desired for the writer, that he may persevere to the end and be found faithful unto death : and with him one other also to be joined, whose trial has been and is the same or greater." And in the same letter, after acknowledging Mr. Turner's kind and successful recommendation of his undertaking to some generous friends at Wakefield and elsewhere, he adds, "I have reason to say, and have said it to more persons than one of late, that I have had the gospel promise of the hundred-fold in the number of friends increased in this world ; and should an evil day of persecution come, they would be a great consolation in it. This, indeed, is what some forebode, especially when our new form of worship is set up." In his next letter, dated April 5, after acknowledging the liberality of Mr. Milnes, and relating the munificence of the gentlemen of Norton, he writes, "We compute that two hundred pounds will nearly fit up and pay the rent of our chapel for two years. Behold then this sum nearly supplied by a few generous hands. I am thankful. But I am sorry to say they are all, one excepted, not of the established church."

In this letter Mr. Lindsey notices to his friend a very honourable invitation which he had lately received to settle with a Dissenting congregation at Norwich, which, however, it did not comport with his present plans and purposes to accept.

As soon as Mr. Lindsey was settled, and especially after he had met with such great encouragement to pursue his primary purpose, he began in good earnest to draw up his Reformed Liturgy, very much upon the plan of Dr. Clarke's, but with considerable variations and improvements adapted to his own more correct and extended views of Christian doctrine, and of the mode of conducting Christian worship. Many of his timid and lukewarm brethren earnestly recommended to him to adhere without any variation to Dr. Clarke's copy, that every innovation might be introduced under the sanction of the venerable name of that learned and eminent theologian. But Mr. Lindsey had advanced too far to be deterred by the fear of calumny, or to adopt error because it was supported by a great name. Indeed, though he was far from wishing to introduce any unnecessary change in the public service, he justly thought that it would be very inconsistent in him, who had resigned a lucrative situation in the established church principally because of his objections to the public liturgy, now that he was at full liberty to choose for himself, to compromise his principles by adopting a form which was open to many objections solely because it was the work of Dr. Samuel Clarke. Rejecting therefore every proposal of this nature, and judiciously resolving upon carrying Dr. Clarke's own principle of reform to what appeared to him to be its proper extent, he requested the assistance of his friend Mr. Turner in this important undertaking; but he chiefly relied upon the able co-operation and prudent advice of his friends Dr. Jebb, Mr. Tyrwhit, and a few other learned and liberal members of the University of Cambridge; and with their aid, in conjunction with his own indefatigable exertions, the Reformed Liturgy was compiled and printed ready for use by the middle of April, 1774.

When it came to be generally known that it was Mr. Lindsey's intention to open a chapel upon principles strictly Unitarian, with a reformed liturgy, great offence was taken by many, and means used, but without effect to, intimidate this magnanimous confessor from the execution of his purpose. It was even intimated to him that the civil power would interpose to frustrate his design. But none of these things moved him; nor could any worldly consideration induce him to abandon what he regarded as the line of

F

duty. " Our church-superiors," says he in a letter to Mr. Turner, dated February 9, " are said to glory in laying everything to
sleep. I doubt not but it will appear that their policy is as much
mistaken as their Christian principle is certainly defective in this
respect. Our design of a reformed liturgy is much spoken
against by them, and highly condemned as forward, schismatical,
and I know not what, and intimations given as if such an attempt
would not be suffered. But these things deter not *one* person,
and I hope they will not others." Of the methods which were
used to intimidate and divert him from his purpose, Mr. Lindsey
mentions an example in a letter to Dr. Jebb, dated February 28:
" If it were not making an obscure man of too much importance,
I might tell you that two of the Commons' House have desired
to see me, and to divert me from a design which will turn that
general compassion now shown towards me into open hostility
and hatred. I wish no other situation but that in which I may
be made instrumental in removing the shocking snares that are in
the way of conscientious men, and the impure idolatries of
Christian worship."

That many of the friends of the established hierarchy, and
that some persons who were of great consideration in the Government, entertained no small anxiety with respect to the consequences of Mr. Lindsey's public secession from the church, there
is great reason to believe. The spirit of inquiry and of reformation was then abroad, and it could not be foreseen how far the
generous contagion would spread. And who could say that
another glorious Bartholomew-day might not be added to the
calendar of English martyrology, and that hundreds might not
be stimulated by the noble example of this truly primitive confessor to resign their preferment, like their predecessors in the
preceding century, for the sake of a good conscience! The time
however was not yet come. And there is no reason to believe
that there ever existed in the minds of men in power a design or
a wish to molest Mr. Lindsey. They had too much understanding, and too accurate a knowledge of human nature and of history, not to be aware that persecution, if it does not extend to

extermination, promotes the interest of the persecuted sect. And in fact Lord North, who was then at the head of the Administration, and the rigour of whose high-church principles was counterbalanced by the suavity of his temper, avowed his wish without hesitation that every one should be permitted to go to heaven in his own way, provided that the public peace was not disturbed. And though, upon the opening of the chapel in Essex Street, an emissary of Government was known for some time to attend the public service regularly, in order to communicate information to persons in power; yet when it was discovered that nothing was either taught or done contrary to the allegiance due to the State, and likewise that few of the dissatisfied clergy were disposed to follow Mr. Lindsey's example, and that the obnoxious principles were not likely to gain over many proselytes, Ministers of State wisely ceased to trouble themselves about Essex chapel, and suffered the new sect quietly to immerge and to find its level in the vast mass of religious dissentients. Nor indeed, if the governing party had been so unwise as to have urged a prosecution, can it be with reason supposed that a Sovereign who began his reign with the memorable declaration that he would " maintain the toleration inviolable;" and who in the course of a long, an agitated, and an eventful administration has never in a single instance violated his promise, would for a moment have lent his countenance to so unjust and cruel a procedure.

But though the tolerant spirit of the times, together with the wisdom and lenity of the superior and more enlightened functionaries of the State, imposed a restraint upon the spirit of persecution, there were not wanting some busy ignorant people in the inferior departments of magistracy, who, " dressed in a little brief authority," were anxious to show their zeal for the church, their loyalty to the crown, and their own official consequence, by crushing Mr. Lindsey's design at the moment of its execution, and by attempting with equal malignity and folly to nullify the provisions of an Act of Parliament by the decrees of a petty sessions. The Westminster Justices hesitated to grant a license for opening the chapel.

F 2

The place was fitted up, the Liturgy was printed, and all was in readiness for performing divine service early in the month of April; but as the Justices did not meet till Easter Tuesday, April 5th, the place could not be legally registered till that day, and it was necessary to defer opening the chapel till the Sunday following. On the day of meeting, application was made in due form to the Justices assembled at Hick's Hall to register the chapel as a place of Dissenting worship. But these gentlemen returned for answer, that they were holding a sessions for the county of Middlesex, and that, the chapel being situated in Westminster, the application for a license must be made to the Westminster magistrates, who would not sit till Monday. This was a great disappointment; and many of Mr. Lindsey's friends urged him to open the chapel without waiting for the license. But his great legal adviser, John Lee, Esq., warmly remonstrated against it, as giving his opponents an undue advantage, and earnestly recommended to him to keep as closely as possible within the limits of the law. It was therefore agreed to defer performing divine service in the chapel till the Sunday following.

On the day appointed, application was made to the Bench of Justices holding their session for Westminster, at Hick's Hall, for a license to open the chapel in Essex Street as a place of worship. What passed upon that occasion was so remarkable and instructive, that I shall set it down as it is detailed in a letter from Mr. Lindsey to Dr. Jebb, dated the very day that the license was promised.

"I have the pleasure of assuring you that our difficulties are over, and we certainly begin (may it be with the divine blessing upon us!) on Sunday next. But we have not succeeded without striking with the great hammer, if I may so speak. For this morning Mr. Johnson, the bookseller, went, according as he was appointed, to Hick's Hall, and was there at the opening of the court. He got the clerk to move for him that he was waiting to have our entry recorded, as the court had given him reason to expect. But Lord Ward, who was that day in the chair, said it was a matter of some deliberation, and must be set over till the next meeting, *i.e.* Saturday. It appeared from hence that they would put us off civilly, and leave us in the lurch at last. I met Johnson coming out of the court, and took him with me to Mr. Lee, who was engaged at Guildhall, where I found him pleading before Chief Justice De Grey. I got to him, however, and told him our situation. He said it did not look well; but that the Chief Justice's Court would soon be up, and he would go immediately to Hick's Hall and see what was to be done. He came like a lion soon; 'desired to see the entry that had been given into the court to license a place of worship for a society of Dissenters; was sorry such unusual obstructions had been put to so legal a demand; that he understood it was said by some that the Justices had a discretionary power in such cases; that they were mistaken; that, on the contrary, they were merely official; and if they refused, a mandamus from the King's Bench would compel them; that he hoped the great Magna Charta of the religious liberty of Englishmen was not now going to be attacked.' Upon this, one or two of the Justices said it was their opinion, and always had been, as Mr. Lee's, that they had no discretionary powers. On something being said concerning the doctrine to be preached, and the officiating minister, that some inquiry was to be made about them, he told them that 'those were subsequent facts and matters of inquiry; that the house of worship was the object before them, and they were bound to make record of it as desired.' After this, on a pause being made, he desired to know 'whether the court would give him the trouble to come again the next day and move the matter and argue it before them, or would now grant it.' The latter was conceded, and our certificate, it was said, should be ready next court day. We begin, however, without it on the authority of our counsel.*

Such was the triumph of firmness and good sense over the narrow spirit of bigotry and persecution. And much to the credit of the improved liberality of the times, and of the Govern-

* The fact, however, was, that the certificate was never granted, nor was the chapel registered or licensed as a place of worship till after the defect had been noticed by Dr. Horsley in his Letters to Dr. Priestley; after which the neglect was immediately and without any difficulty rectified.

ment, this was the only obstruction which Mr. Lindsey ever met with from the civil power during the whole course of his ministry. All difficulties were now surmounted. The vessel was afloat, and commenced its voyage under the happiest auspices and with the most propitious gales.

CHAPTER IV.

FROM THE FIRST OPENING OF THE CHAPEL TO THE PURCHASE OF THE PREMISES AND THE ERECTION OF THE PRESENT BUILD-ING IN ESSEX STREET.

ON Sunday, April 17, 1774, the chapel was opened, and divine service was performed before an audience as numerous as could in reason be expected, and as respectable for rank and character as were ever collected together upon a similar occasion. In a letter to his friend Dr. Jebb, dated the next day,* Mr. Lindsey writes:

* It will be interesting to compare Mr. Lindsey's account of this memorable event with that of his warm friend and supporter the late John Lee, Esq., in a letter of the same date to Mr. Cappe at York :

"After a little difficulty in getting his chapel registered at the Quarter Sessions, which I had the good luck to remove, he entered upon his ministry yesterday. His chapel is a large upper room in Essex House, Essex Street, in a very central part of London, and in my neighbourhood. The place is convenient for the purpose of contain-ing about 300 persons; a greater number would crowd it. He was well attended, con-sidering that no public notice was given of the intended service. There were about ten coaches at the door ; which I was glad of, because it gave a degree of respectableness to the congregation in the eyes of the people living thereabouts. Of those that I knew and remember were Lord Despenser, Dr. Franklin, Dr. Priestley, Dr. Calder, Mr. Shore jun., Mrs. Shore, Mrs. Robert Milnes, Miss Milnes, and Miss Shore ; Dr. Hinck-ley, Dr. Chambers, Dr. Primatt and two or three other clergymen, with a few barris-ters whom you do not know. All the rest were to all appearance persons of condition, and in the whole were I think near two hundred, and mostly of the establishment. We were all pleased with the service and with his manner of performing it. His sermon, which I thought very good, will be printed, and you will of course see it. I begin to con-ceive hopes that his scheme will be patronized, so far at least as to produce him a com-fortable subsistence. Indeed, I hope it will teach those who ought not to have needed such teachings, that Reformation is both a safe and an easy work."

"You will be pleased to hear that everything passed very well yesterday; a larger and much more respectable audience than I could have expected, who behaved with great decency, and in general appeared, and many of them expressed themselves, to be much satisfied with the whole of the service. Some disturbance was apprehended, and forboded to me by great names,—but not the least movement of the kind. The only fault found with it was that it was too small. From the impressions that seemed to be made, and the general seriousness and satisfaction, I am persuaded that this attempt will, through the divine blessing, be of singular usefulness. The contrast between ours and the church service strikes every one. Forgive me for saying, that I should have blushed to have appeared in a white garment. No one seemed in the least to want it. I am happy not to be hampered with anything,—but entirely easy and satisfied with the whole of the service ; a satisfaction never before known. I must again say it, and bless God for it, that we were enabled to begin well. And we only desire to go on as through his blessing we have begun. I must mention one circumstance of yesterday to you and Mrs. J., and confidential friends : that Lord Le Despenser was at our chapel yesterday: whether he will come again we cannot say, but he has subscribed handsomely towards indemnifying us for the expenses of the chapel, &c."*

As Mr. Lindsey's professed design was to gather a congregation from the members of the established church, it was his desire and endeavour that the form of worship should recede no further from that of the establishment than was necessary to edification, and

---

* This nobleman, as might naturally be expected, soon discontinued his attendance. But it was considerate and liberal in him to contribute to the expenses of the chapel at a time when assistance was particularly needed. Other noblemen of still higher rank attended much longer and professed great approbation, but contributed nothing. Not that the late Duke of Richmond, or the present Duke of Norfolk, would have hesitated to have given whatever was right and liberal, if the idea had occurred, or if application had been made o hem. But to attend a place of worship supported by voluntary contribution, was to them a novelty ; and delicacy, perhaps misplaced, prevented the friends of the new sanctuary from suggesting a hint to the illustrious visitors. Such hints have not always been needful: and liberality unsolicited has been sometimes as ample as it was unexpected.

to reconcile it to the pure scriptural doctrine concerning the supremacy and the sole worship of the Father. The clerical dress was retained, with the exception of the surplice only. By the recommendation of his friend Mr. Turner, a prayer was introduced before and after the sermon.* And upon this memorable occasion Mr. Lindsey composed an appropriate discourse, which was immediately published, together with the prayers. The Liturgy also was published at the same time. Both these works, as well as the Apology, had a rapid and extensive sale.†

The subject of the discourse was Ephes. iv. 3 : " Endeavouring to keep the unity of the spirit in the bond of peace ; " and the preacher shows that by unity of spirit is intended " the kind affection, good order, and attention to mutual edification, which ought to subsist among those who profess the doctrine of Christ. The way in which this is to be preserved is 'in the bond of peace.' To illustrate which principle it is observed, that it is a maxim of undoubted truth, that in their religious capacity, mankind are subject only to the authority of God and of their own consciences, —that it has nevertheless been the doctrine of too many in all periods of the church, that peace and unity are not to be attained unless you bring all Christians to be of one opinion in religion,— that when other arguments have failed, the Scripture has been pressed into the hard service of enslaving mankind to one system of religious opinions, though such system has been oft in direct opposition to it,—that God never designed that Christians should be all of one sentiment, but that there should be different sects of Christians and different churches,—that while a friendly,

---

* In a letter to Mr. Turner, dated April 5, Mr. Lindsey says : " I am highly obliged to you for your hint about prayers before and after sermon. The latter I have practised for some years, and shall attend to the other." In a letter, dated June 13, he writes: " I am happy that I adopted the idea which you suggested, of introducing a short prayer of my own before and after sermon. And I am more happy to find that it is not only approved by, but seems to have a good effect in solemnizing the minds of the hearers."

† Of the sermon five hundred copies were disposed of in four days, and of the Liturgy seven hundred copies were sold in six weeks. The Apology passed through four editions.

benevolent temper is cultivated towards each other, the different
sects and churches among Christians, far from being a hurt or
discredit to religion, are an honour, and of singular service to it:
nor can it with truth be said, that different sects of religion in a
country have a tendency to disturb the public peace and quiet.
And though it must not be dissembled that the disputes and
contentions of Christians with each other have caused great
miseries and disturbance in the world, yet the blame lies not on
the mild and gentle doctrine of the gospel, but on the civil
powers who have given life and importance to these disputes by
interfering with them.   But that wise experience has now taught
them a better lesson." The sermon concludes with stating that
" the peculiar reason of forming a separate congregation distinct
from the national church is, that we may be at liberty to worship
God *alone,* after the command and example of our Saviour Christ.
So that if any ask what we are, or for what purpose we are joined
together in a Christian society, our answer is with the apostle,
' We are a people that worship God in the spirit, and make our
boast in Christ Jesus.' Phil. iii. 3."

To this discourse is annexed a summary account of the
Reformed Liturgy used in the chapel in Essex Street: the principal object of which is to vindicate the deviations of this liturgy
from that of Dr. Samuel Clarke, to which many respectable friends
of the author wished him to have strictly confined himself, but
which advice Mr. Lindsey, with his usual correctness of judgment
and firmness of spirit, declined to follow.

Upon this occasion Mr. Lindsey, by the advice of Dr. Jebb
and his Cambridge friends, but as he soon discovered without
due consideration of the subject, pledged himself in pretty strong
language not to introduce disputed points into his public discourses.   " Far will it be from my purpose," says he, " *ever* to
treat of controversial matters from this place." But if popular
and pernicious errors are not to be combated, and if the plain,
simple doctrine of Christianity is not to be taught from the pulpit,
it is difficult to say how public attention is to be excited: how the
mass of hearers are to be instructed, and how truth is to make its

way. In fact it appears that where public teachers have confined themselves to mere moral instruction, and have either not touched at all upon Christian doctrine, or have veiled their real opinions under ambiguous language, the consequence has often been that the teacher by reading and reflection has become enlightened while the hearer has been left in darkness; the preacher has reformed his speculative creed while the hearers have retained all the erroneous and unscriptural notions which their pastor has long ago renounced. And as a natural consequence, when a vacancy has occurred, a successor has not unfrequently been appointed whose system has been directly opposite to that of the person who immediately preceded him.* Those who hold senti-

* Dr. Doddridge's congregation refused to invite Dr. Ashworth, whom he recommended as his successor both in the pulpit and in the academy, and whose sentiments were in perfect unison with his own, and chose a gentleman, a very worthy person, but whose orthodoxy was of a much higher tone than that of his predecessor. A late minister, well remembered by many, made his boast, that though he had officiated twenty years at the same chapel, he defied any of his hearers to know what he believed concerning the person of Christ. And it is a fact of sufficient notoriety, that a flourishing congregation in the metropolis, in appointing a colleague to their respected pastor, who had officiated among them with great acceptance for more than thirty years, fixed their choice upon a person so opposite in sentiment that he would not even hear his colleague preach, or ever join in communion with him. Could such a case have happened had the hearers been properly instructed in their religious principles, and rationally grounded in their Christian faith? It is absurd to say that if these people had been better instructed they would not have been equally serious. How does it appear that they would have been less virtuous if they had been more consistent?

The writer of this note can bear testimony, from his own experience, to the very opposite effects of different modes of public instruction. While he resided in the country as minister of a congregation and divinity tutor in the academy upon Mr. Coward's foundation, he gradually changed his theological views from an affinity to those of Dr. Doddridge, to perfect Unitarianism, and a belief in the proper humanity of Jesus Christ. But not being at that time so clearly convinced as he was afterwards of the duty of an explicit avowal of important truth, he, like many others, satisfied himself with using language which, though not contradictory to, was certainly not explanatory of his new opinions. The consequence was, that when he thought it his duty to resign the connexion, a successor was chosen, a worthy young man, one of his own pupils, but one who in Trinitarian orthodoxy far exceeded all his predecessors from the first foundation of the chapel. Not so when he resigned his place at Hackney to succeed at Essex Street. That intelligent society, trained up under the candid and liberal instructions of Dr. Price and the enlightened zeal of Dr. Priestley, to which his own humble efforts for ten years in the same good cause had not been wanting, when a vacancy was declared, acted in a manner worthy of themselves and of their teachers. To them it was an object of the first consideration to look out for a minister who should be disposed and qualified to support the doctrines in which they had been instructed, and which from conviction they embraced and cherished. Happily divine Providence directed them to a choice which fulfilled their utmost wishes and hopes. And the very

ments to which they give the pompous name of orthodox or evangelical, never decline to avow their systems in the most manly and explicit manner. And they do right while they believe those sentiments to be true and important. How unbecoming, then, is it for those who hold a better and a purer faith to shrink from the public profession and defence of it, and to leave the adversary master of the field! It is a silly objection which is urged by some weak, or timid, or indolent, I will not say interested persons, that speculative preaching, as they call it, tends to diminish a serious and pious disposition, and promote a sectarian spirit. As to the latter part of the objection, let them read Sir George Savile's remark upon the subject of sectaries: and with respect to the former, I confess I could never see how the increase of knowledge had a tendency to produce deterioration of practice; and he would be a very injudicious teacher who did not combine practical exhortation with doctrinal instruction.

"Yesterday," says Mr. Lindsey, in a letter to Dr. Jebb, dated May 23, "I ventured to deviate from the idea which you and my friends with you seemed to entertain as right, of preaching merely practical discourses, and enlarged with much earnestness on John xvii. 3. I find it was acceptable to many, and that it was even looked for, that I should sometimes treat upon the great object and principle on which our new church is formed, in order to confirm some that are already come out, and awaken others to come out of Babylon. But I expect the greatest effects by and by through the nation, from the thunder of yours, of Mr. ——'s,

---

prosperous state of the congregation, which required a larger chapel to accommodate the increasing number of worshippers, demonstrates the energy and, if I may so express it, the *omnipotence* of plain, simple, uncorrupted truth, when taught with openness, with firmness, with ability, and zeal. May this glorious cause continue to prosper among the rising generation there and elsewhere, under the same or a similar able, active, and eloquent ministry, when those who are now passed the burden and the heat of the day, and upon whom the shadows of the evening are fast lengthening themselves out, shall be at rest with their fathers in the land of silence and oblivion! And may the conduct of all who profess to hold the pure and uncorrupted doctrine of Christ, at all times, silently, but powerfully and irresistibly, repel the unfounded and ungenerous charge, so triumphantly advanced by ignorance or malignity, that Unitarian principles and a zeal for truth are inconsistent with seriousness of spirit, with fervour of devotion, and with holiness of life!

and Mr. ——'s apologies, for you can never go out in mute silence and without bearing your testimonies against her witch-craft and idolatries."

Among the earliest hearers of Mr. Lindsey was Mrs. Rayner, a near relation of the Duchess of Northumberland and of Lord Gwydir. This lady was married to a gentleman of large fortune, and was attracted by curiosity and the invitation of a friend to hear the new doctrine at Essex Street, on the day when the chapel was first opened. Through the whole service her eyes were fixed, and her attention riveted upon the preacher; and when it was over, she and Mr. Rayner introduced themselves to Mr. and Mrs. Lindsey, and from that time to the end of life she became a constant hearer at the chapel, and a firm and generous friend to Mr. Lindsey, and to the cause which he supported and for which he suffered. Mrs. Rayner was a lady of open and unaffected manners, of superior intellect, and of a well-informed mind. She possessed unbounded generosity of spirit, and, especially after the death of Mr. Rayner, denied herself almost what was necessary to support her rank and station in life, that she might spend her money in acts of great but not indiscriminate munificence. She became a liberal and powerful patroness of the cause of truth. And to this lady the Christian world is indebted for the publica-tion of one of the most learned and most useful theological works which the age has produced : Dr. Priestley's History of Early Opinions concerning Christ : a work which demonstrates in a manner which never has been and never can be confuted, that from the earliest age of the Christian religion down to the fourth century, and to the time of Athanasius himself, the great body of unlearned Christians were strictly Unitarians, and consequently that this was the original doctrine concerning the person of Christ. This most valuable treatise was a work of great labour and ex-pense, the demand for which would by no means have defrayed the charge of the publication. But Mrs. Rayner, with exemplary generosity, supplied the money, and to her the work is with great propriety dedicated. Many other acts of this lady's princely munificence might be mentioned which almost exceed belief in a selfish and irreligious age. But she sought not worldly applause; and she is now gone where her works and virtues will follow her, to receive their appropriate and everlasting reward.* The cause now began to flourish beyond all expectation. The chapel was always crowded with attentive hearers, so that many who came late were obliged to go away for want of room. Considerable numbers of very respectable names were continually given in as subscribers to the expense of the chapel and to the support of the minister. Among the rest were the late distinguished patriot Sir George Savile, member for Yorkshire; Mr. Serjeant Adair, with his father and mother; the late learned and eminent scripture-critic, Mr. Dodson, the translator of the book of Isaiah; and the present Sir Thomas Bernard, the benevolent treasurer of the Foundling Hospital. Nor must I omit to mention the name of my respected friend Robert Martin Leake, Esq., the present worthy Master of the Report Office in the Court of Chancery, who, being then a young man, and having by reading and reflection emancipated himself from the Trinitarian and high-church prejudices in which he had been educated in his father's house, the late Garter King-at-Arms, was one of the first who called upon Mr. Lindsey at his lodgings in Featherstone Buildings, and encouraged him to persist in his design of opening a chapel for Unitarian worship; and though not then in affluent circumstances, offered a liberal contribution to the object, and has ever since remained a firm and enlightened advocate of the cause: he is now senior trustee of the chapel, and one of the few surviving original founders and supporters of the place.

But nothing of this kind gave Mr. Lindsey more pleasure than

* One instance out of many, and that by no means the greatest, of this benevolent lady's extraordinary munificence is related by Dr. Priestley in his Memoirs, p. 77, London edition. The Doctor mentions that upon his separation from Lord Shelburne he was barely able to support the expense of removal. He adds, "But my situation being intimated to Mrs. Rayner, besides smaller sums with which she occasionally assisted me, she gave me a hundred guineas to defray the expenses of my removal; and deposited with Mrs. Lindsey, which she soon after gave up to me, four hundred guineas, and to this day has never failed giving me every year marks of her friendship. Here is, indeed, I seriously think, one of the first Christian characters I was ever acquainted with, having a cultivated, comprehensive mind, equal to any subject of theology or metaphysics, intrepid in the cause of truth, and most rationally pious."

a letter which he received in the beginning of June from the late
Sir Barnard Turner, who afterwards distinguished himself so much
in quelling the riots in London in 1780, at the head of the London Association. Of this letter the following is an extract communicated by Mr. Lindsey to his friend Mr. Turner, to whom he
knew that it would give the same satisfaction which it gave to
himself.

"I have long been held from associating with any sect of
Christians with that sincerity which my conscience and gratitude
to the Supreme Being tell me are needful in religion, from a
thorough conviction that the adoration of any but the one true
God was highly sinful. It is therefore with the utmost earnestness that I beg to be considered as one of your congregation, and
also that you will do me the favour of accepting my annual subscription of five guineas towards the welfare of the society, and the
making you some amends for the loss and expense to which your
love of truth will make you liable. I shall, besides, be always
ready with cheerfulness to bear a reasonable share of any further
expense that the future exigencies of the society may make necessary."

In reference to this application from Sir Barnard Turner, Mr.
Lindsey expresses himself thus in a letter to Dr. Jebb: "I
have found this institution a means of drawing out, and I hope
will be of encouraging and perfecting, many excellent characters.
Your heart would rejoice in reading a letter I received this very
week from one of these desiring to become a member of our
church. We are still crowded on Sundays."

The satisfaction and comfort which this excellent man experienced upon his deliverance from the galling yoke of an establishment which he disapproved, in the perfect liberty which he enjoyed
of conducting the services of religion in the manner which best
approved itself to his understanding and to his heart, and in the
success of a scheme for the accomplishment of which he had
made such strenuous exertions and such great and costly sacrifices,
a success so far beyond his most sanguine expectations, may be
more easily conceived than described. He often gives vent to the

pious and grateful emotions of his heart in his communications to his confidential friends.

In a letter to Dr. Jebb, dated March 31, a week before he expected to open the chapel, he writes: "No one has more fears or diffidences, and I think justly, of what I do. I sometimes wonder how I came into the service in which I am embarked. But I have met with such friends and encouragement that I go on cheerfully and without fear."

In another letter to the same friend, dated July 24, three months after the grand experiment had been tried, and the success of it was complete, he thus expresses himself : "I have not known what entire quiet of mind and perfect peace with God was for many many years till now; and I would not exchange it for a thousand worlds. Encouraged also as I am that good, extensive good, to glorious Truth does arise and will arise from it. I must have died much in the dark had I been called away before this. How thankful ought I to be for that good Providence which has conducted and preserved me ! You will be glad to hear that last Sunday we had a more respectable audience at the chapel than I ever saw, except the first day. And to-day quite full." So mightily did the word of God, and the cause of pure and uncorrupted Christianity grow and prevail under the ministration of this venerable confessor, and so abundantly did his heart overflow with consolation and delight in the success of his benevolent and pious exertions.

It is not however to be concluded, that all was now sunshine with Mr. Lindsey, and that the season of clouds and darkness was completely over. The tide of prejudice at that time set so strongly against the Unitarian doctrine, that there was some reason to apprehend—at least, many of Mr. Lindsey's friends did apprehend—that some popular disturbance might take place at the opening of a chapel professedly upon Unitarian principles, and that some personal insult might be offered to the minister, or some interruption attempted in the service. This, however, gave Mr. Lindsey little concern. He did not indeed court, but neither did he shun, persecution in the performance of duty. But in truth, though he had received many anonymous libels in the form of letters, he had no considerable apprehension of personal violence. Happily, under the mild administration of the House of Brunswick, religious toleration was the wise and liberal principle of government, and lawless outrage was kept under severe restraint.

It gave Mr. Lindsey more concern that his motives should be mistaken by some of his associated brethren, who regarded the decisive step which he had taken as injurious to the object of their petition, a reformation in the subscription and in the service of the established church. Mr. Lindsey, though he much regretted that offence was taken where none had been intended, consoled himself with the conviction which he felt that his brethren had formed an erroneous judgment in the case, and that his secession from the establishment, so far from being of disservice, would eventually be very beneficial to the cause of the petitioning clergy, by exciting attention to it, and by interesting many in their favour. "You and Jebb," says an eminent leader among the associated clergy, in a letter to Mr. Lindsey, " have obliged the Balguys and Randolphs by your integrity, but none else, though more may commend. It has been the utter ruin of the plan of the petitioners." Mr. Lindsey thought far otherwise. " A few," says he to his friend Dr. Jebb, " of our petitioning friends, and but a few, will have it that my retreat has hurt our cause. But I am emboldened to say, from fact and knowledge in this great city and a wide range elsewhere, that it has and does serve it greatly—nay, has been a great means of keeping it from dying entirely." And upon another occasion, alluding to the same misconception of some of his petitioning friends, he says, "These things must not move us. I hope to be enabled to go on in a way which promises to be of some present use, nay, actually is so already, in removing prejudices and enlarging the minds of some, and may be of unknown benefit."

But nothing appears to have hurt Mr. Lindsey's mind so much as the malignant reports which were industriously circulated by some, that he had been influenced throughout by mercenary views, that he was now in a better situation than that which he had left, and that he had a promise of this before he resigned his benefice. Mr. Lindsey could not but feel indignant at the imputation of motives which his soul abhorred, of which his conscience entirely acquitted him, and to which the whole tenor of his life was a palpable contradiction. Upon this subject he expresses himself with a very becoming and a truly christian spirit in a letter to his kind friend at Wakefield, dated June 13, 1774.

"We have about thirty names upon the list of our society as members, who have signified their intentions, and some of them what they shall contribute. This gentleman's (Sir Barnard Turner's) is *much the largest.* I mention this not as if I had any doubt of a sufficient provision for myself and the society, but that you may know in a general way the whole of our state : because I find that it is said I have already an establishment of four hundred pounds a year, and that I knew what a good exchange I should make when I left Catterick. Such reports we must expect. It is here spread about, and believed by many, that my wife's uncle, at our quitting Catterick, settled 200 pounds a year on me, though he has never seen us, nor admitted us to write a letter to him from that time to this. I believe that with Mr. Shore's and his friend's benefaction, and those of other friends, I have received upwards of four hundred pounds. But upwards of two hundred out of this was given purely to indemnify me for the expenses of fitting up the chapel; its rent, fifty pounds a year : clerk's wages, &c. I am a little sorry I have blotted so much paper and taken up so much of your time on such a subject, but I was desirous you should be acquainted with it. And as I have hitherto done, I desire to keep my hands and heart clear of all mercenary views, though I cannot bind others from imputing them to me."

Mr. Lindsey alludes feelingly to the same reports in his correspondence with Dr. Jebb.* How little foundation there was for

---

* "Nothing," says Mr. Lindsey in a letter to Dr. Jebb, dated May 22nd, "is yet settled with regard to those who are or will be members of our church, and their contributions, though several of them have spoken to me about it. But I am in no hurry on that account. And I wish ever to keep at a distance from the suspicion of attention to money ; though such suspicions have been, are, and will be imputed by those who judge of others by themselves." In another letter, dated June 7th, he writes : "You

them is manifest from the following extract of a letter from a friend, who about that time visited them at their lodgings : " I had the satisfaction of finding our worthy friends in pretty good health and spirit : but by no means in the affluent situation in which common fame in Yorkshire had placed them. The lodgings they are in at present are close, inconvenient, and expensive : nor have they yet been able to meet with any thing more suitable to them. But the cause in which Mr. Lindsey is engaged has power to soften every difficulty, and he has need of such support."

It became now incumbent upon Mr. Lindsey to defend his principles from the press as well as from the pulpit. The Apology was not permitted to pass without animadversion and attempts at refutation. The first who entered the lists was Mr. Burgh of York, a member of the Irish parliament, a young man of some talents, of estimable character, and of liberal political principles, but little versed in theological controversy. He published so early as the month of June, 1774, a work entitled A Scriptural Confutation of the Arguments against the One Godhead of the Father, Son, and Holy Ghost, produced by the Rev. Mr. Lindsey in his late Apology. This treatise as an argumentative work was trifling in the extreme, and must immediately have passed into the oblivion to which it has long been consigned, had it not been supported and puffed off by some persons of note, who no doubt thought it was calculated to make an impression upon the numerous class of readers to whom sounds are a ready substitute for sense.*   Of this work Mr. Lindsey thought it sufficient to take

shall know every thing when I see you, how we go on. In the mean time, though I have the highest cause to be thankful to God's good providence, there is no foundation for reports which some put about with no good design."

* Of Mr. Burgh's argument, the following are curious specimens. Because we read in Scripture of the *grace of God*, and also of the *grace of our Lord Jesus Christ ;* because Paul calls himself a *servant of God*, and also of *Jesus Christ ;* and because the gospel is called the *gospel of God*, and also the *gospel of Christ ;* and " that which is God's is not another's," as the author sagaciously remarks, " therefore Christ is God, one with the Father." Sequel, Pref. p. x. xi. To attempt a refutation of such arguments would be a prostitution of reason. Mr. Lindsey, in a letter to Mr. Turner, dated June 13, 1774, mentions that the pamphlet, then anonymous, had been sent him by the author ten days before. " I really took the book," says he, " to be the work of some methodist at first perusing it, and nothing in it solid or that might require an answer. But I was

a slight notice in the preface to the Sequel to his Apology. In the same preface he also replied, as far as it was judged needful, to two other pamphlets which had been published against his Apology; one of which, by Mr. Bingham of Dorsetshire, was entitled A Vindication of the Doctrine and Liturgy of the Church of England, occasioned by the Apology of Theophilus Lindsey, M.A.: the other by Dr. Randolph, Lady Margaret's Professor of Divinity in the University of Oxford. These treatises were written with more knowledge of the subject than Mr. Burgh's, but their arguments contained nothing of novelty which required particular attention.* The passages of scripture which were alleged by these writers in favour of Trinitarian doctrine and worship, and which had been adverted to in the Apology, were explained in the Sequel.

This able and learned work appeared early in the year 1776. It is much more copious than was originally intended, and contains, as the author expresses it, "a full inquiry into the questions concerning the nature and person of Christ, and what is the

much surprised the other day in conversing with Mr. Mason, to find that he had been privy to the publication, had revised some of the proof sheets, and approved the doctrine in the highest degree. Nay, he told me that Dr. Hurd had just then told him that the writer expressed his own sentiments upon the Trinity. But I could not help telling Mr. Mason that he and his friend were easily pleased. That he boasted too much of the author's freedom from prejudice as being a young man who had never read any controversy on the Trinity : as if we received no prejudices but from reading. Mr. Mason added, 'the book must make a great noise,' which I would easily believe if they cried it up." In a letter to Dr. Jebb, dated June 17th, he writes : "The zeal to propagate *the Layman's* (Mr. Burgh's) pamphlet is most extraordinary. A friend of mine on Sunday, dining with a very high personage, found the book brought to the Lady of the house by a noble Lord of the company, a friend of Mr. Mason. With regard to the two original commenders of it, I declare I am amazed they can find no better salvo for their consciences in the use of our Trinitarian forms. And it has much lessened them both in my estimation. If upon perusal of it you should put a few thoughts together, and be disposed to let them be printed, I should be very glad : not for the importance of the piece itself, but for the vogue which it is to have given to it."

* Save that Mr. Bingham discovered that the word Father, when used by our blessed Saviour in prayer, signifies the first person of the godhead, but when used by us it signifies the same first person, together with two other equal persons, the Son and the Holy Ghost. And that the learned Margaret Professor found out that every thing which the candid Whitby had to say in his " Disquisitiones modestæ," in reply to Bishop Bull, had been "fully answered by Dr. Waterland," though he acknowledges that he had never been able " to obtain a sight of the book." See preface to the Seq. p. xvi. xxi.

G 2

worship due to him ;" also, "a further illustration of some things advanced in the Apology to which objection had been made." In his preface Mr. Lindsey acknowledges his obligations to Dr. Jebb, who had lately resigned his situation and prospects in the church, for his trouble and assistance in revising the greater part of the work.

In this volume, the most elaborate of all Mr. Lindsey's publications, the learned author in his first chapter states the design of his work, and relates the sufferings and the testimony of Mr. Elwall, who was tried for heresy and blasphemy before Judge Denton at the Stafford Assizes, in the reign of George the First ; and gives an account of Hopton Haynes, a zealous and learned Unitarian, the friend of Sir Isaac Newton, with copious extracts from Mr. Haynes's excellent treatise on the attributes of God, which was then very scarce, but which has since been published and very widely circulated by the Unitarian Society. Ch. ii., the author treats at large of the Arian and Socinian worship of Christ, and shows that it has no foundation in the New Testament. Ch. iii., he argues, that the Logos or word is not a divine person or intelligent agent, but that it is the wisdom and power of the Father by which the world was made, and by which Christ and his apostles were inspired and were enabled to perform their mighty works. Ch. iv., this doctrine, concerning the divine Logos, word, or wisdom, is further illustrated by comparing it with various passages in the New Testament, in which Christ is represented as being guided and assisted by the spirit of God, which the learned writer assumes to be the same as the Logos. Ch. v., he examines distinctly and critically those passages in the New Testament which have been supposed to favour the pre-existence of Christ, and particularly those in St. John's gospel. Ch. vi., he argues very forcibly and successfully against the strange and unscriptural doctrine of two Jehovahs, the one supreme, the other subordinate : the latter a great angel who personated the character and assumed the name of the Supreme, who was the medium of all the divine dispensations to mankind, and the immediate object of religious worship to the Jewish church : which angel animated the body of Christ. This hypothesis, which had always been maintained by learned Arians, ancient and modern, had lately been very plausibly stated, and very ably defended, in a learned work by the Reverend Henry Taylor, the Rector of Crawley, under the assumed character of Benjamin Ben Mordecai, a converted Jew. To this treatise Mr. Lindsey makes a calm, detailed, and satisfactory reply. Ch. vii., the work goes on further to plead from the language of Moses and the Prophets, and from the explicit declarations of the Apostles and Evangelists and even of Christ himself, that he was really a man, and that the truth of this doctrine is not impeached by the great and lasting errors of Christians concerning it. Ch. viii., the author comments upon the testimony of the Apostolical Fathers concerning the nature and person of Christ; and, lastly, he concludes with a critical examination of those passages in St. Paul's epistles, in which creation is supposed to be ascribed to Christ, and clearly shows that creation is the proper work of God himself without any instrument or deputy; that this is the uniform doctrine of the scriptures, and that those expressions of Paul which are thought by many to teach a different doctrine, are to be understood of the *new* creation, and of the renovation of the moral world by the gospel of Christ.

In his interpretation of some of the controverted texts all may not be entirely agreed, who nevertheless coincide with the learned and worthy author in his views of the person of Christ. But as long as that important controversy shall continue, Mr. Lindsey's Sequel must always be regarded as a standard work, and as a bright example of free and fearless discussion, blending itself with that amiable spirit of Christianity which softens the asperities of theological controversy, and which allows to all the equal right of private judgment.

From the commencement of his arduous undertaking, and especially from the time when success appeared probable, Mr. Lindsey, modestly diffident of his own powers and qualifications both of body and mind, was anxiously solicitous to secure the aid of an able coadjutor. The first person upon whom he cast his eye was Dr. Jebb, to whom he suggested a hint of the business before he left Yorkshire. But afterwards, when the prospect brightened at Essex Street, and Mr. Lindsey was assured that his friend intended speedily to execute his long-formed determination of resigning his preferment and his prospects in the church, he made the proposal to him in more direct terms.* " I must not forget to add," so he writes in a letter dated October 20, 1775, " as it need be said to yourself alone, that with Mr. Tayleur's, Sir George Savile's and Mr. Smith's subscriptions, our amount, all things paid, is one hundred pounds,† which I should be most glad to share annually, and more that I am sure would accrue with such a coadjutor. I mentioned this formerly, but your plan did not lead to the pastoral line in London ; but I thought I would name it again." Dr. Jebb, however, rather chose the profession of medicine ; and though, after he had retired from the church he was regular in his attendance at the chapel, and retained all his zeal and his activity in the cause of Christian truth, he declined to officiate as a Nonconformist minister.

Mr. Lindsey was also disappointed in his application to another most truly excellent and learned person, eminent for his piety, benevolence, and zeal for truth, whose assistance would have been most acceptable to Mr. Lindsey and to his friends, but who

---

* In the meantime Mr. Lindsey, probably in consequence of Dr. Jebb's delay to secede from the church, appears to have made an overture to Dr. Robertson of Wolverhampton. This is hinted at in a letter to Dr. Jebb, written in May, 1775.

† This was but a very moderate income, even when the necessaries of life were at less than half the price which they bear at present, and far short of what Mr. Lindsey relinquished at Catterick. His willingness to divide this pittance with his colleague is an ample confutation, if such were needful, of the calumnies which represented him as acting from mercenary motives. But the tenor of his whole life demonstrated that his soul disdained the imputation. It is but justice to the liberality of Mr. Lindsey's friends and supporters to add, that his income was rapidly increased, and that he was soon placed in a situation, not only to live with comfort, but in which both he and Mrs. Lindsey could gratify to a considerable extent the favourite wish of their hearts— to do good to others. The third name in Mr. Lindsey's list, Mr. Smith, is probably that of Lord Carrington, who continued his liberal but unostentatious patronage of Mr. Lindsey as Mr. Lindsey lived. And it may now, March, 1812, be added that his lordship's bounty was continued to the widow of the deceased confessor, by contributing largely to an annuity of £100, which was settled upon her for life, to enable that excellent lady to continue her extensive and judicious charities, in which his lordship was joined by a few other friends of Mr. Lindsey, whose names were never made known to Mrs L.

declined the office from principles most honourable to his feelings, and no doubt perfectly satisfactory to his own ingenuous and enlightened mind. Thus this venerable confessor was left to sustain the conflict, and to fight the battle alone. But his God was with him : a good conscience and a good cause bore him up and carried him through, and "his strength was equal to his day." For ten years he continued the sole pastor of a numerous and flourishing congregation, all the members of which held their revered instructor in the highest estimation, and many of them gladdened his heart by their visible improvement in Christian knowledge and virtuous practice.

CHAPTER V.

FROM THE ERECTION OF THE BUILDING IN ESSEX STREET TO THE APPOINTMENT OF DR. DISNEY TO BE THE COLLEAGUE OF MR. LINDSEY, 1783.

As the congregation increased, and the interest appeared likely to be permanent, it became necessary to provide a suitable place of worship; and after much inquiry and deliberation, it was agreed to purchase the premises in Essex Street, which, by the liberal contributions of the friends of the cause,* Mr. Lindsey

* In the foremost rank of these were the generous inhabitants of Norton Hall and Norton House, whose great and unexpected liberality to Mr. Lindsey upon his first coming to town has been before mentioned. Upon the present occasion, having communicated the intelligence to a friend, to whose kind offices he thought himself much indebted for "the friendly disposition of these worthy persons," he adds, "I cannot describe the feelings I had on such an unexpected instance of generous and public spirit, especially when contrasted with some from whom much might have been expected, but who are too poor to do anything." In a letter to the same friend, dated May 14, 1778, after having mentioned Mrs. Lindsey's frequent indispositions, he adds, "but nothing hinders her indefatigable attention to what she takes in hand. It was owing to her that our new chapel was ready so soon. And she is now no less busily engaged in the habitation underneath, which we are to inhabit, and which requires much more to be done at it than we expected ; in short, a new house and chapel might

was enabled to accomplish, and to repair and fit them up in their present commodious form for the purpose of a chapel, and for a residence for himself and Mrs. Lindsey. This great work was completed early in the spring of 1778, and the new chapel was opened March 29. Upon this occasion Mr. Lindsey delivered an excellent discourse from John iv. 23, 24, upon the unity of God and the spirituality of Divine worship, which, with the prayers before and after the sermon, were immediately published.

Among the most zealous advocates of the Divine unity, and for the erection of a place of worship upon the avowed principle that the Father alone is to be worshipped as God, the late William Tayleur, Esq., of Shrewsbury, holds a distinguished place. This gentleman, who by a careful study of the scriptures had become a decided Unitarian forty years before, who had in vain attempted to form a society for Unitarian worship in his own vicinage, and who began to despair that he should ever live to see the accomplishment of his favourite object, concurred most cordially in Mr. Lindsey's design; and though from the remoteness of his residence it was impossible that he should derive any personal benefit, he was nevertheless extremely solicitous that the affairs of the chapel in Essex Street should be placed upon a respectable and permanent foundation. He hoped that the honourable example would be followed by many others both in the metropolis and in the country, and that houses for the worship of the one God would be multiplied through the nation. To this end he contributed very liberally upon the present occasion; and a few years afterwards he had the satisfaction to see his pious and benevolent expectation in some measure realized. A congregation of Unitarian dissenters at Shrewsbury were induced by his exhortations and encouragement to adopt a reformed liturgy; and the last years of the life of this exemplary Christian were consoled and delighted by the quiet possession of a privilege, the hope of which he had hardly permitted himself to indulge, that of joining at stated seasons in the public worship of the one God, the

have been built for much less expense. But it was convenient to have one place to assemble in while the other was building: and we had no idea that the house was in such a ruinous way as we have found it."

Father of all, in the way that his conscience dictated as most rational, scriptural, and edifying.*

Of this excellent person Mr. Lindsey gives the following interesting account in a letter to a friend, dated September 1, 1783, immediately after his return from making him a visit:—

* "It is now forty years," writes this excellent man in a letter to Mr. Lindsey, dated May, 1777, "since I was clearly convinced that the Father alone ought to be worshipped as the only true God. Had any one then told me that I should live to see a society of Christians openly professing that doctrine, meeting together in a chapel of their own, and using a form of prayer avowedly drawn up to perpetuate the honour due to the only true God, I should have treated such a person as a well-meaning visionary. Much yet remains to be done, but what may not be expected from so prosperous a beginning?" In another letter, dated November 13, after having made over £500 in the three per cent. Stock towards building the chapel, Mr. Tayleur adds, " I have many opportunities of declaring that I cannot give my assent to the Athanasian forms of worship, or join in the use of them; but still it is very disagreeable to appear to do this by frequenting the service of the church. I have long sought a remedy against this inconvenience, but hitherto I can find none; for there is no dissenting congregation here, or here-about, who profess to worship the Father as the only true God, or who would not be offended if any of their members should make such a declaration. Could such a congregation be found, I should think it my duty to join them, though I think it too much, at least for an old man, to hear, judge, and pray at the same time: and therefore wish for a form of prayer on the Unitarian plan. I have endeavoured to prevail on some few persons, laymen, who think as I do, to meet one Sunday at least in a month, to read together your liturgy, and to declare openly, without blaming those who are otherwise minded, our reasons for doing this: but hitherto I have met with no success, nor have I much prospect of it till the laity take the matter more to heart than they at present do."

What an exemplary spirit of piety, zeal, and moderation! It is easy to conceive now delighted this worthy man must have been when his own plan, which he had so long laboured in vain to accomplish, was at last, when he was ready to abandon it in despair, unexpectedly carried into effect. Thus we learn not to desist from generous efforts to promote truth and virtue, though they may for a time be ineffectual. This excellent man modestly assigns his reasons for preferring a liturgy to free prayer. Let those blush who judge harshly of their brethren for differing from them in forms of prayer or modes of worship. The prayer of the upright will be accepted, whether it be offered in language which occurs upon the occasion, or in a written or a printed form.

Mr. Tayleur was possessed of a large estate, and his generosity was unbounded. He settled a handsome annuity upon the chapel at Shrewsbury for the support of Unitarian worship. And Dr. Priestley acknowledges himself indebted to the liberality of this gentleman for the most material assistance in the publication of many of his theological works, without which he would not have been able to publish them at all.— Dr. Priestley's Memoirs, p. 104. English edition.

This excellent Christian died May 6, 1796, in the eighty-fourth year of his age. An eloquent and instructive discourse was delivered upon the occasion at the High Street Meeting, in Shrewsbury, by his accomplished friend Theophilus Houlbrooke, LL.B. F.R.S. Ed., originally a clergyman in the established church, but who became one of the honourable band of confessors in the glorious cause of the Divine unity. This sermon was published. It is much to be wished that the learned author had fulfilled his original intention of prefacing his discourse with an account of Mr Tayleur, as the public has in vain waited for the memoir expected from another quarter.

"We took a long flight, you will call it, thence (*i.e.* from Richmond, in Yorkshire), to Shrewsbury; but were well repaid when we arrived there by the sight and society of one of the most valuable of mankind, Mr. Tayleur, in whose house we lodged. He was educated at Westminster, and went off Captain of the school to Christ Church, Oxford, where he resided as student or fellow seven years, a hard and real student all the while; thence to the Temple for nearly as long a space. But an elder brother then dying, and the family estate coming to him, he married the late Sir Rowland Hill's sister and settled at Shrewsbury. An excellent classic scholar both in Geeek and Latin, which he retains, and not unskilled in the Hebrew language. A very good mathematician also. His time and talents have been always much turned, but entirely of late years, to the scriptures, of which he is a great master. A strict Unitarian, but of deep piety at the same time; without which, opinions are of little value. If you have not heard of it you will be glad to know, that some years past, when he could no longer attend the Trinitarian worship of the Church of England, and could not through long association join with edification in extempory prayer, he had service for many Sundays in his own house in which he officiated, at which some gentlemen of the Church of England attended, and some of Mr. Fownes's congregation who preferred a form of prayer; and this continued till Mr. Fownes yielded to the requests of many of his congregation to admit the form they now use, with some additions made by him. One cannot but wish that other gentlemen of the Church of England would follow his example. Were there to be many instances in different places, I apprehend it would be one of the most likely means to put the churchmen on reducing their liturgy nearer the scripture model of worship."

Another very eminent person, who was indeed from the beginning a zealous encourager and supporter of Mr. Lindsey's design, was Richard Kirwan, Esq., F.R.S., the late venerable President of the Royal Society in Ireland; a gentleman of the first eminence in Europe in chemical and geological science, and of whom Dr. Priestley was wont to say, that he was the best general scholar he ever knew, and particularly able in theology. This distinguished philosopher, being from principle and a profound study of the sacred scriptures zealously attached to the great doctrine of the Divine unity, and that the Father alone is the proper object of religious worship, constantly attended Divine service in Mr. Lindsey's chapel during his residence in London.

From the summer of the year 1778, when he took possession of the premises in Essex Street, Mr. Lindsey may be considered as fully settled. All difficulties were completely removed; every thing went on comparatively in a smooth, easy, and equable tenour: and the succeeding years of life were not more diversified than those of other studious persons and ministers of religion commonly are. Mr. Lindsey was in general blessed with a good share of health, and a natural equal flow of good spirits. His circumstances, if not affluent, were at least easy and comfortable. His friends were numerous, and he was in the habit of daily familiar and delightful intercourse with persons of the highest respectability for rank, talent, character, and information. His public services were attended by as large a congregation as the chapel would admit, all of whom revered and loved their venerable pastor, and listened to his words as though he were an apostle of Christ. He was engaged in an office, to himself the most delightful, and to others the most instructive and edifying; at full liberty to search the scriptures without any control, and to speak his sentiments without the least reserve to a people candid, affectionate, and warmly prepossessed in favour of whatever he addressed to them, as the result of his own pious and diligent researches, and of what he seriously and conscientiously believed to be the genuine doctrine of Christ. Happy in a consort who felt a lively sympathy in all his sorrows and his joys, whose principles were in perfect unison with his own, and whose prudence, activity, and energy of mind relieved him from every secular care, and left him at perfect liberty to devote all the powers of his mind to the great object in which his whole soul was engaged. If ever any person resigned a situation of ease and affluence from principles the most pure and disinterested, with expectations the most humble, and with prospects the most gloomy and uninviting, it was Mr. Lindsey. And if any person ever experienced the accomplishment of the evangelical promise, that he who should voluntarily forsake all for Christ and for his words, should even in the present life receive remuneration a hundred fold, Mr. Lindsey was the man. Of this mark of divine goodness this truly excellent man, who from his cradle had been taught to see the hand of God in every thing, was most deeply sensible; and without any affectation of humility, or parade of piety, he was ever most ready upon every proper occasion, and especially in correspondence with his intimate friends, to express the gratitude and admiration which he felt for blessings so far beyond his expectations and deserts.

In the autumn of the year 1778, Mr. Lindsey was seized with a violent fever, which for some days excited the greatest alarm amongst his friends, lest they should lose their revered and beloved instructor, while, for a time,

> the important die
> Of life and death spun doubtful, ere it fell
> And turned up, life.

The pious and becoming posture of his mind upon this trying occasion he thus describes in a letter to his friend Mr. Turner, dated October 4, 1778.

"I never remember to have had an illness, and I have had many, for which I could not see reason to thank the hand that sent it. I have reason to say so of this last on many accounts; but I would add to *you* on this: because it has given me such convincing proofs not only of the tenderness of my old friends, but of the kindness and attachment of all the congregation to their minister; and of others not so nearly connected. I desire the help of your prayers that I may live, while I do live, if it so please God, to be useful in promoting the truth of the gospel." After expressing his great concern at Mrs. Turner's illness, and his joy at her recovery, he adds, "I do not know whether the tender husband or wife that is a by-stander, does not endure more than the patient on the sick bed. My wife I am persuaded

slept as little as I did for the three weeks nearly that I was confined to a bed; and during all that space, when my head was so
apprehensive and sore with continual watchfulness, that the least
noise was a torture to me, she admitted no one into the room but
the physicians. During my illness happily she kept very well;
since she has been much otherwise, which is not to be wondered
at, considering what she underwent, but I bless God she is now
tolerably recovered."

May the writer of this memoir be permitted to mention, that
soon after this, in January, 1779, being at that time the minister
of a congregation in the country, and upon a visit in London, he
was taken by a friend to attend the evening service in Mr.
Lindsey's chapel? The subject of the discourse was a good
conscience; and the seriousness and gravity with which it was
treated confirmed him in the opinion which he had already formed
from the perusal of some of Dr. Priestley's writings, that it was
possible for a Socinian to be a good man. At the same time he
felt a very sincere concern, that persons so highly respectable as
Mr. Lindsey and Dr. Priestley, should entertain opinions so
grossly erroneous as he then conceived, and so disparaging to the
doctrines of the gospel. This he ignorantly imputed to the little
attention which they paid to the subject of theology. Little did
he then suspect that further and more diligent and impartial
inquiry would induce him to embrace a system from which his
mind at that time shrunk with horror. And had it been foretold
to him that in the course of years, and the revolution of events,
he should himself become the disciple, the friend, the successor,
and the biographer of the person who was then speaking; that
it should fall to his lot from that very pulpit to pronounce before
a crowded assembly of weeping mourners the funeral oration of
Theophilus Lindsey, he would have regarded it as an event almost
without the wide circle of possibilities, and as incredible as the
incidents of an Arabian tale. So strange are the vicissitudes of
human life, and so little does man know of what lies before him,
or of the path in which the mysterious wisdom of divine providence
may conduct him.

At the time when Mr. Lindsey came to settle in London the American contest was carrying on with the greatest animosity. It was an awful crisis for the country. The nation was torn asunder by the conflicting parties, and it was on all sides portended that the separation of the colonies must be inevitably followed by national bankruptcy, if not with the loss of national independence. Not to be deeply interested in a state of affairs so gloomy and alarming, would have indicated a deficiency in some of the most generous and honourable feelings of human nature. Mr. Lindsey felt deeply for the miseries of his country, and for the errors or misconduct of the government. And though, standing at the head of a religious party which was exposed to popular prejudice, and amenable to the laws of the land, he wisely abstained from rendering himself personally obnoxious by taking a public part in political meetings; and though, being chiefly intent upon the great object which he had in view, to restore the simplicity of Christian truth, he seldom or never made the pulpit the vehicle of party politics, he nevertheless thought and felt as a man and a Briton, and hesitated not to express his opinions upon all proper occasions with freedom and warmth. The part he took in the political contests may easily be inferred from his intimacy with Dr. Priestley, Dr. Jebb, Dr. Price, Dr. Franklin, Mr. John Lee, and many other eminent writers and partisans of the times : and Mr. Lindsey was one of those patriotic alarmists who augured much worse of the issue of the contest than the event justified, and who perhaps attributed worse motives to the authors of these unfortunate measures than in fact they deserved. " For my own part," says he, in a letter to Dr. Jebb, dated June, 1774, " I must own I have been so much dejected at the present measures and condition of our country, that it has broken my rest and peace both night and day. Instead of teachers of knowledge, wisdom, virtue, and true religion, which we might and ought to have been, to be a nation the most debauched in principle and practice, exerting its powers to extinguish light and liberty wherever its vast power reaches, is a melancholy reverse of what we expected."

Happily the American war terminated in the independence of

the United States: and this event, contrary to the predictions of boding politicians, so far from proving the ruin of the two countries, has been found by experience to be the greatest blessing which could have happened to both. America for upwards of twenty years has enjoyed peace and liberty, both civil and religious, to an extent unknown in the world before. And Britain, exonerated from the expense and trouble of governing a distant empire, and forming a liberal commercial connexion with her emancipated colonies, far from sinking into bankruptcy and servitude, soon emerged from her difficulties and rose to a state of opulence and prosperity unparalleled in the annals of history. Thus she stood the admiration and envy of the world, till the portentous Revolution of France involved her, as some think unwisely, and as others believe inevitably, in a contest infinitely more hazardous, and the termination of which it is impossible to foresee.*

The gentle and pacific spirit of Mr. Lindsey was averse to all personal and angry controversy: nevertheless, he regarded it as his duty to watch over the cause of which he had avowed himself the advocate, and particularly to notice any remarks which might be made upon his own publications, and which might give birth to any further corrections or illustrations of his arguments. The feeble and intemperate attacks of Burgh and Randolph had been sufficiently exposed by the Rev. A. Temple, M.A., a worthy clergyman of Richmond in Yorkshire, and solid evidence produced by him to prove that the universal church for a good part of the two first centuries was decidedly Unitarian. This gentleman, however, was not satisfied with Mr. Lindsey's interpretation of the proem to St. John's gospel; and in the year 1776, he published a pamphlet entitled "Objections to Mr. Lindsey's Interpretation of the first fourteen verses of St. John's gospel, &c." And two years afterwards another pamphlet was published entitled "A Letter to Dr. Jebb about the unlawfulness of all religious Addresses to Jesus Christ." These works gave rise to a publication by Mr. Lindsey, in the year 1779, entitled "Two Disserta-

* This was written in 1812. The unexpected issue of this disastrous conflict is now well known.

tions, i. On the Preface to St. John's gospel. ii. On Praying
to Jesus Christ." In the first of these Dissertations the learned
writer has alleged further evidence in favour of the interpretation
of this difficult passage, which, after Le Clerc, Lardner, and
others, he had advanced in the Sequel to his Apology, viz., "that
the Logos in this Preface to St. John's gospel is not Christ, but
the word, wisdom, and power of God, communicated to him and
manifested by him." This interpretation, though adopted by
many learned moderns, differs from that of the Polish Socinians,
who by the Logos understand Jesus Christ, who at the commencement of his ministry was admitted like his great predecessor
Moses to intercourse with God, from whom he received his commission, and by whom he was appointed to introduce that great
change in the moral world which is figuratively represented by
the new creation. This hypothesis has been lately revived and
ably defended by Mr. Cappe in the first volume of his ingenious
and learned Dissertations, and the arguments on both sides are
stated and abridged in the notes to the Improved Version of the
New Testament. In the second Dissertation Mr. Lindsey shows
with great force of reasoning that religious worship is not due to
Jesus Christ. For, that God is one person, the sole object of
prayer—that Jesus Christ is a man, and not God—that he never
taught men to worship or pray to himself—that the worship of
Christ is not deducible from his offices and powers—that the
apostles never teach that prayer is to be offered to him—and that
there is no sufficient precedent or example of praying to Christ
recorded in the New Testament: under which head the learned
writer gives an able, and, in general, a very satisfactory analysis
of those texts which are commonly produced in favour of the
worship of Jesus Christ. This pamphlet concludes with a postscript by Dr. Jebb, in which, though he denies the assertion of
the letter-writer that he had referred to Mr. Lindsey's book in
support of his opinions in the pamphlet containing the reasons
for his resignation, he adds, "I will freely own that I entirely
assent, both in general and particular, to the arguments by which
Mr. Lindsey establishes the proper Unity of God, as well as to

those by which he demonstrates the offering of addresses to Christ Jesus to be destitute of all scripture foundation : and that notwithstanding what his opponents have objected, I am persuaded he has sufficiently, and very ably, proved these points."

In the year 1781, Mr. Lindsey published a small work in duodecimo, called "The Catechist,"* or an Inquiry into the Doctrine of the Scriptures concerning the Only True God, and Object of Religious Worship. In the preface he obviates the insinuation of Mr. Gibbon, that the evangelist John had borrowed the doctrine of the Logos from the philosophy of Plato. The work itself is cast into the form of dialogues between Artemon, an Unitarian Christian, and Eusebes, a virtuous inquirer after truth, who being dissatisfied with the popular opinions in which he was educated, is solicitous to gain information concerning the character of God, and the proper object of religious worship. The dialogue is well supported, and the argument is treated clearly, popularly, and concisely, of which the following is a fair specimen. In the sixth dialogue the question proposed is, "Whether Christ had not two natures, so that he was God and man at the same time, and all the depreciating things which he speaks of himself as being a creature belonging to his human nature only, as it is called ? " Artemon replies, " The supposition of Christ's having

---

* " The title Catechist," says Mr. Lindsey, in a note to a work published two years afterwards, " prefixed to the work, and which occurred to the writer from the idea of the famous Origen being Catechist of the church of Alexandria, has, it seems, misled and disappointed some persons, as if it were a composition fitted only for very young persons : whereas it was intended, whether it will answer the purpose others must judge, for those of mature age, who have not had sufficient leisure to attend to the subject ; not without striving at the same time to make the whole plain to ordinary capacities." (Historical View, Pref. p. 1.) In a letter to Mr. Cappe, dated October 22, 1782, Mr. Lindsey, says, " The title has long displeased me. It was taken up indiscreetly and in haste at first. A grave man the other day told me that he thought it related only to children, and therefore had not sent for it. As soon therefore as I have got off my hands what engages me at present, I shall profit by ycur hints, and new monld the work in some measure, adding the second part to it, and, if life be continued, may add other parts, and particularly consider the doctrine of the pre-existence in the same way." The title which the learned author proposed to give to the new-modelled work was, " Dialogues concerning the True God, and the Object of Religious Worship." He did not, however, complete his design, the demand for the work not being sufficient to encourage a second edition until it was taken into the catalogue of the Unitarian Society.

H

two natures, a divine and a human nature, taketh for granted the very thing in question which ought to be proved.

"It is a supposal which has no countenance whatever in the sacred writings. Our Saviour most assuredly used no reserve or ambiguity in what he said of himself. When he averred that he received life from the Father and Creator of all things, that he could do nothing of himself, he meant what he said most sincerely, and would have us so to understand him. When he prayed to God for help and strength, he stood in need of what he prayed for, and wanted that assistance which was given him.

"It is a thing in itself utterly impossible that a being should be God and man; Creator and creature; self-existent, eternal, in-dependent, and limited, dependent, and having beginning of existence at the same time; omniscient and omnipotent, and yet ignorant and weak. These things are not compatible: we should be shocked at their absurdity, if they were not instilled into us before we began to make use of our reason, and if many were not afterwards afraid to make use of it about them, suffering them-selves to be dazzled by great names and authorities, and imposed on by high antiquity, which can give no prescription to what is unintelligible and impossible. In short, this doctrine of Christ being possessed of two natures, is the fiction * of ingenious men, determined at all events to believe Christ to be a different being from what he really was and uniformly declared himself to be; by which they solve such difficulties of scripture as they cannot other-wise get over, and endeavour to prove him to be the Most High God, in spite of his own most express and constant declarations to the contrary. And as there is no reasoning with such persons, they are to be considered and pitied, as being under a debility of mind in this respect, however sensible and rational in all others."

From the commencement of Mr. Lindsey's connection with the congregation in Essex Street, it had been his earnest desire to obtain an associate whose principles, views, and feelings were con-genial with his own, mighty in the scriptures, zealous and intrepid

* See Mr. Lindsey's Answer to Mr. Robinson, p. 172, note.

in the cause of the Divine Unity, who might actively co-operate with him in diffusing the light of Christian truth. While he could entertain the least hope of engaging the able assistance of Dr. Jebb, he could fix his attention upon no other person. But when every expectation of this kind vanished upon the determination of his learned and pious friend to enter upon the profession of medicine, his views and endeavours were directed to another most excellent and amiable person, a very respectable and learned member of the University of Cambridge; but in this application he was now also disappointed. He was almost ready to give up the point in despair, when to his great surprise and joy he received a letter from the Rev. Dr. John Disney, the rector of Panton, and vicar of Swinderby, in the diocese of Lincoln, an intimate friend, and a near relation by marriage, informing him of his resolution to resign his situation in the church, and offering to unite with him in officiating to the congregation in Essex Street. This was in the autumn of the year 1782. Nothing could be more agreeable to Mr. Lindsey than this proposal. He had indeed long been acquainted with Dr. Disney's scruples; but while his friend could reconcile himself to continuing in the church, Mr. Lindsey did not conceive it to be his duty officiously to solicit him to quit his preferment; especially as he knew how offensive this step would be to Dr. Disney's own connections, and particularly to the venerable archdeacon of Cleveland, whose daughter he had married. The trustees of the chapel and the friends of Mr. Lindsey cordially concurred with the wishes of their beloved pastor, who with his usual liberality offered his colleague, who had a growing family, a certain income nearly equal to that which he had resigned. And in return, some of his friends, subscribers to the chapel, had the consideration to increase their annual subscriptions; and Mrs. Rayner, with a liberality peculiarly her own, added to her former annual donation fifty pounds a year, which she continued till Mr. Lindsey resigned his pastoral office at the chapel. Of Mr. Lindsey's feelings upon this happy occasion we may form a judgment from the following expressions of them in correspondence with his friends. " I must not delay to tell you,"

says he, in a letter to a friend, * dated November 28, 1792, "lest
you should hear of it less directly, that Dr. Disney, who left us
last week, was here somewhat more than a fortnight, and during
that interval resigned two livings to the Bishop of Lincoln, preached
afterwards with great acceptance both parts of the day to our
congregation, and the next day was approved as my colleague by
as many of the benefactors to our building as were in town.
This you will believe has made me very happy. I am the more
so, because it was an event unlooked for a few months ago. In
the autumn, when I was at his house at Swinderby, I was in treaty
with another friend and very eminent person to become my colleague. But I said not a syllable of it to Dr. Disney, for I knew
how sore he was; and for six years past have never by letter or in
conversation touched the subject of conformity." The Doctor,
however, having heard by other means that this negotiation was
at an end, "wrote to me," continues Mr. Lindsey, "to offer himself, and the result has been as I have told you. I have been
enabled to allow him something handsome, and some few friends
have come forward to enable me, and so I trust everything will
turn out as we wish it. We expect them in January. They have
a journey first to make to the good archdeacon, who thinks that
the original sin lies with me in drawing his son-in-law out of the
church. But I have told you the truth and nothing but the
truth."

In a letter to Mr. Turner, dated January 1, 1783, Mr. Lindsey
writes: "My new colleague is this week arrived with his wife and
three children. The enclosed (viz. Dr. Disney's Reasons for re-

---

* The Rev. Dr. Toulmin, then minister of a small congregation of Protestant Dissenters at Taunton, now settled with a very large and flourishing society of Unitarian
Christians at Birmingham, the same which formerly enjoyed the privilege of Dr. Priestley's instructions. In this place persecution has produced its usual effect of multiplying
the persecuted sect. Under the prudent, affectionate, and pious labours of their present
venerable minister, and of his able and equally zealous colleague, the Reverend John
Kentish, the cause of pure uncorrupted truth, and of serious and practical religion, without
which knowledge is of no use, is advancing with a celerity most encouraging, and
almost without example. Dr. Toulmin for many years kept up a regular correspondence
with Mr. Lindsey, of which he has had the goodness to permit the author to avail himself in drawing up this Memoir. N.B. This amiable and useful man died July 23,
1815, universally beloved and regretted. He is succeeded in office by the Rev. James
Yates, well known by his able and learned reply to Dr. Wardlaw, of Glasgow.

signing the Rectory of Panton, and the Vicarage of Swinderby) which I present you with in his name, will give you pleasure, as a mark of good sense and a good heart, and likely to do good in our common cause. I am the more pleased with this connection, as it was both unthought of and unexpected."

CHAPTER VI.

MR. LINDSEY PUBLISHES HIS HISTORICAL VIEW. SOME ACCOUNT
OF DR. WILLIAM ROBERTSON. SOCIETY FOR PROMOTING THE
KNOWLEDGE OF THE SCRIPTURES.

In the spring of 1783, Mr. Lindsey being now more at liberty, committed to the press a work, the materials of which he had been collecting for some years. This work is entitled, "An Historical View of the State of the Unitarian Doctrine and Worship from the Reformation to our own Times; with some Account of the Obstructions it has met with at different Periods." This is an elaborate work, and one of the most interesting and important of Mr. Lindsey's publications.* The professed design of it is to

* The plan and title of this work is somewhat different from the author's original intention, as announced to his friend Mr. Cappe, in a letter dated October 22, 1783.
"The title of my intended work will be, Impediments to the Acknowledgment and Worship of the One Living and True God the Father, caused by (or arising from) Christians themselves, especially Socinians and Unitarians, from the Reformation to our own Times.
"Chap. I. will contain,—
"1. The state of the Unitarian doctrine at the Reformation.
"2. The state of the Unitarian doctrine in England at that time.
— "Under the last section will be an opportunity of comparing the advantages enjoyed from the liberal interpretations of scripture given on the point in question, with the narrow and systematic turn of our interpreters in general.
"Chap. II. will contain,—
"1. Impediments from Socinus, and Socinians properly speaking. This will be a

establish the great truth, that the One Almighty Father of the universe is the only God of Christians; and that he alone is the proper Object of worship. With this view the author intermixes illustrations of scripture with historical facts, many of which are little known, and are well calculated to excite the attention of those who are interested in theological inquiries, in detecting the corruptions and in recovering the genuine doctrines of the Christian religion.

"These facts," says Mr. Lindsey, Pref. p. 5, "it is apprehended, will be reckoned curious by such as wish to know what passes and has passed upon the stage of this world of ours, concerning a point of so sublime a nature, the diversity of opinions that have been entertained upon it, the warm passions it has excited, and the singular events to which it has sometimes given occasion, in whatever light they look upon the religion of Christ. But to those who believe that religion to come from God, it is presumed they will appear both important and curious.

"The history of virtuous, upright minds and inquirers after truth, emerging out of the long night of anti-christian darkness, seeking the great Source of being and benevolent Father of all, and having found him, yielding themselves to torture and death rather than disown him, rather than not confess and maintain,

large discussion. Socinus will be proved as he is really believed to be, an idolater; and consequences will be intimated with respect to other Christians.

"2. Impediments from English Unitarians. Mr. Firmin; a good deal concerning him, and the Unitarians of his day.

"3. Impediments from Dr. Clarke, Bishop Hoadley, &c.

"4. Impediments from Mr. Tucker, who was a complete Unitarian, but, out of good though mistaken motives, endeavoured to quiet himself and others by giving an Unitarian sense to Trinitarian language.

"Chap. III. will consider—

"1. The general pleas for Unitarians attending Trinitarian worship which they disapprove.

"2. The part they ought to take."

One cannot help wishing that the learned and pious author had more completely executed his plan, especially under the two last divisions. This is indeed an interesting and a painful subject; concerning which it is greatly to be feared that many err, not for want of knowledge, but of firmness of mind. For, of what avail is the still small voice of reason and duty in opposition to the loud clamours of self-interest, fashion, and the estimation of the world? How few lay it seriously to heart, that a day is coming when the *Man of Nazareth* will be "ashamed of those who are now ashamed of him!"

and declare to others his transcendent majesty and excellency, and superiority to the things he has made, presents the most instructive, awful, and animating spectacle and lesson of all others, tending to inspire the reader with the like unshaken courage and love of truth, and loyalty to the righteous and moral Governor of the world.

"It would be great satisfaction to be made an instrument in any the least degree, to lead others out of the mazes of impenetrable mystery and polytheism to this parent Mind, *to the first Good, first Perfect, and first Fair,* alone worthy of the highest love, adoration, and gratitude."

In pursuance of his design, the worthy author begins with representing the state of the Unitarian doctrine at the beginning of the Reformation, and exhibiting the superior advantages then enjoyed for understanding the scriptures in this respect. He then notices the promising state of the Unitarian doctrine in England at the time of the Reformation, with the violent means used to suppress it. He next treats of the worship of Jesus Christ by Socinus and his followers, and particularly enlarges upon the controversy on this subject between Faustus Socinus and Francis David, and upon the severity exercised towards David and others, for refusing to acknowledge Christ as an object of religious worship. In this chapter, Mr. Lindsey introduces a section in reply to some severe and unfounded remarks of Bishop Newton upon the Unitarians. The succeeding chapter exhibits the state of the Unitarian doctrine in the reign of Queen Elizabeth and of the Stuarts; and the author here explains the cause of the great silence concerning the Divine Unity during this period, and gives some account of that truly eminent confessor John Biddle, M.A., of the University of Oxford, who, for the profession of his principles, was banished by Cromwell to the Scilly Islands, and afterwards died in prison. Then follows an account of the state of the Unitarian doctrine and worship from the Restoration to the close of the seventeenth century, in which is included a brief memoir of the celebrated Mr. Thomas Firmin, merchant of London, a disciple of Biddle, and his protector and friend; a man eminently useful in his day, the friend of Whichcote, Burnet, and Tillotson, an avowed and zealous Unitarian, but who hesitated not to conform to the worship of the established church, justifying his conduct, but surely erroneously, upon the principles of Dr. Wallis and the Oxford divines in the controversy with Dr. Sherlock, that the three persons in the Trinity were nothing more than three different characters or relations of one and the same Being. In the following chapter the author describes the state of the Unitarian doctrine and worship in the eighteenth century: and here he gives a particular account of the opinions and writings of Emlyn, of Whiston, of Dr. Samuel Clarke, of Bishop Hoadley, of Sir Isaac Newton, and of Abraham Tucker, the author of a curious and profound work entitled, " The Light of Nature pursued, by Edward Search, Esq." The concluding chapter contains a relation of some circumstances favourable of late years to the progress of the doctrine of the Divine Unity, in which the worthy author, after representing the benefit accruing to the cause of truth from an open defence and maintenance of it, records some recent public declarations in favour of the Unitarian doctrine and worship, by an open and avowed separation from the worship of the Church of England. And in particular, he relates the circumstances of the first rise of the church of Unitarian Christians assembling in the chapel in Essex Street, to which he annexes a brief memoir of some eminent persons who had honourably, and from a sense of duty, avowed Unitarian principles, and some of whom had for conscience' sake resigned lucrative situations and fair prospects of preferment in the national church. In this honourable catalogue are the highly respected names of Dr. Robertson, Dr. John Jebb, Dr. Chambers, Mr. Tyrwhitt, of Jesus College, Cambridge; Mr. Evanson, Mr. Maty, Mr. Harris, and Dr. Disney.*

* The following letter from the late learned and venerable Bishop of Carlisle, Dr. Edmund Law, was received by Mr. Lindsey in return for a present of this valuable work, dated Cambridge, September 23, 1783 :

"Dear Sir,—I received the favour of your Historical View, and read it with satisfaction. You appear to have cleared up all the passages of scripture usually alleged in favour of the contrary opinion, and to have exhausted the subject. As a small return

Of the first of these venerable worthies, Mr. Lindsey thus writes in the concluding paragraph of the Introduction : "Whilst I am finishing this sheet, I have an account sent me from Wolverhampton of the decease of my ingenious, amiable friend, Dr. Robertson, mentioned near the close of the following work.. He was born in Dublin, October 16, 1705, and died May 20, 1783." Of this truly eminent person, "this venerable father of Unitarian Nonconformity of our own days," as he is styled by Mr. Lindsey, I will here subjoin a few anecdotes which. may serve to illustrate the uncommon excellence of his character. The following account of him is given by the late celebrated Thomas Hollis, Esq., under the fictitious name of Pierce Delver, which he assumed in his correspondence with Mr. Lindsey, in a letter dated February 2, 1768. It appears that Mr. Hollis had requested an interview with Dr. Robertson.

"The Reverend William Robertson, author of a work entitled, An Attempt to explain the Words, Reason, &c., &c., was with a certain person lately at his own desire, and stayed with that person from eleven till two. That person talked him over closely, so as to get informed of his family, education, situation throughout life, and present views. He found him to be in all respects a learned, ingenious, cheerful, polite man; a voluntary martyr to the Candid Disquisitions, and religious liberty. He presented him with ten guineas, assured him of all his general good offices, with open doors at all times; and though very sensible, yet a *suckling* to the world, suggested to him the likeliest means of his attaining some civil post, by what interest he possesses. At parting, Mr. Robertson was please to say, he should esteem that day as

for the obligation, I must desire your acceptance of a new Cumberland edition of my Theory, *purged of some ancient prejudices relative to pre-existence*, &c. I have recommended to my executors to procure a publication of Dr. Bullock's two Discourses which clear up the doctrine of atonement, and which I think I communicated to you formerly. The Bishop of Clonfert was returned to Ireland before your letter reached us. He would have been delighted with seeing your account of his favourite author A. Tucker, whose work I have often said wanted methodizing and abridging to be of more general use. My compliments to your worthy coadjutor, and to my old friend Dr. Jebb. That all the success and satisfaction may attend your labours to which they are so justly entitled, is the most hearty wish of your sincere friend and servant,

"E. C."

one of the most interesting of his whole life. And indeed so, in a certain sense, he might say, as the informations given him must necessarily appear new, many of them useful and determining.

" He is of a Scottish family, born in Ireland, was bred regularly for the church, was some years at school in Dublin, where his father lived, under Mr. Hutcheson, the after celebrated Scottish Professor at Glasgow,—studied several years in Glasgow, was presented, so soon as he was capable of holding them, to Ravilly and other adjoining livings, by a then bishop, his patron. These livings are worth, on my poor memory, about £150 a year. On them he resided till about the year 1760, when he resigned them on account of his scruples in relation to some parts of the public service. Some art was used to induce him to resign these livings on his evidencing those scruples, with promise, in case he did quietly, of providing for him decently in some way suitable to himself. On such resignation, no care was taken of him, but, at best, much coolness shown towards him ; nor will, he thinks, and one person believes, any care be taken of him. Before his scruples he was a favourite of Lord Primate Stone, who recommended him to Dr. Robinson, then Lord Bishop of Ferns. Became a favourite of the Bishop's, who offered him the livings mentioned in his letter, value, I think, about nett £80 a year, £40 a year being allowed for a curate, with promise of further countenance. And he thinks, had he continued in the church and in favour of the bishop, now Lord Primate of Armagh, he should be probably possessed of church preferment at this time to the amount of £1000 a year. When he waited on his patron under scruples, he was told, ' You are a madman : you do not know the world.'

" He has several children which are all tolerably settled, save one daughter single, who lives with another married. Himself alone has no subsistence. After having sought it years at Dublin in vain, he came over here in August last, to that end, with tolerable recommendations to two persons of some influence and will to assist him. These, however, had the indiscretion at best to tender it on the church line, to the amount of £100 a year or so ! which he declined at once, and so matters rest with him at present. One person has put him on a new plan, and hopes it may issue to subsistence. He is aged sixty-three, middle-sized, and tolerably hearty. The same person recommended to him to maintain his cheerfulness, and was thanked for so doing. " My dear sir, I scribble off-hand and tired, but you cannot, I think, but perceive a colossus of a good man. In our age, he should indeed be miserable. There is great simplicity with ease in his behaviour; but I suspect under it, for my time was but short with him considering what I had to throw out to him, strong parts."

The pains which this respectable gentleman took to serve this worthy friend in procuring for him some civil establishment, were however unsuccessful. But in the same year a provision was made for him by the Merchant-Taylors Company of London, who presented Dr. Robertson to the office of head-master of the free grammar school at Wolverhampton, in Staffordshire. A laborious employment, and not very lucrative at best; and at this time charged with an annuity to a superannuated incumbent who had retired, and who lived some years afterwards. To this humble station did the venerable confessor repair, now in his grand climacteric, when an office requiring less exertion might have better suited his advanced age ; and here he resided content and thankful for fifteen years, discharging the duties of his office with great reputation ; and though in this situation he survived all his children, and was left *alone and unpropped*, he still retained, as Mr. Lindsey expresses it, " that serenity and cheerful trust in the' divine Providence, which can only belong to the virtuous and innocent mind."* But the malice of bigotry pursued him even into this retreat.

* In a letter to Mr. Lindsey, dated March 9, 1769, Pierce Delver (Mr. Hollis) communicates to his friend the following interesting intelligence concerning this venerable confessor :
" Dr. Robertson, I believe, at first thought the school in Staffordshire to be better circumstanced than it really was ; and afterwards having been chosen to it with great good will and earnestness of the trustees of it, he then thought it a kind of shame to decline it. A little before the Doctor went out of town, he communicated to me the following singular and very fine anecdote, but in his own finer manner : ' 'I hat a country clergyman, of a good look and great simplicity of manners, had then lately

It has been before stated, p. 28, upon Mr. Lindsey's own authority, that no consideration pressed more strongly upon his mind, nor urged him more forcibly to resolve upon his resignation, than the sentiments expressed by Dr. Robertson in his letter to the Bishop of Ferns. And when at last Mr. Lindsey had given up his preferment, and had succeeded so far beyond his expectation in opening a chapel in Essex Street and establishing an interest which offered a good prospect of permanence, Dr. Robertson appears to have been one of the first persons to whom he directed his thoughts and wishes as an associate in his labours. To this he was prompted more perhaps by motives of veneration and gratitude, than by his usual sense of propriety and expedience; for Dr. Robertson, though vigorous and active for his years, and not unwilling to listen to the application, must at that time have been turned of seventy. To this application Mr. Lindsey appears to allude in a letter to Dr. Jebb, dated May 10, 1775.

" R. was to have preached for me the last Sunday afternoon; but on Friday he came to tell me he was not quite provided. He is, however, to do the duty on Sunday next. I shall be glad to engage him if approved by our congregation, and have told him so. But as what I can allow him will not be sufficient for his support, he is looking out for some that may be consistent with it. N.B. Half of what I at present receive from our subscrip-

called upon him one morning at his lodgings, and asked him if his name was Robert-son? On being answered in the affirmative, he seized his hand, shook it heartily, said he had heard much of him, had read and approved his book, rejoiced to see him more than any man in England, and that having brought fourscore pounds to town to lay out by way of addition to some Stock which he already possessed in the Funds, there it was, pulling out a bag of money from his pocket and laying it upon the table by Dr. Robertson,—he could never dispose of it so usefully, so excellently, as to him. The Doctor, astonished, entreated him many times to put up his bag again, for that he had no need of it, being without want : which at length, with very great reluctance, he did, after having repeatedly exclaimed, Why! man, I have no use for it; at least take a part.' The name of this clergyman was William Hopkins, of Cuckfield, a gentleman, it seems, who has long since distinguished himself for good sense, learning, and public spirit, by his writings. Archbishops of England ! Ireland ! who declare difference of opinion from your small sect to be a *misfortune*, match, if ye can, in your like, this pair ! I could not help saying to Dr. Robertson, that for both's sake, I thought he should have taken ten guineas."

So far Pierce Delver. After Mr. Lindsey's resignation, when he came to reside in London, Mr. Hopkins became his friend and correspondent. A few of this excellent man's letters are inserted in the Appendix, No. VII.

tions, the expenses of the chapel deducted, I propose to give him if we engage."

What steps were afterwards taken do not appear.   For when Dr. Jebb had fixed to leave the church and to remove from Cambridge, Mr. Lindsey could think of no other colleague till he had peremptorily declined.   After this, Mr. Lindsey's attention appears to have been again turned towards his venerable friend at Wolverhampton, who thus addresses him in a letter dated April 5, 1778:

" Some weeks ago I had prepared boxes, and had actually packed up some of my luggage, and was saying to myself, Transmigratio hinc sit felix, faustaque! when I was privately informed that there were some people here consulting together what methods they should take in putting the laws in execution against me for teaching a school without a license.   The Company of Merchant-Taylors, London, who presented me to this school, 1768, had a bill filed against them in Chancery three years ago, by some very troublesome people of this town, to compel them to give an account of the issues and profits of the manor of Rushock, which was bequeathed in trust to them for the support of the school.   The Company have set forth in their answer, that they have expended £1,200 upon this school more than they received out of the estate. And this I verily believe to be true.   I have, therefore, upon every occasion vindicated the Company, and have spoken my mind very freely here with respect to the persons who are plaintiffs in this suit.   This, I find, has drawn upon me their displeasure; and as religion must be brought into every dispute, public and private, they have now, I am told, taken it into their heads to prosecute me on account of non-subscription.   To this indeed, I believe, they have been instigated by some orthodox clergymen, whose zeal is without much knowledge.—And shall I now decline the contest?   No!—I am resolved either to gain the victory over these assailants, or to fall gloriously in defending the most noble privilege of human nature: LIBERTY OF THOUGHT !   To fly now would look like cowardice.   I cannot, therefore, avoid abiding the event.   If they should proceed, you shall be informed of every step

taken on either side.   The cause between the Company and their
accusers is to be heard by the Lord Chancellor next Term.   If he
makes a decree, as is expected, it may either animate or discourage
these warm gentlemen.   A little time will therefore determine
that.   I long to be with you, but I think it is my duty in present
circumstances to continue here a little longer at least.   I am but
poorly in health; both the gout and stone have been lately very
pungent.   But submission to my God, gratitude to my friends,
afford the greatest comfort to your most obliged and most affectionate, W.R."

Who can read this excellent letter without admiring the piety,
the fortitude, the magnanimity of this extraordinary man, this
aged confessor, this veteran champion of Christian truth?   How
dignified, how sublime, does Dr. Robertson appear, at the age of
seventy-three, clad in the armour of innocence and truth; collecting the remaining vigour of his powers, firmly resolved to stand
his ground in the day of trial, and to perish in the conflict, rather
than tarnish the honours of his former years, or to recede a tittle
from that good confession to which he had cheerfully sacrificed all
his temporal possessions and prospects!   In comparison with this
Christian hero, how mean, how contemptible do his persecutors
appear, insidiously and maliciously plotting in their dark cabals
to deprive an old man of his bread, and to consign him to the
horrors of a gaol!   And why?   Was it because he had offended
against the laws of eternal justice and committed crimes worthy
of bonds and imprisonment?   Was Dr. Robertson a bad neighbour, a faithless friend, a dishonest citizen, a disloyal subject?
This was not even pretended.   What was it then that provoked
the zeal, that roused the malignant passions of these holy inquisitors?   It was this: that Dr. Robertson professed himself a
worshiper of the Father only; of that Being whom Jesus wor-
shiped, and of whom he speaks as his Father and our Father, as
his God and our God.   For the sake of this object, he had quitted
his situation and all his hopes and prospects in a church where
this pure primitive worship was not allowed, and had cast himself
and a large family upon the wide world to seek their bread, with-

out any friend but a good conscience, and without any patronage or protection but that of divine Providence. His enemies " could find nothing against him, except it were touching the law of his God." The crime charged upon this venerable confessor was the same which was alleged against the apostle before him; "after the way which they called heresy, so did he worship the God of his fathers." O Persecution, what a hideous fiend art thou in every shape, in every place, and in every age! But never, surely, more hideous, more disgusting, nor more contemptible, than when enlisted in the service of men calling themselves Christians, to fasten thy venomous fangs upon such a character as Dr. Robertson.

Happily, in this case the success of the enterprise did not correspond with the malignity of the purpose. A flourishing school of Papists subsisted in the neighbourhood, zealously patronized by the lord of the domain, the same nobleman who being chairman to the bench of Westminster justices demurred to register Mr. Lindsey's chapel, Lord Dudley and Ward; and bigotry herself did not think it decent to prosecute a Protestant clergyman for keeping a school, while a popish seminary was left unmolested. Happily the danger of such persecutions is now passed; and in this enlightened age, and in this tolerant reign, both Protestants and Catholics are protected by law in the exercise of that indefeasible right, that primary duty of parents to educate their children in the principles and habits which they judge to be most conducive to their virtue and happiness. But now let this excellent man tell his own story in his letter to Mr. Lindsey, dated April 27, 1778.

" I congratulate you most heartily upon getting again into your chapel. But I hope you have too much prudence to go to dwell in the house till it gets the next summer's seasoning at least. My friend Mrs. Abernethy tells me she has got a seat in the chapel, and invites me to sit there. *But you invite me to a higher station.* It is possible I may accept of both. This day was our visitation, to which I was cited. I expected articles would have been exhibited against me, but none appeared. Our Official very

civilly invited me to dine with him, and placed me next himself.
I asked him if he had heard anything of the design against me
that was whispered about. He made no direct answer to my
question, but said I might be quite easy in that respect. There
is a popish school set up in our town within this half year,—but
one of much greater importance within two miles of us, kept in a
house in which the Lords Dudley resided, and was set up by the
late lord, whose lady was suspected of popery, for that purpose.
This school is supported by large contributions from Catholics
both at home and abroad, and contains now one hundred and
fifty scholars, who are taught, and most of them clothed and fed,
gratis. Now I find that a prosecution could not be carried on
with any decency against me, without obliging the same persons
to prosecute the masters and supporters of the popish school upon
the same principles, and this design they know would meet with
all possible discouragement from the ruling powers. Therefore,
under the protection of popery, wonderful event! I find myself
safe. It was the profound policy of the counsellors of James II.
to grant an universal toleration to all dissenters from the established
church, amongst whom were included the Papists, and thus popery
became tolerated at least, and highly encouraged. Protestant
dissenters are more the objects of popish persecution than the
established episcopalians. But though the devil shows sometimes
as an angel of light, yet he is a devil still, and only puts on that
appearance that he may the more effectually deceive, and in the
end more surely destroy."*

* This expression may be thought harsh, and to savour of a persecuting spirit, in
one who was himself at that very time threatened with persecution. But let it be
recollected, that the venerable septuagenarian was born in the reign of the last of the
Stuarts, who earnestly sought to set aside the Act of Succession and to introduce a
popish successor. And through the reigns of the two first princes of the House of
Hanover the Papists were regarded, and as a body justly, as enemies to the family upon
the throne, and decided partisans of a popish Pretender; and were, therefore, properly
considered by the friends of civil and religious liberty as political enemies; who, if they
gained the ascendency, would subvert the government and religion of the country, and
introduce popery, tyranny, and persecution. The state of things is now materially
changed. The Pretender's family is extinct; and the present generation of English
Catholics are as good and loyal subjects as the Protestants, and equally entitled to civil
rights and to religious liberty. And though popery, as a system of faith and an
enormous corruption of Christianity, ought still to be attacked by every argument of

In September, 1783, a society, was instituted "for promoting the knowledge of the Scriptures." The meetings were held at Essex House. Among the original members of the society were Mr. Lindsey, Dr. Disney, who accepted the office of Secretary, Dr. Jebb, Dr. Kippis, Dr. Price, Dr. Calder, Mr. Dodson, Mr. Lee, &c. in London; and in the country, Mr. Taylcur of Shrewsbury, who generously remitted £100 to the society for immediate use, and entered himself as a subscriber of five guineas annually; Mr. Shore, and Mr. Newton of Norton, Mr. Turner, Dr. Priestley, Dr. Toulmin, Dr. Law, bishop of Carlisle, and others, in all about thirty or forty members. The society limited its object to the illustration of the Scriptures, and declined all tracts which were wholly controversial, or which were formal defences or confutations of specific doctrines. A very able sketch of the society's plan was drawn up by Dr. Jebb, in which he states and illustrates what he calls the *analytic* plan of interpretation which the society proposed to pursue and to recommend, viz., Having selected a passage of scripture for the purpose of illustration, to begin with discussing preliminary questions relating to the connexion, &c. These being settled, the judicious interpreter is to proceed, by settling the text by a comparison of various readings; by accurate translation, division, and punctuation; by a concise well-digested commentary; by notes philological and explanatory; and finally, by adding doctrinal and moral conclusions. This, which is unquestionably a most excellent plan of interpretation,

reason and scripture, the professors of that corrupt religion ought not to be laid under political restraint. Many of the Catholics themselves have learned in the school of adversity the true principles of religious liberty. And the Christian petition for universal religious freedom, originating with that eminent patriot and clergyman of the established church the Reverend Christopher Wyvill, presented to Parliament in June, 1810, and ably supported by Samuel Whitbread, Esq., and W. Smith, Esq., was signed not only by Protestants of all denominations but by many gentlemen of distinction among the Catholics. Popery, as a political system, is no longer an object of terror. Babylon the great is fallen. In this event the professors of rational Christianity must rejoice, and the friends of civil and religious liberty must share in the triumph. But this is a very different thing from insulting the individuals of the catholic persuasion. And nothing, surely, can be more ungenerous than rejoicing in the calamities of the aged and respectable pontiff; who is now (1812) a victim to a merciless tyranny. We exult in the fall of an anti-christian domination; but we pity the sufferings of the man, and execrate the cruelty of the oppressor.

I

was laid down as a general rule, without meaning to require
from their correspondents a rigid conformity to it, or to any other
specific model; but to admit any communication which tended
to the advancement of scriptural knowledge.

This society did not flourish in the degree nor to the extent of
the desires and expectations of its learned and benevolent founders.*
Its members were never numerous, and they were very sparing
in their contributions : the plan was too circumscribed, and
interfered too much with the larger, the more comprehensive,
and more useful plan of the Theological Repository, at that time
resumed by Dr. Priestley : and after languishing a few years, it
was altogether given up. Not, however, without bequeathing
a valuable legacy to the theological student, consisting of two
volumes of Commentaries and Essays. Among these are a curious
dissertation of Mr. Lindsey's upon John xiv. 1–3 ; and a
gleaning of remarks on Mr. Travis's attempt to revive the exploded
text of 1 John v. 7. A translation with notes, by Mr. Dodson,
of the twelve first chapters of Isaiah, and likewise of the fifty-
second and fifty-third chapters, which were all afterwards republished by that learned writer in a complete translation of the whole
book, with notes. Another communication was added by Mr.
Dodson in the second volume, in the form of a letter to Mr.
Evanson, in defence of his hypothesis concerning the spurious-
ness of the gospels of Matthew, Mark, and John. Also two
inestimable dissertations of the Rev. Robert Tyrwhitt, one upon
the "Creation of all things by Jesus Christ," and the other upon
the "Resurrection of the dead through the Man Jesus Christ."
The bulk of the second volume is made up of remarks, many
of them very ingenious, upon select passages in the Old Testament,
by the late Rev. Henry More, of Leskiard in Cornwall.

* "This circular letter which our secretary sends," says Mr. Lindsey in a letter
to Mr. Turner, dated December 5, 1785. "will but too much prove that our society
does not flourish at present. Not that we receive no contributions to it; but unless
they have something original in them, and are ingenious, it would not answer our
design to give them admission. You have well earned your dismission from such
labours, though we cannot but lament it."

CHAPTER VII.

CONTROVERSY WITH ROBERT ROBINSON. ANALYSIS OF THE VIN-
DICIÆ PRIESTLEIANÆ. MISUNDERSTANDING AND RECON-
CILIATION WITH DR. RICHARD PRICE.

In the beginning of the year 1776 the late celebrated Robert
Robinson, minister of a Baptist congregation at Cambridge, published a book entitled "A Plea for the Divinity of our Lord Jesus
Christ." This treatise, written with great ingenuity, and which
breathes throughout a most amiable spirit of candour, is considered by many as one of the most plausible and imposing
defences of the popular doctrine concerning the person of Christ
which ever issued from the press. So far indeed as argument is
concerned, it is egregiously trifling, and contains a sort of defence
of the deity of the Son of God which the learned Trinitarians, the
Bulls and Waterlands of a former age, would have blushed to
avow. It consists chiefly of a collection of texts arranged under
different heads as suited the author's purpose, without any inquiry
into their genuineness, without any attention to the connection,
and even without any attempt to ascertain the correctness of the
translation. These texts so arranged, the worthy author commented
upon and explained agreeably to his own preconceived opinions,
and with all the confidence of inspiration itself. He even goes so
far as to denounce Jesus and his apostles as "idiots and im-
postors," if they intended any other meaning than what he was
pleased to annex to their language.* This specious and dog-

* "Notwithstanding so many reasons for precision, Jesus Christ declares, All things
that the Father hath are mine, a very dangerous proposition if he were not God."
Robinson's Plea, p. 14. Again, p. 17: "If they who ascribe the perfections of deity
to Jesus Christ have fallen into an error, they have been led into it by the writers of
the New Testament. If Jesus Christ be God, the ascription of the perfections of God
to him is proper; if he be not, the apostles are chargeable with weakness or wickedness, and either would destroy their claims to inspiration." Further, p. 18: "Con-

I 2

matical style, combined with much ingenuity, and wit, and eloquence, and accompanied with great liberality towards those who
held a different position, and particularly with many expressions
of marked respect to Mr. Lindsey and Dr. Jebb, rendered the
treatise extremely popular, and made a considerable impression
upon many who ought to have been better informed; but who
were not forward to pry with too curious an eye into the validity
of arguments in support of doctrines which they dare not dis-
believe. "Accordingly," says Mr. Robinson's biographer, "a pro-
fusion of compliments followed the publication, as well from
several dignitaries of the church as from the dissenters. Dr.
Hinchcliffe, bishop of Peterborough, Dr. Hallifax, afterwards
bishop of Gloucester, Dr. Goddard, master of Clare Hall, Dr.
Ogden, Woodwardian professor, Dr. Cooke, provost of King's
College, Dr. Beadon, afterwards bishop of Gloucester, at that time
public orator, and Dr. Tucker, dean of Gloucester, courted his
acquaintance. And it was pretty generally agreed that the Plea
was the best defence of the divinity of Christ which had been
published." Handsome compliments likewise were paid to the
author by ministers of his own persuasion, particularly Dr.
Stennet, Dr. Evans, Daniel Turner, and several others of the
moderate Calvinists. The Rev. Josiah Thompson, late of. Clapham, in particular, writes, "I have read your Plea with singular
pleasure, but not more than I expected from it. Everything you
write never fails to entertain and delight me." This good man

sider now into what contradictions these writers must fall if Jesus Christ be not God.
They contradict one another: they contradict themselves. They degrade writings
which they pretend are inspired, below the lowest scribbling of the meanest authors."
  Such is the censure which this ingenious and well-meaning but mistaken writer
passes upon Jesus and his apostles if they did not mean to teach the doctrine which he
imputes to them, not a suspicion of which ever entered. into their imaginations, not a
single trace of which is to be discovered in their discourses or in their writings; and
from the very idea of which they would have recoiled with horror.
  "The few who examine and decide for themselves," says Mr. Lindsey, "are not to
be dazzled and overawed by these confident declarations, knowing that mortals are
oftentimes most ignorant where they are most presumptuous and assured. But it is
not so with others; especially if their prejudices lean that way already. Such violent
language overpowers them before they are aware of it, and puts an end to all cool and
fair inquiry, so that they will hear no reason from those of a contrary sentiment; and
it will be well if even their resentments are not instantly kindled against them."
—Exam. of Robinson's Plea, p. 4..

showed the Plea to Dr. Furneaux and Dr. Kippis; but though these learned and judicious divines express themselves in hand-some and becoming terms of the author's superior abilities, and his great talents for original composition, they understood the controversy too well to pay any compliment to his argument.*

Of the admirers of this celebrated Defence of the Divinity of Christ, though not in the number of Mr. Robinson's corre-spondents, the learned Archdeacon Blackburne is one of the most conspicuous. This eminent divine, who, it is plain, had paid more attention to the subject of Christian liberty than of theolo-gical controversy, thought but slightly of the arguments contained in Mr. Lindsey's Apology; and at the same time, he had too much good sense to be satisfied with the superficial replies of Burgh and Randolph. But after he had read Mr. Robinson's pamphlet, which he did not see till it came to a second edition, the good archdeacon, in the warmth of his zeal, began to think that the controversy was by this unanswerable work completely settled, that Unitarianism was now silenced for ever, and that all her learned advocates were humbled in the dust by " the sling and the stone" of this new champion of the orthodox faith. But let the worthy dignitary speak for himself.

In a tract written in the year 1782, and printed in an Appendix to the Memoir of his Life, (prefixed to an edition of the Arch-deacon's Works in seven volumes, in the year 1804, published by his son, the Reverend Francis Blackburne,) entitled an Answer to the Question, "Why are you not a Socinian?" Mr. Blackburne expresses himself thus: "When Mr. Lindsey's Apology came out I read it, and thought some things in it well enough. In other passages he seemed to me to be infirm in his proofs; I then read several answers to him, which, among a few tolerable hits, had a considerable mixture of weakness and absurdity. About five years ago, I know not what chance threw in my way a pamphlet entitled A Plea for the Divinity of our Lord Jesus Christ. I perused this pamphlet with care and attention, and was both surprised and concerned to find so many of my friend Lindsey's arguments and

* See Dyer's Life of Robert Robinson, p. 109.

positions totally subverted, *a fundamentis,* provided the pleadings, reasonings, and authorities were well grounded. To prove this to myself I consulted a number of the texts he had cited, and found his superstructure bottomed upon a rock. It is now six years since this pamphlet was first published. I have looked in every news-paper, review, magazine, &c., I met with, and could never find an answer to it either from Mr. Lindsey, Dr. Jebb, Dr. Priestley, or even Mr. Evanson, who I think is one of the best writers among the Socinians, either ancient or modern. Indeed, so far as con-cerns the Socinians, I think it unanswerable." *

Such was the judgment of the venerable Archdeacon of Cleve-land; and in this judgment be was supported by the multitude, who always find it to be less trouble to take a doctrine upon trust than to examine its evidence with care. Thus was this spirited assailant for many years left master of the field, and his work not being answered was of course reckoned unanswerable.

In the meantime the Unitarian divines were not negligent of what was passing, nor inattentive to the temporary triumph of orthodoxy in one of the chief seats of science and learning. Mr. Lindsey and Dr. Jebb were the principal persons whose writings were attacked in this popular publication; and the author with much good nature had sent to each of those gentlemen a copy of his work, accompanied with letters professing his high regard for their talents, their learning, and their character, and apologizing for any expression which might through inadvertency have dropped from his pen, and which was capable of being construed into per-sonal disrespect. Courteous answers were of course returned.† But neither of the gentlemen so addressed entertained at that time any thoughts of writing a confutation of the Plea; Dr. Jebb

---

* Whether the archdeacon was ever convinced of the futility of the arguments of the " Plea," by that forcible train of reasoning which converted the candid author him-self, does not appear. His worthy biographer concludes the contrary. It appears, says he, that in the year 1785 an Examination of Mr. Robinson's Plea was published by the Rev. T. Lindsey, but without a name, and by him pr-sented to Mr. Blackburne. We have not, however, been able to discover that the archdeacon's sentiments of Mr. Robinson's work underwent any change, as he recommended the serious perusal of it to some young clergymen, a very few weeks before his death. Blackburne's Works, vol. i. Memoir, p. cxxvi.

† Dyer's Life of Robinson, p. 116.

being fully engaged in preparing for the new profession to which his views were then directed, and Mr. Lindsey being always averse to personal controversy, and neither of them regarding this superficial attack as deserving of a serious reply.

The " Plea," however, excited greater attention, and made a deeper impression than these gentlemen expected, and than its intrinsic merits deserved, and it soon became apparent that a reply of some kind was advisable. Mr. Lindsey, conceiving that, as the author resided at Cambridge, an answer to his work would come with the best effect from " that famous seat of learning," inquired from time to time of some of his literary and theological friends at the university whether any notice was likely to be taken from the press of this new " Plea," which for a time had so much vogue. All, however, that he could learn was, "that it was looked upon as so very superficial, and had so little argument in it, that it could not long deceive any one, and needed no confutation."*

Mr. Lindsey's learned friends probably thought, and indeed justly, that his own writings having been the principal object of attack in the " Plea," it was more particularly incumbent upon him to draw up a reply; and they knew that they could rely with confidence upon his prudence, his learning, his zeal, and his moderation. Mr. Lindsey himself, perhaps, was conscious that

* Examination of Robinson's Plea, p. 3. A brief account of the origin of this publication is contained in the following extract from a letter to Mr. Cappe, dated early in the year 1785, in which Mr. Lindsey requests Mr. Cappe to apply to Dr. Leechman, the principal of the University of Glasgow, for some authentic account of Professor Hutcheson.

" Did you ever read Mr. Robinson, minister of Cambridge's Plea for the Divinity of our Lord Jesus Christ, printed first in 1776, which has undergone three editions? Mr. Archdeacon Blackburne has often asked me, in triumph, how we could go on in Essex-street without confuting this work? It is also much commended by several dignitaries in the church; and held as gospel very generally among dissenters. I have been formerly and often pressed to take some notice of it. I asked the Cambridge men at the time and since, but they declined. Very much importuned by some persons lately, I have undertaken it, and am actually in the press. Unless I put my name to the work, about which I am not decided, not loving to appear in controversy, the title will be," &c. In another letter to the same friend, dated the 25th of February, he says, " I often wonder at myself, and am often not a little drooping, to think how I should venture on the public, when certain persons, so much more able and capable, are silent. But then it recurs, that it is fit something should be opposed to such triumphant non-sense and declamation, which seems well received because many know no better."

the task properly devolved upon him ; and his sense of duty, and zeal for the cause which was, as he thought, so petulantly and dogmatically impugned, overcame his natural aversion to personal controversy, and determined him at length to put on the harness, and to enter the lists with his courteous but presuming opponent, and in the year 1785 he published, anonymously, " An Examination of Mr. Robinson of Cambridge's Plea for the Divinity of our Lord Jesus Christ, by a late Member of the University."

In his preface, Mr. Lindsey remarks, that " the Author here examined has seldom given himself the trouble of doing anything more than barely to bring together texts of Scripture, without explaining them, or even showing how they apply to his purpose in proving Jesus Christ to be truly and properly God; presuming that it would be taken for granted, at sight and upon his authority, that they prove the point for which he assigned them ; so that the title of this tract of mine might with very great propriety have been, 'An Explanation of all the Texts of Scripture produced by Mr. Robinson in Proof of the Divinity of Jesus Christ.' How far it may afford anything new or useful the reader will judge."

The learned writer, in his Examination of the Plea, pursues Mr. Robinson's method, and examines and sifts his popular opponent's defence of the divinity of Christ argument by argument, and text by text. Accordingly, he inquires in order whether the sacred writers speak of God in peculiar appropriated terms,— whether Jesus Christ is the Supreme God,—whether the same titles are given to Christ in the Christian Scriptures which are given to God in the Jewish Scriptures,—whether the perfections which are ascribed to Christ are the same with those which are ascribed to the Supreme God,—whether the like worship is given, or commanded to be given, in the Scriptures to Jesus Christ as to Almighty God,—whether there be any passages in the Old Testament, and applied to Jesus Christ in the New, which prove Jesus Christ to be Jehovah the Supreme God,—whether the Scriptures which foretell the destruction of idolatry by the Gospel have not been fulfilled, although Jesus Christ be wrongly worshipped as God,—whether, if Jesus Christ be not the Supreme

God, Mahomet has written more clearly on the nature of Jesus Christ than the Apostles have,—whether numberless passages of Scripture have no sense, or a very absurd one, if Jesus Christ be a mere man,—and, finally, what is the source of men's erroneous opinions concerning the person of Christ, according to the author of the "Plea." After having with great ability and learning discussed these important questions, explained and illustrated the several texts, confuted his opponent's arguments, and occasionally animadverted with a warmth and severity more than was usual with him upon the presumption, the ignorance, and the dogmatical spirit of the writer, and particularly upon his unbecoming abuse of the sacred writers if their meaning is different from what he chooses to represent, Mr. Lindsey concludes his treatise with some pertinent observations upon the inattention of the author of the "Plea" to those numerous passages of Scripture which in direct terms exclude Christ and every other person from all pretensions to deity,—on the general tenor of the Scriptures, from which no man of plain understanding would ever suspect more gods than one to be therein revealed,—and on the great injury which is done to true religion and the gospel by such representations of it.

The success of this Examination was complete. From the time that it was published no person who had the least pretension to Biblical learning was heard to open his lips in defence of this famous Plea for the Divinity of Christ; not a syllable was written in confutation of the Reply. Those who would not retract were at least compelled to be silent; and it seemed to be universally conceded, that if the divinity of Christ was to be defended at all, it must be upon a very different ground from that which was occupied by this much vaunted performance.

The impression made by the Examination upon the ingenuous mind of the author of the Plea was very considerable. Mr. Robinson was stung to the quick by the grave, and, as his conscience must have testified, the not unmerited rebuke of his unknown opponent. His friends urged him, his opponents challenged him, to stand upon his defence, or to fulfil his promise,

—that "if ever he discovered his deception he would retract his error." He resolved, however, to keep a prudent silence. "I do not intend," says he, in a letter to a friend, "to answer the anonymous examiner. He hath not touched my arguments; and his spirit is bitter and contemptuous. His faith stands on criticisms; and my argument is, that if the doctrine required critical proof, it is not popular, and therefore not divine. Yes, they will have the last word, and let them."* This amiable man, however, soon recovered the tenor of his mind; and wisely profiting by rebuke, he paid greater attention to the important question, not disdaining to call in the aid of sober and just criticism, and in a short time reformed his opinion and became decidedly anti-trinitarian. This is a known fact. I shall mention but one proof of it. In a letter to a friend, dated March 4, 1789, speaking of an aged minister who had applied for relief to the Baptist-board, he says:—"Instead of sending him charity they sent him faith, and informed him that they had made a law not to relieve any except they subscribed a creed, a human creed which

* See Dyer's Life of Robinson, p. 113. It is said to have been a favourite maxim of this extraordinary man at one time of his life "Criticism is a good thing in its place; but woe to the system which depends upon it!" And from this it has been weakly inferred by some of Mr. Robinson's admirers, whose zeal exceeded their knowledge, that a doctrine supported by criticism must be erroneous, because, forsooth, the common people could not understand it. These wise men, it seems, are not aware that the main object of Scripture criticism is to discover the sense which would be most obvious to those for whose immediate use the Scriptures were written, which must no doubt be the true sense, however contrary to modern ideas and prejudices. That Mr. Robinson was not serious in this sarcastic reflection upon criticism or that he afterwards thought more rationally upon the subject, is evident from the following extract of a letter to a friend:—

"I have remarked only a few of the many ministers who are sincerely studying the New Testament, the four gospels I mean. I want a man who vindicates the book, and ascertains the fact that the history of the incarnation is not an addition; and this, *by sober just criticism.* I do not want authorities of great names; I want reasons to convince my understanding,—I want one who gives me the genuine doctrine of the four gospels, before the epistles were written; a man as familiar with Palestine as with his own country. I do not want *a quoter of texts* and a packer of ecclesiastical news; I want a good sound logician, who knows how to reason, and who is no novice,—a cool, deliberate, honest disciple of Jesus, who pauses and weighs, and admits the refining fire of inquiry to burn freely." Speaking of Mr. Winchester, who taught the doctrine of universal salvation, he says of his opponents:—"They preach and print against him. They pretend that God is of their temper, and will not bate a day of eternity. *They never knew what criticism was;* and they do nothing but chaunt for ever, and for ever, and for ever. Poor honies! Servants who know not what their Lord doeth."—Dyer's Life of Robinson, p. 287, 289.

they sent him; and the first article of which is :—There are three
divine persons in the Unity of the godhead! Absolute nonsense!
supported by tyranny over men's consciences."*
It is not quite clear to what distance from the standard of
orthodoxy this ingenuous and inquisitive man carried his speculations upon the subject of the person of Christ. "For many
years," says one of Mr. Robinson's family and congregation in a
letter to Dr. Priestley, dated three days after his decease, "but
especially for the last two or three of his life, he taught the
doctrine of the unity of the great Cause of all things expressly
and effectually." He had promised himself much pleasure from
an interview with Dr. Priestley; and in a letter addressed to Dr.
Priestley a few weeks before the interview, and the only one
which Mr. Robinson ever wrote to him, he says: "I am indebted
to you for the little I know of rational defensible Christianity.
But for your friendly aid I fear I should have gone from enthusiasm to deism : but a faith founded on evidence rests upon a
rock." In the admirable sermon which Dr. Priestley preached
and published on the melancholy occasion of the sudden death of
this excellent man, the author expatiating upon the character
of his deceased friend justly remarks, that "what most of all
distinguished Mr. Robinson was his earnest love of truth, and
his laborious search after it. Notwithstanding his long attachment to the doctrine of the Trinity, yet continuing to read and
think on the subject, he came at length to change his opinion, and
before he died he was one of the most zealous Unitarians. The
subject of the Divine Unity was ever uppermost in his mind, and
he urged it not only in season, but, as you would observe, out
of season. Such also was his power of persuasion, such the
excellence of his character and the just esteem in which he
was held, that in time his congregation came almost universally to
embrace his opinions, as I was myself informed about a year ago,
by one of them who had himself† been a Trinitarian, but who

* Dyer's Life of Robinson, p. 300–301.
† Dr. Priestley's Sermon on the Death of the Rev. R. Robinson, p. 20-21. This
excellent man was found dead in his bed on Wednesday morning, June 9, 1790, after
having preached twice at Birmingham the Lord's day before.

was then a Unitarian." Dr. Priestley in a letter to a friend,
expressing his delight in Mr. Robinson's conversation and his
disappointment in his preaching, says " His discourse was unconnected and desultory, and his manner of treating the Trinity
savoured rather of burlesque than serious reasoning. He attacked
orthodoxy more pointedly and sarcastically than I ever did in
my life."*

Upon the whole, it is evident that Dr. Priestley and his friends
regarded Mr. Robinson as decidedly an Unitarian in the sense in
which Dr Priestley always used the word, that is, as a believer in
the simple humanity of Jesus Christ. And there can be no doubt
that these were the sentiments which he expressed in his last visit
at Birmingham. Nor does it appear that Mr. Robinson was ever
inclined to the Arian hypothesis concerning the person of Christ·
His plea for the divinity of Jesus Christ is framed more upon
the Sabellian than the high Arian scheme; and he tells Dr. Jebb,
in a letter written at the time of its first publication, " It is not impossible that our sentiments, much as they seem to differ, may,
after all, differ less than they appear to do."† And in this
very treatise he scouts the Arian doctrine as utterly unscriptural
and inadmissible.‡

---

* Dyer's Life of Robinson, p. 397.   † Ibid. p. 118.

‡ In reply to the proposition which he puts into the mouth of a supposed opponent,
" That God may enable an inferior being to create a world ; that Jesus Christ is such a
delegated God ; " he answers, " My concern is not with what God *may* do, but
with what he declares he *has* done. I AM JEHOVAH, AND THERE IS NO GOD BESIDES
ME. I AM GOD, AND THERE IS NONE LIKE ME. YEA, THERE IS NO GOD, I KNOW NOT
ANY. This is the God of my Bible. But besides this God there is in my proposition
another God a delegated God. Here are two Gods. Here is a supreme God. and
a subordinate God ; a natural God, and an artificial God ; a great God, and a little God.
A Philosopher has ONE God, a Jew has ONE God, but a Christian it seems has
TWO Gods. What a world of difficulties belong to this propo-ition ! Is this delegated
God entitled to worship ? The idea of a God without a title to religious worship
is an idea inadmissible. Is all worship to be paid to the subordinate God, or does the
supreme God claim any ? Which acts of devotion belong to the one, and which to the
other ? A mistake would be dangerous, and I have no guide. Every inspired writer
forsakes me. Jesus Christ, it seems, created all things in heaven and earth ; and
a Creator, it seems, proves by creating his eternal power and godhead. The proposition
says, God *may* empower a creature to create. Perhaps he may : but God declares
he hath not done so. *Hast thou not heard that the Lord, the everlasting God, the
Creator of the ends of the earth, fainteth not,* &c. I am then obliged to reject

It is however certain, that Dr. Priestley must have been misinformed with respect to the state of Mr. Robinson's congregation; for, though many of them had become decided Unitarians, many, and perhaps the majority, thought differently. And this mixture of jarring and inconsistent opinions in a religious society is always to be expected where the eloquence of the speaker, and not the truth of principles, is the bond of union. The advocates of Mr. Robinson's expiring orthodoxy maintain that he never did in the pulpit directly avow the doctrine of the mere humanity of Jesus Christ; and that, if he professed this opinion at Birmingham either in the pulpit or in the parlour, it is to be recollected that at that time he laboured under great infirmity both of body and mind; and that of this he was himself so very sensible, that to a person who was then introduced to him he made the affecting declaration, " You are only come to see the shadow of Robert Robinson."* It is argued therefore, and with some degree of plausibility, that, in this debilitated state of health and intellect, it is not easy to collect the last deliberate result of the calm judgment and mature reflection of his better days. It is however said that Mr. Robinson had avowed Unitarian principles in conversation before his constitution was impaired: at the same time he might not be so far confirmed in these principles, or think them of such great importance, as to feel it to be his duty explicitly to avow and to defend them before a mixed assembly of persons holding a great diversity of sentiments.

Dr. Priestley, in his Defences of Unitarianism, for the year 1786, having taken occasion, from his controversy with Dr. Horne, then dean of Canterbury and president of Magdalen College, Oxford, afterwards bishop of Norwich, to address a series of

the notion of a subordinate God, a delegated Creator and to admit that the living and true God united himself to the man Jesus."—Robinson's Plea, p. 66-68.

It seems very improbable. that a person who argues so forcibly and unanswerably against the Arian hypothesis should himself soon afterwards become an Arian. The natural process of such a mind, after discarding the divinity of Christ, would be to adopt that of his simple humanity. Such was the progress of Mr. Lindsey's reflections and such probably was that of Robert Robinson.

* Dyer's Life of Robinson, p. 397.

letters to the young men who are in a course of education at the Universities of Oxford and Cambridge, upon subscription to articles, the doctrine of the Trinity, and on the difficulties attending an open acknowledgment of the truth, a smart letter in reply to Dr. Priestley was published under the signature of an Undergraduate, which was however soon discovered to have proceeded from the pen of the worthy President of Magdalen. To this letter the learned champion of the Unitarian faith made a very suitable and spirited answer in his Defences of Unitarianism for the succeeding year, under the impression that the pamphlet had been really written by a youth of the lowest form in the University. But Dr. Horne, though a good-natured man, and upon the whole a candid disputant, had occasionally followed the illiberal practice introduced by those controversial *bravos*, who having first entered the lists with Dr. Priestley, soon discovered that it was by much the easiest and shortest method of dealing with their formidable antagonist to assume a lofty and supercilious air, and to arraign his literary character, instead of disproving his stubborn facts, and refuting his potent arguments. In this crisis Mr. Lindsey generously stood forward in defence of his insulted friend; and in the year 1788 he published a volume entitled "Vindiciæ Priestleianæ, an Address to the Students at Oxford and Cambridge, occasioned by a Letter to Dr. Priestley from a Person calling himself an Undergraduate, &c." "The idea of drawing up this tract first arose," as he informs his readers in the preface, "from observing a studied affectation in many persons of treating Dr. Priestley's theological and metaphysical writings with slight and contempt, and an endeavour in others particularly to infuse the like sentiments of him in the rising generation.

"I had no view therein," continues Mr. Lindsey, "was I capable of it, of lending him any aid against the attacks made upon him, as if he were in danger of being overpowered by his opponents. For he is more than equal to a whole host of them, which they have all experienced in their turns; Bishop Horsley, one of the most violent of them, the least of all excepted. But

I thought it might be possible for another to suggest some circumstances, and to say certain things in his behalf, which he would never think of offering, and which indeed could not so properly come from himself, by which the edge of prejudice might be taken off, and a juster estimate formed of him and his writings."

In the progress of the work the learned author vidicates Dr. Priestley's conduct in addressing his letters to the youth of the two universities, and represents subscription to articles and creeds as a grievance which had long been complained of. He enters at large into the defence of his friend's character as a philosopher and a theologian. In the department of philosophy he introduces a very high encomium upon him by Mr. Kirwan, the late venerable and learned president of the Royal Society of Ireland, drawn up in the year 1787, of which I shall take leave to transcribe an extract.

"To enumerate Dr. Priestley's discoveries," says this eminent philosopher, "would be to enter into a detail of most of those that have been made within the last fifteen years. How many invisible fluids whose existence evaded the sagacity of fore-going ages has he made known to us! To him pharmacy is indebted for the method of making artificial mineral waters, as well as for a shorter method of preparing other medicines; metallurgy, for more powerful and cheaper solvents; and chemistry, for such a variety of discoveries as it would be tedious to recite: discoveries which have new modelled that science, and drawn to it and to this country the attention of all Europe."

Mr. Lindsey adds, "that Dr. Priestley's genius is equal to all subjects; that he is remarkable for selecting only the strongest and most suitable arguments, and applying and arranging them with exquisite method and simplicity, and seldom to fail to work conviction in the unprejudiced mind."

He then proceeds to vindicate a declaration of Dr. Priestley's in his debate with Dr. Price, that he could not pretend to say when his creed would be fixed; a declaration which the soi-disant undergraduate affects to ridicule, but which Mr. Lindsey plainly

proves to be a truly just and philosophic maxim, and confirms
by the testimony of Archbishop Tillotson, who mentions it to
the commendation of his deceased friend, Dr. Whichcote, " that he
was so wise as to be willing to learn to the last."

The learned author next proceeds to justify Dr. Priestley's
sentiments concerning the inspiration of the Scriptures, the imperfection of the Mosaic account of the fall of man, and the
occasional inaccuracy of the apostle Paul's reasonings.   And upon
these subjects he introduces some curious extracts from a work
of the celebrated Castellio, but little known, entitled " De arte
dubitandi et confitendi, ignorandi et sciendi," and which was
published by Wetstein at the end of the second volume of his
New Testament. " The title itself," says Mr. Lindsey, " has
more in it to be learned than you find in many large books.
For it is no ordinary attainment to know when to doubt, and
when to be assured, and when to be ignorant."

In the course of this excellent little treatise, amongst other
pertinent observations, the learned and liberal writer remarks,
that " men with difficulty admit at first, what they have been
ignorant of, however most true it be. For, as Christ says,
those that are used to old wine do not immediately take to
the new, though it be better.   But we must not be discouraged in
our attempts, when persuaded of the truth of what we have
to offer, if we would in earnest serve mankind. Otherwise, if we
go on in the same track with those who have never benefited
the world, we shall, like them, be wholly useless."

The Dean of Canterbury having in his undergraduate's letter
represented Dr. Priestley's notion concerning the simple humanity
of Christ to be as incredible as the " stories of the Alcoran,"*
Mr. Lindsey remonstrates upon the indecorum of the remark,
and shows that the simple humanity of Jesus is the doctrine both
of the Hebrew and the Christian Scriptures ; and he cites a
passage from the Last Sentiments of Pere le Courayer, a work of
that celebrated Catholic refugee given by the author to the
late Princess Amelia, and bequeathed by her to Dr. Bell the pub-

* Undergraduate's Letter to Dr. Priestley, p. 25.

lisher, in which that learned divine avows his opinion concerning the person of Christ, which nearly coincides with the proper Unitarian doctrine.

This excellent man was under the necessity of leaving France on account of a treatise which he published in vindication of the validity of English episcopal ordination. " He was a person," says Mr. Lindsey, "of remarkable simplicity of manners and sweetness of disposition, and of a constant, even cheerfulness, befitting the innocence of his life, and his well-grounded hope of exchanging it for a better. I lived formerly for months together under the same roof with him, in a noble family who had been his friendly protectors from the time of his being forced to fly his country for his religious opinions." This venerable man lived to the age of ninety-three, and continued to the end of his life in the communion of the Roman church.*

In reply to the supposed undergraduate, Mr. Lindsey further pleads, that Christ being a human person, his power and knowledge were necessarily limited, and that Dr. Priestley is right in ascribing to him the frailties and moral imperfection and peccability of human nature. Also, that the question concerning his miraculous conception has nothing to do with his qualification for his office. He maintains, that Dr. Horne errs widely from the doctrine of the New Testament, in his notions concerning the atonement and intercession of Christ. And he justly rebukes the worthy President of Magdalen for the false and invidious light in which he has represented Dr. Priestley's opinions concerning the nature of the soul and the state of the dead, which nevertheless were perfectly consonant to the doctrine of the holy Scriptures, and had been very zealously supported by Luther, the great reformer, and more lately by two very learned dignitaries of the established church not long since deceased, viz. Dr. Law, Bishop of Carlisle, and Archdeacon Blackburne, to both of whom he pays a tribute of deserved applause. The work closes with some just animadversions upon Dr. Horne's fanciful interpretation of many pas-

---

* See an excellent letter from this amiable and learned ecclesiastic to Mr. Lindsey, Appendix, No. IX.

K

sages of Scripture, and particularly of his strange and extravagant commentary upon the book of Psalms, in which he applies almost everything to Christ which the writer addresses to the Supreme Being; and a neat and very proper form of reply is proposed from the students of the University to Dr. Horne. A postscript is added, containing a very high and justly merited character of Dr. Priestley's History of Early Opinions concerning Christ.

To the large account which I have already given of this work, I will take leave to add a short extract which exhibits a striking view of the feelings and character of the pious and benevolent author. He is remarking upon the sad and sombre view of the physical and moral state of the world, which the learned Bishop Butler exhibits in his celebrated Treatise upon the Analogy of Religion, Natural and Revealed. Of this eminent prelate, Mr. Lindsey had some personal knowledge; and he speaks of him as a person that had great piety, but of a gloomy cast, and tending to superstition, which he seems to have caught from reading the lives of Romish saints. He always appeared dissatisfied with the public state of things and of the world; which probably originated in the erroneous opinions which he entertained of the character of the Divine Being, and of his governing providence. In his Analogy he represents the world as having the appearance of a ruin, and that mankind, according to the Scriptures, are in a state of degradation.*

* Mr. Lindsey occasionally met this respectable prelate at the Duchess of Somerset's. The following extract from a letter written by the Bishop to the Duchess soon after his promotion to the see of Durham, and which she transmits to Mr. Lindsey in a letter dated July 23, 1751, exhibits, as the noble writer expresses it, "a pleasing picture" of the Bishop's mind.

"I had a long letter last Friday," says her Grace, "from the good Bishop of Durham, and will transcribe a paragraph of it, as I think you will like to know what his thoughts are amidst the novelty of pomp which surrounds him.

"'I had a mind to see Auckland before I wrote to your Grace; and as you take so kind a part in everything which contributes to my satisfaction, I am sure you will be pleased to hear that the place is a very agreeable one, and fully answering expectations, except that one of the chief prospects, which is very pretty (the river Wear, with hills much diversified rising above it), is too bare of wood. The park not much amiss as to that. But I am obliged to pale it anew all round, the old pale being quite decayed. This will give an opportunity, with which indeed I am much pleased, to take in forty or fifty acres competently wooded, though with that enlargement it will scarce be sufficient for the hospitality of the country. These, with some little improvements and

Upon this, Mr. Lindsey remarks, p. 253, "Surely this is an exhibition of the dark side of things, giving a partial and untrue account of our present state." He adds, p. 254, " Far, very far, is it from being a miserable world that we now live in, but very much the contrary: nor, I apprehend, has there ever been any the least reason to call it so in general, however some individuals may have suffered much in it."

" For my own part," says he, p. 256, " I am bound to say, that my condition has been most happy from the beginning of my existence to the present day. Happily preserved from great cala-mities, I have not been exempt from hardships, reverses, and sick-nesses ; but the kind hand of Providence has been discernible in them all, leading to good by them. I have most particularly cause to speak well of those of my fellow-beings whom I have been acquainted with, and among whom my lot has been cast ; and I would desire no better company for ever than those I have known, and loved, and esteemed, and heard, and read of, especially when divested more of all selfishness and *terrene concretions*, as Edward Search calls them, which we expect, nay, rather are per-suaded, will take place in our future progressive state. Indeed, was there to be no such state, and all was to end here, though so dark and abrupt a conclusion of the fair promising scene is not

very great repairs, take up my leisure time. Thus, madam, I seem to have laid out a very long life for myself; yet in reality everything I see puts me in mind of the shortness and uncertainty of it: the arms and inscriptions of my predecessors, what they did, and what they neglected, and, from accidental circumstances, the very place itself, and the rooms I walk through and sit in : and when I consider in one view the many things of the kind I have just mentioned which I have upon my hands, I feel the burlesque of being employed in this manner at my time of life. But in another view, and taking in all circumstances, these things, as trifling as they may appear, no less than things of greater importance, seem to put upon me to do, or at least to begin : whether I am to live to complete any or all of them, is not my concern.' "

The Duchess adds, in a style that does credit to her piety, " I thought this so pleasing a picture of this excellent prelate's mind, that I could not deny you or myself the satisfaction of sending you a copy of it. Libertines may lay schemes and talk as much as they please of happiness, but it can only reside in the breast of the sincere, humble Christian."

It may not be amiss to add, as one proof among thousands of the vanity of human grandeur, or, to use Mr. Burke's memorable language, "what nothings we are and what nothings we pursue," that this excellent prelate enjoyed his splendid preferment but for a short time. He was translated to the see of Durham in 1750, and died at Bath of a decline in June, 1752, within less than a year after he had written the above letter, and in the sixtieth year of his age.

credible, and would be wholly unaccountable, I must for my part
take my leave and depart as a well-satisfied guest : *satur conviva
recederem :* thankful that I had passed so many happy days, and
lived, and seen, and experienced so much of the goodness of my
Creator, and been favoured with the knowledge of so many
amiable and valuable characters among my species, though concerned to take a farewell for ever of the one and the other, and to
know nothing any more."

Mr. Lindsey having in this work connected the name of Dr.
Price with that Bishop Butler, p. 249, as having "fallen into and
adhered fixedly to this gloomy and unscriptural doctrine, that
repentance alone is not sufficient to restore sinful mortals to the
favour of their Maker ;" and having, contrary to his usual moderation of language, ascribed this to their "not keeping strictly to
the doctrine of Scripture concerning the Divine Unity and the
proper humanity of Christ, there delivered in the clearest characters to all who come not to the reading of it *under a rooted and
fixed contrary persuasion ;* " and having in other parts of his book
expressed himself in terms which bore rather hard upon his Arian
brethren, this unprovoked attack drew from Dr. Price, who felt
himself not a little hurt upon the occasion, the following spirited
letter to Mr. Lindsey, dated Hackney, May 26, 1788 :—

"Dear Sir,—I know not how to avoid writing to you a few
lines to return you thanks for your book in defence of our friend
Dr. Priestley. I have read it with pleasure, and been instructed
by it. If, contrary to my apprehensions, the Socinian doctrine is
true, I wish you success in your endeavours to propagate it ; but
whether true or not, good must be done by all fair and candid
discussions of it.—You have done me honour by joining me to
Dr. Butler : but will you excuse me if I tell you that I am sorry
that, in your animadversions on him, you have not intimated that
I do not think as he does on the subject of worshipping Christ,
and that I have given an account of the Divine character and
government, and human life, very different from that which you
censure ? I am afraid that, from your not distinguishing between
him and me, those who read you only will be led to very wrong

ideas of my sentiments on these points, and also on the dignity of Christ, and our redemption by him.

" My convictions, generally, are only a preponderance on one side, attended with a feeling of difficulties ; and I am often ready to wish I was more assured of the truth of my opinions. But in forming this wish I am checked by reflecting, that this assurance is most enjoyed by those who are most in the wrong,—Trinitarians, Calvinists, Papists, &c. ; and that were I possessed of it with respect to my opinion of the dignity and offices of Christ, I might possibly be led to a sad loss of candour by charging Socinians, as you do Arians, with ' resisting an evidence so insurmountable that all the rational are seeing it every day more and more,' p. 189, and ' so vast that every eye must see it that is not wholly blinded by prejudice,' p. 177. And also by saying of some of the ablest and best men who differ from me, but of whom I have every reason to believe that they inquire as fairly and as diligently as myself, that ' they see things through a mist,' that they are ' ignorant and gloomy,' that ' they have narrow minds bound down to a system,' and ' have never properly searched the Scriptures to see what Christianity is.'

" I am, dear Sir,

" With affectionate and sincere respect, yours,

" RICHARD PRICE."

The venerable advocate of the Unitarian doctrine felt the justice of the rebuke, and immediately returned the following answer :

" Dear Sir,—As there is no one living for whom I have a higher respect and esteem than yourself, I am proportionably concerned that you think yourself at all intended or involved in what I say of Bishop Butler and his system. To make what reparation I can, if my book should ever come to a second edition, I will either omit your name entirely, p. 249, and I now wish I had done it ; or, when I publish Part II., which I hope to be able to do in the course of the next year, I will do that justice which is due to your very different sentiments to those of Bishop Butler.

" For that perhaps too vaunting style in which I speak of Christ being purely one of the human race, and of no other order of beings, I make some apology to my young men, p. 168, and am sorry that any conclusion should be drawn from it but that of speaking from the fullness of my own mind, without the least thought of casting blame on those of different sentiments, or impeaching their judgments or understandings."

This letter gave complete satisfaction to the ingenuous and liberal mind of Dr. Price, and produced in return the following candid reply, dated June 2, 1788 :—

" Dear Sir,—Accept my best thanks for your kind letter. It is extremely satisfactory to me, and leaves in my mind no room for any other sentiments than those of affection and respect which I have always entertained for you. If my letter discovered any degree of unreasonable sensibility, I hope you will forgive me. Indeed, I care not what strong expressions of dislike are applied to my opinions concerning Christ, provided they are properly represented, and I am not understood to hold that he is *almost equal to the Supreme God*, a sentiment at which I shudder, and which probably no Arian now holds."

Thus did these two Christian worthies of congenial spirits, equally lovers of truth, of virtue, of unrestrained freedom of inquiry, and of political and religious liberty, by mutual forbearance, explanation, and concession, put an end to the misunderstanding which for a short time cast a cloud upon their countenance and interrupted their accustomed harmony.

Mr. Lindsey, agreeably to his promise, performed his *amende honorable* in the Introduction to his Second Address to the Students of Oxford and Cambridge, published in the year 1790, where, p. xxx, he "takes blame to himself for having in the former part, without just grounds, included Dr. Price in Bishop Butler's gloomy conclusions concerning the character of the moral governor of the world, whose notions in this respect that excellent person is as far from approving, as from countenancing the Bishop's metaphysical, superficial way of introducing two new deities among Christians, without ever in any proper way consulting the Bible about them." Mr. Lindsey adds, " I should indeed be in pain if in anything of importance to morals I should differ from Dr. Price, whose judgment and heart I must ever honour; who from the first of my coming to settle in this great city has been one of my chief friends, and whom to know is the same as to esteem and love."

CHAPTER VIII.

ANALYSIS OF MR. LINDSEY'S SECOND ADDRESS. DR. WATTS'S UNITARIANISM. MR. LINDSEY'S ALARM AT DR. PRIESTLEY'S BOLD ASSERTIONS, AND ULTIMATE CONVERSION TO HIS DOCTRINES.

"THE Second Address to the Students of Oxford and Cambridge, relating to Jesus Christ and the Origin of the great Errors concerning him," was originally designed to trace the invention of these errors to the honest enthusiasm of Justin Martyr, and to exhibit a list of false readings and mistranslations of the English Bible which contribute to support them. But in the meantime, the Rev. John Hawkins having published his Bampton Lectures, which contained some curious arguments in favour of the doctrine of the Trinity, Mr. Lindsey regarded it as not travelling much out of his road to introduce a few animadversions upon this gentleman's doctrine, and to exhibit to serious and inquiring youth a better mode of reasoning from the evangelical writings.

The doctrine of the Trinity, as Mr. Hawkins describes it, maintains the existence of "three efficient, living, intelligent persons, the sovereign causes and rulers of all things;" and he strangely presumes that this was the doctrine of the church previously to the publication of the holy writings; and that, if this fact be allowed, the Scriptures "are sufficiently full and intelligible;" but if otherwise, they contain "more than enough to perplex and misguide the readers, and to lead them into errors of the first magnitude."* So that, upon Mr. Hawkins's hypothesis, the Scriptures do not teach the doctrine of the Trinity, but only allude to it, and that obscurely. From whence it follows, that no one who takes his creed from the New Testament only, will believe in the doctrine of the Trinity.

Mr. Lindsey, justly regarding it as a vain attempt to reason with a person who advanced an hypothesis so arbitrary and unfounded, thought that he should engage the attention of his readers to better purpose by presenting them with "a sample of the right method of interpreting the sacred writings." Accordingly, he exhibits in his first chapter the evidence concerning the person of Christ contained in the four Evangelists and in the Acts of the Apostles, and thanks Mr. Hawkins for putting him upon the inquiry; as, says he, " it has given me an opportunity of drawing forth and exhibiting, even beyond my own expectation, the most overwhelming evidence of the following facts, clear and plain to every understanding, and which all men who believe the Scriptures sooner or later must bow down to and acknowledge : namely,

" 1. That there is ONE GOD, one single person who is God, the sole Creator and Sovereign Lord of all things.

" 2. That the holy Jesus was a man of the Jewish nation, the servant of this God, highly honoured and distinguished by him.

" 3. That the Spirit, or Holy Spirit, was not a person or intelligent being, but only the extraordinary power or gift of God, first to our Lord Jesus Christ himself in his lifetime, and afterwards to the apostles and many of the first Christians, to impower them to preach and propagate the gospel with success."†

In the second chapter the learned author produces evidence to prove, "that Justin Martyr was the first person who ascribed divinity to Christ, by maintaining, that before his works of creation God produced from himself a rational power or agent, in scripture

---

* Mr. Lindsey's Second Address, Introd. p. vi. Hawkins's Discourses at the Bampton Lecture, p. 59.

† Ibid. p. xix.

God the Word, the Son, &c., who was his instrument in the creation, and his substitute and representative afterwards in the appearances made to the patriarchs, and at the giving of the law to Moses, and was afterwards united to the man Christ Jesus."*

Justin Martyr was a Platonic philosopher, an honest and zealous inquirer after truth. He embraced Christianity as a more excellent system of philosophy than that of Plato, but he wished to reconcile his new doctrine as nearly as possible to his former opinions. And some peculiarities in the phraseology both of the Jewish and Christian Scriptures being, as he imagined, favourable to his hypothesis, he easily persuaded himself that this hypothesis was true; and the rather, because the doctrine which he maintained exalted, as he thought, the person and the character of the founder of the Christian philosophy, and entirely effaced the reproach to which the Christian religion was exposed from the low birth, the humble circumstances, and the ignominious death of its author. This hypothesis he defends in a dialogue, real or fictitious, with one Trypho, a Jew, whom he introduces as declaring that his whole nation expected the Messiah to be a mere human being, brought into the world in the ordinary way: and that " it was to them a thing unheard of, and the height of folly, to suppose him to have pre-existed before the ages as a God, and to have submitted afterwards to have been born and to become man."† Justin, however, undertakes to prove the truth of the doctrine, which to the Jewish nation appeared so extravagant. And to this end he appeals to their own Scriptures in a series of arguments which Mr. Lindsey has detailed, and which have been borrowed from age to age by all who have adopted a similar opinion, viz.: That it is to the Son that God speaks when he says, " Let us make man ;" that Christ was the Jehovah who appeared to Abraham ; and that he was the angel who spake to Moses in the burning bush, and who delivered the law from Mount Sinai. Nor does this Christian philosopher appeal either to the authority of Christ or his apostles for the truth of his doctrine or the correctness of his interpretation, but

---

* Lindsey's Second Address, Introd. p. xx.
† Justin Martyr, Opp. p. 143, 144. Lindsey's Second Address, p. 153.

without any hesitation he declares himself inspired to explain the Scriptures of the Old Testament, and expects his readers to believe it upon his own word.

"I shall tell you plain fact," says he, "without any art or embellishment of words, for which I have no talent. But it hath pleased God of his especial favour to impart to me the gift of understanding his Scriptures. And of this his grace to me I call all to partake freely and without reward, lest for not communicating so great a benefit to others I should myself be condemned in the judgment which the Creator of the world will exercise by our Lord Jesus Christ."*

Mr. Lindsey upon this, with his usual candour and judgment, remarks, that "as Justin was a person of unquestioned probity, we cannot doubt of his sincerity in believing himself to have had an extraordinary insight into the Scriptures given him by the Almighty, though he most wretchedly imposed upon himself in it. His alleging that he himself was inspired is no proof to us of it; and we can no more admit any new revelation from his own word without the stamp of divine authority, than we can pay respect to the waking dreams and revelations of Baron Swedenborg."†

The Third Part of the work contains a copious catalogue of False Readings and Mistranslations in the English Bible which countenance the doctrine of the divinity of Christ; in the room of which the learned writer substitutes those readings which are supported by the best authorities, and the translations which

---

* Justin. Dialog. cum Tryphon, p. 154. Second Address, p. 176.

† Second Address, pp. 177, 178. Mr. Lindsey, in a note, mentions an anecdote which he had "received from a person of great worth and credit: that a friend of his several years ago walking with Baron Swedenborg along Cheapside, the baron suddenly bowed very low down to the ground; when the gentleman lifting him up and asking what he was about, the baron replied by asking him if he did not see Moses pass by, and told him that he had bowed to him." After this anecdote, one may easily admit that the baron himself was a sincere believer in his own doctrines and visions. But that any persons who are not in the same state of mind can be induced to give credit to his extravagant reveries, and to profess themselves his disciples, is a problem of very difficult solution. It is not, however, more wonderful than the confidence which has been placed of late years in the inspiration of Richard Brothers and Johanna Southcote, and that not only by persons of the lowest rank in society, but by men of sense and education. How lamentable is it that religion, which is the most rational thing in the world, should thus, by the errors and weaknesses of its friends and advocates, be brought into contempt and made the laughing-stock of unbelievers !

appear to him to be the most correct. This very valuable portion of his work was afterwards re-published in a separate pamphlet, in order to give it a more extensive circulation.

In the First Part of this Second Address to the Youth of the two Universities, Mr. Lindsey introduces some curious and affecting passages from Dr. Watts's "Solemn Address to the Great and Ever-blessed God, on a Review of what he had written in the Trinitarian Controversy." It is well known that this learned and pious writer (who paid very great attention to the question), in the latter part of his life receded very far from those mystical opinions concerning the doctrine of the Trinity, and particularly the person of Christ, which he held in his youth. His well-known volume of Hymns and Spiritual Songs, so much used in Calvinistic congregations, was published when he was very young, and contains many expressions and many sentiments from which, though regarded by great numbers as the standard of Christian verity, his judgment revolted in maturer years, and which he would gladly have altered if he had been permitted by the proprietors of the copyright, who knew their own interest too well to admit the proposed improvements.

His sentiments concerning the person of Christ were believed by many to approximate very nearly to those of the old Socinians. But it is not certain that Dr. Watts ever regarded himself as a Socinian.

On the contrary, there can be little doubt that, owing to early prejudice, he would to the latest day of his life have started from the imputation with horror. How nearly soever his opinions might really approach to the Socinian scheme, possibly he himself apprehended that he still kept at an inaccessible distance from them, by contending for a mystical personal union by which a true and proper deity was communicated to the human nature of Christ. Absurd as this supposition is in itself, and as it must be viewed by all unprejudiced minds, it did not appear in that light to Dr. Watts, nor to many others who, influenced by his authority, have since embraced the same strange hypothesis. He and they were

serious believers in this modern notion, and have thought that they
have discovered in it a salvo for their falling orthodoxy. And they
have no doubt as good a right as others to retain and to defend
their own system. Dr. Watts's latest opinions concerning the
Trinity are supposed to have been contained in some papers prepared for the press, which were left to the discretion of Dr. Jennings
and Dr. Doddridge, and which were committed to the flames (very
much, as the author of this Memoir has been credibly informed,
against the judgment and inclination of the latter), probably
because it was suspected that they would give offence to the zealots
of orthodoxy. At any rate, Dr. Watts's last sentiments concerning
the person of Christ cannot, perhaps, now be absolutely ascertained ; but the feelings of his humble, pious, and inquisitive mind
are beautifully exhibited in that devout Address to the Deity from
which Mr. Lindsey has made some copious extracts, of which the
following are an interesting specimen :—

 " Hadst thou informed me, gracious Father, in any place of thy
word that this divine doctrine is not to be understood by men, and
yet they were required to believe it, I would have subdued all my
curiosity to faith. But I cannot find thou hast anywhere forbid
me to understand it, or make these inquiries. I have, therefore,
been long searching into this divine doctrine, that I may pay thee
due honour with understanding. Surely I ought to know the God
whom I worship, whether he be one pure and simple being, or
whether thou art a threefold deity, consisting of the Father, the
Son, and the Holy Spirit.

 " Thou hast called the poor and the ignorant, the mean and
foolish things of this world, to the knowledge of thyself and thy
Son. But how can such weak creatures ever take in so strange,
so difficult, and so abstruse a doctrine as this, in the explication
and defence whereof, multitudes of men, even men of learning and
piety, have lost themselves in infinite subtilties of disputes and
endless mazes of darkness ? And can this strange and perplexing
notion of three real persons going to make up one true God be so
necessary and so important a part of that Christian doctrine which,

in the Old Testament and the New, is represented as so plain and easy even to the meanest understandings ? "*

* See Mr. Lindsey's Second Address, pp. 5, 6. The extracts are taken from a work published in 1785, entitled, " The Life of the Rev. Isaac Watts, D.D., by Samuel Johnson, LL.D., with Notes, containing Animadversions and Additions. '

The following extract from a letter written by the late Reverend and learned Samuel Merivale, of Exeter, to Dr. Priestley at Leeds, exhibits the most authentic account of Dr. Watts's last sentiments concerning the person of Christ ; from which it appears that, in Dr. Lardner's estimation, Dr. Watts became in the strict and proper sense of the word an Unitarian.

" What I mentioned to Mr. Aikin" (the late Rev. Dr. Aikin, Professor of Divinity at Warrington) " concerning Dr. Watts, I had from Dr. Lardner, who told it me as a thing known to few, though without enjoining me secrecy.—Having mentioned in the course of my correspondence with the latter the difficulty of fixing my sentiments with regard to the person of Christ, though I had formerly thought the doctrine of his pre-existence sufficiently proved by Dr. Clarke, Dr. Watts, and others, he replies, ' I think Dr. Watts never was an Arian, to his honour be it spoken. When he first wrote of the Trinity, I reckoned he believed three equal divine persons. But in the latter part of his life, for several years before his death, and before he was seized with an imbecility of his faculties, he was an *Unitarian*. How he came to be so I cannot certainly say, but I think it was the result of his own meditations on the Scriptures. He was very desirous to promote that opinion, and wrote a great deal upon the subject. But his papers fell into good hands (menning Mr. Neal's), and they did not think them fit for publication. I also saw some of them.' "

" As there seemed some ambiguity in the word *Unitarian*, though I knew very well in how strict a sense the Doctor generally used it, and being aware that Dr. Watts in his later publications quite gave up the notion of a threefold Deity, though he contended earnestly for the pre-existence of Christ's human soul, originally possessed of powers superangelical, on which, however, he is silent in his Solemn Address to the Deity, printed in the quarto edition of his Works, I begged leave to be informed, whether in his unpublished papers he had appeared to have given up that point; in answer to which Dr. Lardner wrote :—

" ' I question whether you have anywhere in print Dr. Watts's last thoughts upon the Trinity. They were known to very few. My nephew Neal, an understanding gentleman, was intimate with Dr. Watts, and often with the family where he lived. Sometimes in an evening when they were alone, he would talk to his friends in the family of his new thoughts concerning the person of Christ, and their great importance ; and that, if he should be able to recommend them to the world, it would be the most considerable thing that ever he performed. My nephew, therefore, came to me and told me of it, and that the family was greatly concerned to hear him talk so much of the importance of these sentiments. I told my nephew that Dr. Watts was in the right in saying they were important, but I was of opinion that he was unable to recommend them to the public, because he had never been used to a proper way of reasoning on such a subject. So it proved. My nephew, being executor, had the papers, and showed me some of them. Dr. Watts had written a good deal, but they were not fit to be published. DR. WATTS'S LAST THOUGHTS WERE COMPLETELY UNITARIAN.' "

One cannot help regretting that such should have been the judgment of Dr. Lardner, and such the decision of the executors with respect to the publication of Dr. Watts's last essays upon a subject on which he had thought and written so much. The judgment of Dr. Doddridge, one of the trustees for Dr. Watts's papers, himself a professed Trinitarian, but a lover of truth and a friend to inquiry, was, as I have mentioned above, very different, and, as many think, more correct. How interesting

Dr. Priestley, who was very sensible that his ardent spirit, his haste in writing, and his reluctance to revise and to correct, occasionally betrayed him into inaccuracy in his reasonings and sometimes in his facts, and into an unguardedness of language of which his enemies were glad to avail themselves to the utmost, was accustomed to submit his more important publications to the cooler judgment of his calm and prudent friend, and very frequently he yielded at discretion to every erasure or alteration which Mr. Lindsey recommended. But he was not always equally passive. Where he believed the cause of truth to be at stake, no advice of friends, no earnest expostulation, no serious representation of the offence which would be taken, or the supposed injury which might accrue to himself or to the cause, could deter the learned, zealous, and inflexible detector of the corruptions of Christianity from exhibiting what he believed to be important truth, and from exposing what he thought gross and pernicious error, in language the most direct and explicit, without giving himself the least concern about personal consequences, or the offence which might be taken by the political supporters of corrupt systems or the partisans of orthodox creeds.

And it is happy for the interest of rational Christianity that this intrepid champion of truth had the resolution at times to persist in his own judgment, in opposition to the remonstrances of his less informed and more timid friends. In the year 1784, Dr. Priestley, then residing at Birmingham, resumed the Theological Repository, a work which had been discontinued for upwards of twelve years, chiefly it should seem with a view to bring forward for open discussion some original ideas which he had long entertained concerning inspiration, the gradual formation and improvement of the character of Christ, and the history of the miraculous conception. These papers, as usual, he put into the hands of Mr. Lindsey for his perusal and correction. And it is amusing to see how anxious this venerable confessor, who had

and instructive would it have been to have traced the mind of this great and good man through the various steps of his progress, from the darkest shades of error to the clear light of rational and evangelical truth !

exposed himself to so much hazard by the frank and unreserved avowal of the proper humanity of Jesus Christ, was to warn his friend, and to save him from the odium which he apprehended would accrue from pursuing this principle to its just consequences, which at any rate could not be so obnoxious as the principle itself. For, if Jesus Christ be in truth one of the human race, can anything be more reasonable than to admit that his character, however exalted, was the result of the discipline through which he passed; and that his inspiration, how superior soever to that of other prophets and messengers of God, did not extend beyond the purposes of his mission, and might leave him involved in the common misapprehensions of his contemporaries and countrymen upon physiological or philosophical subjects? And as to the case of the miraculous conception, which is a mere insulated fact upon which no one important conclusion depends, it is surely a very fair question of historical research.

These questions, however, were at that time quite new, and the discussion of them alarmed Mr. Lindsey lest it should be attended with ill consequences to his friend, by creating enemies, injuring his character, or impeding his usefulness. In a letter to Mr. Cappe, dated Dec. 2, 1784, in reference to the papers in the Theological Repository concerning the inspiration of Moses and of Christ, he adds: "He was so good as to send me the whole; but I expressed myself so vehemently against the latter part, that he yielded to defer the publication in the first number, but I apprehend it will be brought forward in the next.

" Concerning it I would first say, in general, that granting him to have proved his fact, that our Saviour was as much in the dark as the most vulgar among the Jews about possessions, and believed them in the gross literal sense ; and if also he was in ignorance of the Scriptures of the Old Testament and misapplied them :

" Yet our friend has no call whatever to tell this to the world, because it would increase the prejudices of multitudes against him, and hinder others less indisposed from reading his works.

" I do not, moreover, apprehend that the persuasion of Christ being an infallible teacher, and perfectly sinless, does now stand in the way of any one's embracing Christianity. If our friend had been pushed upon this point in the way of controversy, I should have said nothing against his delivering the sense of his own mind; but as things now stand, to go on to attack a character held in such different universal estimation, unprovoked, seems to me likely to do harm and no good.

"But still more will the outcry be increased against him, if it should appear that he has not proved his facts, and made good his accusation; which may be reasonably questioned in some instances. And not only myself, but Dr. Jebb, and one other whom I have consulted, are persuaded that his chief argument fails him, when he would prove Christ's mistaken imperfect citation of the Old Testament similar to that of the rest of his country-men, from Luke xxiv. 27.

"I own I am unwilling that he should let anything fall from his pen that might co-operate with the endeavours of many to prevent the reading of his works, which are so calculated to open the eyes of many, and have had and have that effect with all that can be brought to read them."

These animadversions, which are tinged with something which appears more like asperity than was usual with Mr. Lindsey, prove at least, that if he was partial to the merits of his inquisitive and learned friend, he was not blind to his failings, and that he did not hastily adopt all his opinions. Nor was he deficient in that sure criterion of true and virtuous friendship, faithful reproof where he thought it needful; for there can be no doubt that the sentiments which he here expresses to Mr. Cappe he had pre-viously expressed in language at least equally strong to Dr. Priestley himself.

Yet, after all, it may be doubted whether the over-cautious spirit of the friendly monitor, and his anxious apprehension lest the uncommon boldness of his friend's remarks should swell the tide of popular prejudice against him, have not induced him to overcharge the picture. Dr. Priestley was as far as his friend could be from desiring to *make an unprovoked attack upon the character of Christ*. But holding the character of Jesus perhaps in as high estimation as Mr. Lindsey himself, he did not think it necessary to presume, nor did he find evidence to prove, that our Lord, being in all other respects a man like other men, was born into the world a perfect character, or that his character was miraculously superinduced. On the contrary, believing that Jesus was in all respects like unto his brethren, and pursuing his principles to their just consequences, he argued that our Saviour came into the world with the frailties and infirmities of a human being, moral as well as physical, and that, by the peculiar process of mental discipline to which he was subjected, he grew up to that consummate dignity and elevation of character under which he appears in the writings of the evangelists. And this truly Christian philosopher believed it to be not only a more rational way of accounting for the excellence of our Lord's character, and more agreeable to the language of the New Testament, which represents him as growing in wisdom and in favour with God and man, but, in truth, more honourable to our Lord himself, that his perfect moral excellence should be the result of his own exertion, vigilance, and fortitude, rather than of a supernatural operation. And upon this supposition, the example of Jesus becomes far more interesting and efficacious than upon the common hypothesis. Dr. Priestley's doctrine was new and original, and at first very obnoxious and startling even to those who thought with him upon most subjects. And as his generous mind was above courting popularity, he took no pains to avoid offensive language in expressing his ideas: but in the present day, the alarm having subsided, and a cooler examination of the subject having taken place, it would I believe be hard to find any considerate and consistent Unitarian who does not adopt Dr. Priestley's ideas concerning the formation of our Lord's moral character, and who does not rejoice that he did not yield to the *prudent timidity* of his worthy but less adventurous friends. Mr. Lindsey acknowledges to his learned correspondent that " he had not then paid much attention to the subject." Afterwards, when he reflected more deliberately upon it, there is reason to believe

L

that his alarm ceased, and that he became convinced that his difference with his friend was more nominal than real.

Whether, as Dr. Priestley apprehends, our Lord was mistaken with respect to the cause of epilepsy and insanity, or whether, as Mr. Farmer maintains, knowing the falsehood of the popular opinion, he still thought fit, and indeed found it necessary, to use the popular language, is a more doubtful question than that concerning the natural perfection of our Lord's character. But surely it is a question highly worthy of public discussion among those who are desirous of obviating objections to the credibility of the New Testament. The language of Jesus to those who were believed to be possessed by demons, that is, by human ghosts, and especially in the case of the Gadarene demoniac, Luke viii., is hardly reconcilable to the simplicity and sincerity of our Lord's -character, if he at the same time knew that the symptoms were occasioned by natural disorder, not by demoniacal possession; nor can it be regarded as any objection to his prophetic authority, or to the reality of the miracle, that his inspiration did not extend to the knowledge of the nature and causes of the diseases which he was empowered to heal. On the contrary, it may be urged with great appearance of truth, that it cannot with any reason be admitted that our Lord was so grossly ignorant of the state of the dead, as to believe that the souls of bad men were permitted to enter into the bodies of living men and to torment them. Upon the whole, with the exception of the case of the Gadarene demoniac, it seems more easy to admit that our Lord used the popular language without adopting the popular philosophy, than to suppose him chargeable with such an egregious error upon a subject so closely connected with the proper object of his mission. The contrary hypothesis is, however, more generally adopted by those who inquire freely into the subject, as I believe I am warranted to say it certainly was by Mr. Lindsey, notwithstanding the alarm he expresses at his friend's insinuation, that "our Saviour was as much in the dark as the most vulgar among the Jews, about possessions; and believed them in the gross literal sense."

That our Lord misunderstood and misapplied the prophecies of the Old Testament, relating to the Messiah, is a position maintained by Dr. Priestley, which did not meet with the general concurrence of those who were disposed to think with him upon other subjects. Dr. Jebb and Mr. Lindsey had some reason to say that "here his main argument failed him." Our Lord so expressly asserts his knowledge of the true sense and application of the prophetic Scriptures; he so frequently interprets, without the least hesitation, and with the highest tone of authority, those prophecies which relate to the Messiah; he so gravely rebukes his disciples for not understanding what he had so plainly and repeatedly taught; and after his resurrection he so explicitly assumes an authority to "open their understandings that they might understand the Scriptures;" that to deny to Jesus a power which he so directly challenges, looks like an attack upon his veracity, and is little less than charging him with vanity and arrogance. Nor are we by the necessity of the case driven to this conclusion. For it is not allowed that Dr. Priestley, though he has attempted it, as indeed his argument required, has succeeded in any one instance in proving that our Lord has actually fallen into error, in his explanation and application of the prophetic Scriptures. This, however, is a fair and interesting topic of discussion; and the friends of scriptural knowledge will rejoice to have the question set in a satisfactory light.

Dr. Priestley, unawed by the remonstrances of his friends, and fearless of personal consequences in the pursuit of Christian truth, and in the detection and exposure of the corruptions of the Christian doctrine, or of the sacred text, and justly thinking that nothing would prove more favourable to the discovery of truth than fair and animated discussion, proceeded in his open and manly way, under the signature of Ebionita in the Theological Repository, to urge his objections against the narrative of the Miraculous Conception in the introductory chapters to the gospels of Matthew and Luke. This bold attack upon an article of faith which had maintained its ground undisputed for upwards of a thousand years, not only renewed the clamours of bigots against the

insolence and•impiety of the hardy assailant, but excited considerable apprehensions among many professed friends to free inquiry,
who not only feared that the author's own reputation might suffer,
and his writings be brought into discredit, and that his usefulness
might thereby be greatly impeded, but that the credibility of the
gospel history itself might be impeached, if so large a portion of
it should be regarded as spurious. Nor were the apprehensions
of any one upon this occasion more vivid than those of the venerable subject of the present Memoir; who thus expresses his
feelings and his fears, in confidence, to his learned and estimable
friend, the Rev. Newcome Cappe, at York.

April 30, 1785. " I wish some able hand would send him
some remarks on his account of the miraculous conception; for
no one I believe would sooner relinquish any opinion, was he
made to see cause for it. A friend told me that he thought the
doctor seemed moved, when he remarked to him that an extraordinary event of that kind might be most important in forming
the character of Christ, by inducing his parents to pay particular
attention to him in this respect, and by the early impressions it
might make upon his own mind; neither of which had occurred
to him. However, whether he or any one retains or rejects the
notion, is of little consequence. A man may be most fully persuaded that Jesus is the Christ, whether he holds him as the son
of Mary, or of Joseph also. Only I have much wished Dr.
Priestley could restrain himself from appearing the patron of the
latter opinion, lest it might hurt his usefulness in preventing the
reading of his many valuable theological writings."

These are the natural and liberal reflections of Mr. Lindsey's
candid mind upon the first proposal of the subject. But his own
correct feelings appear to have been in some degree aggravated,
and, if I may so express it, *acidified,* by the less candid observations which he occasionally heard from others. He thus expresses
himself in a letter to his friend at York, dated December 8,
1785:

" I am exceedingly gratified by your leaving your letter to
Dr. Priestley unsealed, and permitting me the perusal of it.

When you but barely intimated your sentiment at York, but now much more from your further enlargement upon it, I think I see a new light thrown upon our Saviour's language and manner of address to Almighty God throughout the gospels, though I have not considered yet at all, how the idea of his extraordinary birth at times pervades the language of his apostles concerning him. I shall, however, most earnestly long for your full discussion of the subject, and I hope it will please Providence that nothing will prevent your going on to finish this disquisition in the manner in which you have planned it. I do not, however, imagine, as you formerly expressed yourself, that the suggestion of any argument of this kind will have such an effect on our friend as to work any change in his sentiments; though I hope, if he attends to it, as I trust he will, the remarks on Ebionita pointing out so many mistakes, and several less fair (however undesigned) methods of application to his readers, will prevent him exhibiting his opinion in such a disgusting form, and with so wrong a spirit, in his greater work now printing.

" Besides the ardour of his own natural temper, I am sure that he has been hurried on further than that would have carried his judicious mind, by the vehemence of some persons about him, so as to look upon the miraculous conception as one of the great corruptions of Christianity. So that he set out without weighing the consequences; and as his method of treating the subject did not affect himself nor disturb him, he thought it would be the same with others. And having happily got over the outcries raised against him on other like points, as he conceived, he believed it would be the same here. I will, however, entertain hope that your most candid but strong manner, at the conclusion of your letter, of representing to him your own and the opinions of others concerning his treating the subject, will prevail with him to treat the matter with a better temper, as not a day passes but I meet with one or other friends that earnestly wish it for his own, and for the truth's sake."

Dr. Priestley, in his essay upon the Miraculous Conception, in the Repository, expresses his sentiments upon this subject, as upon all others, unequivocally, and without disguise; and certainly, though not with the intention to give offence, yet without any precaution to guard against it. But surely his language, and his manner of treating the subject, hardly deserve the severe censure of making "unfair applications to his readers, and of exhibiting his opinion in a disgusting form, and with a wrong spirit." In an argument so novel, the prejudices of some would undoubtedly be shocked. But there were many who, though not converted to his opinion, were by no means offended with the argument or the spirit of the writer, but rather admired the ingenuity which could give plausibility to an hypothesis in their apprehension so un-founded, and so inconsistent with what they judged to be the plain declaration of the New Testament. Such was unquestion-ably the first impression upon the ingenuous mind of Mr. Lindsey; and nothing but a too great facility in yielding his own judgment to that of his friends, could have induced him to think and to express himself with such unusual asperity upon the temper and spirit of his honest and able fellow-labourer in the field of truth.

It is, however, of more consequence to remark, how widely Mr. Lindsey differed from his inquisitive friend upon the subject of the miraculous conception, and how unlikely he was at that time ever to be reconciled to his sentiments. But an upright inquirer will never think it too late to learn, and will be always ready to embrace doctrines the most opposite to his pre-conceived opinions, if after mature examination he sees reason to believe that they are founded in truth. Such was the character of the venerable subject of this Memoir; and in the following extract from a letter to his friend Mr. Cappe, he expresses himself in a more hesitating tone.

April 10, 1787. "I am much concerned to find you have such a multiplicity of business and of avocations; but I hope you will steal time to give us your arguments for the miraculous conception, which I have not hitherto seen any cause to give up, though some inconsistencies with which the evidence for it is encumbered have disturbed me a little; and I should be happy to see your further positive scriptural proofs for it made out at full length." In a letter dated nine months before, in July, 1786, Mr. Lindsey had importunately urged the same request : "I cannot conclude without entreating you, my most worthy friend, to give us, and give the public, your valuable thoughts on the miraculous conception. If Dr. Jebb had been alive, he would have joined with me, and would have told you it was a duty for you to do it. *He had not attended much to the argument;* but he had no doubt about the fact, or the genuineness of those scriptures which relate to it, any more than you have. Adieu. But I beg you will think of this seriously and in earnest."

Notwithstanding, however, these repeated and urgent calls, the oracle remained silent. Whatever might be the reason, whether, upon further inquiry, he found that, when he first promised the answer, like his precursor Dr. Jebb, *he had not attended much to the argument,* or from some other unknown cause, this truly learned and acute theologian, who was looked up to as the only person competent to advocate the sinking cause of the suspected narrative, declined to enter the lists,* and the historian and detector of the corruptions of Christianity was left the undisputed master of the field. His venerable friend, thus deserted by his principal ally, after a few more ineffectual struggles, found himself compelled, by the power of truth and the irresistible force of argument, to lay down his arms and surrender at discretion; and, like the man of Tarsus, to become the champion of the faith which he once disapproved. In other words, Mr. Lindsey, upon further consideration of the subject, and seeing no satisfactory reply to his friend's arguments, gave up, though not without some reluctance, his belief in the miraculous conception : and in the next edition of his Liturgy, in the year 1789, he

---

* Mr. Cappe's first remarks upon Dr. Priestley were published in the fifth volume of the Theological Repository, under the signature of Nazaræus. The principal object was to prove that the miracle, though in its own nature necessarily private might nevertheless have its use. Dr. Priestley in the same volume adverts to this objection, in a paper signed Nazarenus. Whether Mr. Cappe, like his ingenuous correspondent, ever abandoned the miraculous conception, does not appear from any of his posthumous publications. The "Connected History of the Life of Christ," published by his excellent widow, leaves the fact in a state of considerable doubt.

omitted that creed erroneously called the Creed of the Apostles, which contains this unscriptural article.

This doctrine, that Jesus of Nazareth, the great prophet of the Most High, was the son of Joseph and Mary, which was so alarming when it was first asserted by Dr. Priestley, is now perfectly familiarized, and is, I believe, generally received by those who maintain the proper humanity of Jesus Christ. Indeed the direct assertion of Luke, which can by no fair and legitimate criticism be set aside, that our Lord had just completed his thirtieth year,* in the fifteenth year of Tiberius, fixes the birth of Christ at least two years after Herod's death. This single undeniable chronological fact at once invalidates the introductory narrative to Matthew and Luke. And the uselessness of the train of splendid miracles there recorded; the very little attention which they excited to the object of them; the apparent fabulousness of many of the circumstances; the irrelevance, not to say the absurdity, of the quotations from the Old Testament; the inconsistency of the two narratives with each other; the entire omission of the whole transaction by Mark and John; the want of the introduction to Matthew in the Ebionite copies, and to Luke in those of Marcion; the rejection of the miraculous conception by the Gnostics, with whose system it would so well have harmonized, and by the Ebionites or Jewish Christians, whose history supplied so many prior accounts of miraculous births; the prevailing desire of Christians to aggrandize their Master, and in every possible way to diminish the disgrace of his extraction and the reproach of his cross; and, in fine, the general credit given to the narrative in distant countries, and the discredit under which it laboured in those regions which are represented as the very scenes of these extraordinary events; all concur to establish the conclusion, that the introductory narratives to Matthew and Luke were not written by the evangelists to whom they are ascribed. By whom they were written, and at what time they were prefixed to their respective histories, it may not be easy to ascertain; but

* Αρχιμαι ων ιτων τριακοντα, est *incipio jam esse tricenarius,* quod non dicitur nisi post impletum annum tricessimum.—Grotius.

as we are certain, from the date of Luke's history, that the facts cannot be true, we may be equally certain that they could not have been related by the apostle of Jesus, or the faithful and accurate companion of Paul.

CHAPTER IX.

UNITARIAN LITURGY ADOPTED BY THE CONGREGATION AT THE KING'S CHAPEL AT BOSTON IN NEW ENGLAND. MR. LINDSEY CORRESPONDS WITH DR. FREEMAN, MR. VANDERKEMP, ETC. PROGRESS AND PRESENT STATE OF THE UNITARIAN CHURCHES IN AMERICA.

THE grand theological controversies which excited so much attention, and were conducted with so much animosity, in England, could not fail to attract notice in America, and especially in the New England States, where a manliness of character, a decency of morals, and a serious though not universally enlightened spirit of piety, dispose the minds of considerable numbers to religious inquiries, and where freedom of investigation suffers no restraint from the civil power. It was with great pleasure that Mr. Lindsey received information in the year 1786, from a respectable correspondent (the Rev. J. Smith, afterwards Librarian to the University of Cambridge in New England), that the principal Episcopalian church in Boston had consented to the introduction of a Liturgy reformed nearly upon the plan of that which had been adopted in Essex Street, and perfectly Unitarian.* The minister of this

* In Mr. Freeman's first letter to Mr. Lindsey, dated July 7, 1786, he tells his venerable correspondent, " The Liturgy of our church was during a long time unpopular. But your approbation, the note of Dr. Price annexed to a letter of Dr. Lush, and the mention which Dr. Priestley is pleased to make of it in his sermon upon the fifth of

congregation, which assembled at what was called the King's
Chapel, was the Rev. James Freeman, and is described by his
friend as "a young man of a great deal of knowledge and good
sense, and of an excellent disposition." Some of his hearers left
him on account of the change introduced into the service; but the
majority adhered to him, and the congregation flourished under
him. He was for some time under considerable embarrassment
for want of episcopal ordination, upon which some of his hearers
laid much stress, though in the estimation of the more judicious
members of his congregation, as well as of Mr. Freeman himself,
it was rather a matter of expedience than necessity. To avoid,
however, giving unnecessary offence, he applied for orders first to
Bishop Seabury, who had lately been consecrated by the non-juring

November, have raised it in esteem. It now seems to be acknowledged that that book
cannot be very absurd which is praised by gentlemen of such great learning and
abilities, who have been so long known and so justly admired in this country. I
wish the work was more worthy of your approbation. I can only say that I endeavoured to make it so by attempting to introduce your Liturgy entire. But the people of
the chapel were not ripe for so great a change. Some defects and improprieties I was
under the necessity of retaining, for the sake of inducing them to omit the most exceptionable parts of the old service, the Athanasian prayers. Perhaps in some future day,
when their minds become more enlightened, they may consent to a further alteration."

The writer of this Memoir is happy to add, that the day of increased light and
liberality, foretold by this enlightened reformer, is now arrived, and that Dr. Freeman
has himself lived to see his own prediction verified. In a new edition of the Boston
Liturgy, printed in the year 1811, a copy of which the writer has had the honour to
receive as a present from the ministers, wardens, and vestry of the King's Chapel,
nothing is to be found which is inconsistent with the purest principles of Unitarian
worship as such, and with a very few alterations, chiefly verbal, it might be made
perfectly unobjectionable. May it long be the efficacious means of supporting the
purity and simplicity of Christian worship, and diffusing a spirit of rational piety!

Mr. Freeman further proceeds to state the progress which Unitarian principles were
making in the United States, and particularly in New England. This he imputes to
the many excellent books published in England, and to Mr. Lindsey's works in
particular, which were much read and with great effect. The sermons and conversation
of some clergymen in New England also contributed their share; and amongst these he
mentions the Rev. Mr. Hazlitt, a pious, zealous, and intelligent English minister, who
after his return to England settled at Wem, in Shropshire. Mr. Freeman speaks of
himself as particularly indebted to the instructions and conversation of this respectable
person. "I bless the day," says he, "when that honest man first landed in this
country." In another letter, dated June, 1789, Mr. Freeman writes, "Before Mr.
Hazlitt came to Boston, the Trinitarian doxology was almost universally used. That
honest, good man prevailed upon several respectable ministers to omit it. Since his
departure, the number of those who repeat only scriptural doxologies has greatly
increased, so that there are now many churches in which the worship is strictly
Unitarian."

bishops of Scotland, and who exercised his jurisdiction over the episcopal churches in Connecticut. But this prelate, being a rigid Calvinist, would not lay hands upon his suspected brother. Application was then made to Dr. Provost, who had been elected bishop of the province of New York, and who, together with Dr. White, had been consecrated to the episcopal office by the prelates of the Church of England. This gentleman, who had been a pupil of Dr. Jebb, was a man of great learning, of liberal sentiments, and of deep piety. At the Convention of the Episcopal clergy at Philadelphia, he had himself proposed a very important alteration in the Litany, viz., to leave out the invocations to the Son, the Holy Ghost, and the Trinity; and to retain only the first, which is addressed "to God the Father Almighty, the Maker of heaven and earth." To this worthy prelate, therefore, the members of the congregation at the King's Chapel repeatedly applied to obtain episcopal ordination for their respected minister. But the bishop, perhaps unwilling to give offence to his weaker brethren, referred the matter to the next Convention at Philadelphia; which determined Mr. Freeman's friends, who had reason to apprehend that, whatever might be the information and liberality of some individuals, the majority would decide against him, to ordain their own pastor at home. This solemn rite, therefore, was performed, with the previous approbation of many persons of high character and worth who had been consulted upon the occasion, on Sunday, the 18th of November, 1787, according to a form suggested by Governor Bowdoin, a gentleman whose learning, good sense, and merit, as Mr. Freeman expresses it in his letter to Mr. Lindsey, "would give a sanction to any sentiment which he espouses," though the honourable Governor was not a member of the King's Chapel congregation. "The whole ceremony," says Mr. Freeman, "was performed with great decency and solemnity in the presence of a very numerous assembly. Deep attention was impressed upon every countenance, and many of the advocates for religious liberty, of our own and other churches, could not forbear expressing their sensibility by tears of joy." The form used upon this interesting occasion is published by Mr. Lindsey in his Vindiciæ Priestleianæ, who there expresses his entire approbation of it. All difficulties were at length surmounted : the remaining scruples of those who were advocates for episcopal ordination gradually subsided,* and the cause of the congregation continued to flourish under the auspices of this pious and exemplary preacher for upwards of twenty years. Since January, 1809, Mr. (now Dr.) Freeman has been associated with a colleague, the Reverend Samuel Cary, who, if we may judge by the specimen of his talents and spirit in the sermon which he delivered on the day of his ordination, and by the esteem and affection expressed in the charge of his revered associate, is worthy of the honourable situation which he occupies, and

---

* In tenderness to the prejudices of some worthy members of the congregation, a vote was passed by the society, that Mr. Freeman's ordination should be confirmed by an episcopal imposition of hands, if it could be at any future time conveniently procured without sacrificing their own religious sentiments. But a circumstance occurred shortly afterwards which contributed more effectually to overrule the scruples of those who were unsatisfied, than anything which Mr. Freeman or his friends could say or write upon the subject. This was the ordination of a clergyman at Boston, by Bishop Seabury.

"If any prejudices remained upon the minds of my people in favour of episcopal ordination," says Mr. Freeman in a letter to Mr. Lindsey, dated October 15, 1788, "what you say in your book, the Vindiciæ Priestleianæ, would effectually remove them. But they are already cured of all prepossessions of that nature. I mentioned in a former letter that Bishop Seabury had ordained a priest in Boston. The members of my congregation in general attended. They were so shocked with the service, particularly with that part where the bishop pretends to communicate the Holy Ghost and the power of forgiving sins, which he accompanied with the action of breathing on the candidate, that they now congratulate me upon having escaped what they consider as little short of blasphemy. Few of them had ever read, or at least attentively considered, the Ordination service. Since they have heard it, I have frequently been seriously asked by them, whether I would have submitted to so absurd a form. I confess that I am convinced I should have acted wrong if I had done it. I shudder when I reflect to what moral danger I exposed myself in soliciting ordination of the American bishops, for I certainly never believed that they had the power of conveying the Holy Spirit."

Bishop Seabury might be, and probably was, a very honest man. How far his wisdom kept pace with his honesty, the following anecdote may assist the reader to judge. This venerable prelate, after having been invested, or imagined himself to be invested, with extraordinary powers by the manual imposition of a few obscure priests in Scotland, when he had returned to Connecticut, wrote to Dr. Styles, the president of the college, the learned friend and correspondent of Dr. Price, that it was his intention to be at the annual meeting of the Institution, but that he "hoped he should be received with proper distinction, and that his precedency would be allowed in the place allotted to him." To which the learned president sent back a courteous answer : "That they should be very glad to see Bishop Seabury, but that he could not promise him any such mark of distinction as he expected. One thing, however, he could engage for, and would assure him of, that he would meet with a hundred and ninety-one as good bishops as himself."

is well qualified to carry on the cause in which his excellent colleague has been so long and so successfully engaged. May this holy cause continue to prosper in their hands, and when the chief Shepherd shall appear may they receive a crown of glory !*

As a further means of diffusing the important doctrines of the proper Unity of God, and the simple humanity of Jesus Christ, Mr. Lindsey made a present of his own and of Dr. Priestley's Theological Works to the library of Harvard College, in the University of Cambridge in New England; for which, "as a very valuable and acceptable present," he received the thanks of the President and Fellows. These books were read with great avidity by the students. But though there is great reason to believe that the seed thus sown took deep root, and that in many instances it produced a correspondent harvest; and though many persons eminent for rank and talent in the New England States † openly avowed the Unitarian creed, it does not appear that any numerous societies of Christians have hitherto followed the example of the congregation at the King's Chapel in making a public profession of the Unitarian doctrine.

* This sincere and ardent wish it was not the will of Providence to ratify. Mr. Cary's connection with his affectionate flock and his revered colleague was of very short duration. In the autumn of 1815, he fell into a deep decline from a neglected cold ; and being advised to try a milder climate, he came to England with his wife in October. For a few days he appeared a little revived ; but the disorder soon returned with increased violence, and on Sunday, October 22, he expired at Royston, on his road to London, in the thirtieth year of his age. He was interred in the burial-ground belonging to the Unitarian chapel, at Hackney, and the service, by his particular desire, was performed by the minister of Essex-Street chapel, who delivered a discourse upon the melancholy occasion upon the next Lord's-day. Mrs. Cary, whose Christian fortitude and pious resignation under this severe trial was the admiration of all her friends, returned to Boston in the spring. The removal of such a person as Mr. Cary, in the prime of life, and in the midst of usefulness, is one of the unsearchable mysteries of Divine Providence.

† "Governor Bowdoin," says Mr. Lindsey's worthy correspondent, "is a critic in biblical learning. General Knox, one of the most distinguished officers in the late war, is an admirer of such authors as Edward Search. General Lincoln, our present worthy Lieutenant-governor, appears uniformly and openly the friend of those doctrines that you approve. There are many others, besides, in our legislature, of similar sentiments. While so many of our great men are thus on the side of truth and free inquiry, they will necessarily influence many of the common people. As we have no establishment to oppose, the same zeal which is felt in England cannot be expected in this country ; but rational Christianity will, I doubt not, make a rapid, though not very visible progress." This letter was written in 1788.

In March, 1792, an Unitarian congregation was formed at
Portland, a considerable town of the district of Maine, in the
north-eastern part of the State of Massachusetts. The worthy
founder of this society was the Reverend Thomas Oxnard, a man
of good talents, of sincere piety, and of ardent zeal, who had for
some years officiated as minister of the episcopalian church at
Portland, and who had been convinced of the truth of the
Unitarian doctrine by reading the works of Dr. Priestley and
Mr. Lindsey, with which he had been supplied by his friend
Mr. Freeman. Through the same means, and by the public and
private instructions of this good man, in the course of a few years,
many other persons of property and respectability of character
embraced and avowed the same principles. "I cannot," says
this worthy man, in a letter dated November, 1788, " express to
you the avidity with which these Unitarian publications are sought
after. Our friends here are clearly convinced that the Unitarian
doctrine will soon become the prevailing opinion in this country;
which must afford great pleasure to those good men Mr. Lindsey
and Dr. Priestley. Three years ago I did not know a single
Unitarian in this part of the country besides myself: and now,
entirely from the various publications you have furnished, a
decent society might be collected from this and the neighbouring
towns. When you again write to Mr. Lindsey, you may assure
him in the most positive terms that his and Dr. Priestley's
publications have had, and probably will have, great effects in
this part of the country; which I am sure must afford him great
satisfaction."

Agreeably to this account, the doctrine of the proper Unity of
God made a progress so rapid in the town and vicinage of Portland, that in the beginning of the year 1792, an effort was made
to introduce a reformed Liturgy into the episcopal church; which
being resisted by one or two leading members of the congregation,
the Unitarians, who constituted a considerable majority of the
society, seceded from the rest; and forming themselves into a
separate church, they chose the Reverend Mr. Oxnard to be their
minister; and being denied the use of the episcopal chapel, they

assembled for religious worship at one of the public school-houses which was large and commodious, and where they carried on the worship of the One God with increasing popularity and success.

About the same time another society for Unitarian worship was formed at Saco, a populous village about twenty miles distant from Portland, under the auspices of Mr. Thatcher, a gentleman of considerable property and of excellent character, who was repeatedly returned as representative in Congress for the northern district of the State of Massachusetts. Mr. Thatcher, it is said, was originally an unbeliever; but possessing a candid and inquisitive mind, he became a very sincere and rational Christian in consequence of reading Dr. Priestley's works; and, as Mr. Lindsey's correspondent expresses it, " the influence of our divine religion became very evident in his life and manners." This gentleman, by his conversation, his occasional publications, by lending Unitarian books, and by the great influence of his moral and religious character, contributed much to diffuse rational and pure Christianity in the vicinity of his residence, and formed at Saco a congregation of Unitarian Christians which was for some time connected with that at Portland, but afterwards became sufficiently numerous and respectable to maintain a separate minister. In England the spirit of the times is more liberal than the spirit of the laws. In America it is the reverse; and the bigotry of individuals sometimes labours to counteract the unlimited freedom of faith and worship, which is the glory of the Constitution of the United States. The active zeal of Mr. Thatcher, in promoting the worship of One God in opposition to unscriptural formularies and creeds, excited the malignant efforts of some of his bigoted neighbours to oppose his re-election to a seat in Congress. But the high character, the approved patriotism, and the distinguished talents of that honourable gentleman secured him an easy triumph over the mean attacks of ignorance and envy, and he was again returned by a great majority.

Upon the formation of the first Unitarian society in the district of Maine, Mr. Lindsey's intelligent correspondent makes the following just and important observations, in a letter dated May 21, 1792 :—

" I consider the establishment of this society as an event peculiarly favourable to the progress of Unitarianism in this country. The eastern division of this State, commonly called the province of Maine, of which Portland is the capital, is one of the most flourishing parts of the United States. It is rapidly increasing in population and in wealth. Portland, which under the name of Falmouth was almost totally destroyed during the last war, has now become a large and respectable town, and bids fair in the course of half a century to rival Boston. Like other capital towns, it will probably influence the opinions of the surrounding country. It may be expected, therefore, that Unitarianism will grow with its growth, and be widely diffused. What favours this expectation is, that one of the ministers of the town, a very liberal and enlightened man, is upon very good terms with the Unitarian society, and not disposed to discountenance them. In sentiment he professes to be a Sabellian. The other ministers in the neighbourhood are in general ignorant, and some of them vicious. The consequence is, that there is less appearance of religion in the province of Maine than in any other part of New England. I have no doubt, therefore, that a number of Unitarians possessing that purity of morals for which they are generally distinguished will have a great effect, not only in diffusing rational sentiments, but also in reforming the practice of their fellow-citizens. I give this not merely as my own opinion, but as the opinion of some gentlemen who are best informed in the State of the province of Maine. The establishment of a rational Christian society, and the happy changes which are to be expected in future, must, sir, in a great measure be ascribed to the books which you have sent over. What, therefore, must be your triumph when you reflect that you have enlightened the minds of your fellow-christians, and that you will probably be the means of turning many to righteousness ! "

How far this worthy and ardent correspondent of Mr. Lindsey

was warranted in the sanguine expectations he expresses of the success and beneficial effects of the Unitarian doctrine in the New England States, does not very distinctly appear. In 1788, he states to his venerable friend, that the Socinian scheme is less frightful than it was some years ago, and begins to have some public advocates. The only minister, however, who then preached in favour of it was Mr. Bentley, of Salem, a fellow-collegian and intimate friend of the writer, who describes him as "a young man of a bold independent mind, of strong natural powers, and of more skill in the learned languages than any person of his years in the State." This gentleman had the good fortune to be connected with a congregation uncommonly liberal, who were not alarmed at any improvements, and who were pleased with the introduction of Bishop Lowth's translation of Isaiah, and of other improved translations of the prophetic Scriptures, in preference to the common English version, which was a liberty that few of the ministers in New England would be allowed to take. In 1793, Unitarianism remained at Portland in the state in which it had been settled the preceding year: but the clergy in the neigh-bourhood of Saco having passed a censure upon these opinions as unsound and heretical, the consequence of this attack was an able defence of the doctrine by its advocates in that vicinage, and a subscription for building an Unitarian church. In the year 1794, the same respectable correspondent communicates to his venerable friend the progress which the doctrine and worship of the One true God, the Father, were making in the southern districts of the State of Massachusetts. "The counties of Plymouth, Barnstable, and Bristol, were the first part of New England settled by the English; and till the year 1692, when they were annexed.to Massachusetts, constituted a distinct province. The first settlers were a religious and industrious people, of more candid minds and less disposed to persecution than the settlers of Massachusetts. Though the country is barren, yet it has become one of the most populous districts of the United States. The inhabitants are enlightened and virtuous. Crimes are unknown; and there has not been a capital execution for upwards of sixty years. Such characters are valuable acquisitions to the cause of truth. It must give you pleasure, therefore, to learn that two ministers, one in the county of Plymouth, and the other in the county of Barnstable, have lately come forward and openly opposed the doctrine of the Trinity. Their preaching has made a deep impression, and converts have been multiplied. In Barnstable county in particular, there is a very large body of Unitarians."

This letter was written not long after the worthy writer had received intelligence of Mr. Lindsey's resignation of the pastoral office on account, not of declining health, but of advanced age; and I cannot deny myself the gratification of transcribing Dr. Freeman's excellent and judicious reflections upon that occasion: "I fervently pray, dear sir, that your health may long be preserved, and that your old age may be as happy as the meridian of your life has been active and useful. You now enjoy the fruits of your labours. You have reclaimed many from the errors of idolatry and superstition. You have diffused knowledge and truth not only in England but in America. But what is most to your honour, though you have displayed all the zeal of a reformer, yet you have possessed none of that bitterness of spirit with which reformers are too often infected. In your numerous works I find no harsh expressions or malignant censures. I contemplate this part of your character with peculiar pleasure; and though I am conscious I am frequently more angry with error and bigotry than a Christian ought to be, yet I ardently desire to imitate your candour and mildness of temper. Excuse this praise; it is suggested to me by your two last excellent discourses." This is a high and at the same time a discriminating and justly merited eulogy, and must no doubt have been gratifying to the venerable person to whom it was addressed; whose great humility would, however, lead him to disclaim in part, at least, his title to it.

In a letter dated May 24, 1796, the amiable and candid writer expresses some little doubt whether his zeal may not have induced him inadvertently to exaggerate the success of Unitarian principles in the United States; and he endeavours to give a correct account of the actual state of the public mind upon this subject. As this is the last of Dr. Freeman's letters upon the state of Unitarianism in America which is in my possession, and as it contains a more general view of the case than he had before exhibited, I shall make no apology for the length of the extract:

"I consider it," says this intelligent correspondent to his venerable friend, "as one of the most happy effects which have resulted from my feeble exertions in the Unitarian cause, that they have introduced me to the knowledge and friendship of some of the most valuable characters of the present age; men of enlightened heads, of pious and benevolent hearts; 'quibuscum vivere amem, quibuscum obire libens.'

"Though it is a standing article of most of our social libraries, that nothing of a controversial nature should be purchased, yet any book which is presented is freely accepted. I have found means, therefore, of introducing into them some of the Unitarian tracts with which you have kindly furnished me. There are few perons who have not read them with avidity; and when read, they cannot fail to make an impression upon the minds of many. From these and other causes, the Unitarian doctrine appears to be still upon the increase. I am acquainted with a number of ministers, particularly in the southern part of this State, who avow and publicly preach this sentiment. There are others more cautious, who content themselves with leading their hearers by a course of rational but prudent sermons gradually and insensibly to embrace it. Though this latter mode is not what I entirely approve, yet it produces good effects. For the people are thus kept out of the reach of false opinions, and are prepared for the impressions which will be made on them by more bold and ardent successors, who will probably be raised up when these timid characters are removed off the stage. In the eastern part of this State, or what is called the district of Maine, the Unitarian doctrine also makes progress, as I have just been informed by a worthy and judicious minister from that quarter. The clergy are generally the first who begin to speculate: but the people soon follow, where they are so much accustomed to read and inquire.

M 2

"In the accounts which I give you of the state of religious opinions in this country, I always endeavour not to exaggerate, sensible that every zealous man (and I confess that I am zealous) is naturally disposed to rate his own party as highly as he can. It is possible that Unitarianism may be losing ground in one quarter while it is gaining it in another, and that I may not perceive or may not attend to the former. Indeed, I confess and lament that the opinion is scarcely known in the largest part of this vast republic. It flourishes chiefly in New England; but not much in Connecticut, Rhode Island, New Hampshire, and the western counties of Massachusetts. A few seeds have been sown in Vermont, and an abundant harvest has been produced in the vicinity of Boston and the counties directly south of it. In Pennsylvania much may be expected from the labours of Dr. Priestley."

It was in the year 1796 that this letter was written; and though it cannot reasonably be doubted that the important doctrines of the unrivalled supremacy and sole worship of the Father, and of the proper humanity of Jesus Christ, have since that time been gradually advancing in a country so favourable to freedom of inquiry; yet it may justly be questioned whether the progress of truth has been quite so rapid, visible, or extensive, as the zeal of this ingenuous and ardent lover of truth prompted him to expect. Dr. Priestley's personal ministry in the United States was attended with very little apparent success. In Northumberland, where he resided, he collected but few proselytes; and in Philadelphia, where the chapel in which he preached was at first crowded with the principal characters in the United States, he was afterwards for some reason or other almost deserted. Yet here his labours were not wholly ineffectual. Since Dr. Priestley's decease, a small but highly respectable congregation has been formed, in which, till a regular minister can be procured, a few of the most intelligent and best informed members conduct the service by turns; and the society, upon the whole, is increasing, though some who once professed zeal in the cause have turned their backs upon it. The Unitarians in Philadelphia have erected a chapel for religious worship, to which many of different persuasions contributed liberally.

Another Unitarian congregation has been formed at Olden-barneveld, a new settlement in the back country of the State of New York, under the patronage of Colonel Mappa, a gentleman of a truly respectable character, and of considerable property and influence in that district, aided by the exertions of the Rev. Frederic Adrian Vanderkemp, a learned and pious emigrant from Holland, whose zeal for the doctrine of the Divine Unity has exposed him to many difficulties and privations. This church was, for a few years, under the pastoral inspection of the Reverend John Sherman, who in the year 1805 was dismissed, on account of his Unitarian principles, from his office as minister of the first church at Mansfield, in Connecticut, where he had officiated upwards of eight years with great and increasing accept-ance and success. . Of the circumstances which led to this separation, and of the inquisitorial spirit which was exerted against him by the bigoted clergy in his neighbourhood, he published a plain and affecting account, a copy of which now lies before me. And if some expressions of irritation have escaped him, which it would perhaps have been better to omit, it requires but little charity to make allowance for them where the provoca-tion was so great and unmerited.

This gentleman, in consequence of an attentive perusal of the works of Mr. Lindsey and Dr. Priestley, became a sincere and zealous convert to the doctrine of the proper Unity and sole Supremacy of God, to the simple humanity of Jesus Christ, and to the appropriation of religious worship to the Father only. A doctrine of such high importance, and so materially differing from the popular creed, he justly conceived it to be his duty to avow and teach.* And, in the first place, he communicated his change

---

* This worthy confessor's plain and artless narrative of the feelings of his mind upon this occasion is well deserving of being here transcribed, and may it make a due im-pression upon all who are placed in similar circumstances, and called out to similar trials !

" Settled," says he, " in the sentiment that God is one person only, and that Jesus Christ is a being distinct from God, dependent upon him for his existence and all his

of sentiments to the congregation with which he was connected;
when, to his great surprise and satisfaction, he found that, with a
single exception, they were all earnestly desirous that he should
continue his connection with them, and that each should quietly
allow to others the right of private judgment in this and every
other case. This, however, did not satisfy his clerical brethren,
with whom, as residing in the neighbourhood, he had joined in a
voluntary association. Being duly informed by Deacon Southworth, the dissatisfied member before alluded to, of his reverend
pastor's departure from the faith, they first in a formal session,
held in October, 1804, excluded him from their society, and dis-
avowed ministerial connection with him. And in this measure
was no injustice; for the associated ministers had as good a right

powers, I was involved in much trial and perplexity of mind with respect to the course
which duty required me to pursue. I was aware of the prejudices of my brethren in the
ministry, and foresaw that, should my sentiments be made public, they would certainly
exert themselves to destroy my ministerial and Christian standing; that my standing
with the people of my charge, whose confidence I was so happy as to possess, would
be endangered, if not by their own prejudices, yet by the influence and exertions of
others; and, considering the state of the American churches, that I could hardly expect
an invitation to minister to any people on this side of the Atlantic. Poverty, a diminution
of my usefulness, and the unhappy condition of my beloved family, stared me in the face,
and conjured me to be silent respecting my opinions.
    " On the other hand, I considered that, having avowed different sentiments at my
ordination, it could not be reconciled to a frank and open honesty to allow the world
to be deceived as to my real belief;—that it is the duty of the minister of the gospel
to instruct men in the knowledge of its important doctrines;—that I was accountable
to God for my conduct in this matter, who requires of stewards that a man be found
faithful, and who certainly must desire his people to be acquainted with the truth, or
he would never have revealed it;—that no reformation from prevailing errors could take
place if those who are acquainted with the truth should, through the fear of persecution,
conceal it from public view;—and, finally, that it is base, and unbecoming the dignity
of man, in this 19th century of the Christian era, in this land of liberty and free
inquiry, to bow down to popular absurdities and superstitions, and quietly to abandon
the inalienable right of private judgment. These considerations determined me to put
all temporal things at hazard, and to place my trust in that wise Providence which had
always been kind, and which will either deliver us from the evil, or inspire us with
fortitude to endure it." Upon these generous and pious principles did this Christian
confessor act throughout the whole of this arduous conflict; and however his ignorant
and malignant persecutors might injure his good name, and deprive him and his family
of the comforts of society, and leave them destitute of the necessaries of life, they could
not rob him of the inestimable treasure of an approving conscience. How rapidly and
extensively must the cause of Christian truth prevail, if all who were convinced of it
possessed the fortitude and zeal of Mr. Sherman ! But this is an elevation of character
to which every one cannot attain. Different persons have different gifts, and are
called to different duties. Let every one judge impartially for himself, and candidly
for others.

to judge of the truth and importance of their opinions as Mr.
Sherman of his. But the zeal of these pious inquisitors did not
stop here: they wrote an official letter to the church at Mansfield,
stating that they had judged it to be their duty to withdraw from
their heretical brother their own ministerial connection, and pretty
plainly intimating their expectation that the society would follow
their example, and dismiss their pastor, who stood convicted by
his own confession of many capital errors. This advice, though
treated with merited neglect by a majority of the church, nevertheless made a considerable impression upon a small number of
feeble-minded members, who, in April, 1805, addressed a letter to
the *venerable* Association, expressing their dissatisfaction with their
worthy pastor for denying, as they express it, that "the *man*
Christ Jesus is truly and properly GOD;" which, say they, "is a
doctrine which we cannot be persuaded to give up but with the
Bible which contains it." And they further profess that "the
doctrine of a trinity of persons in the Godhead, as *held by
Calvinistic divines for ages,* is a doctrine clearly taught in the
holy Scriptures;" and that, "however mysterious and incomprehensible, it lies at the very basis of Christianity." Under these
difficulties, they implore the advice of the reverend Association.
But notwithstanding all the activity of Deacon Southworth, and
the artifices and intrigues of some bigots in the neighbourhood,
only ten signatures could be procured to this address. Such,
however, was the eagerness of the venerable body, and such their
zeal to exterminate heresy, that they immediately directed an
answer to be sent to the complainants, advising them to have
recourse to a Council or Consociation, which is an ecclesiastical
court, consisting of ministers and messengers, and invested by
law with great and indefinite powers. But as the *Consociation*
was to consist in a great measure of the same ministers of whom
the *Association* was formed, who had already prejudged the cause;
and as the congregation at Mansfield had never acknowledged the
jurisdiction of this court, they rejected the advice with the contempt it deserved. Nevertheless, as this worthy confessor saw
that his unrelenting adversaries were determined to pursue every

possible method to disturb the peace of the society, and to accomplish his ruin, and being desirous of preventing the disastrous consequences of religious discord, he came to the resolution of resigning his pastoral office. This resolution he communicated to his friends; and at his desire the church and congregation concurred with him in inviting, according to the custom of the country, a *mutual* council of respectable ministers to give their advice in the case, and, if they should judge it expedient, to grant Mr. Sherman an honourable dismission and recommendation.

This council assembled in October, 1805, and Mr. Sherman first stated his case and the reasons which led him to wish to resign his connection with the congregation at Mansfield. After which, a deputation from the church, that is, from the communicants,* were heard on their own behalf; who stated that,

---

* It may not perhaps be known to the generality of readers, that in the strict Independent form of church government, the whole power of ecclesiastical discipline, the entire management of the property, and the sole right of choosing or dismissing a minister, is vested in the church, that is, in the body of communicants, of those who have been admitted into the communion of that church in particular, according to its prescribed forms, or who have been received by regular dismission from other churches. Mere subscribers have no vote, however numerous and opulent. Mr. Howard, the celebrated philanthropist, was the richest member and the most liberal supporter of the congregation at Bedford; he also joined statedly in communion with the church: but not having been regularly admitted into the church, he was only regarded as an occasional communicant; and in the choice of a minister not the least attention was paid to his expressed opinion and desire, and a minister was chosen who was by no means acceptable to him.

In Northamptonshire I recollect another instance in which a venerable minister of irreproachable character, of most amiable manners and unimpeached orthodoxy, was dismissed from his office by the church under some trifling pretence, in opposition to the sense of by far the most respectable part of the congregation. His friends appealed to a court of law to reinstate their respected minister in his office. But Lord Mansfield, who, whatever might be his political delinquencies, was a most liberal and impartial judge in all cases in which the rights of Protestant Dissenters were concerned, demanded to see the writings of the place; and finding that they vested the communicants with the discretionary power of choosing and deposing a minister, he dismissed the cause immediately, and the worthy veteran was obliged to resign his claims. Another chapel, however, was provided for him, where he continued to officiate, and was supported by his friends as long as he lived.

In America, it is presumed that where the Independent form of church government prevails this principle is in general maintained. But in Connecticut they have strangely deviated from the original freedom of the separate churches, by the institution of what is called the Consociation, a sort of spiritual court, which was established in Connecticut in the beginning of the last century. This court has power to interfere "upon all occasions ecclesiastical," and its censures are authorized and supported by the civil power. Each Consociation consists of ministers and

though the discontented party did not constitute more than one third of the *church*, yet they plainly perceived that their design was first to exclude their pastor, and then to excommunicate their brethren. That, in order to prevent this schism, they had offered to the complainants either that they should remain unmolested with the majority; or that the majority, for the sake of peace, should dismiss their pastor, in order to remain unmolested with them; or, if this would not satisfy their opponents, Mr. Sherman's friends would retain and maintain their own minister, and let the discontented party have theirs. This concession however, liberal as it was, did not satisfy the dissidents. Lastly, a deputation from the *congregation* were heard before the Council, who stated that not less than nine-tenths of the society were well satisfied with their minister, and had no desire to part with him, or to restrain him in his inquiries. "Being," as they express it, "tenacious of the right of private judgment, they wish to indulge their minister in the same : neither would they wish that he should act the hypocrite to gain the approbation of any man; and they apprehend that, in case Mr. Sherman is dismissed, the society will soon be found in a most unhappy situation, not likely to be settled with another minister for many years."

Notwithstanding, however, these strong facts, this noble profession, and this conciliatory spirit, the *prudent* Council proceed, as a matter of expediency, to dismiss Mr. Sherman from his connection with the society; and while they bear honourable testimony to his character and talents, and "recommend him to the kind reception of those who may see fit to employ him," they cautiously subjoin that they "do not consider themselves as giving their approbation of Mr. Sherman's *peculiar phraseology* or *circumstantial difference* of sentiment on the subject of the

messengers from every congregation which belongs to it. But no congregation is compelled to join it. As far as its power extends, it is properly a court of inquisition ; and in some cases the members have discovered too much of an inquisitorial spirit.— N.B. 1820 : it is said that in consequence of the popular party having gained the ascendancy in the State of Connecticut, these inquisitorial courts have been put

Trinity." And in their subsequent advice to Mr. Sherman they admonish him to "guard against a bold spirit of speculation, and an inordinate love of novelty."

It is not a little curious to contrast those differences of opinion which this venerable Council coolly describe under the soft expressions of *peculiar phraseology* and a *circumstantial difference* of sentiment. The man whom they gravely caution against a bold spirit of speculation and inordinate love of novelty, asserts the doctrine that there is One God, the sole object of religious worship, and one mediator between God and men, the man Christ Jesus, who is the prophet and messenger of God. While his orthodox opponents, to accommodate whom the Council think it expedient to dismiss their exemplary pastor, maintain as a doctrine essential to salvation, and which they " can never give up but with the Bible which contains it," that " the man Jesus is truly and properly God." Is the venerable Council serious in stating differences so glaring and so substantial as these, as nothing more than a "peculiar phraseology," and a " circumstantial difference " of sentiment ? No ! No ! Opinions such as these can no more harmonize with each other than light and darkness, than Christ and Belial. They who hold doctrines so diametrically opposite cannot be fellow-worshippers in the same temple. It was expedient that they should separate. So far the Council judged right. But the difficulty lies in discovering the expedience, the justice, the common sense of making the greater submit to the less; in deciding in opposition to the declared principles and wishes of two-thirds of the church and nine-tenths of the congregation. It is not to be doubted that the members of this Council were upright and honourable men. But as the case now stands it is impossible to approve of their decision. Why is the majority to be sacrificed to the minority ? Why is the upright conscientious inquirer after truth to fall a victim to bigotry, ignorance, and intolerance ? This surely is a miserable way of promoting either truth or peace. So the members of this truly respectable but too timid and cautious Council have themselves seen reason to acknowledge; and one of them at least has amply redeemed his character, and has himself very lately become a fellow-sufferer in the cause of truth.*

* This gentleman is the Rev. Abiel Abbot, late pastor of the first church in Coventry, in the state of Connecticut, where he was settled in February, 1795, and continued to exercise his ministry peaceably and acceptably for fifteen years. In February, 1810, some of the members of his church discovered in their worthy pastor symptoms of heresy, and after some discussion the church applied for advice to the Association, which assembled in October, who again referred them to the Consociation, which assembled in April, 1811. The Consociation summoned the worthy pastor to reply to the charge : but Mr. Abbot protested against their jurisdiction ; neither himself, nor the church of which he was pastor, nor the congregation, having ever joined the Consociation, or acknowledged its authority. The society likewise entered a similar protest. The Consociation, however, nothing daunted, voted its own competency and authority, and in their way proceeded to examine the merits of the case ; the result of which was, that the Rev. Abiel Abbot does neither preach nor believe the doctrine of the sacred Trinity ; that he does neither preach nor believe the divinity of Jesus Christ ; that he does neither preach nor believe the doctrine of the atonement by the blood of Christ, nor of justification by his imputed righteousness ; and that doctrines contrary to these, and subversive of the Christian's faith and hope, are by him taught and inculcated. Voted, That the man who neither believes nor preaches the doctrine specified, is disqualified for the office of the gospel ministry ; for he has essentially renounced the Scriptures, has made shipwreck of faith, has denied the Messiah, &c. The Council, therefore, *feel themselves required by Jesus Christ*, the great God and Saviour, &c., to declare, and they hereby do declare, that the ministerial relation between the Rev. A. A. and the first church at Coventry ought to be, and is dissolved, &c.

Such, at the commencement of the nineteenth century, was the language, and such were the extravagant claims, of an assembly of Protestant Christian ministers assuming the title of the Consociation of the county of Tolland, in the State of Connecticut. Neither the Fathers of the Council of Trent, nor those of Nice, nor of any intervening Council, whether General or Special, ever pretended to higher authority, nor made a bolder claim to inspiration or infallibility.

Mr. Abbot, however, and his friends, the great majority of his society, not feeling themselves inclined to submit to the dictates of the inspired Council, resolved that the unwarranted censure of the Consociation should have no effect upon their mutual connection ; and he still continued to officiate among them as before. Nevertheless, to guard on the one hand against the interposition of the secular arm, and on the other to testify his respect to the Council itself, the members of which were individually respectable, this amiable and persecuted confessor thought it advisable to invite a mutual Council of grave and learned divines from the State of Massachusetts to deliberate how far it was his duty to respect the decision of the Tolland Consociation. The very sensible and pious answer of Dr. Osgood, who declined attending, contains many very just and pertinent observations. "For myself," says he, "I have little faith in, or respect for, Ecclesiastical Councils. I have long thought them unauthorized in Scripture, and for the most part worse than useless, excepting as mere referees or arbiters mutually chosen by parties at variance to settle their disputes." Speaking of the censure of the Consociation, he adds : "It is indeed a most extraordinary procedure in this land of republican liberty, where all Ecclesiastical Establishments are explicitly disclaimed. This consideration, however, assures you, that though the tongues and pens of Ecclesiastical Councils be as free and unrestrained as those of any other description of citizens, yet they have no power to execute their decrees ; and you have no more reason to tremble at the anathema of the Consociation of Tolland county, than

Mr. Sherman being thus dismissed from a congregation where he had passed eight years in harmony and usefulness, now found himself cast out upon the world destitute almost of the necessaries of life, and under the ban of a powerful party, who were determined to the utmost to obstruct his future exertions, and to drive him from the ministry. Happily, though the will was good, the power was wanting. The pastor and the congregation appear to have regarded it as their duty to acquiesce in the decision of the Council, however painful: and in an affecting address which was presented by the society to Mr. Sherman, they express their deep regret at the unexpected dissolution of their connection, when they most wished for its continuance,—when they most wanted his ministerial services and friendly counsels, —and when he stood highest in their esteem, and had engaged their warmest affections. This address was voted November 12, 1805, and the answer to it is dated from Oldenbarneveld, January 1, 1806. Mr. Sherman's talents were not suffered to remain long unemployed; and he appears almost immediately

at a bull of the Roman Pontiff. It might therefore, perhaps, be advisable to let it pass with as little notice ; suffering it to have no other effect than to render you a better Christian and a better man."

These are the observations and advice of a wise and good man ; which perhaps it would have been most prudent to have followed. The mutual Council, however, convened by Mr. Abbot and his friends, assembled at Coventry, on the 15th of June, 1811, the venerable Dr. Lathrop in the chair ; and after due deliberation they conclude that " the Consociation had no right to dissolve the connection between the pastor and society, the great majority of whom manifest a warm attachment to his person and ministry; but that from considerations of expediency they do dissolve it, and declare that it is dissolved accordingly." Thus again we see the sacred cause of Christian truth sacrificed to a mean and temporizing policy ; and the faithful champion of truth, the amiable, useful, and beloved pastor torn from his weeping flock, and consigned to poverty and solitude for the sake of preserving a hollow, deceitful, temporary peace. But this cannot last long ; nor can such a measure be approved by the great Head of the Church. Of this strange event, the virtuous sufferer has published a fair and interesting narrative, which is written with a temper and spirit truly Christian. " I will bring," says he, "no railing accusation. The men from whom I have differed, I have loved : the men from whom I have suffered, I have respected ; and to none am I conscious, to this hour, of feeling an unfriendly sentiment. From the heart I wish them grace, mercy, and peace." It is, however, but justice to the members of this, perhaps, too cautious Council, to add, that they do not presume to judge of the faith of their unfortunate brother ; that they express the highest respect for his moral character, and that they cordially recommend him to the pastoral office in some other church. And if there be, as I am sure there is, a love of truth, virtue, and liberty, in the New England States, this able, honest, and pious sufferer for truth will not be suffered to remain long in silence and seclusion.

after his dismission to have been invited to undertake the pastoral charge of the small congregation which had been collected chiefly by the labours of the excellent Adrian Vanderkemp. And to enable him to remove his family to this distance, he received a very handsome pecuniary present from his friends at Mansfield, which he acknowledges with warm gratitude. At last this respectable society seems to have roused itself from its slumber, and to have taken the step which it might have been expected that their affection would have dictated immediately upon their worthy pastor's dismission. The church and the congregation invite him to resume the pastoral office at Mansfield. This invitation was dated December 19, but it was then too late. A scene of greater usefulness had, in his estimation, opened before him, and to this consideration he regarded it as his duty to sacrifice personal gratification and social enjoyment. But in his reply to this application, he introduces a very judicious summary of the evidence of the Unitarian doctrine, and concludes with expressing his grateful sense of the kindness of his friends, and with a very impressive address to the youth of the congregation.* For some years afterwards Mr. Sherman remained at Oldenbarneveld; and in a letter to Mrs. Lindsey, dated November 5, 1807, the worthy Mr. Vanderkemp expresses himself thus favourably of the exertions and success of his respected coadjutor:

* The conclusion of this worthy confessor's address to the youth of his late congregation of Mansfield is so excellent, that no apology can be necessary for inserting it.
" To the great question in dispute undoubtedly your minds are also directed. The subject is of primary importance, and demands your serious and attentive consideration. Surely you ought to know whether you are to be the worshippers of Three Gods, or of One God only. Let me exhort you to search the Scriptures diligently on this point, and see whether they teach you that three divine persons, three distinct moral agents, make, when added together, only one individual being. Should the result of your investigation comport with the doctrine which I have taught you from the Scriptures, I wish you may be duly impressed with the importance of openly avowing it, and appearing as its advocates; that as you rise into public life you will never be ashamed of the interesting truth, but boldly and faithfully stand in its defence, though the multitude should be against you. Let your zeal, however, be well tempered with Christian charity. Be moderate and candid, liberal and catholic, in your treatment of those who may differ. Above all, always remember that the best orthodoxy is a faithful observance of the sacred precepts of that One God, whom you profess and acknowledge."

"It must fill Mr. Lindsey's heart with gladness that his labours are blessed here in the wilderness, through the means of those whom he enlightened and confirmed in the gospel doctrine by his writings. Our pastor, with his amiable and worthy wife, has the greatest reason for gratitude to the Divine Being, being beloved, respected, and useful in spreading religious knowledge far and wide. Our situation, in a religious point of view, is very gratifying. Notwithstanding, our pastor has to struggle with furious bigotry and ignorant superstition, which blacken his character and slander his innocence, while infidelity has her adherents through the whole country. That kind of writings are spread everywhere, and peddled round the country by hawkers in the wilderness, sometimes under spurious titles. Volney and Paine and Hollis are found in miserable cots and hovels, while it is often difficult to meet the sacred Scriptures. This evil has been nursed through the misconduct of high-flying Calvinist teachers in New England, in choosing their missionaries from the most stupid and bigoted; perhaps from necessity : while men of talents among them decline the task. It is therefore not surprising that our pastor is heard with delight wherever there remains any claim to virtue and religion. His plain affable manners, his energetic manner of preaching, his vast superiority over his antagonists in disputes whenever they attack him, increase his influence every day. He preaches in the week twenty miles round, and is sanguine in his expectations that he shall form another society twelve miles from hence. Few weeks are passing in which some one or other of the vicinity do not join our church, and those by far the most respectable among them. Disney's tracts and Seddon's sermons have operated a great deal of good : so too have the works of my worthy friend, who now ere long shall receive the glorious reward of his labours. Our minister has instituted a school of moral instruction, in which every subject of natural and revealed religion is discussed freely."

In a letter dated April, 1809, Mr. Vanderkemp writes in a less sanguine, yet not altogether discouraging strain : "The gospel cause gains slowly here and at Philadelphia. We have at length succeeded to re-engage our worthy minister," who it should seem was about to leave them for want of necessary support for his family. " His ministerial labours are not in vain. Well supplied with a tolerable library, he has seen it enlarged, by Mr. J. Priestley and Mr. J. Taylor from Philadelphia, by some valuable additions. He deserves fully this encouragement. His talents are bright : his sermons are plain and persuasive ; his prayers devout and ardent ;—and his conduct struck his slanderers dumb. Unfortunately, whether it were owing to the inability of the congregation at Oldenbarneveld to raise an adequate income for the support of their worthy pastor ; or whether, as is often the case with persons of genius, and whose minds are devoted to intellectual pursuits, there might be on his part too little attention paid to economical arrangements ; in the next account we learn that Mr. Sherman was under the necessity of dissolving his connection with this society, and that the flock was at that time left without a shepherd, and in a state by no means encouraging. " The best that I can say about our situation is," says the excellent Mr. Vanderkemp, in a letter to Mrs. Lindsey, dated August, 1810, " that we are in a very torpid state. Since March we have had no minister. Though a few doubled their subscriptions, though twice we took the defalcations of others on our account, we could not raise a sum adequate to his salary : so the connection was dissolved, to our great grief and the irreparable loss of this community. We have resolved, however, and continue steadfastly our religious meetings. Some of us have engaged to read in turns ; so that we are edified sometimes by Clarke and Tillotson, sometimes by Blair, and sometimes by Lindsey, Priestley, Price, and Toulmin."*

---

* In a letter which I received from Mr. Sherman, dated Oldenbarneveld, August 25, 1818, he states that his sole reason for resigning his connection with the congregation, was the necessity of providing for a large and growing family. He now keeps a flourishing academical school, by the profits of which his circumstances have been retrieved : and he expresses a hope that, if life be spared, he may again be called to preach the gospel of the grace of God. Mr. S. likewise states, in justification of the Council at Mansfield, that it was at his own desire that he was dismissed;—this fact, however, should have been more clearly stated in his publication.

Of the present state of the Unitarian doctrine in the district (now the State) of Maine, the author of this Memoir is not informed. Whether the congregation at Portland collected by the worthy Mr. Oxnard, or that at Saco, under the patronage of the truly excellent Mr. Thatcher, still exist, or in what state they now are, he has not heard. At Hallowell, the first families in the place are in their principles decidedly Unitarian; and it is hoped that they will find some opportunity of erecting an altar to the ONE GOD, and that by the powerful influence of instruction and example they will diffuse the blessings of national religion in a district which, under their auspices, is rapidly rising into opulence and distinction.

In the State of Massachusetts, and particularly in the environs of Boston, the great cause of Christian truth is making a silent but rapid and irresistible progress. From the inquisitive and liberal spirit which prevails in the University of Cambridge, which has never been checked at any time, but which there is reason to expect will receive every requisite aid and encouragement from the present learned and accomplished Principal, Dr. Kirkland, the happiest consequences may be expected to ensue.

The edition of Griesbach's Greek Testament with select various readings, and with the accurate and laborious author's latest corrections, a copy of which was procured in Germany by the late reverend, learned, and eloquent Joseph S. Buckminster, which under his inspection was elegantly and correctly reprinted in America as a text-book for the students of Harvard College, cannot fail to contribute essentially to the true interpretation of the sacred oracles. And a large and beautiful impression of the Improved Version, with the Notes, published by my intelligent, learned, and valuable friend and correspondent Mr. W. Wells, of Boston, whose zeal for truth is beyond all praise, will, it is hoped, contribute to the better understanding of difficult and doubtful passages in holy writ. The Monthly Anthology, the General Repository, and of late the Christian Disciple, and other valuable periodical publications conducted by gentlemen of distinguished talents and liberality, tend very much to diffuse a spirit of inquiry.

Bigotry is discountenanced; and divine worship in many of the principal churches at Boston is carried on upon principles strictly, if not avowedly, Unitarian.* Being myself a friend to in-

* A very correct, certainly not a partial account of the present state of professed Unitarianism in the State of the Massachusetts, and particularly in Boston, has lately been published in the Monthly Repository for March and April, 1812, in a letter addressed by my highly esteemed friend the Reverend Francis Parkman, of Boston, to the Reverend John Grundy, in reply to a flattering account of the state of Unitarianism in Boston and its vicinity, contained in the Appendix to Mr. Grundy's eloquent discourse at the opening of a new place of worship at Liverpool. This account appears to have been communicated to my worthy friend by some person whose zeal in a good cause led him to see the objects of his wish in rather too favourable a light.—See Appendix, No. X.

The following extract from a letter written by a minister in America to his friend in England, dated October, 1810, though somewhat long, will, it is hoped, be found both entertaining and important; it will throw much light upon the state of religion in Boston, and may give rise to some useful reflections :—

"On my return home I spent the Sabbath at Templeton, and I preached twice. There are not more than forty or fifty families near the meeting; but they come in all directions from the woods and mountains in such numbers as to make altogether a goodly company. There being in almost every parish, especially in Massachusetts and Connecticut, a settled minister always of good morals, and generally of real piety, to administer divine ordinances to them and lead them in the way of truth and duty, can scarcely fail having a good influence upon the people at large, in preserving them from that gross ignorance and grievous profligacy so prevalent in many countries that are called Christian. Nothing would satisfy my son but I must, whilst in Boston, have my picture drawn; this cut up my time so very much, I could not attend so many of their private meetings as I otherwise should. It was the General Election for the State; the Democrats gained the ascendency. I heard the election sermon preached by Dr. P., a very warm Federalist. He made it his business to expose the nefarious proceedings of the opposite party—in truth, a most copious subject; and was heard by the people in the galleries with high approbation, and almost clapping. The Convention Sermon (i.e. the sermon preached before the General Assembly of Ministers) was preached by Dr. Porter. Full two hundred ministers were in town. Their public business is transacted in the Court-house. The Convention has no ecclesiastical authority. Their proceedings and resolutions are merely advisory, but are not without considerable effect. The principal thing that came before them was a complaint against some missionaries for going into parishes where there were settled ministers, holding meetings without their knowledge, and even in opposition to their advice. The conduct of the missionaries was highly disapproved. The Monday after the General Election for the State, there is always a sermon preached to the Artillery Company. Mr. L., I was informed, gave them an excellent discourse, but I did not hear it. I went to the meeting door but the crowd was so great that I did not go in. The two Legislative bodies, the Governor, and a number of the principal gentlemen and clergy, after the service was over, dined at Fanuel Hall, a large building over the market-house, where they have their town meetings and transact their town business. Mr. Jackson, the late British Minister, was there. I was invited to dine with them, but I declined it. I was, however, introduced to Mr. Jackson at his lodgings, and once dined with him at Mr. B.'s. Mrs. Jackson, with four other ladies were there; the rest of the party were gentlemen, about thirty in all. We had a splendid entertainment. Two courses of all the delicacies money could procure. Among the rest, a dish of green peas, the first brought to market, which, the papers said, cost four dollars a bushel. The

N

genuousness and candour, I could wish to see all who are truly Unitarians openly such, and to teach the doctrine of the simple

Bostonians paid Mr. Jackson great attention, and where much pleased with his behaviour while among them. I preached for Dr. E., Mr. B., Mr. L., and Mr. F., at the Stone chapel. The last-mentioned gentleman was never episcopally ordained; of course, the ministers who have been so never exchange with him. In this place the Governor used to worship when the State was a British colony. It is a large stone building, just like an English church. The other three are large and costly buildings, and have numerous assemblies meet in them. The galleries were designed principally for Negroes; but there is now a meeting built for the Africans to worship in by themselves. A mulatto minister preaches to them. There are said to be eleven or twelve hundred people of colour in the town. It was Communion-day at Mr. B.'s; there were about one hundred and fifty communicants. At Dr. E.'s, there must have been two hundred. Never did I see such a display of plate on the Communion-table. At Dr. E.'s, there were five or six flagons, which held from three to four quarts each; six tankards, each containing a full quart; two dozen of cups of various sizes and forms, with six large plates for the bread; all handsome, and as bright as silver can be made. No person of a grain of sense can suppose these things to be of any importance. But as many of these people display great opulence in their own houses, I see nothing improper in their expending a portion of their superfluous wealth upon the house of God. A charity sermon is preached once a quarter for the benefit of the poor belonging to the Congregational societies in this town. The ministers of that denomination preach it in their turns, and the money is equally divided among the societies for distribution. About fourteen hundred dollars are collected in this way in the year. Mr. C. preached an excellent discourse, and is in truth a charming preacher; being remarkably serious and sensible, and universally liked. The place was quite full, though it will accommodate upwards of two thousand people. There is always a collection at the Convention Sermon for the relief of poor ministers and their families. About six hundred dollars were collected on that occasion. Though the people in Boston have lost much of their ancient rigidity respecting the Sabbath, great attention is paid to that day. Few resort into the country, and those who do, go early in the morning that they may not be noticed. Very few visit on that day, and but few are to be seen in the streets, except when going to or from public worship, and then the streets are crowded. At sunset their Sabbath is considered as ended; the gentlemen often visit their friends, and the ladies sometimes take their work. In religious families the Saturday evenings are observed with strictness; but some, as might be expected, under pretence of keeping Saturday evening in preference to the other, keep neither. It is customary in the gayest, and even the most profligate, to connect themselves with some religious society, so far as to contribute to its support, and occasionally to attend. This is necessary if they would be thought of any consequence in society, and even to preserve themselves from ridicule and reproach. Dr. E., who has been a minister at Boston above thirty years, tells me he never knew a greater regard paid to religion in that town than now, nor does he think there ever was in his time more real goodness among them. On election day I dined with about thirty gentlemen at Mr. P.'s, one of the deacons of Dr. E.'s church. We had a most sumptuous entertainment. When they had drunk two or three glasses of wine after dinner, the company dispersed. This I find is a pretty general practice, and thus all temptation to drink to excess is avoided. Their graces before and after meals are generally longer than with you. That office is assigned to the minister of the host, or to the oldest minister present. Episcopalianism is at most only upon a level with other denominations. The Bostonians are very commendable for keeping very much to their own places of worship, and for speaking of their own minister as one of the best preachers in the town. The clergy seem to be comfortably supported, their salaries being from 1,500 to 2,000 dollars a year, and

indivisible Unity of God as well as to. practise the rites of Unitarian worship. But I will not presume to judge for another.

they are constantly receiving. handsome presents. They very. generally wear in the. summer a silk gown and cassock, with a band; in the winter a cloth one; and altogether their worship is kept up in a splendid style. The pulpits throughout the country will hold from four to six ministers; and in Boston their rich cushions and curtains, or Venetian blinds, ornamental pillars and splendid chandeliers, give their meetings a. magnificent appearance. I think those which have been lately built are too large; a. minister must have a good voice. to fill them. Boston is said to contain 30,000 people, and is increasing very fast. The ground on which the town stands is greatly elevated on the south-west. It makes a noble appearance from the country. The State House on Beacon Hill is a magnificent structure. All their Meetings have steeples with one bell. That to the new Meeting in Park Street is very lofty, and one of the handsomest I ever saw. It stands on high ground at the top of the Mall, is seen all round the country, and indeed beyond the lighthouse far into Massachusetts Bay. The High Calvinists, who built this Meeting, expected to have lessened the other congregations, but I am told they have not yet done it. Should they get a popular minister, I have no doubt there will be a large society: the disposition of the people for attending public worship being such that I expect all their meetings will be well attended. In the old part of the town the streets are narrow and crooked, but are much improved and improving in that respect. Formerly, they were much exposed to depredations from fire, the houses being mostly built of wood. The danger from this quarter is lessening daily, as no buildings higher than fourteen feet are permitted to be erected of wood now. The town stands on a peninsula, joining to the main land only by a narrow neck on the south. They were, therefore, obliged to make use of boats to get to and from town. But since the war, five bridges have been built over the different waters that surround Boston and Charleston, which are a vast convenience to the inhabitants. .These bridges are all built of wood, and some of them are above a mile in length. The ministers of Boston and that vicinity discover considerable accuracy and taste in their compositions, and, generally speaking, may be considered as well furnished divines. Dr. O. is a man of very strong powers of mind; and though his distinguishes himself upon all public occasions, and especially those of a political nature, his general manner of preaching is very pious and edifying. The clergy are invited. to a great many good dinners. A Boston merchant would hardly think of making a dinner for his friends without inviting three or four clergymen. Some that I once knew I believe injured their health and shortened their days by eating and drinking too much. Those now on the stage do not give into any excess."

For this long, but curious and interesting extract, I trust that the reader will require no apology. I will only add two brief reflections. First, that the ministers of the Church of England are not the only persons who dislike itinerant intruders into parishes which are served by regular clergymen. The spirit of all establishments is the same, whether the favoured sect be Episcopalian, Presbyterian, or Congregational. Secondly—may it be permitted to put the question without offence?—Can it upon the common principles of human nature be reasonably expected of a body of clergy, nursed in the lap of ease and affluence, and placed in a station of such high secular consideration and comfort as that of the ministers of Boston, that they should come forward and, by an open profession of unpopular truth, voluntarily risk the loss of all their temporal dignity and comfort, and incur the contempt and enmity of many who are now their warmest admirers and friends? I say not this by way of disparagement to the present body of ministers in Boston and its neighbourhood. Some of these I have the pleasure to call my friends, and I know them to be possessed of talents the most distinguished, of piety the most fervent, and of benevolence and zeal the most ardent, active, and laudable; and of the rest I have heard a most favourable character. It is

N 2

There may possibly be reasons for caution which do not occur to me, and of which I am not competent to judge. The time must however come, perhaps it is near, when truth will no longer endure confinement, but will burst forth in all her glory. The dull hollow rumbling at the bottom of the sea, which is scarcely noticed by the inattentive traveller who is gliding carelessly over the solid plate of ice which encrusts the surface, is, to the wary and experienced observer, a sure presage of the speedy and sudden explosion of the immense superincumbent mass, and of the restoration of the imprisoned waves to their native freedom, to the consternation and often to the utter destruction of those who refuse to listen to the friendly premonition.*

APPENDIX to CHAPTER IX.

I HAVE republished this chapter without any material alterations; though I have learned with regret that some worthy persons have taken offence at it, and that it has given birth to a warm, not to say an angry, controversy on the other side of the Atlantic.

It should seem that many who claim the honourable title of Unitarians in the American States, are very desirous to have

the situation, not the men, which excites my apprehension. And who will venture to say of himself that his virtue would be equal to the trial? Yet still it cannot reasonably be hoped that truth will make any visible and rapid progress till her advocates rise above the fear of man and the love of ease, and are willing, with the Apostles of Christ, and the reformers of every age, to forsake all and to sacrifice their dearest interests in her glorious cause. The encouragement and success which such faithful confessors would meet with in that populous and opulent city would, I doubt not, be very great. The harvest truly is plenteous; it is ripe and ready to be gathered in. Highly honoured will that servant be to whom the great Master of the field shall communicate a portion of his energetic spirit, and shall say, " Put in thy sickle and reap."

* See the interesting narrative of the very narrow escape of two Moravian missionaries in travelling over the ice, in consequence of neglecting the advice of some friendly Esquimaux, in the History of the Mission of the United Brethren to Labrador.

it known that they are not " Unitarians in Mr. Belsham's sense of the word." Of this I have no right to complain : I never desired to set myself up as the head of a party : nor have I the slightest pretensions to it ; being nothing more than a humble disciple in the school of Lardner, of Lindsey, and of Priestley ; having learned of them and of a few others, particularly Locke, how to read and examine the Scriptures, and being a follower of them so far as they appear to me to be followers of Christ and his Apostles. But I do complain of palpable misrepresentation of my opinions, and of an exaggerated account of my sentiments concerning the person of Christ, to which I am by no means disposed to subscribe.

In perfect concurrence with the first-named venerable men, I believe that Jesus of Nazareth was a human being, in all respects like unto his brethren, only distinguished from the rest of mankind as the greatest of all the prophets of God, chosen by the Most High to be the founder of a new and universal dispensation, the prince and the leader of life, the first begotten from the dead, to whom the spirit was communicated without measure. By which I mean, that he was fully instructed in the nature, object, and extent of his divine mission, and that he was endowed with a voluntary power of working those miracles which were necessary to excite attention, and to demonstrate the divinity of his mission.

In this definition of Unitarianism I perfectly harmonize with Dr. Lardner, Mr. Lindsey, and Dr. Priestley : it is no more my definition than it is theirs : and I have no right to the honour of being represented as its author. They who disclaim Unitarianism according to my definition, disclaim the Unitarianism of Lardner, Lindsey, and Priestley—men of the greatest distinction for theological learning, for their researches into the Scripture, and for the unblemished sanctity of their character.

I agree with Mr. Lindsey and Dr. Priestley in rejecting upon critical grounds the story of the miraculous conception, and in believing that Jesus Christ was the son of Joseph and Mary. And being in all respects like other men, he must originally have been a peccable, or he could not have been a moral agent : and the perfection of his character was owing to moral discipline. Though he was a Son, he learned obedience by the things he suffered : and he grew in wisdom as he grew in stature. And though inspired with a perfect knowledge of everything relating to his divine mission, it would be absurd to suppose that a human being was inspired with omniscience. In those philosophical, historical, and other topics which were not immediately connected with the objects of his mission, he probably entertained opinions similar to those of his countrymen in similar circumstances. This is all that is meant when it is said that Jesus was fallible: and in this conclusion all consistent believers in the proper humanity of Jesus Christ must agree. Dr. Priestley thought that Jesus had erred in the interpretation of Scripture prophecy, and in the case of the Gospel demoniacs. I do not completely agree with my late learned and pious friend in all his conclusions upon these subjects: but if they were true, they would not at all affect the authority of Christ in those points to which his divine mission properly extended.

If Unitarianism is a belief in the existence of one God only, in opposition to a plurality of deities, I am decidedly of opinion, with Dr. Lardner, Mr. Lindsey, and Dr. Priestley, that genuine Arians have no claim to the title of Unitarians. Dr. Lardner, with all his mildness, had such a dislike to Arianism that he could hardly speak of it with temper. "Dr. Watts," says he, " to his honour be it spoken, never was an Arian." And though he lived in an age when Arianism was triumphant, so profound was his knowledge of Christian antiquity, and so clear his discernment of Scripture theology, that it was a well-known maxim with him, "The pride of Arianism will have a fall." Mr. Lindsey, " to his honour be it spoken," never was an Arian. Dr. Priestley and others descended from the heights of orthodoxy to the plains of Unitarianism through the medium of Arianism. I am therefore very far from intending the slightest disparagement to those who hold the Arian doctrine, as I myself for many years very honestly did, with perhaps a slight modification of what is now called the indwelling scheme, in whatever language I may now think it right to enter my protest against it. No one surely who thinks rightly concerning the Unity of God will ever admit that Dr. Clarke's scheme of an eternally begotten Logos, or the proper Arian doctrine of a created Logos, who is the sole former, preserver, and governor of the whole created universe, which completely excludes God from all concern in his works, is consistent with just notions of the Unity of the Supreme Being. Upon both these hypotheses, if the Father is nominally God, the Logos is really and the only God. And as to modern Arianism, such as that of Dr. Price, which supposes the Logos to

be only the former, supporter, governor and judge of this world, or
of the planetary system, if ever polytheism existed in the world,
this doctrine is such. For not only does it exclude God from his
works like the theories of Arius and Dr. Clarke, so far as this
world is concerned; but it naturally and necessarily leads to the
conclusion that there are as many Logi as there are systems,
and that each Logos is endowed with infinitely more power than all
the gods and goddesses of the heathen world put together; who
yet were also subject to one great Supreme. Arianism therefore is
polytheism in its strictest sense. But modern Arians, as if they
were determined to recede as far as possible from the letter of
Scripture, having thus deified their Lord and Master, and
raised him into the situation of a substitute for the Supreme
Being, strangely, and in direct opposition to the dictates of
common sense and to the plainest language of Scripture, deny him
the worship and homage due to the rank and character to which
they have elevated him. For while the Scripture expressly requires
that we shall worship and bow down and kneel before the Lord our
Maker, for HE IS OUR GOD; the modern Arian replies, " No,
we will not worship the Lord our Maker, for he is not our God;
and to worship him would be an act of downright idolatry: but we
will worship our Maker's Maker, for he alone is our God: " a
strange doctrine; for which if any one can find any foundation
in the Scripture, he must read with very different eyes from mine.
It is indeed astonishing that so many wise and good men should
be so blind to the plain consequences of their own opinions,
and should fancy that they are Unitarians, when they believe
not only in two, but in two hundred thousand gods. But, as
Dr. Price says, we are apt to wonder at one another: and it is
almost impossible to make sufficient allowance for the strength of
early prejudice and the influence of fixed principles. But at
least I think it will be allowed me that, while I entertain these
sentiments of the Arian hypothesis, I cannot very consistently
class Arians with Unitarians.* As to the very modern doctrine

* Nothing can be more extraordinary and unaccountable than the zeal with which
modern Arians explode the worship of Jesus Christ. For upwards of twenty years of
my life I was an Arian or a Clarkist. I believed that the spirit, the Logos which
animated the body of Christ, was the maker of heaven and earth and sea, and all
things therein: I believed that he was my maker, supporter, benefactor and governor,
in whom I lived and moved and existed: I believed that he descended from his
celestial glories; that he became incarnate; that he took the form of a servant;
and, that by undergoing the severest pains of body and mind, he satisfied Divine

of the simple pre-existence of Christ, the abettors of it have certainly no claim to the title of Arians, but have a very good right to be numbered with Unitarians, though, as I think, under a cloud of error.

No small share of credit is 'claimed by many on both sides the Atlantic for being what they call practical preachers, and for not troubling their hearers with what they represent as speculative notions. And not unfrequently a sarcasm or an inuendo is thrown out against those of their brethren who think it their duty to instruct, as well as to exhort. If such practical teachers satisfy their own consciences, and are useful to others, it is well. Happy is he who condemneth not himself in the thing that he alloweth. Theirs is comparatively an easy task. Others are placed in circumstances of greater difficulty and severer trial. Enlightened by a serious, long, and painful study of the Scriptures in the knowledge of the truth as it is in Jesus, they feel themselves not only called to resign their most cherished prejudices, but to abandon their dearest connections, to exchange

justice and expiated the sins of men. I believed that after his resurrection he ascended into heaven; that he resumed his original glory; and that he ever lives to make intercession for us, in the usual sense of the words. I believed that the first duty of a Christian was to commit his immortal interests into the hands of Christ, who was ever willing to take the charge of them; and who was always at hand to sympathize, to strengthen, to console, to advise, and to keep what was committed to him to that day. With these views of Christ, was it possible to suppress the feelings of veneration, of gratitude, of hope, of confidence, of joy and the like; or to restrain the natural expressions of those feelings, in the language of prayer and praise? It was utterly impossible. And never shall I forget the delight with which I have a thousand and a thousand times repeated the language of Grove's Sacramental Meditations: " Do I not love thee, O my Saviour! thou knowest all things, thou knowes't that I love thee. I love thee, O Jesus! but not as I would, not as I ought to love thee," &c. Or of that beautiful hymn of Dr. Doddridge:

" Do I not love thee, O my Lord ?
  Then let me nothing love;
  Be dead, my heart, to every joy,
  If Jesus cannot move."

And even now I hardly dare trust my feelings with those recollections; even though, in consequence of having acquired correcter notions of the person of Christ, I am fully convinced that our exalted Master would not think himself honoured by those affections and addresses which are alone due to his Father and our Father, to his God and our God. But how it is that modern Arians can possibly entertain these sentiments of Jesus Christ, and yet refuse him the correspondent homage; and not only so, but make their boast of it, and glory in it as a circumstance which entitles them to the honourable title of Unitarians, is utterly beyond my comprehension. When I entertained their sentiments concerning the person and offices of Christ, I should rather have said, " Perish Unitarianism ! if it requires a sacrifice so costly as that of the affection and homage which are due to the Redeemer."

affluence for poverty, and reputation for contempt. Being themselves happily possessed of the simplicity of evangelical truth,
discerning its inestimable value, and feeling its enlivening and
consolatory power, they believe it to be their duty to enter their
solemn protest against popular and prevailing errors, and to be as
explicit in teaching God's sacred truth, as others are in publishing
their unscriptural and pernicious errors. In thus fearlessly obey-
ing the dictates of conscience they often incur severe privations,
and are censured and even abandoned by some from whom they
would have expected more liberal treatment. It is however
enough for them that God knows their heart; and that his approbation will make ample amends for every loss which they may
sustain, for every pang which they endure, for all the calumny
and reproach which they encounter from the world, and .from
the unkind censures of their mistaken brethren. If they are
honoured as the humblest instruments of promoting the truth of
God and the purity of the Gospel, none of these things move
them.

As to the rest, I trust that this discussion has been the happy
means of promoting the great cause of the proper Unity and the
sole unrivalled glory of God in the United States. I am happy
to learn that ministers both of the Arian and Unitarian persuasions are now in the habit of openly professing the doctrines
which they believe : and I do not wonder that, in consequence of
this fearless integrity in a land of perfect religious liberty, Christian truth is flashing like lightning through that highly favoured
empire, from Boston to Baltimore, and from Philadelphia to the
Illinois. And I doubt not that in less than a century the belief
of one God even the Father, and of one Mediator between God
and man, the MAN Christ Jesus, will become the prevailing religion
of the Western world.*

* The admirable discourse of the Rev. W. E. Channing, delivered at the ordination
of the Rev. Jared Sparks, the respectable minister of the new Unitarian church at
Baltimore, in May, 1819, and the explicit language used upon that occasion, are amply
sufficient to redeem the liberal theologians in America from the censure of concealing
what they believe to be the truth : and the discussion excited by this eloquent address
cannot fail to be greatly conducive to the cause of free inquiry and·the propagation of
Christian knowledge.

CHAPTER X.

ACCOUNT OF THE NEW COLLEGE AT HACKNEY. THE AUTHOR'S
INTRODUCTION TO, AND INTIMACY WITH, MR. LINDSEY AND
DR. PRIESTLEY. LONDON UNITARIAN SOCIETY. WESTERN
UNITARIAN SOCIETY. REV. TIMOTHY KENRICK. UNITARIAN
FUND SOCIETY.

FROM this long but I trust not irrelevant nor uninteresting digression concerning the present state of the Unitarian doctrine
in America, it is now time to return to the venerable subject of
the present Memoir.

In the year 1786, the Dissenting Academical Institutions at
Exeter, Warrington, and Hoxton, having been lately dissolved,
and no place of education for Dissenting ministers remaining
where freedom of inquiry upon theological questions was allowed,
excepting that at Daventry, which was by no means equal to supply
the demands of the Nonconformist churches, some gentlemen in
London formed a plan for erecting an Academical Institution in
the vicinity of London for the purposes of general education, and to
supersede the necessity of sending the sons of Dissenting parents
to the English Universities, where they are under an obligation of
subscribing to articles which they do not believe, and of attending
upon forms of worship which they do not approve. The design
was generous and noble; and it could not have failed to produce
the most beneficial and permanent effects, had the wisdom of the
execution been proportionate to the beneficence of the plan, and
to the disinterested liberality, the zeal, and the public spirit of
the original founders. The Dissenters through the country took
up the case most warmly, and subscribed most liberally; so that,
if the sums raised had been judiciously applied, an institution
might have been founded and endowed which would have bid
defiance to opposition and calumny, and the duration of which

would have been equal with that of the nation. Some have objected to its vicinity to London: but the true and conclusive answer to this is, that other very flourishing Academical Institutions have existed, and do exist, in the vicinity of the metropolis: there is, therefore, no impossibility, physical or moral, why an Institution of this kind, established upon liberal principles, and aided by a vigorous system of discipline, might not have been equally successful. And the advantages of the vicinity of London are obvious and numerous, particularly as it affords the greatest facility of obtaining the best means of instruction in every art and science. If the funds of the Institution had been permanently established and economically applied, any error, however great, in the internal management might have been corrected without affecting its existence. It was a grand experiment; in the conduct of which it might reasonably be expected that, from the want of experience, errors would arise without any imputation of blame to individuals. And from my own knowledge of the case, having been personally connected with the Institution for the last seven years of its existence, I will presume to say that it did not fail from any deficiency in attention or zeal, either on the part of the committees or the tutors. The spirit of the times was against the Institution; and the mania of the French Revolution, which began so well and ended so ill, pervaded all ranks of society, and produced a general spirit of insubordination. The ferment of the times gave birth to insidious and even to daring attacks upon natural and revealed religion, which produced mischievous effects upon uninformed and undisciplined minds. And the founders of the Institution, with the best intentions in the world, introduced a principle which they held up to the public as the peculiar and distinguishing excellence of the plan, and which was to render this Institution paramount in discipline and order to all others; but which, in fact, sapped the very foundation of all discipline, and was the bane of all salutary authority, viz., that a superintending committee should be always at hand to watch over the conduct of the students, and to support the authority of the tutors. This regulation, in fact, left the tutors totally destitute of all authority; for whatever happened amiss, they had no other power to rectify but by an appeal to this committee. Every one who is in the least degree acquainted with the dispositions of young men, must see at once that such a constitution is directly and necessarily productive of anarchy. And in.fact it did produce it to a considerable degree; and it was owing to the principles and habits which many of the students brought with them to the college, that this spirit was not more prevalent.

Yet, after all, everything might have been rectified had the funds been properly managed. The principal, and in truth the only, cause of the failure of the Institution was the unfortunate purchase of the estate at Hackney, which involved the committee in an expense of building and a load of debt, which the funds of the Institution never were, nor could have been able to support. The creditors became clamorous, and it was necessary to sell the estate to great disadvantage in order to pay off the debt.

The principal of this debt has been long since discharged; and by the accumulating interest of the residuary funds, during the suspension of the Institution, under the management of the worthy and respectable treasurer, John Towgood, Esq., a sum has been raised sufficient to discharge the interest of the debts, and to relieve the College honourably and faithfully from every just demand upon its assets. A considerable permanent fund still remains, agreeably to the resolution of the General Meeting, July 1, 1786,*

---

* The resolution is expressed in the following words, extracted from the minutes annexed to the discourse delivered by Dr. Price, in April, 1787, before the supporters of the College, viz. : "That one-third of the present and future donations, benefactions, and bequests to the new Academical Institution in the neighbourhood of London, the same not being annual subscriptions, shall go to create a Permanent Fund, the capital whereof shall be preserved for ever INVIOLABLE and INALIENABLE, in the hands of Trustees." A subsequent resolution purports, " That the annual income arising from the Permanent Fund shall ALONE be paid from time to time as it arises towards the support of the said institution, in such manner as the General Committee shall direct. Or if the said institution shall at any time hereafter be dissolved, or be discontinued for the space of three years, to the founding or to the support of any other academical institution, or of any institution preparatory to such among the Protestant Dissenters for the liberal education of youth in any part of England or Wales; or in giving exhibitions to students for the ministry, or in supporting one

which is now vested in public securities in the names of four trustees; the dividends upon which are applied by them to the purposes for which that fund was appropriated.

Of this Institution, Mr. Lindsey was from the beginning a sincere well-wisher and an active and liberal supporter : no one more ardently desired its success, nor did any one more sincerely lament the circumstances which led to its suspension.

It was his connection with this Institution which first introduced the writer of this Memoir into an intimacy with the revered friend who is the subject of it. As a minister whose principles were known to be what is commonly called Evangelical, the author of this Memoir had been appointed, in the year 1781, Theologial Tutor in the Academy at Daventry, which was a continuation of the Academy under the late pious and celebrated Dr. Doddridge at Northampton, and was supported by the trustees of the late William Coward, Esq., who bequeathed a considerable estate for the education of Dissenting ministers, and for other religious purposes.* The office of pastor of the Independent

or more tutors at any such institution or institutions within the same limits as the General Committee shall direct."

As the annual subscriptions have been discontinued for many years, the only persons who now have any interest in or control over the funds of the institution are the Life-Governors, out of whose donations the Permanent Fund has been formed.

* William Coward, Esq., was a merchant in London, a man of large property, and a zealous Calvinist. He left his great fortune to pious purposes, intending, however, that it should be limited to the support of the Calvinistic doctrine. But the professional gentleman who drew up the will, who was a man of great talent and liberality, expressed it in such terms as to leave the trustees at full liberty to apply it to the support of whatever they might judge to be the cause of Christ among Protestant Dissenters. The trustees consist of three Dissenting ministers and one lay gentleman; and when a vacancy occurs, the survivors appoint a successor; and this important trust has always hitherto been filled by persons of high respectability. • For many years this fund supported two very respectable and flourishing institutions for the education of Dissenting ministers; one in the vicinity of London, first under the direction of Dr. David Jennings, and afterwards of Dr. Savage, and Dr. Kippis, and Dr. Rees; the other in the country, first at Northampton, under the care of Dr. Doddridge, and afterwards at Daventry, under Dr. Ashworth, the Rev. T. Robins, and finally the writer of this Memoir. And it was during this interval that Mr. Coward's trust was in the meridian of its glory. To them the whole Dissenting interest looked up as its patrons and benefactors; and from one or other of their institutions most of the respectable congregations were supplied with well-educated ministers. Indeed, it may be questioned whether more good has ever been done for so great a length of time at so moderate an expense. For though they exerted themselves to the utmost of the powers with which they were vested, the allowance which they were able to make to

congregation at Daventry was at that time held in connection,
with the office of divinity tutor, and to this he was also invited.
The Unitarian controversy, revived with so much animation by
the writings of Mr. Lindsey and Dr. Priestley, and brought home
so closely to the feelings by the truly christian and disinterested
conduct of the former in the resignation of his vicarage, was at
that time in its zenith. And the tutor regarding it as a question,
of the highest importance, conceiving it to be his duty to state it
fairly before the theological students, and observing that the,
question concerning the simple humanity of Christ, which was
now become the great controversy of the age, was scarcely glanced
at in Dr. Doddridge's Lectures, which were the text-book of the
Institution, he determined to draw up a new course of lectures
upon the subject. And to this he was impelled by an additional
motive, namely, the hope of putting a speedy termination to this
newly-revived controversy; since whatever respect he entertained
for the abilities, the learning, and the character of the great
champions of the Unitarian faith, he felt a perfect confidence that
their arguments would be found capable of an easy and satisfactory reply; and, whatever might be the errors of his own
education, he had been happily instructed and firmly fixed in
the grand principle that freedom of investigation must ultimately
be favourable to truth. The method which he pursued in
instituting this inquiry he has detailed at large in another place.
It is, therefore, sufficient at present to mention that he first
selected all the texts of the New Testament upon which the

the tutors was never such as to enable them to make any considerable provision for
their families, never amounting, I believe, upon an average, including board, tutors'
salaries, house-rent, &c., to more than 30*l.* a-head for each pupil, and in the country not
so much. But there was no complaint, and the tutors performed the duties of their
office with cheerfulness, looking for remuneration of a different kind, having never
entered upon the Dissenting ministry with the expectation of aggrandizing their
fortune. In the year 1785, upon the resignation of the tutors of the Hoxton
Academy, Mr. Coward's trustees, feeling the support of two institutions as a burden
too oppressive, determined upon uniting them together at Daventry, under the charge of
the writer of this Memoir, under whose direction the united institution remained till
his resignation in 1789; after which it was placed for some years under the care of the
Rev. John Horsley, at Northampton; and upon his resignation it was removed to
Wymondely, in Hertfordshire.

controversy is allowed to depend; most certainly not omitting any which appeared to him favourable to the pre-existence and divinity of Jesus Christ. These he arranged under distinct heads; and under each text, he introduced the explanations of the most approved commentators of the Trinitarian, Arian, Socinian, and Unitarian hypotheses, very rarely introducing any theological comments of his own, choosing rather to leave the remarks of the different expositors to make their own impression upon the minds of his pupils. The labour was considerable; but it was not thought burdensome either by the teacher or the learner; the consciousness of honest unbiassed inquiry, and the gradual opening of light, was ample compensation for all. But the result was widely different from what had been expected. First, the pupils, whose ingenuous minds, not so firmly bound by prejudice, were more open to conviction, began to discard the errors of education; and some of them, much to the regret of their worthy friends, and not least to that of their tutor, became decided Unitarians. The tutor's habits of thinking were more firmly riveted; and though from the beginning of the inquiry he was a little surprised at discovering so few direct, and, as he thought, unequivocal, assertions of his favourite doctrine, and though in the process of his labours he found himself obliged to abandon one text because it was spurious, another because it admitted of a different and more probable interpretation, and so on, and was thus driven by degrees out of his strongholds; yet such was the ascendency which the associations of education had obtained over his mind, that he does not believe it would have been in the power of argument to have subdued it, had not the nature of his office, which made it necessary for him to repeat the lectures to successive classes, and which thereby compelled his attention again and again to the subject, eventually, and almost imperceptibly, overruled his original prepossessions, and brought him over to the faith to which he had certainly no previous partiality, to the profession of which he had no interest to induce him, and which he had fondly flattered himself that he should without much difficulty have overthrown. Those who have never changed their opinions, who are not much in the habit of inquiry, or who have not watched the vacillations of the mind when it is deliberating upon subjects of high importance, when it is anxious to form a correct judgment, when much depends upon the decision, and when it once begins to suspect as erroneous what it has long regarded as sacred and essential truth, may wonder that the teacher should be so long in making up his own mind, and that he should not be able to mark the day and the hour of his conversion. The fact is, that he was not himself aware of it, till, upon the repetition of a sermon which he had preached a few years before, and in which the pre-existence of Christ and its concomitant doctrines were assumed as facts, he found himself so embarrassed from beginning to end by his sceptical doubts, that he determined from that time to desist. from teaching what he now first discovered that he no longer believed. This was in the autumn of 1788. And conceiving that, his mind being now made up upon the subject, it was his duty no longer to hold his peace, but to bear his public testimony to the truth ; and at the same time being conscious that he no longer possessed the qualifications which were deemed essential to the offices he sustained, and regarding it as both unhandsome and unjust to put his friends under the disagreeable necessity of dismissing him from his office, which they probably would have thought it their duty to do ; at least, being fully persuaded that it was right to give them their option in the case, he determined to resign both the Academy and the congregation. His resignation of the former he sent in to the trustees in January, 1789, requesting them to keep it concealed till March, as it would be impossible for him to leave his situation till Midsummer; and he had no desire to make himself the topic of conversation till it became absolutely necessary. The trustees, with great propriety, expressed their acceptance of the resignation, in a respectful letter of form by the late excellent and benevolent Joseph Paice, Esq., the lay trustee, accompanied with a kind, affectionate, sympathetic letter of his own—like himself.* Nor were the rest of the trustees deficient in expressions of sympathy and friendship.

In March, 1789, the writer of this Memoir went up to London to officiate at the ordination of his friend and pupil the Rev. Edmund Butcher,† at Leather Lane, and for a few days he resided in lodgings in Essex Street. It was upon this occasion that he took the liberty of introducing himself to the venerable patriarch of the Unitarian church. His visit was short: as a stranger he was received with the politeness and benignity which were inseparable from Mr. Lindsey; but nothing confidential passed. It was a visit of form, perhaps it may be said of curiosity, not, it is hoped, wholly unwarrantable in the new proselyte to see the holy confessor and champion of truth, whose doctrine he had embraced, and whose dignified example he had endeavoured, in his humble measure, to follow. But his intended resignation was not then known; and he did not choose to be the first notifier of it to this excellent man. While he continued with Mr. Lindsey, a gentleman came in, who, without knowing the stranger present, announced to Mr. Lindsey that the ordination was to take place at which that stranger was to officiate. Upon this solemnity Mr. Lindsey attended: but no further personal intercourse passed between them while the writer of this Memoir continued in town; and he returned into the country gratified with the opportunity

* Of this gentleman, so long and so well known in London, and so highly esteemed for his amiable manners, his unimpeachable integrity, and his unbounded, disinterested, and almost romantic benevolence, an elegant Memoir was printed by his intimate friend and executor, James Gibson, Esq., addressed to Mr. Gibson's only child. Mr. Paice was a Dissenter upon principle; and for many years a distinguished ornament of the highly respectable congregation at Carter Lane, under the pastoral care of Mr. Pickard, and Mr. Tayler, and now of the Rev. Joseph Barrett. He was eminently pious, and of a truly catholic spirit. He died on the fourth of September 1810, and on the 16th of the same month, an excellent and impressive discourse was delivered upon the occasion by the Rev. T. Tayler, at Carter Lane, before a numerous, respectable and much-affected auditory, at whose request it was given to the public.

† This gentleman in the course of a few years was obliged to resign his office on account of ill health and the weakness of his voice. Happily, by the blessing of Divine Providence, on the use of proper means, he gradually recovered both. He is now the respected and useful minister of a congregation of liberal Dissenters at Sidmouth; and having upon more mature investigation seen reason to abandon the system of Arianism, to which he was formerly much attached, he very honourably made a public profession of his conversion to the pure Unitarian doctrine, in a sermon preached before the Western Unitarian Society two years ago, 1810.

O

which he had enjoyed of visiting Exeter House, but little expecting that this interview would be introductory to the happy intimacy with which he was afterwards honoured by its distinguished inhabitants.

For at that time Unitarianism was far from being a popular doctrine; and the highest ambition of the tutor, when he quitted a connection which had existed for eight years, with great harmony and comfort, and to which from principle and from habit he was fondly attached, was to reside in a cottage in the vicinity of Birmingham, where he had many kind and excellent friends, and where he flattered himself that he should enjoy the society and the interesting and instructive conversation of Dr. Priestley. But Divine Providence ruled otherwise. It was thought by many of the respectable friends and supporters of the New College at Hackney that his labours might be of use to that rising Institution. Some, indeed, of the old school objected to the new proselyte; and his own expectations of usefulness or of comfort, in a situation so materially different from that which he had left, were not sanguine. But being now in an unconnected and insulated state, he had nothing to lose, and he sacrificed nothing, though his labours might be in vain. He was urged by many respectable persons to embark in the undertaking. Many objections were obviated, sacrifices made, and difficulties removed, to make room for him. Dr. Priestley and Mr. Lindsey both concurred in pressing his acceptance; and, what perhaps weighed more than all the rest, a prospect was opened, by residing in the neighbourhood of London, of cultivating the friendship of Mr. Lindsey. This, it must be confessed, was the favourite wish of his heart; and in the accomplishment of this wish his mind was completely gratified, and every sacrifice which he had been called upon to confer upon the altar of truth and integrity was compensated a hundred-fold. He settled at the College in August, 1789; and from that time his intimacy with the venerable subject of this Memoir commenced, and continued without interruption or abatement till the end of his days. Two years afterwards, in the year 1791, Dr. Priestley, the most spotless and innocent of men, as well as the most sagacious of philosophers, and the most laborious and ingenuous of theologians, having been driven from his home by the insane riots at Birmingham, and having been invited to succeed his learned and virtuous friend Dr. Price in the pastoral care of the congregation at Hackney, he voluntarily and gratuitously undertook to deliver to the students at the College his admirable lectures upon history and chemistry. This was the consummation of every wish which the writer of this Memoir could form for intellectual, moral, and social felicity and improvement. To be received into the familiar intercourse and admitted to share the confidence of these venerable men, whose honourable exertions and generous sacrifices in the cause of truth had placed them so much above the level of ordinary characters, and even of celebrated divines, was a blessing to which he had indeed earnestly aspired, but the enjoyment of which he had never ventured to anticipate. Few days passed without some personal intercourse with one or other of these estimable men, and often with both. And the usual topics of conversation, besides the great events of the time which arrested everyone's attention, were some subject in theology, some passage of Scripture, the elucidation of some point of doctrine, the solution of some objection, the present slow progress of Christian truth, the anticipation of a day of greater light and knowledge, and happiness and peace. The friends did not entirely agree in opinion upon all points; but the discussions, sometimes animated, were always amicable, for all were lovers of truth, and they sought after no other object. To discover truth was to gain the victory.

> How oft did they talk down the summer's sun,
> How often thawed and shortened winter's eve,
> By conflict kind, that struck out latent truth ! *

* It is pleasing to see that the society which was so truly interesting to the writer of the Memoir, contributed, in a considerable degree, to the gratification of the other parties. Upon this subject Dr. Priestley thus expresses himself in the Memoir of his Life, p. 107 :—

"On the whole, I spent my time even more happily at Hackney than I had ever done before; having every advantage for my philosophical and theological studies in some respect superior to what I had enjoyed at Birmingham, especially from my easy access to Mr. Lindsey, and my frequent intercourse with Mr. Belsham, Professor of Divinity in the New College, near which I lived. Never, on this side the grave, do I

But this felicity was too pure to last : and in a short time these two eminent veterans in the service, whose friendship had been the growth of thirty years, and whose writings had, for the greater part of that time, been the food and sustenance of the revived primitive Unitarian Church, were destined to be separated, never to see each other's face again. But of this more hereafter.

In the year 1791 was formed the Unitarian Society for Promoting Christian Knowledge and the Practice of Virtue by the Distribution of Books. The object of this Society was two-fold :— the first was, that the few who then professed the unpopular doctrine of the unrivalled supremacy of God, and that the Father alone is to be worshipped, and the simple humanity of Jesus Christ, might have some common bond of union, that they might know and support one another, and that they might thus publish their profession to the world, and excite that serious inquiry which would lead to the diffusion of truth. The second object of the Society was, to print and circulate, at a cheap rate, books which were judged to be best calculated to propagate right views of the Christian doctrine, and to apply it to the direction of the practice. It was proposed at first to combine this Society with that for promoting the Knowledge of the Scriptures, of which some account has been already given. But this combination was opposed by Mr. Lindsey and Dr. Priestley, who thought it best that the Societies should be kept distinct ; and as the writer of this Memoir was the person who first suggested the plan, it was allotted to him to draw up the preamble to the rules. And as the object of the Society was by no means to collect a great number of subscribers, but chiefly to form an association of those who thought it right to lay aside all ambiguity of language, and to make a solemn public profession of their belief in the proper Unity of God and of the simple humanity of Jesus Christ, in opposition both to the Trinitarian doctrine of Three Persons in the Deity and to the Arian hypothesis of a created Maker,

expect to enjoy myself so much as I did by the fireside of Mr. Lindsey, conversing with him and Mrs. Lindsey on theological and other subjects ; or in my frequent walks with Mr. Belsham, whose views of most important subjects were, like Mr. Lindsey's, the same with my own.''

Preserver, and Governor of the world, it was judged expedient to express this article in the preamble in the most explicit manner. This was objected to by some, as narrowing too much the ground of the Society, which, as they thought, ought to be made as extensive as possible. But the objection was easily overruled, it being the main intention and design of the Society to make a solemn, public, and explicit avowal of what in the estimation of its members was Christian truth; to enter a protest against the errors of the day; to unite those who held the same principles, and who were scattered up and down in different parts of the country, in one common bond of union; and to encourage them to hold fast their profession, and to stand by and support one another.

A much more plausible objection against the preamble was urged from the introduction of the word *idolatrous*. The obnoxious sentence is thus expressed : " While, therefore, many well-meaning persons are propagating with zeal opinions which the members of this Society judge to be unscriptural and *idolatrous*, they think it their duty to oppose the further progress of such pernicious errors, and publicly to avow their firm attachment to the doctrine of the Unity of God, of his unrivalled and undivided authority and dominion," &c. Now, as the proper definition of idolatry is the worship of a being who is not truly God, and more especially the worship of a deified man, nothing can be more evident than that the worship of Christ must, in the estimation of Unitarians, be in that sense idolatrous; and no persons are more ready to allow this consequence than Trinitarians themselves are, upon the supposition that their doctrine is erroneous. Yet nothing appears to give greater offence than the use of this epithet by the Unitarians, though they adopt it chiefly to excite the attention of their fellow-christians to the importance of the question; and are at the same time solicitous to point out the wide difference between Christian and Pagan idolatry ; the former being solely an error of judgment, upon the culpability of which they presume not to decide; while the other is essentially connected with the most odious vices, is branded in Scripture with the most contemptuous epithets, and justly threatened with the most awful punishments.

The introduction of this expression into the preamble gave very great offence to many of the friends of the infant Institution, and it was very seriously debated whether it should be retained or not. Perhaps it might have been prudent to omit it, as the doctrine which the Society desired to hold forth as their common faith might have been expressed with equal distinctness and precision without it. But as it had been introduced, many were unwilling to abandon it : they even considered the omission of it as little less than a dereliction of principle. Among these were Mr. Lindsey, Dr. Priestley, Mr. Russel, of Birmingham ; and Mr. Tayleur, of Shrewsbury. On the other side were some gentlemen of Cambridge and elsewhere, whose names would have been an ornament to the Society, but who either declined joining it, or withdrew from it when they heard that it was decided to retain the offensive epithet. And, in fact, some who still continued in the Society were not well pleased with the expression, which they regarded as having a tendency to fix an opprobrium upon their fellow-christians.*

* As the preamble to the Rules of the Unitarian Society is not of any great length, and has been the subject of much discussion, it may not be amiss to introduce it in this place :

"Christianity, proceeding from God, must be of infinite importance ; and a more essential service cannot be rendered to mankind, than to advance the interests of truth and virtue ; to promote peace, liberty, and good order in society ; to accelerate the improvement of the species ; and to exalt the character and secure the greatest ultimate happiness of individuals, by disseminating the right principles of religion, and by exciting the attention of men to the genuine doctrines of revelation.

"This is the chief object of THE UNITARIAN SOCIETY FOR PROMOTING CHRISTIAN KNOWLEDGE AND THE PRACTICE OF VIRTUE, BY DISTRIBUTING *such* BOOKS as appears to the members of the Society to contain the most rational views of the Gospel, and to be most free from the errors by which it has most been sullied and obscured. Error, voluntary or involuntary, so far as it extends, must have a pernicious influence. The members of this Society think, therefore, that they are doing signal service to the cause of truth and good morals, by endeavouring to clear the Christian system from all foreign incumbrances, and by representing the doctrines of revelation in their primitive simplicity. Truth must ultimately be serviceable to virtue.

"The fundamental principles of this Society are, That there is but ONE GOD, the SOLE Former, Supporter, and Governor of the universe, the ONLY proper object of religious worship ; and that there is one Mediator between God and men, the MAN Christ Jesus, who was commissioned by God to instruct men in their duty, and to reveal the doctrine of a future life.

"The beneficial influence of these truths upon the moral conduct of men will be in proportion to the confidence with which they are received into the mind, and the attention with which they are regarded. Consequently, all foreign opinions which men have attached to this primitive system of Christian doctrine, and which tend to

The first annual dinner of the Unitarian Society was held at the King's Head, in the Poultry, in April, 1791 : the number assembled was between forty and fifty: among these were Mr. Lindsey, Dr. Priestley, Dr. Kippis, &c., and several eminent political characters were also present who were not members of the Society. It was at a time when the French Revolution was in its glory, when it excited the highest hopes, and when its success was the object of the most cordial wishes of the best friends to civil and religious liberty in this country. Mr. Burke had published his celebrated book six months before; and Dr. Priestley and Mr. (now Sir James) Mackintosh and others had written or were preparing answers to it. The subject so occupied the public attention, that it almost engrossed the conversation in every company. Unfortunately, upon this occasion many political toasts were given; and, amongst others, " Mr. Burke, and thanks to him for the discussion which he has provoked." And still more unfortunately for the Society, they were published the next day in some of the morning papers, from which they were transferred into the *Moniteur* and other French journals. The right

divert their thoughts from these fundamental principles, are in a degree injurious to the cause of religion and virtue. While, therefore, many well-meaning persons are propagating with zeal opinions which the members of this Society judge to be unscriptural and idolatrous, they think it their duty to oppose the further progress of such pernicious errors, and publicly to avow their firm attachment to the doctrine of the UNITY of GOD, of His UNRIVALLED and UNDIVIDED authority and dominion ; and their belief that Jesus Christ, the most distinguished of the prophets, is the CREATURE and MESSENGER of God, and not his EQUAL nor his VICEGERENT in the formation and government of the world, nor CO-PARTNER with him in divine honours, as some have strangely supposed. And they are desirous to try the experiment, whether the cause of true religion and virtue may not be most effectually promoted upon proper Unitarian principles ; and whether the plain unadulterated truths of Christianity, when fairly taught and inculcated, be not of themselves sufficient to form the minds of those who sincerely embrace them to that true dignity and excellence of character to which the gospel was intended to elevate them.

" Rational Christians have hitherto been too cautious of publicly acknowledging their principles, and this disgraceful timidity has been prejudicial to the progress of truth and virtue. It is now high time that the friends of genuine Christianity should stand forth and avow themselves. The number of such, it is hoped, will be found to be much greater than many apprehend. And their example, if accompanied with, and recommended by, a correspondent purity of life and morals, will naturally attract the attention of others, and produce that freedom of inquiry, that liberal discussion, and that fearless profession of principles embraced after due examination, which can be formidable to nothing but to error and vice, and which must eventually be subservient to the cause of truth and virtue, and to the best interests of mankind."

honourable gentleman whose name had been introduced with such distinction animadverted upon the meeting the next day in the House of Commons with great indignation. And twelve months afterwards, when a petition was presented to the House, which, though it originated with the Unitarian Society, had been signed by persons of all persuasions, Churchmen and Dissenters, for the repeal of the penal laws relating to religion ; though it was intro- duced and supported by Mr. Fox with all his super-eminent powers of reason and eloquence, it was most vehemently opposed by Mr. Burke, who made the house merry, and at the same time alarmed their prejudices, by reading and commenting upon the toasts which had been given at the dinner, and which he, with some humour, described as the articles of the Unitarian creed. This *faux pas* of the Society at its commencement, in mixing politics with religion, gave much and reasonable offence to many of its friends and absent members, and induced the Society afterwards to hold their meetings more privately, to decline all publicity in their proceedings, and to determine that, as a body formed upon a religious principle and directed solely to a religious object, they would not intermeddle with temporary politics.

This Society, the dawn of which was thus ushered in with clouds, soon emerged from its obscurity. It was joined by numbers of high respectability in different parts of the kingdom, who were not afraid or ashamed to be enrolled in the catalogue of Christians who were the avowed worshippers of the One God, the Father, through the one Mediator between God and man, the Man Christ Jesus. And the success of the Society, thus constituted, greatly exceeded the most sanguine expectations of those by whom it was originally formed. It made Unitarians known to one another. It diffused the doctrines of uncorrupted Christianity, by the ex- tensive circulation of books which were calculated to check the progress of popular errors. It encouraged the public profession of these long-neglected truths. And, what was of the greatest importance, it gave birth to many similar societies in different parts of the country, some of which are in a state as prosperous, or even more more so, than the London Society itself.

The first of these *affiliated* societies was the Western Unitarian Society, which was formed under the auspices of that truly excellent man, the late Reverend Timothy Kenrick, of Exeter, a gentleman equally distinguished by the soundness of his judgment, the accuracy of his learning, the piety and rectitude of his character, and the warmth and inflexibility of his zeal in the cause of truth, virtue, and liberty. Having after long and rigorous inquiry seen reason to adopt the doctrine of the proper humanity of Jesus Christ and the unrivalled supremacy of the Father, he regarded it as an imperious duty to bear his testimony to the truth, to communicate the light which he had received, and to eradicate from the minds of the people of his charge the deeply-rooted errors which they had derived from the writings and instructions of the learned Peirce and the venerable Towgood, of a second and inferior God, a delegated Creator, Preserver, and Governor of the Universe. This erroneous and unscriptural doctrine Mr. Kenrick gradually undermined by judicious discourses and plain and practical expositions from the pulpit, and attacked still more directly in the familiar lectures which he delivered to the young men of his congregation, and by the formation and zealous support of the Western Unitarian Society. He saw with much regret that few young persons were in a train of education for the Christian ministry among the rational Dissenters. And he himself opened an institution for that purpose at Exeter, in connection with the Reverend Joseph Bretland, and received students into his family, gave up his time and labour to their instruction, and boarded them upon terms from which it was impossible for him to gain anything. He can hardly be said to have done justice to his own family in thus expending his time, his talents, his vigour, and even his substance, with so little prospect of adequate remuneration. But this was to him an object of light consideration, in comparison with the great end he had constantly in view—the diffusion of Christian truth, and the extrication of the Christian doctrine from the mass of rubbish in which it has been for many centuries overwhelmed. In this great work he met with much opposition; with opposition from those who, from early habit and education, were sincerely and zealously attached to the errors which he was labouring to eradicate, and who of course believed it to be their duty to oppose him in all his measures; and with opposition from some wise men of the world, who, though their opinions perhaps were not much at variance with his own, did not think it *prudent* to excite religious dis-sensions and to give public offence; arguing in the same way, and acting upon the same principles, as the first opposers of the Reformation, and even of Christianity itself. Mr. Kenrick's vigorous mind was in no respect daunted by this opposition; but persevering in his object with inflexible resolution, he ultimately obtained complete success. It pleased the Almighty, in his mysterious providence, to put a stop to this excellent man's exertions by an awful and unexpected stroke in the midst of his career. While in full possession of his health and faculties, and rejoicing in the increasing success of his pious and benevolent schemes, he was suddenly cut off by an apoplectic seizure at Wrexham, in Denbighshire, August 22, 1804, in the forty-fifth year of his age. The success of Mr. Kenrick's labours in his congregation appeared by their choice of a successor of similar ability and zeal in promoting the same great and good cause of Christian truth, the Reverend Dr. Lant Carpenter—and in his Academical Institution by the reverence and affection in which his name and character are held by his pupils, and by their zeal and usefulness in the respectable stations which they occupy in the Dissenting churches. The Western Unitarian Society has continued to flourish since Mr. Kenrick's decease, and Arianism seems to be nearly expelled from one of her strongest citadels. Mr. Kenrick left three sons, the eldest of them, after his father's decease, passed a few years at Birmingham under the tuition of the Reverend John Kentish, his father's friend; and, having afterwards finished a brilliant career at the University of Glasgow, is now settled as a tutor in the College at York, an Institution of deservedly high reputation, under the able direction of the Reverend Charles Wellbeloved. And at this Institution Mr. Kenrick's youngest son is in a course of education for the

ministry.* Two volumes of posthumous Sermons and three of
Exposition of the Evangelists, published at the desire of his
congregation, are ample proofs how well qualified the learned and
pious author was to teach the pure, uncorrupted doctrine of Christ.
Let the reader pardon what it is hoped may be considered as a
not totally irrelevant digression, which the author has introduced
to testify his respect and veneration for one in whose education he
had the honour to sustain no inconsiderable share, and with whom
he had afterwards the happiness to be connected as a colleague, a
friend, and a brother.

> His saltem accumulem donis, et fungar inani
> Munere."

The Southern Unitarian Society was formed soon after the
Western, and a few years afterwards the Northern and other
similar societies. These gave birth to Unitarian Tract Societies
in different parts of the kingdom, the design of which was to
distribute small tracts for the purpose of diffusing just principles
of religion among the inferior classes of society. With these
have been united what are called Christian Tract Societies, which
are intended to spread among the inferior classes interesting little
compositions wholly practical and entirely unconnected with controversy. These societies have met with great encouragement,
and many have contributed to them who by no means agree in
sentiment with the original founders of these useful associations.
But the Society which at present holds the foremost rank, and
engages the most general and the warmest support of the
Unitarian body, is that which is called the Unitarian Fund
Society; the professed object of which is to encourage popular
preaching, and to engage missionaries to visit different parts of
the country, and, wherever there is an opening, to preach pure
and uncorrupted Christianity in opposition to popular and prevailing errors. Some of the ministers employed in these missions,

* The Reverend George Kenrick is now (1820) settled with a respectable congregation at Hull, where he is discharging his official duties with a zeal and activity
worthy of the descendant of such a father.

though not possessing the advantage of regular education, are
men of very popular talents and very extensive information; and
by the great success with which their labours have been attended
they have abundantly proved that simple unsophisticated truth
has charms to captivate even the most ordinary minds, when it is
exhibited to them in a clear and affecting light, and have demonstrated the fallacy of the commonly received opinion that Unitarianism is not a religion for the common people. This being a
new experiment, in which unlearned ministers were chiefly employed, many of the more learned and regular members of the
Unitarian body stood aloof, and declined to give countenance to a
proceeding, of the prudence and propriety of which they stood in
doubt. Some do not even yet approve it; and others who wish
well to the design do not regard it as within the field of their
personal exertions. But after the success which has attended the
efforts of this Society, no person who is a real friend to the cause
can consistently be hostile to its principle. How far the venerable
patriarch of Unitarianism, who is the subject of this Memoir,
would have patronised a society of this description, cannot now
be ascertained. That he was in the highest degree favourable to
the main object of it, is evident from the following extract from a
letter to a friend, dated October 23, 1789 : " I find that your
son's account of the Unitarian street-preachers is true, and that
he was with Dr. Priestley at Manchester when he saw them. It
will be very desirable to have their numbers increased. We want
much to have the common people applied to, as enough has been
done, and is continually doing, for the learned and the higher
ranks."

The parent Institution, the London Unitarian Society, still
exists upon a very respectable footing; and though its numbers
may not be so large, nor its funds so ample, nor its proceedings
attended with so much *éclat*, as those of some associations of
later date, it still retains the honour of having set the first
example of a society publicly professing Unitarian principles, and
constituted with an avowed design of supporting and diffusing
them. One of its main objects no longer exists. The title of

Unitarian, then a term of general reproach, is now, in consequence of the extensive diffusion of Unitarian principles, become a mark of honour, and is courted rather than shunned. The Society still continues to distribute, every year, a very considerable number of Unitarian books and tracts. And if its numbers should decline, of which however there is no immediate prospect, the members of the Society, whose only object is to promote the cause of truth, and who have no personal or party interest to consult, will rejoice to see it superseded by any institution which promises to be of greater utility to the general cause.

CHAPTER XI.

ANALYSIS OF THE CONVERSATIONS UPON CHRISTIAN IDOLATRY. THE DUKE OF GRAFTON CORRESPONDS AND VISITS MR. LINDSEY, AND ATTENDS UNITARIAN WORSHIP. A BRIEF ACCOUNT OF THE PROGRESS OF THE DUKE'S OPINIONS, AND OF HIS REASONS AND MOTIVES FOR SECEDING FROM THE ESTABLISHED FORM. REFLECTIONS.

THE introduction of the charge of idolatry into the Society's Preamble having been much misunderstood and given great offence; to obviate the objections, and to correct the error, Mr. Lindsey published a small work, in octavo, in 1792, entitled " Conversations upon Christian Idolatry." The scene is laid in the house of Marcellinus, a gentleman of large fortune and great liberality of sentiment, and the conversation is supposed to have taken place in his library after breakfast, between himself; Volusian, an eminent barrister and moderate churchman ; Synesius, a person of great worth, who seldom attended public worship,

but who was a zealous friend to a religious establishment; and
Photinus, an enlightened and zealous Unitarian, who writes an
account of the conversations to his friend Victorin. And the
author leads his reader to understand that the whole transaction
had some foundation in fact.

The dialogue begins with some severe animadversions upon the
late disgraceful riots at Birmingham, the whole blame of which
Marcellinus imputes to the operation of the Test Act, and other
laws against the Dissenters; but is interrupted by Volusian, who,
while he expresses his entire disapprobation of the Test Laws, and
his indignation at the insults and injuries offered to Dr. Priestley,
nevertheless expresses his suspicion, that " Dr. Priestley had
contributed to excite the bad spirit which, however wrongly, had
appeared against him ;" and particularly by his late sermon at
Hackney, in which he had " bluntly and peremptorily declared
the worship of Jesus Christ to be idolatrous." Marcellinus
defends Dr. P. upon his own principles, and represents him as
" worthy to be remembered as a benefactor to mankind, particularly for the light which he has thrown upon theological subjects."
But Volusian, without impeaching his moral character, regards a
restless love of novelty as " evidently his failing ;" and " having
been bred up in the belief that Jesus Christ is God, and to be
worshipped, he cannot endure the rudeness and impertinence of
the man who tells him that he is an idolater." Here Photinus
interposes, and puts the question seriously to Volusian, " whether
he had ever searched the Scriptures to know how many Gods
there are, and whether Jesus Christ was one." This leads
Volusian to the confession, that " he had not made the Scriptures
his particular study ;" —that, " in general, these theological
matters are left to be settled by the divines, those especially of
the upper ranks ;" and that, " at his time of life, he had no
leisure, and less relish, for such intricate inquiries." This
confession introduces from Photinus a serious remonstrance, and
an earnest exhortation to study the Scriptures for himself, in
which he would very soon attain entire satisfaction concerning the
God he is to worship. This ends the first conversation.

Volusian, much impressed with his friend's advice, goes home for a week under pretence of business, but passes the greater part of his time in reading and studying the Scriptures with the greatest attention; in consequence of which he becomes a sincere proselyte to the faith, that there is but One God, the Father, the only proper Object of religious worship, and that Jesus Christ is the servant and faithful messenger of God, but not the object of worship; and, upon his return, he embraces the earliest opportunity of communicating his conversion to his friends. This constitutes the subject of the second day's conversation; in which Volusian is almost the only speaker, and details to his friends the principal arguments, both from the Old Testament and the New, by which he was led to the conviction that " God is strictly One, one person: and the blessed Jesus nothing but his favoured creature and servant." " Still, however wrong, he could not look upon himself as an idolater in the worship he had hitherto paid to Jesus Christ; and though mistaken, he could not look upon himself to have been a wicked man, which that language implies."

This, of course, forms the subject of the third day's conversation, in which Photinus replies at large to Volusian's objection, that "idolatry is represented in the sacred writings as a heinous sin, an idea which he could not entertain of any who are sincere, however erroneous, in their worship of Jesus Christ." Photinus very justly remarks, that the idolatry against which the judgments of God were denounced, was that of the heathen, which was not a mere "speculative error, but attended with the most shocking vice and immorality;" whereas "nothing of this kind can be charged on the idolatrous worship of Christians, though the Almighty and Infinite Being is dishonoured and degraded by it." And in answer to the question of Volusian, "to show wherein their idolatry lies," he states, that " idolatry consists in paying divine honours to a creature;" the doing which is a direct violation of the first commandment in the decalogue, which is not only not repealed, but is solemnly confirmed by Christ. If, therefore, Jesus Christ be a creature, " to call him God, and to worship him, can be nothing less than idolatry." Synesius now interposing the observation, " that the members of the Church of England are not idolaters; because, though charged with worshipping three Gods, they are themselves persuaded that they worship only One," Photinus replies, that " if men's own thoughts will exculpate them, there never was such a thing as idolatry in the world ;" for all idolaters, the worshippers, for example, of the Virgin Mary, are persuaded that their worship is allowed by God. "Our convictions concerning actions cannot make that right which is in itself wrong, though they will excuse us in doing it, in proportion to the insuperable ignorance under which we labour." And in answer to Volusian's expression of anxiety at the great prevalence of Christian idolatry, Photinus reminds his friends of the innocence of those who, through the errors of education, are involuntarily involved in it; but adds, that "how far those are innocent who, believing Jesus Christ to be a creature, do, nevertheless, customarily join with others in the worship of him as the Supreme God, is a very serious question." He then observes, and produces some very remarkable instances to prove, that the most orthodox in our own country have had no scruple of terming the worship of Christ to be idolatrous if he be a creature ;* and after a few general remarks the conversation closes.

The fourth conversation discusses the question which Volusian tells his friends presses with much weight upon his mind, viz., "how a person should act upon discovering that the established

* See Waterland's Defence, p. 231, 252. Dr. Hughes' Sermon at Salter's Hall, vol. ii. p. 8. Whitaker's Origin of Arianism, p. 4. 5. The expressions of the last-cited author are very remarkable. " If." says he, " this doctrine of the Trinity be false, then nine-tenths of the Christians throughout every age, and every country, are guilty of idolatry, of idolatry more gross than that of the Papists at present; because, not merely the worship of saints and angels in subordination to God, but the worship of a creature along with the Creator; placing him equally with God on the throne of the universe; giving God a partner in his empire, and so deposing God from half his sovereignty." These are the words of a zealous Trinitarian : surely, then, it becomes every one who offers divine worship to Jesus Christ. well to consider the ground upon which he stands : much more does it become the decided believer in the proper Unity of the great Object of worship, to flee from that which must in his own estimation, and even in that of those who are themselves worshippers of Christ, be gross idolatry.

worship of the country in which he was bred, was idolatrous?"
Synesius gives it as his opinion, that public worship should be
abandoned altogether. For "all right worship is in the heart,
and the moment you mix with others in the worship of God, you
are in danger of being misled by a thousand fancies, and idle
superstitious forms and practices." Photinus, in reply, vindicates
public worship as a duty, enjoined even by natural religion, to
keep up the knowledge of him in ourselves and others, and to
cherish in our breasts that attention to him which is necessary
for our present right conduct and comfort, and to qualify us for
his favour hereafter;" that it was expressly required under the
Mosaic institution, and authorized by the example of Christ, and
the practice of the apostles. Synesius, conceding this point to
Photinus, contends, nevertheless, for joining in the established
worship, "out of the general principle of doing homage to the
Creator. If there be any which you cannot conscientiously join
in and repeat, you have only to adopt what you like, and pass
over the rest, leaving it to those who are edified by it." Photinus
allows that, for lesser matters, it would be peevish and hyper-
critical to dissent; but he maintains, and he supports his argument by the authority of Archdeacon Paley, that, with respect
to the Object of worship, "there seems to be no latitude." And
having been charged by Synesius with having spoken disrespect-
fully of the public Liturgy, he expresses high approbation of it
as an excellent form of prayer; but at the same time enters his
strong protest against many parts of the Litany, in particular,
"which is ordered to be read every Wednesday, Friday, and
Sunday, throughout the year;" in which "a variety of beings are
addressed in a manner utterly inconsistent with the first commandment; and our Saviour, in particular, "is worshipped as the
Supreme God; and is addressed in such gross degrading language, as nothing but custom from early youth could reconcile
any to use;" and he concludes his argument with asserting that
all worship, excepting that addressed to the Supreme Being, is a
direct violation of our Lord's express precept to his apostles,
that they should teach men to observe all things whatsoever he

P

commanded them. Volusian, who, through the whole of this conversation had been a hearer only, now expresses his obligations to Synesius and Photinus for their temperate discussion of this important subject, and declares his entire conviction "that he can no longer with a quiet mind continue to frequent the worship of the Church of England, or say one thing with his mouth to the all-seeing God, while his heart and better knowledge mean another." Here the conversation ends.

In the beginning of the next letter, Photinus describes to his correspondent Victorin, the rise and progress of idolatry in the Christian church, and represents how very imperfectly the Reformation recovered the great body of Christians from this enormous error. He then proceeds to relate the subjects of the fifth day's conversation, which Volusian begins with expressing his hope that the public sentiment would soon change, and a corresponding change be adopted in the public forms of worship. Marcellinus expresses very little expectation of this happy event, and relates to his friend the steps which Dr. Samuel Clarke had taken to reform the Liturgy, and the approbation of his plan by Archbishop Herring; and in reply to the animadversion of Volusian, he defends the character of Dr. Clarke in continuing to officiate in the church; which, however, it is not improbable that he might have relinquished, if he had not succeeded in his plan of reform. And to the inquiry of Volusian, how it would be advisable to act, especially in the country, with regard to public worship, Photinus refers, with high approbation, to the conduct of a gentleman, Mr. Tayleur, of Shrewsbury, who had used the Reformed Liturgy first in his own house, and afterwards in a separate place of worship; an example which had been followed by some others, and which it was hoped would continue to spread. The conversation concludes with an interesting quotation from a late publication, by a gentleman who had, upon principle, retired from his connection with the Established Church. "Christian reader, this is no matter of barren speculation; it strikes directly on our conduct through life, on a point of serious importance. The public worship of God we all consider as a duty of indispensable obligation : and whether we shall perform this worship in the way most acceptable to him, and most conformable to the precepts of the sacred writings, or in that way which best suits our indolence, or coincides with our interest; whether we shall pay to God the homage of an upright heart, or with gross negligence and solemn mockery publicly repeat what we cannot understand, and join in professing what we do not believe ; are subjects of inquiry which (however easy to determine) every Christian, of whatever denomination, must acknowledge to be of high concern."

In this work a question of considerable importance is treated with great judgment, impartiality, and moderation ; the characters of the speakers are well sustained, and every argument and objection are allowed their due weight. And no person can rise from a serious and attentive perusal of the Conversations upon Christian Idolatry without feeling the conviction that, whatever allowance may be made for error, which is the result of invincible prejudice, it is the indispensable duty of every one who believes in the Unity and Supremacy of God, and that he is the proper and sole Object of religious worship, and in the simple humanity of Jesus Christ, the servant and messenger of God, to withdraw from worship which must to him necessarily be, and appear, idolatrous, and, wherever opportunity presents, to join with those, however small their number, however humble their condition, who, agreeably to the precept of their Great Master, associate for the worship of God the Father only.

Some years before the venerable subject of this Memoir retired from his office at Essex Street chapel, his ministry was statedly attended by the late Duke of Grafton. This illustrious nobleman appears, after his retirement from public life, upon the accession of the famous Coalition Ministry in 1783, to have devoted a very considerable portion of his leisure hours to serious inquiry into the evidences of divine revelation, and into the contents of the holy Scriptures. To this he was impelled, as he himself declares in the papers which he drew up and printed chiefly for the in-

formation of his family, by the suspicion which his intercourse
with the world raised in him, and which the observation of every
day confirmed, that many persons, in the more elevated ranks of
life especially, had little or no belief in the truth of the Christian
religion. The result of this inquiry was, that the Christian religion
had been promulgated to mankind by a person sent by, and acting
under, the authority of the Supreme Being; and that this religion,
having been corrupted from very early times by various means,
and these corruptions having been mistaken for essential parts of
it, had been the cause of rendering the whole religion incredible
to many men of sense. The noble inquirer soon discovered that
one of the plainest precepts, both of the Jewish and Christian
revelations, was the worship of one God; and that the public
forms of worship in all the established churches in Christendom,
not excepting that of our own country, contained a grievous
deviation from this fundamental precept by prescribing the
worship of two other persons, called the Son and the Holy Ghost,
jointly with that of the Almighty Father, as being in all respects
equal to him and consubstantial with him. And it soon occurred
to the inquisitive mind of this virtuous nobleman that this was
not a speculative discovery of little practical importance, but that
to one who was a firm believer in the divine origin of the Christian
religion, it was attended with very serious consequences. Convinced upon the highest authority that Christianity required the
worship of one God only, the Duke could no longer satisfy his
mind to attend the worship of three Gods; and it became a
subject of anxious and even distressing inquiry, how far it was his
duty, in the situation and rank which he held in his country, not
only to desert the established mode of worship, but to join a
separate congregation, whose sole and professed bond of union
and ground of dissent was the worship of the Father only. Upon
this subject, and upon some others of a personal kind, this nobleman opened a confidential correspondence with the venerable
founder of the Essex Street congregation; in consequence of
which, his difficulties being satisfactorily removed, he became a
regular attendant at the chapel in Essex Street, and continued a

serious and exemplary worshipper there till bad health and increasing infirmities confined him at home.

It was not till some time after the Duke became a worshipper in Essex Street chapel that his peculiar intimacy and personal intercourse with the venerable pastor commenced, which continued unabated through the remainder of Mr. Lindsey's life. This will be evident from the following extract of a letter from his Grace, dated June 4, 1789:—"The Duke of Grafton is much gratified by the acquaintance of Mr. Lindsey; and though he would be very desirous to profit from it by taking the liberty of calling on him now and then for half-an-hour's conversation on serious subjects, he would at the same time be very unhappy to obtrude on his time. But if Mr. Lindsey is so obliging as to allow him that advantage, the D. of G. would be much obliged to him if he would point out about what time of the morning or evening he is commonly least engaged, and at which he is most likely to be found at leisure." The Duke after this became a frequent morning visitor at Essex House, and to the end of life he maintained a character worthy of his profession. After a long and painful decline, the Duke expired at Euston, Suffolk, March 14, 1811. A sermon was preached upon the afflicting occasion at Essex Street chapel on the 24th by the author of this Memoir, which was afterwards published, and which contains some further particulars of this venerable and lamented nobleman.

The Duke of Grafton at different times set down in writing the result of his inquiries and his own reflections upon them. These extended from the year 1788 to the year 1797, and they contain a simple and interesting account of the progress of a virtuous and intelligent inquirer in his pursuit after truth. These papers were printed in his own lifetime, but not published. A few copies were given by his Grace to select friends, but they were principally intended for the use of his own family. And he desires that six copies may be given to each of his children, hoping that these may remind them of the true and honest sentiments of their father at different times in his better days, and that they may accustom themselves thereby to improve their lives more and more every day by a study of the Scriptures.

The first paper is dated December, 1788. The Duke was at that time, from the best search he was able to make into the holy writings, confirmed in the belief that "there is but one God only, who ought to be acknowledged and worshipped as such by all his creatures, and that he is the Creator and Governor of the universe." But at this time he appears not to have completely made up his mind upon the subject of the pre-existence of Christ. "I do," says he, "most sincerely believe in Jesus Christ, and am convinced that he was the Messiah, and sent by our Heavenly Father that the glad tidings should be made known to all mankind." The noble writer adds: "Whether Christ pre-existed at all or not, in what manner, or from what time, I find in Scripture no sufficient ground or necessity to make this point a matter of faith, and this both comforts and rejoiceth me. It may not, perhaps, be displeasing to God that pious or learned and well-intentioned persons should ruminate and form their conjectures upon these high subjects; but I conceive that no man should offer, for the belief of others, his opinions on them, but with the utmost deference, and adducing proof from Scripture sufficient to justify his way of thinking." He concludes this paper with great humility and piety in the following words: "If I am in any error, and under any mistake in these sentiments, I earnestly beg of Almighty God that I may be convinced of it, and that he will pardon me in my ignorance, and that he will enlighten my understanding by his Holy Spirit, and lead me into the way of truth, establishing me in the same more and more every day." In a sort of postscript to this paper, the Duke expresses his "humble judgment" that the example of Christ is more impressive and efficacious upon the supposition of his "having been a man liable as we are to all the weakness of human nature, but to whom God gave not the spirit by measure."

In another paper, dated December 25, 1789, his Grace remarks, "that the service for the Lord's Supper is not cleared from some things which deter numbers from joining in that holy rite. A few omissions in the prayers would render this service very suitable to comprehend large denominations of Christians, who cannot join with the congregation at present and acquit themselves to their own consciences, and who cannot bring their minds to do as I have this day done, by joining devoutly where I could, and in humble silence submitting myself, where I could not join, to the direction of that light which it has pleased God to grant unto me."

This practice of joining in a religious service in many respects so very exceptionable, and, as a Unitarian must think, even idolatrous, cannot perhaps be strictly justified, even with the mental reservation which this virtuous nobleman exercised when he joined in the solemnity. But it is most evident that he acted under a sense of duty; and that, far from condemning those who could not in conscience join in communion with the Established Church, he wishes that the service might be so altered as to obviate their objections. Surely, then, it ill becomes those who judge perhaps more correctly, and who act more consistently in abstaining from such worship, to censure others with severity who think it their duty to attend what they justly deem a corrupt, and in many respects an unscriptural form of worship, rather than entirely forego the benefit of religious institutions, or exhibit an example of the total neglect of Christian ordinances which may be misunderstood, and may mislead the lower orders of society. Happy is he who condemneth not himself in the thing which he alloweth. Let every one be a severe judge of his own conduct, and candid in his estimate of others.

In a paper dated December 30, 1790, the noble writer declares his now firm conviction, that "Jesus was a man, one in our own nature, and that his example and precepts were designed to direct us in our duty, as well as to afford the greatest possible consolation and encouragement in the regular discharge of it."

In the next paper, which is dated January, 1791, the Duke, having stated that he by no means would be understood to represent the proper humanity of Christ as a doctrine essential to salvation, adds, "Yet I cannot but think that a belief in the divinity of Christ, and the invocation of him as God, is displeasing to the Almighty, as breaking his first great and unrepealed command; and that every man who wilfully neglects to inquire has much to answer for; and much more those who have presumed to fetter his creatures by *forcing* them in their belief. Let ministers and teachers of religion, let fathers of families and others who are *enforcing* the belief of a mystical union in the Godhead, let them be aware, that they are using a most unwarrantable authority over the consciences of their fellow-creatures, for which they will ultimately have to answer to the Father of our Lord Jesus Christ, to the One only true God, who on this very head has been pleased to style himself a jealous God; and also that if they should be in an error, as I conceive them to be, they become dangerously responsible for the restraints which they have presumed to lay upon the consciences of others."

I transcribe the whole of the memorandum dated March 5, 1791, as expressive both of this virtuous nobleman's enlightened views and deep humility. "On the truth of the Christian dispensation and religion I confidently rest my hopes of immortality; and, with thankfulness for so great a boon, I trust to the mercy of God towards me, who stand so much in need of it."

In a paper dated January 1, 1792, the Duke expresses a belief that the exaltation of Christ to dominion and authority was the consequence of his submission to those sufferings which "were so efficacious, perhaps so necessary, to his own glory and to the future happiness of mankind." His mind seems at this time to have been perplexed with some obscure notion of the unscriptural doctrines of meritorious sufferings, and of the external authority of Jesus Christ; which, however, he regards as a mystery which "it will probably never be given to man in the present state" to understand, and which therefore "must consequently be ranked among those articles the belief of which cannot be necessary to salvation."

In a paper dated April 21, of the same year, the Duke represents himself as differing from some with whom he generally agrees, in believing that Jesus Christ in his present state can hear and help us. At the same time he adds : "I presume, and do firmly believe, that he would be offended at being addressed by any of his followers as an object of that divine worship which, as I conceive, the Scriptures represent to be due only to the Almighty Father and Creator, the ever-living God."

The difference upon this subject between his Grace and the theological friends to whom he refers, was probably merely nominal. Agreeing with the noble writer in the great principle that Jesus Christ is not the proper object of worship, they would be far from presuming to limit the extent of his knowledge or his power in his present exalted state.

In a paper dated June 10, of the same year, the Duke, after expressing his firm belief in the inspiration of the prophets, and of the information communicated to the apostles by the instructions of Christ and the gifts of the Holy Spirit, proceeds to state his objections to " the notion generally inculcated concerning the perpetual inspiration of the apostles and evangelists, which," says he, " I humbly conceive has much more assisted the cause of infidelity : which, in its turn, will recede in proportion as our divines, becoming every day more liberal in their opinions, shall advance to a candid admission that the apostles were fallible, and not at all times directed by the Holy Spirit."

In a paper dated June 10, 1794, the noble writer states, that his "own unenlightened reason had ever revolted against the church doctrine of original sin, as wholly incompatible with the attributes of a benevolent and omnipotent God." He adds: "And my mind received great comfort when I found that Scripture, so far from justifying an idea so derogatory to the honour and glory of the Deity, does, through its whole tenor, furnish ample ground for concluding against this sad and, I trust, unsupported doctrine." After this, he proceeds to state some of those passages which, in his view, appeared to be most irreconcilable to this popular opinion, particularly Matt. xviii. 3, xix. 4; Luke xviii. 17.

The paper dated March, 1795, contains rather an elaborate

disquisition upon the subject of the redemption of sinners by the
death of Christ, which seems to have pressed very much upon the
mind of the noble writer. He discards the common notion of
vicarious suffering and satisfaction. He conceives that "Scripture
redemption consists in a deliverance from the practice and guilt of
sin to be effected by sincere repentance, followed by total amend-
ment of life, to which the merciful goodness of God has vouch-
safed to annex the forgiveness of all past sins and offences." "That
which propitiates God is the forsaking of sin and newness of
life. If so, may not Christ, who teaches us this method of being
reconciled, be fairly and properly called the *propitiation* of our
sins ?"

In a paper dated April 17, 1796, the noble writer expresses his
decided conviction, that if doctrines are unintelligible, the belief of
them cannot be necessary to salvation. "Arrogant indeed," says
he, "is the theology of those who would enforce the belief of
superstitious or inexplicable opinions as divine truths, annexing
the hard *alternative* of eternal punishment. Far otherwise, I
believe, speaks the conciliating language of the gospel of our
benevolent Lord and Master."

The paper dated March 14, 1797, represents the expectation of
a future life, founded on the natural immortality of the soul, as
involved in inextricable difficulties; "whereas he who believes
in the truth of Christianity, and who confides in the assurances of
the gospel, has no occasion to fly to any metaphysical disquisitions,
for he feels at once that God, who was able to create him originally,
has promised through Jesus Christ to raise him again to life at
the last day; that he who has done the first has equally power
to perform the second, and has given an irrefragable proof of it
by the resurrection of Jesus himself from the dead."

The conclusion, which, though it has no date, appears to have
been written in the year 1797, begins with a most ingenuous
and affecting apology to the noble writer's friends, acquaintance,
and to *the world in general,* for embracing a form of public worship
differing essentially from that of the church in which he was
bred; expressing his deep sense of the responsibility which he

incurred by it, his entire satisfaction in the choice which he had made, his earnest regret that he had not turned his serious attention to the subject of religion earlier in life, and his ardent desire that what he writes may be instrumental in rousing others to an earlier attachment to the pure religion of the gospel. As this introduction has been cited at length in the discourse which was published by the author of this Memoir upon occasion of the lamented decease of the noble Duke, it is unnecessary to repeat it here.

The noble writer goes on to animadvert upon the egregious error of those who, regarding religion chiefly as an engine of state, expect to establish good order by the help of it, without "reviewing the Articles and Liturgy, and presenting to the people a purer Christianity, not liable to the formidable attacks which are daily made upon the present system." The remainder of this paper is taken up in commenting upon the first Article in the Church of England, which teaches that "in the Unity of the Godhead there be three persons of one substance, power, and eternity, the Father, the Son, and the Holy Ghost;" and in showing how repugnant this doctrine is to the declaration of the apostle, that "there is One God, and one Mediator between God and men, the MAN Christ Jesus." After this, the noble writer severely condemns the damnatory clauses of the Athanasian Creed, which, though it still remains as a creed required from those who profess to be of the Church of England, had no existence till a hundred years after the Council of Nice, and was not admitted even into the Church of Rome till the tenth century.

Having expatiated somewhat at large upon these subjects, he adds: "My objections are weighty against the Article of the church on *original* or *birth* sin, against the doctrine maintained relative to good works done before justification having the nature of sin, against that on predestination, and some others. But I trust I have said enough, without now entering on these, to prove that, if I be in the wrong, it is with an honest and firm desire of searching for the truth." "It is from the Scriptures alone," continues this illustrious inquirer after truth, and with these remarks he closes his interesting volume, " It is from the Scriptures alone that we can know the revealed will of God; and it is from thence I venture to draw my justification for wishing to join in communion with a church which will admit of no article of faith that is not expressed in the very words of Scripture; no creed which disclaims the right of private judgment in the concern of religion, and still, more, which allows the right of persecuting any human creature for conscience' sake."

As there is little reason to expect that these interesting papers will be soon published, the writer of this Memoir thought that it would be acceptable to his readers to exhibit this brief abstract of their contents, accompanied with a few specimens of the observations themselves; and in so doing he is convinced that he complies with the expressed desire of the noble writer, that "not only his friends and acquaintance, but THE WORLD IN GENERAL, might know that he embraced a form of public worship essentially different from that of the church in which he was bred, not hastily and through levity, but with all the consideration and investigation which so awful a decision required; " and that what he wrote " might be instrumental in rousing others to an earlier attachment to the pure religion of the gospel, and to remember their Creator in the days of their youth." And it cannot be doubted that the noble writer's vindication of his conduct must be perfectly satisfactory to every serious, liberal, and enlightened mind, how strange and unaccountable soever such conduct and such reasoning may appear to a gay and a thoughtless world.

Indeed, that a person of the Duke of Grafton's elevated rank in society, who had filled the principal offices of the state, and who was allied by birth, and associated by habits of familiar intercourse, with the first nobility of the land, should, in the vigour of life, sit down calmly to study the Scriptures; that, in consequence of this, he should embrace a system of Christianity widely different from the popular creed; that, impelled by a commanding sense of duty, he should secede from the church established by law, in which he had been educated, and to the

worship and constitution of which he was affectionately attached;
that he should publicly unite himself to a society of Christians
not then tolerated by the state, which existed by connivance only,
and the principles of which are held in public disrepute; whose
primary principle and professed bond is the unrivalled supremacy
and the sole worship of God the Father, as revealed and taught
by his faithful servant and messenger Jesus Christ,—indicates
perhaps as pure a principle of integrity, and as high a degree
of mental vigour and Christian fortitude, as can be conceived to
exist. It may even be questioned whether the noble sacrifice
made by Mr. Lindsey of all his preferments in the church and his
prospects in life, or the calm and dignified self-possession of Dr.
Priestley under calumny and persecution, discovered a more
generous and intrepid spirit in the cause of truth. In all
the changes of their fortune, and amidst the severest trials of
their constancy, these Christian heroes were encompassed with
friends who stood by them, who kept them in countenance,
who protected them from, or who shared with them in, the con-
tumely and the insult of their misguided opponents. But the
Duke of Grafton stood alone—the Abdiel of the sacred cause.
He had no one to join him, no one to stand by him, no one
to share in the reproach; and yet he persevered. And though he
fully understood, and feelingly describes, the delicacy and responsibility of his situation, he at the same time attests the
unspeakable satisfaction which he experienced from a faithful
adherence to the dictates of an enlightened conscience. Had the
Duke been a religionist only, and without inquiry or discrimination
continued a believer in the popular creed and a frequenter of the
established worship, his conversion, so far from being a subject of
reproach, would have been blazoned to the world with every mark
of honour and applause. Nor would he have wanted associates
even among persons of his own rank, who generally, and almost
unavoidably, confounding the Christian religion with the creeds
and catechisms and other articles of human device to which
they are accustomed, when they become religious too often
degenerate into narrow bigots to the tenets of their childhood.

But the Duke of Grafton disdained to take his religion upon trust. His superior mind examined the Scripture for itself. And having discovered Truth, he valued it most highly; he held it fast, and would upon no consideration part with it. By an habitual attendance upon a form of public worship addressed exclusively to the One God, even the Father, he calmly but firmly avowed his principles; and to all who had the happiness of knowing him, he exhibited their powerful and beneficial influence in a virtuous and Christian life.

Some have affected to believe that this virtuous nobleman was not thoroughly consistent, and that he did not carry his principles to their proper extent. Suffice it to say, in reply to these ungenerous insinuations, that the Duke of Grafton at all times acted up to his own ideas of consistency and rectitude, though his judgment might not entirely correspond with that of his accusers. Let such persons recollect what this illustrious nobleman did, before they presume to arraign him for what he did not. And it may not be unbecoming those who are so very sharp-sighted in discovering a mote in the eye of another, to consider well whether there may not at the same time be a beam in their own.

CHAPTER XII.

MR. LINDSEY PUBLISHES A NEW AND REFORMED EDITION OF HIS
LITURGY; RESIGNS HIS OFFICE AT ESSEX-STREET CHAPEL.
HIS FAREWELL SERMON PUBLISHED, BUT NOT PREACHED.
INTERESTS HIMSELF IN FAVOUR OF THOSE WHO SUFFERED
BY UNJUST STATE PROSECUTIONS. CASES OF FYSHE PALMER,
MUIR, AND WINTERBOTHAM.

EARLY in the year 1793, Mr. Lindsey, at that time approaching the term assigned by the sacred writer as the usual limit of human life, or at least of the active and useful portion of it, and

being secretly but firmly resolved, though in a high state of health
and vigour, corporeal and intellectual, to retire from public service
in his seventieth year, he revised and printed a fourth edition of
the Reformed Liturgy, that he might bequeath it to his bereaved
flock, as containing the last corrections, and the most approved
sentiments, of their faithful and affectionate pastor.   He introduced it with a sermon delivered upon the occasion in the month
of April in that year, and which he afterwards published.   In
this sermon, after giving a judicious account of the duty, the
reasonableness, and the efficacy of prayer, he proceeds to state
the nature and the grounds of the alterations which he had made
in this new edition of the Reformed Liturgy.   They were indeed
not inconsiderable.   He had omitted what is called the Apostles'
Creed, and the three invocations in the Litany.

After stating the preference which the society in Essex Street
give to forms of prayer, he observes that "one capital inconvenience belongs to this mode of worship, viz. that forms of
prayer drawn up in one age, through greater improvements made
by the study of the sacred writings, may become improper to be
used; and things of this nature once established, are too apt on
that very account to be held sacred, and by no means to be
changed: by which serious thinking persons are often brought
into great difficulties.   The proper remedy would be, frequently
to revise public devotional forms of human institution, and to
correct and bring them nearer to the Scripture model."   And
having glanced at the ineffectual attempts which had been made in
the seventeenth and eighteenth centuries for the reformation of
the established Liturgy, he reminds his readers that Dr. Samuel
Clarke's amendments of the Book of Common Prayer had been
adopted by the society in Essex-Street chapel,* but not without

* Mr. Lindsey observes in a note, that it is very probable that Dr. Clarke's Reformed
Liturgy was approved by King George II., certainly by his consort Queen Caroline;
that Dr. Herring, Archbishop of Canterbury, gave it the fullest and highest com-
mendations in a letter to the amiable and excellent Dr. Jortin ; and that it also received
very signal tokens of approbation from a learned and venerable prelate, lately deceased
(probably Bishop Law), the intimate friend of Dr. Jortin.   "And I cannot suffer
myself to doubt," continues the venerable writer, "that whenever the people of Great
Britain shall calmly weigh the reasons offered, they will be earnest to attain such an

" some alterations and improvements in the different editions of the Reformed Liturgy," which had hitherto met with the approbation of the Society; he had no doubt that the same approbation would be extended to the changes introduced into the present edition; the reasons for which he proceeds to state :

" The first omission is that of the Creed, concerning which I would observe to you that I had thought of leaving it out when our worship first began in this place; but it was retained at the suggestion of judicious friends, lest without further examination or inquiry we should on that account be represented as a society of mere Deists, and other Christians be deterred from uniting with us. But I persuade myself that it has been long seen that there are no grounds for such an imputation."

The author then proceeds to assign the following reasons for not continuing this Creed as a part of public worship. " 1. It was not written by the apostles, and therefore is of no authority. 2. It is very wrong and unwarrantable to put persons upon making a profession of their faith in assemblies for Christian worship. 3. No man, or number of men together, have any authority to make a creed for others. 4. The imposition of creeds in all ages has been the cause of great mischief and dissension,

important alteration in their public form of prayer, so easily accomplished : a circumstance fervently wished for by many of the clergy of the Church of England twenty years ago, when I ceased to be one of them, and now much longed for by many of its lay members."

May I be permitted to suggest, how much wiser it would be, in the present critical period, when the church is alarmed, and not without reason, at the rapid growth of Nonconformity in various shapes, instead of anxiously devising means to shore up a system of doctrine and worship, which no effort of human ingenuity can support in opposition to the liberal and inquisitive spirit of this enlightened period, to open the doors of the Established Church to learned and conscientious inquirers, by substituting the Scriptures in the place of the Articles, and reforming the Liturgy upon the plan of Dr. Clarke's, so as to contain nothing unscriptural, or offensive to the judicious and serious worshipper? The Church of England would then be built upon a rock, and might bid defiance to all assailants. Nor would it then exhibit the extraordinary phenomenon of the whole body of the clergy setting themselves in array against the laudable efforts of a humble individual for the instruction of the poor, assigning for their conduct this singular reason, that of a system which teaches the Scriptures only, without the aid of the Catechism and Liturgy, " the natural consequence must be to alienate the minds of the people from, or render them indifferent to," the " doctrine and discipline of the Established Church."—See the Preamble to the Catalogue of Subscribers to the National Society for the Education of the Poor, in the *Morning Chronicle* for Dec. 28, 1811.

and a constant snare to honest minds who are tied down to them.

"The other omission is in the beginning of the Litany, where the three invocations are changed into one. Many persons of high estimation for learning, judgment, and piety, favourers of Dr. Clarke's Liturgy, have always esteemed it a great oversight and blemish therein, that when that celebrated person rejected the Trinity from the Liturgy he should so far accommodate himself to the doctrine he exploded as to retain three different invocations in form, which carry to common heedless persons a sort of appearance of the Trinity."

The Liturgy thus amended was glady accepted by Mr. Lindsey's congregation, and continued to be used in the chapel till the year 1802, when it was superseded by a Liturgy drawn up and intro-duced by his successor, the Rev. Dr. John Disney. But though this Liturgy was judicious, unexceptionable, and, as many thought, in some respects an improvement upon the former, yet, from the modern style of the language, and other circumstances, and particularly from its wide deviation from the established Liturgy, it was not so acceptable to the congregation as that of the venerable founder of the society. And upon the choice of a successor to Dr. Disney, upon that gentleman's resignation in the year 1805, the general wish of the Trustees and the congrega-tion was expressed to resume Mr. Lindsey's Liturgy, which was accordingly acceded to ; and a few alterations, chiefly verbal, being made, to which that excellent person gave a cordial assent, a new edition was printed, a copy of which was locked up with the writings of the chapel, and a resolution passed that no further alterations should be made, nor any new form of worship be introduced, without the express consent of a majority of the Trustees.*

Mr. Lindsey having now completely made up his mind upon

---

* This cannot with justice be regarded as any infringement upon the rights of con-science ; for, as the Trustees have the disposal of the chapel property, they have a right to annex what terms they please to the grant, consistently with the tenor of the trust with which they are invested. And this condition was approved by the original grantor of the premises, Mr. Lindsey, who was then living.

the subject of his resignation, in the beginning of the summer addressed a circular letter to the Trustees, of which the following is an extract:

"Dear Sir,—I beg leave to address you in the capacity of a Trustee for the chapel in Essex Street, and to inform you of my intention of resigning my office of minister of it.

"My advanced age and growing infirmities have for some time intimated to me the rightness and necessity of this step; but as I was enabled to perform the service, I thought it my duty to accomplish two points previous to my retiring from my station."

The points to which the writer alludes, were a renewal of the Trust, and a complete repair of the whole premises, which had been done in the best manner possible. Having stated these circumstances for the information of the Trustees, Mr. Lindsey adds: "I have fixed the middle of July next for the time of my resignation; and I am happy in having a candidate as a successor in my colleague, Dr. Disney, whose zeal for the principle upon which the society was founded, and whose abilities, assiduity, and acceptableness to you and the congregation, in the discharge of his duty, have been for a long time ascertained."

In this simple and unostentatious manner did this pious veteran resign his connection with a congregation which he had served faithfully for nearly twenty years, during which period he had enjoyed the unintermitted veneration and attachment of every member of the society, both old and young, and had been witness to the progress of those principles, to the propagation of which his life had been devoted, and for the sake of which he had made the greatest sacrifices, to an extent far exceeding his most sanguine expectation, both in his own society and in the world, and in a great measure by means of his own labours and writings.

To Mr. Lindsey's letter of resignation, the Trustees of the chapel returned the following appropriate and respectful answer:

"The Trustees for the chapel in Essex Street, at this time in

London, having received a circular letter from the Reverend Mr.
Lindsey, declaring his intention to resign his office as minister
of that chapel on the fifteenth day of July next, resolve: That,
together with their sincere regret on the occasion, their very
affectionate acknowledgments, in the names of themselves and
the absent Trustees, be presented to him for the rare and noble
example which he gave to the professors of genuine Christianity, when he sacrificed the honours and emoluments of the
Established Church, in compliance with the dictates of his conscience; for his active zeal in the cause of truth, manifested by
the institution of the religious society in Essex Street; for the
able and distinterested services by which he has raised it to its
present state of prosperity; for the distinguished spirit of
benevolence and piety which hath uniformly marked his discharge of the duties of his office, and endeared him to all
under his pastoral care; and also for his attention to the future
prosperity of the institution, by introducing to the society his
worthy colleague, the Reverend Dr. Disney."

Upon this interesting occasion Mr. Lindsey composed a
judicious and suitable discourse, which, however, he would not
trust himself to deliver from the pulpit, finding himself, as he
expresses it, "too tenderly impressed with taking leave of so
many indulgent friends, to be capable of personally addressing
them with any tolerable degree of vigour."* This discourse,
therefore, was published and distributed among his friends,
and to the members of his congregation. In the exordium
he states, that "having now attained the term of life when
the human faculties naturally lose their vigour and decay, and
being in the twentieth year of his happy services as their minister,
it is now time to withdraw, and meet the unavoidable infirmities
of nature in a private station;" and having assigned his reasons

---

* In a letter to Dr. Toulmin, dated July 8, 1783, Mr. Lindsey thus expresses
himself: "I take my final leave of the pulpit in this chapel on Sunday next, in the
morning, and shall endeavour to say something suitable, though without any hint of
bidding farewell, which my own nerves would not bear; and many kind friends of
those who are not yet gone into the country say, that they must keep away from the
chapel if I do anything of this kind."

why he declined the pressing solicitations of many of his friends
to continue public services, with any additional assistance that
he might require, he takes for his text those words in the Lord's
Prayer, " Thy kingdom," or rather, " Thy reign come," professing
his ardent wish upon this occasion to impress his readers with a
sense of the importance of the principle by which we distinguish
ourselves from other Christians, and of the obligations which it
lays upon us to the practice of piety and all virtue.   In the
progress of his discourse, the pious and learned writer professes
to show that the gospel being from God, it must prevail ;—
that its success is to be gradual ;—that a principal obstacle
to the progress of the gospel is the making of Jesus Christ
the Supreme God, and worshipping him.   Here he introduces
a brief history of the long and lasting corruption of so fundamental a doctrine of the gospel as the Unity of God, and of its
revival after a seemingly total extinction of it; and shows that
this corrupt doctrine concerning Christ is the cause of atheism and
infidelity among Christians ; from which he infers that it is only
by the revival and spreading of the strict doctrine of the Divine
Unity that the kingdom of God, or the gospel of Christ, can
be fully established in the world :—and upon this the venerable
writer justly and forcibly remarks, that " it is not any religious
sentiment, any opinion of our own, which is frequently objected
to us, that excites our zeal.   In contending for the strict Unity
of God, and that Jesus, his messenger to us, was a man like
ourselves, we contend for the gospel itself, as in this enlightened
age serious and rational inquirers are not likely to be reconciled
to any other form of Christianity."*

* Under this head the venerable writer remarks, " You will perceive that your
duty to Christ and to truth requires you to do nothing whereby you may encourage such undue sentiments of him, especially not to frequent the worship of him as
God, when you are absolutely convinced that he is not entitled to such regards, and
expressly requires you to pay them to God only."
In a note, the author observes that " the apostle Paul, in his adjudication of a case
where any doubt remained upon the mind concerning the lawfulness of an action
has given it entirely against compliance.   Whatever is not of faith is of sin :'
Rom. xiv. 14, 22, 23.   He adds : " It must be owned, however, that there may be
peculiar situations in life, which may incline some to doubt whether greater good may
not accrue from an Unitarian Christian sometimes attending Trinitarian worship.   The

Having thus established the great importance of the Unitarian doctrine, this venerable apostle of primitive truth proceeds to state that holiness of life is indispensably necessary for promoting the success of the gospel; and especially " the most perfect benevolence towards all other Christians, and all men." He laments over the prevalence of an intolerant spirit among Christians in all ages, and particularly alludes to the disgraceful scenes which had been lately acted at Birmingham. " He flatters himself, notwithstanding, that this hostile, barbarous temper is by no means generally prevalent, but that a spirit of candour and gentle forbearance is gone forth and spreading itself silently through the nation;" of which, " the place of public worship in which we assemble is no small proof. Although it is founded upon the principle of the worship of the church established being directed to wrong objects, and such as we cannot conscientiously frequent, there is not perhaps a Christian society in this great city, for its numbers, more respectable or more respected than ours; and such it has been from the very first of its institution." The pious writer adds, what it is to be hoped that all his successors in office, and all who do now or who may hereafter join in the religious services of that society, of which he was the founder, will practically remember: " I have no doubt of our going on to be more and more respected, whilst we adhere to the just and liberal principle with which we first set out, and from which I have never knowingly deviated, viz. never to arraign or condemn other churches or Christian

instances can be but rare. But where this is done, the persons should act without disguise, and let their real sentiments be known—as in the remarkable case of the captain of the army of the King of Syria: 2 Kings v. 17. 18. The safe side, however, is to refrain entirely."

The question is indeed of very difficult solution. The case of Naaman, to which the writer alludes, will scarcely be allowed to have much weight in the decision. The Syrian courtier states his own purpose: and the prophet, having no authority over a heathen, dismisses him courteously. But this will by no means amount to a justification of a Unitarian joining habitually in Trinitarian worship. How far this may be lawful when no other worship is accessible, is a question of great nicety of which every one must form a judgment for himself; nor has any one a right to arraign the conduct of another. Happy is he who condemneth not himself in the thing which he alloweth.

societies, for their different worship or opinions, who have a right to judge for themselves as much as you have."

The conclusion is interesting and very appropriate. It is too long to be wholly transcribed, but it is hoped that no apology will be thought necessary for inserting a few extracts.

"And now, brethren, I bid you finally farewell. And having for many years earnestly desired and endeavoured, however weakly, to serve you in the gospel of our Lord Jesus Christ, and to promote your virtue and everlasting happiness, I commit you to God and his overruling providence; for, however diligently others may plant and water, the increase and the fruits are to be expected from him.

" I can never be sufficiently thankful to the bounty of Divine Providence in raising up a number of serious and generous friends, when alone, and destitute of all means to set on foot this place of worship, to concur in the design, and for all the support continued by them and others to the present day.

" Happy, thrice happy, if both they who have been called away before us, and we that are left, may be found worthy objects of the Divine mercy, and meet together at the resurrection of the last day, never to be separated more ! And as no energies in the cause of truth and virtue are lost, we may perhaps have the felicity to perceive that we, in our narrow spheres, have been honoured with being made instruments of good in the hands of our Maker. And particularly, that our humble and honest testimony against so early and lasting a corruption of the honour and worship due to him alone, had its beneficial effects in the great scheme of his providence, in bringing forward that more perfect state of things which we look for, when knowledge shall increase, and benevolence be universal."

Such were the pious and benevolent sentiments which this venerable teacher of truth and righteousness expressed and endeavoured to inculcate upon the minds of his congregation when he took his final leave of the pulpit, and closed those public and paternal addresses of which they had so often been the attentive and delighted hearers.

Some of Mr. Lindsey's friends who were witnesses to his almost unabated vigour, both of body and mind, could hardly excuse him for thus prematurely, as they thought, withdrawing himself from an office the duties of which he was so fully competent to discharge. But this resignation of his public ministry was no hasty step. It had long been a settled principle with Mr. Lindsey and his friend Dr. Priestley, and, to the best of the author's recollection, of their common friend Dr. Price, that at the age of seventy it was expedient for ministers to retire from public service, even though their faculties should appear to be in full vigour, and that they should not wait till resignation became necessary in consequence of bodily or of mental decay. After the age of threescore and ten, the faculties cannot long remain unimpaired, and the decline of physical or intellectual capacity is often more apparent to others than to a person himself. Often were they accustomed to speak with regret of ministers whose age and infirmities would have made retirement eligible, but who were necessitated to continue in office for the sake of a scanty subsistence; and still more did they deplore the case of those whose incapacity and incompetency to the duties of their office were obvious to every one but themselves. They disapproved the injudicious partiality of friends who were urging aged ministers to official duties to which their strength was not equal; and they highly applauded the discretion and firmness of those ministers who, like their late friend the learned Hugh Farmer, having once resigned the pulpit upon account of age and infirmity, resolutely declined, upon any consideration whatever, officiating again in public. Upon this principle Mr. Lindsey thought proper to act; and having, for reasons which he judged satisfactory, taken leave of his public charge, he took leave of it for ever, and could never be persuaded to ascend the pulpit again.*

* Upon this subject Mr. Lindsey thus expresses himself, in a letter to a friend, dated June 13, 1793: "I ought not to keep secret any longer from you what was known to one or two friends a year ago, and lately been signified to the Trustees of the chapel, that I intend very soon to resign my office of minister in it. On the first of July I enter into my seventieth year; and though I have cause of all thankfulness for the health and strength I enjoy, being able tolerably to go through the duty, yet I find infirmities coming, and have had some nervous spasms, particularly in my head, that have long

The venerable subject of this Memoir, though neither his judgment nor his inclination led him to take a prominent part in the politics of the time, was nevertheless a warm advocate for civil and religious liberty, and his generous feelings and principles upon this most interesting of all subjects he scorned to disguise. He sympathized deeply with those political characters who, whatever indiscretions some of them might be chargeable with, suffered from that which, in Mr. Lindsey's estimation, was the overstrained rigour of the law both in Scotland and England, penalties far beyond the demerit of any crime which could be proved against them. Among these sufferers, the person on whose behalf Mr. Lindsey was in the highest degree interested was the Reverend Thomas Fyshe Palmer, a gentleman descended from a respectable and opulent family in Bedfordshire, who, having been destined to take orders in the Established Church, had been educated at the University of Cambridge, and was a Fellow of Queen's College. This gentleman, in consequence of perusing the writings of Dr. Priestley and Mr. Lindsey, became a decided Unitarian ; and being a man of an ardent, active spirit, he devoted himself to the propagation of those principles which to him appeared scriptural and evangelical. In the year 1792, he was preacher of the Unitarian doctrine in Scotland, where his official labours were chiefly employed in the town of Dundee, in which a considerable society of Unitarian worshippers had been formed by the united exertions of himself, Messrs. Christie, Millar, and other respectable

satisfied me that it is right to retire with a good grace. I have recommended my worthy colleague, and he will certainly be chosen to succeed me. But we shall continue to live on in our present situation. For the whole premises being purchased, and the chapel, &c., built by money collected by me from various friends, with not less than five hundred pounds of our own, and the accommodations, &c., being much owing to my wife's attention, skill, and daily superintendence, when I gave up the fee of the whole, which was vested in me, and made choice of the Trustees in the trust-deed, which perpetuates the premises for the proper uses, they settled the house rent-free to my wife 'or her life.'

To the same purpose Mr. Lindsey writes to another friend, September 9, 1793 : " We shall still continue to reside in the house in Essex Street ; for the Trustees of the chapel would not appoint a successor, but under the limitation of my enjoying the house, &c.. for life, as was appointed in the original trust-deed for my wife if I had died the minister and she had survived me. This was thought reasonable, as by collections from our friends, with no small sum of our own, we had purchased, built, and furnishe the premises."

inhabitants. Mr. Fyshe Palmer was a man of excellent under-standing, unimpeachable morals, and of great simplicity of character; and being a zealous friend to liberty, and upon all occasions ardent, he, perhaps inconsiderately, was concerned in the republication of an Address to the People of Scotland concerning the Reform of Parliament, for which, in the autumn of 1793, he was tried by the Circuit Court of Justiciary; and being convicted, a sentence of banishment was passed upon him, which was inter-preted and executed as a sentence of transportation for seven years to Botany Bay. After this inhuman sentence, Mr. Palmer experienced very rigorous treatment. He was confined for some weeks in the common gaol of Perth, from which, without any previous notice, he was hurried away at four o'clock in the morn-ing, in the month of November, and taken on board a cutter, which brought him to London, where he and Mr. Muir, a gentle-man of the Faculty of Advocates in Scotland (who, for a similar offence, had been subjected to a still severer sentence), were for some time lodged in Newgate, and were afterwards confined in the hulks at Woolwich, where they were treated by the governor with much humanity, and were allowed all the accommodations which their situation would admit.* They were permitted to see their

* "Mr. Muir and Mr. Palmer," says Mr. Lindsey, in a letter to Dr. Toulmin, dated December 14, 1793, "are on board the hulks with the felons, and many of my friends have been to see them. I also hear from Mr. Palmer, and have sent him some books. Neither of them, I believe, is in want of anything, the place considered. But the situa-tion is, upon the whole, horrible. Mr. Palmer, however, is most cheerful in the midst of it, and Mr. Muir not otherwise." In another letter to the same friend, dated January 10, 1794, Mr. Lindsey writes: "Since I last wrote, opinions have varied about the destiny of Mr. Palmer and Mr. Muir, as the Scotch judges have, upon revisal, adhered to the sentence pronounced upon them. Mr. Palmer's health and spirits are most cheerful; Mr. Muir far from well in health since the cold weather set in; both of them supported by their integrity and future hopes. Some friends who visited the hulks on Wednesday had a commission from some others to offer a purse to Mr. Palmer and Mr. Muir. The former declined taking anything, but Mr. Muir thankfully accepted it." Mr. Palmer afterwards saw reason to alter his mind, and accepted the proffered kindness of his friends. In a subsequent letter, Mr. Lindsey informs his friend that the amount of the contribution was between five and six hundred pounds, and that it was vested in the hands of a committee of seven for the benefit of Messrs. Palmer, Muir, Skirving, and even Margarot, "who, as a joint sufferer, was not to be overlooked, though his general character was not so high as the others." How true this observation of Mr. Lindsey's was, and how justly this person was entitled to participate in the bounty of Mr. Palmer's friends, those who were witnesses to his conduct to that gentleman on board the transport in the passage to South Wales could properly appreciate.

friends. Here they were visited by Mr. Lindsey and Dr. Priestley, and by many other virtuous friends of liberty and reform, who contributed by their sympathy to alleviate their sufferings, and who, with others, raised a very handsome subscription to provide necessaries for their voyage and requisites to their future establish-ment when they had reached the place of their destination. The extreme inhumanity of the sentence passed upon these reformers, and the unparalleled severity of the penalty annexed by the barbarous law of North Britain to an offence which, if proved to its utmost extent, was punishable in the South only by a few months' imprisonment, considered in connection with the excellent characters of the defendants, who could not in reason be regarded as capable of intentionally involving the country in confusion and anarchy, excited general indignation and horror; and that not only in England, but in foreign countries.

"The trial of the Scottish advocate, T. Muir," says a respect-able writer in the *Altona Journal*, A.D. 1794, "who, for various endeavours to effect a reform of the Parliament of his country, was condemned to be transported to Botany Bay, must excite in the breast of every German an esteem for his native land. We here see a man sent to Botany Bay on account of an accusation to which a German court of justice would have been ashamed to listen."

The legality of the sentence was called in question by many distinguished advocates at the Scotch bar; the punishment for leasing-making, *i.e.* libelling, being expressed by the word *banish-ment* in the Scotch statute, not transportation to another country. Upon this ground, when Parliament was assembled in the begin-ning of 1794, various motions were introduced by an honourable member eminently learned in Scotch jurisprudence, William Adam, Esq., with a view to a revision of the Scottish law relating to sedition; to an inquiry into the legality of the sentence; and, finally, to the regulations of the Justiciary Courts of Scotland. These motions were overruled; but from the interest which many persons of great weight and influence in the country appeared to take in the fate of the prisoners, the sufferers and their friends fondly flattered themselves with the hope that the punishment would be mitigated.* But the Administration of that day had determined upon ruling by a system of terror, unprecedented since the accession of the House of Brunswick: and while the conduct of the Scottish courts of justice was under discussion in Parliament, in the month of March, 1794, these two upright and respectable sufferers, and others in the same predicament, were hurried on board the Surprise, a Government transport, and despatched to Botany Bay, among a crowd of felons of various descriptions, who were for their crimes condemned to the same punishment.† The treatment of Mr. Fyshe Palmer on board this ship was so gross and

---

* "The sentence against Mr. Muir and Mr. Palmer," says Mr. Lindsey in his letter to Dr. Toulmin, dated February 20th, "is so unjust, that I can hardly persuade myself still that it will be executed, at least till their case has undergone the intended parliamentary discussion. My friends say this is hoping against hope. At present they are at Portsmouth, and it is said are to remain there a fortnight." In a letter dated March 8th, Mr. Lindsey writes: "I hear that Mr. Palmer was not quite so well at Portsmouth on board the ship, and that their fare and accommodations were not such as were expected. However, some of my friends still flatter me with hope that Government will not take such a bold step as to send these men away whilst the legality of their sentence is questioned, and its discussion pending in the national legislature." These flattering hopes, however, proved abortive. And in a letter to the same friend, dated May 3, 1794, Mr. Lindsey states, that they had then actually set sail, and taken leave of their native country, never, alas! to return again. "A letter from Mr. Scott this day mentions the whole fleet being at length out of sight yesterday morning, with a very fair wind down the channel; and whatever some intend, I trust a good Providence carries some to Botany Bay for most important purposes of human virtue and happiness."

The correspondent from whom Mr. Lindsey received this intelligence was the Reverend Russell Scott, of Portsmouth, a gentleman of most active benevolence, who was indefatigable in offices of kindness to these persecuted reformers while the ship which conveyed them remained at Spithead. "Mr. Scott cannot enough be commended," says Mr. Lindsey to Dr. Toulmin, "for his exertions to serve those worthy martyrs, and to see them accommodated with everything needful."

† "The case of men of education and reflection," says Dr. Priestley, "and who act from the best intentions with respect to the community, committing only what state policy requires to be considered as crimes, but which are allowed on all hands to imply no moral turpitude so as to render them unfit for heaven and happiness hereafter, is not to be confounded with that of common felons. There was nothing in the conduct of Louis XIV. and his ministers that appeared so shocking, so contrary to all ideas of justice, humanity, and decency, and that contributed more to render their memory execrated, than sending such men as Mr. Marolles, and other eminent Protestants, who are now revered as saints and martyrs, to the galleys, along with the vilest miscreants. Compared with this, the punishment of death would be mercy. I trust that, in time, the Scots in general will think these measures a disgrace to their country."—Dr. Priestley's Fast Serm., 1794. Pref. p. xviii. note.

inhuman, as to excite a suspicion that it was never intended that he should reach the place of their destination alive; nor would it have been possible for him to have survived the hardships he endured, had it not been for the humane attentions of James Ellis, a young person who, from affection and sympathy, volunteered his services to Mr. Palmer, and accompanied him to the colony as a free settler. Mr. Palmer's own affecting narrative of the barbarous severities which he encountered on his passage, is contained in a letter to Mr. Lindsey, immediately after his arrival in New South Wales, and is inserted in the Appendix.*

This excellent man lived to complete the period assigned by his sentence for his banishment in this dreary country, enduring many hardships, but highly respected by all who were themselves respectable in this motley community. When the term limited for his residence was expired, he, and the faithful companion of his fortunes, James Ellis, fitted out a small ship to convey them to England, meaning in their way to carry on some advantageous traffic in the islands of the Southern ocean; but their little barque was not equal to the undertaking, and in a gale of wind it was wrecked upon the coast of Golam, one of the Ladrone islands belonging to Spain, with which this country was then at war. The Spanish governor made prisoners of the ship's crew, and during his imprisonment Mr. Fyshe Palmer fell a victim to a fever.

Mr. Lindsey interested himself very feelingly in behalf of many

---

* See Appendix, No. XI. In order to justify the severities used to Mr. Palmer, and even the infliction of capital punishment if that had been resorted to, the most infamous calumnies were industriously circulated against that virtuous sufferer, viz. that he was exciting the felons to seize the ship and to take it to America; a report which, for a time, gained too easy credit, but which, as it afterwards appeared, had not the least foundation in truth. "Serious apprehensions," says Mr. Lindsey in a letter to Dr. Toulmin, dated November 8, "are entertained by Mr. Palmer and Mr. Skirving's friends—I am concerned to mention it—that they have been engaged in some mutinous intention of rising and seizing the ship on their parting from the grand fleet, and going off to America; I wish there may be no truth in this report." In a succeeding letter, dated December 15, Mr. Lindsey expresses his conviction that these worthy men were wrongfully accused. "There is reason to believe that there have been disturbances on board the Surprise, and that Messrs. Palmer and Skirving have been very injuriously accused, as principally concerned in fomenting of them.

other respectable characters, who at this period suffered by the
harsh measures of Mr. Pitt's Administration. The Reverend
William Winterbotham, minister of a Calvinistic congregation at
Plymouth Dock, was accused of uttering seditious language in
two discourses which he delivered from the pulpit; and upon the
slightest evidence, such was the ferment of the times, he was
found guilty, and sentenced to four years' imprisonment in
Newgate. "I have not read Mr. Winterbotham's trial," says Mr.
Lindsey, in a letter to Dr. Toulmin, dated February 8, 1794,
"but lawyers, and others whom I have seen, declare that there
never was a more iniquitous verdict." It reminded many of the
conviction of Mr. Rosewell, a Presbyterian minister in the reign
of Charles II., for treasonable words uttered in the pulpit,
upon the evidence of two notorious prostitutes; concerning
which, a noble lord who had attended the trial, immediately
reported to the King at the levee, that he had just seen one of
His Majesty's subjects, a man of learning and piety, convicted
of high treason upon evidence on which he would not hang a
dog. And when Jefferies came in soon afterwards, and bragged
to the King of the feat which he had performed in inducing the
jury to convict Rosewell, the King ordered him to arrest the
judgment, and the prisoner was soon afterwards set at liberty.
It was hoped by the friends of liberty and justice, that a sentence
so glaringly outraging every feeling of equity and humanity
as that passed upon Mr. Winterbotham, would not have been
carried into execution. But the Administration were inexorable;
not a single day of confinement was remitted; and the innocent
sufferer was compelled to drink the cup of bitterness to the very
dregs. During his confinement he was visited occasionally by
Mr. Lindsey, who, by his kind sympathy, and by his own great
liberality, and his influence with his good and generous friends,
and particularly the excellent Mrs. Rayner, contributed very
materially to the mitigation of Mr. Winterbotham's sufferings.*

* The following extract from a letter of Mr. Winterbotham's, dated Plymouth, August
31, 1802, will show the grateful sense which that gentleman entertained of the kindness of Mr. Lindsey and his other benefactors:
"Reverend and Dear Sir,—Although I am far separated from you, and possess but

CHAPTER XIII.

DR. PRIESTLEY EMIGRATES TO AMERICA. HIS REASONS FOR
THIS MEASURE. MR. LINDSEY'S JUDGMENT IN THE CASE.
DR. PRIESTLEY'S FAREWELL SERMON AT HACKNEY. LETTERS
TO MR. LINDSEY FROM GRAVESEND, DEAL, AND FALMOUTH.
ARRIVES AT NEW YORK. HIS RECEPTION IN AMERICA.

THE time was now arrived in which the venerable subject of
this Memoir was destined to experience the severest privation
which had ever yet fallen to his lot, by the emigration of the
approved friend of his heart, his fellow-labourer and fellow-sufferer
in the cause of divine truth, Dr. Priestley, to America. This
memorable event took place in the spring of 1794. In the
preface to his Fast Sermon preached in February that year,

few opportunities of intercourse with you, yet my heart ever contemplates you with
affection and gratitude ; nor, indeed, can it be otherwise : for while I feel myself
surrounded with comforts, I cannot, I trust, ever forget the man to whose kindness so
many of them are owing. Indeed, my dear sir, your name, and that of dear Mrs.
Rayner, borne by my two eldest boys, has added pleasure even to the sensations they
naturally inspire, and a parent's heart has dared to indulge the hope that they may
one day imitate the virtues of those after whom they have been called.

"Permit me here to thank you also for the present of your last publication. I have
perused it with pleasure and profit, although every sentiment therein may not accord
with my own. And I feel thankful to the Father of Mercy, who thus kindly continues
to you the faculties of the mind so entire, while your advanced period of life forbids the
more active labours of the house of God.

"Whatever differences of opinion may exist between us on religious subjects, I hope
and trust that I shall be enabled to imitate that sincerity of soul of which you have
given me and the world so bright an example. My heart, I can truly say, is alive to
the duties and the importance of Christianity, and I trust that I am not altogether a
stranger to its pleasures. I continue my public labours, and my aim amidst my little
flock has been to cultivate that mind that was in Christ Jesus, and to promote those
dispositions which render obedience to the divine will delightful. I do not labour in
vain, although my success is not adequate to my wishes.

"I trust I shall yet have an opportunity of seeing you in the flesh : but if this
favour is denied, I will cherish and indulge the pleasing hope of meeting you in the world
of spirits, and enjoying your friendship in a state of immortality through the ages of an
eternal world."

It is to be remembered that Mr. Winterbotham is a minister of the Calvinistic
persuasion. The letter does great credit to the head and to the heart of the writer ; it
shows that the spirit of Christianity is not limited to any sect or party of Christians.

Dr. Priestley states the reasons which induced him to leave his country: the principal of which were, the removal of his sons, the transfer of the greater part of his property to America, and the apprehended insecurity of his own person in consequence of the rancorous spirit of the times, and the violent measures of the Administration. Dr. Priestley naturally enough concluded that the same bitter and tyrannical spirit which dictated or enforced the cruel and unjust sentences upon Muir, Palmer, and Winterbotham, and especially the latter, who was convicted upon evidence the most suspicious, of an offence of which no reasonable person could believe him guilty, and condemned to four years' confinement in Newgate, might, upon a similar pretext, which could never be wanting if it was sought for, deprive him of his liberty, or expose him to political persecution. It is not, indeed, probable that the Government of the country, who knew his innocence, ever meant to disgrace itself by the direct prosecution of the most enlightened and most virtuous of its philosophers. It was sufficient for them that a hireling crew had raised against him a popular hue and cry; and it cannot be doubted that the men then in power would have been better pleased if, after having been burned out of his house by a hired mob of ruffians at Birmingham, he had fled the kingdom, instead of finding an honourable asylum at Hackney. Warned, however, by the terrible example of 1780, and even by that of the late riots at Birmingham, there is no reason to believe that they would have encouraged a mob in the vicinity of the metropolis to have pulled down Dr. Priestley's house a second time. And in fact, though the venerable sufferer met with a few personal insults at his first settlement at Clapton from some of the lowest of the rabble, that spirit had entirely subsided; and had he chosen to have remained at Hackney, it cannot be doubted that he would have lived in equal security and tranquillity with the rest of his fellow-citizens; admired, beloved, and revered, by a numerous, respectable, and continually increasing circle of hearers, pupils, and friends. But the high spirit of Dr. Priestley could not brook to hold his liberty and security upon what appeared to him to be so precarious a tenure; and he therefore resolved to seek an asylum in a country where, if civilization has not attained to so high a polish as in older countries, thoughts, and words, and consciences are free; and no restraint is laid upon freedom of inquiry, latitude of disquisition, or openness of profession upon the most important subjects of religion or politics. It was not, however, without much regret that this much-injured man bid adieu to his native country, nor without indulging the fond hope that he might eventually return and end his days in peace in the land which gave him birth. But the circumstance which most touched his feelings was the loss of the society of his old, tried, and beloved friend, Mr. Lindsey, "in whose absence," says he, "I shall for some time at least find all the world a blank." *

But though many of Dr. Priestley's friends, those especially who resided in the vicinity of Hackney, and who were naturally

* The concluding paragraph of this interesting preface is so truly characteristic of Dr. Priestley's amiable, affectionate, and ingenuous mind, that I trust I shall be excused for inserting it here.

"The sentence of Mr. Winterbotham for delivering from the pulpit what I am persuaded he never did deliver, and which similar evidence might have drawn upon myself, or any other Dissenting minister who was an object of general dislike, has something in it still more alarming. But I trust that conscious innocence would support me, as it does him, under whatever prejudiced or violent men might do to me, as well as say of me. But I see no occasion to expose myself to danger without any prospect of doing good, or to continue any longer in a country in which I am so unjustly become the object of general dislike, and not retire to another where I have reason to think I shall be better received. And I trust that the same good providence which has attended me hitherto and made me happy in my present situation, and all my former ones, will attend and bless me in what may still lie before me. In all events the will of God be done!

"I cannot refrain from repeating again, that I leave my native country with real regret, never expecting to find anywhere else society so suited to my disposition and habits; such friends as I have here, whose attachment has been more than a balance to all the abuse I have met with from others; and especially to replace one particular Christian friend, in whose absence I shall, for some time at least, find all the world a blank. Still less can I expect to resume my favourite pursuits with anything like the advantages I enjoy here. In leaving this country I also abandon a source of maintenance which I can but ill bear to lose. I can, however, truly say, that I leave it without any resentment or ill-will. On the contrary, I sincerely wish my countrymen all happiness; and when the time for reflection, which my absence may accelerate, shall come, my countrymen I am confident will do me more justice. They will be convinced that every suspicion which they have been led to entertain to my disadvantage has been ill-founded, and that I have even some claims to their gratitude and esteem. In this case I shall look with satisfaction to the time when, if my life be prolonged, I may visit my friends in this country; and perhaps I may, notwithstanding my removal for the present, find a grave, as I believe is naturally the wish of every man, in the land that gave me birth."

most anxious to retain him in the country, allowed perhaps too little weight to the arguments for emigration; there were others, possibly equally well informed, and certainly not less interested in the result of his deliberation, who thought him fully justified in the resolution which he adopted of abandoning, at least for the present, a country which no longer knew how to appreciate his transcendent merits, and in which his property, and even his person, was believed to be no longer safe. In the number of these was the venerable subject of this Memoir, to whom the emigration of Dr. Priestley must have been a most afflicting event. He thus expresses himself upon the subject in a letter to Dr. Toulmin, dated January 10, 1794, before Dr. Priestley had made up his mind to leave the country :—

"We have seen Dr. Priestley very frequently of late, as also Mrs. Priestley, and they are both very well. If his sons do well in America, I have no doubt of his following them, but do not apprehend that he will remove thither at any time but upon some opening or prospect of being provided for, so as to be useful in his own way as a teacher of philosophy. He is now preaching at Hackney a course of lectures on the Evidences of the Mosaic and Christian Revelations, which he intends afterwards to print; and which, from what I have seen of the former, will be most useful and highly seasonable at a period when many in this country, and the greater part upon the continent, count all revealed religion as a fable, which might be well intended at first, but has proved most destructive to the morals and happiness of mankind."

In his next letter to the same friend, dated February 8, 1794, he thus communicates the intelligence of Dr. Priestley's final resolution :—" I return your son's two letters, which I like much, as everything which comes from him.* They show a good mind,

---

* The Reverend Henry Toulmin, who was settled with a large and respectable congregation in Lancashire. This gentleman, when a violent spirit, not discountenanced by the Administration of the day, broke out against the Dissenters, and particularly the rational Dissenters, soon after the riots at Birmingham, emigrated with his family to America, and after some time settled at Kentucky, where he was appointed to the high office of Secretary of State, with a salary of about eighty pounds a year; but this being

sensible, active, and ever attentive to the proper business of his journeyings. At Dr. Priestley's request, I let him take them home with him a day or two since to show to Mrs. Priestley, as they are every day more and more interested in what relates to America; and I now believe, in the course of not many months, will both of them remove thither. This full decision I have come to the knowledge of since I last wrote, though I have for some time suspected it. It will cut off a great source of the highest satisfaction to me, amongst many others. But I hope it will be for his greater good and contentment upon the whole, as his family have gone before him; and I have for some time thought that his chief business was done here, and we were no longer worthy of him, and that he may be of eminent service to that other country, retaining still in great vigour his powers of body and mind; and there can be no doubt of the intimate friend of Franklin's being there well received."

In this manly way does Mr. Lindsey express his approbation of his friend's emigration, though mixed with deep regret. In the following extract of a letter to Dr. Toulmin, dated February 20, it appears that other intimate and judicious friends of Dr. Priestley entertained similar sentiments: "The Doctor has received letters which are very encouraging. The family of V—— here, who have two sons (that were both the Doctor's pupils) in America, one well settled in Philadelphia, the other in Kennebec, but who is part of the year at Boston, all advise and rather press him to

thought too extravagant, it was reduced to fifty. The Governor of the State was Mr. Toulmin's friend. He had been a Baptist minister, and a colonel in the army. His revenues were in proportion to those of the Secretary. The fact is that he was a man of a liberal and enlightened mind; and while he continued at the head of the Government, he and his Secretary introduced many wise and salutary regulations, and contributed to the utmost of their power to establish order and tranquillity in a state of society which was but a few degrees removed from a state of nature and barbarism. But their patriotic Administration was not permitted to continue long. After a few years, in consequence of one of those political revolutions to which empires are liable, another party gained the ascendency,—the Administration was changed, and the Governor and Secretary retired to private stations. The President of the United States, however, Mr. Jefferson, to whom the abilities and merits of Mr. Toulmin were well known, soon afterwards appointed him to the office of Judge in a district of the United States upon the river Mobille, which he now fills with great reputation to himself and advantage to the community.

go, though greatly grieved to lose him hence. As to the Doctor, his purpose is certainly fixed to leave England towards April, and he is making preparations for the purpose."

In a letter to the same correspondent, dated March 8, Mr. Lindsey states: "You will be pleased to know that our friend, though we cannot think of losing him without deep concern, has taken places for himself, Mrs. Priestley, and two servants, in the Sansom, which is to be ready to sail the latter end of this or the very beginning of next month. Happily, the other persons, all of them emigrants, who are going in the same ship, are known to him or his friends."

On the 21st of February, 1794, Dr. Priestley sent in his letter of resignation to the congregation at Hackney, to which, after some time, when they found all efforts to induce him to remain with them unavailing and hopeless, they returned an answer expressive of their veneration and gratitude for his person and his labours, their poignant regret at the dissolution of the connection, and their affectionate good wishes for his future welfare. On the 30th of March, he delivered to a crowded auditory a farewell discourse from Acts xx. 32. The subject of it was the "Use of Christianity, especially in Difficult Times." It begins with stating "the great design of the gospel to raise the sons of men to the high character and honour of sons of God, and make them heirs of a happy immortality;" it represents "the situation of Dissenters, and especially of Unitarian Dissenters, at that time, as calling in a particular manner for the exercise of Christian principles; and that the insult and outrage to which they were then exposed, though not to be desired, was most favourable to the cultivation of that temper of mind which is most eminently Christian, to the virtues of patience, fortitude, forgiveness, and heavenly-mindedness." The preacher then shows how much superior these virtues are to that courage and zeal which is so generally applauded in heroes and martyrs, and of how much more difficult attainment; and in the true spirit of Christian philosophy he remarks, that "we shall be the less disturbed at the malignity of others when we consider that our enemies, as well as our friends, are acting the

R 2

part assigned them by the Supreme Ruler of the universe; that they are in their proper place as well as we in ours, though, being instigated by their own bad dispositions, this is no apology for their conduct; and that the plan of the great drama in which we are all actors is so arranged that good will finally result from the evil which we experience in ourselves or see in others." He adds, that "all the opposition we meet with makes part of the useful and necessary discipline of life, and no great character could be formed, or any great good be done, without it;—our Saviour, the apostles, the reformers from popery, the Puritans, and Nonconformists, were equally exposed to it. And shall we complain? We must not forget that it is only by discipline, and often very severe discipline too, that great and excellent characters are ever formed; and there is a source of satisfaction, even in adversity, or nearly connected with it, that persons in prosperity and affluence have no idea of."

In proof of this observation, he cites his own example: " Of this I am myself not without some experience. My violent expulsion from a favourite situation at Birmingham was to appearance sufficiently disastrous; and I was not without feeling it to be so. Yet I have had more than a recompence, internal and external, so as to make me consider it even now as no evil upon the whole; and I am far from wishing, if it were possible, that it might not have happened." The preacher then proceeds to show " that a state of suffering is a state of usefulness, no less than one of most active exertion." Also, that "such a state of persecution as that to which *we* are exposed will tend to purge our societies of lukewarm and unworthy members; of men who prefer the world and the things of it to the cause of truth and a good conscience—and such are many of the richer sort among us and in all societies— men who, by associating with other rich and worldly-minded men, and especially those who are within the influence of a court and the honours and emoluments derived from it, catch too much of their spirit, become assimilated to their manners, and adopt their views. Let all such go to their proper place ;— we want them not; —we want not even their wealth. True Christianity does not sup-

pose nor require it. But in all cases of persecution, some of the
most wealthy have proved the most zealous." It is further remarked that " true Christians, devoid of superstition, will meet for
public worship and edify one another, even without the aid or
expense of regular ministers;—in situations in which ministers
cannot be had, Christian laymen will, I hope, have the good sense
to do themselves everything which has been usually done by their
ministers; and this excellent lesson will be taught more effectually
in a season of adversity than of prosperity." "It is our pride
that, as Unitarians, our religion has been so far from being
befriended, that it has in all ages been frowned upon by the civil
magistrate; and yet in these seemingly unfavourable circumstances it has constantly gained ground." As an evidence of
their having imbibed the true spirit of Christianity, the preacher
recommends that his hearers should "exert themselves in their
several spheres to extend the knowledge of 'it to others, and not to
imagine that this is the business of ministers only. Gladly," continues he, " would unbelievers have it to say that all men of sense
are with them. On the contrary, I am confident that men of real
knowledge and reflection, as well as men of virtue and integrity—
men who have given the most serious attention to the subject, and
men of the most upright and unbiassed minds—are with us. But
to recommend Christianity to men of reason and reflection, it
must be made to appear a rational thing. Men cannot embrace
as sacred truths anything at which their common sense revolts."
Hence he infers that it is our duty, "if we have any real value for
Christianity, to exert ourselves to free it from those great incumbrances which have already done it the greatest injury, and have
endangered its very existence." He congratulates the congregation
upon its honourable denomination of an Unitarian society, and
augurs the happiest effects from the public avowal of their Christian principles. "The opinions," says he, "of single persons are
often overlooked or disregarded, but a Christian church is a city
set on a hill that cannot be hid."

And the congregation having, chiefly upon his recommendation,
chosen as his successor the writer of this Memoir, the preacher

is pleased to say, "I cannot conclude this discourse without expressing my satisfaction in your choice of my successor:" and after expressing, in language which it does not become the writer to repeat, his persuasion that this successor would carry on plans of instruction, public and private, on the same principles with himself, he adds, "By making choice of such a person, you have greatly lessened the pain that I shall feel from our separation. It will appear to me that I am still with you in his person. May the connection be long and happy!"

Having thus finished what he had to say to his regular audience, he closes his discourse with addressing a few hints of advice to the numerous strangers which thronged to hear him upon this interesting occasion. The introduction to this address is most judicious and conciliatory. "Most of you, I presume, are come hither from an innocent curiosity to see and hear a person of whom you have heard much evil, and perhaps some good, and whom you do not expect to hear or see any more. Others, though I hope not many, may have come for some less innocent purpose. These, let them have come whenever they please, must have found themselves disappointed, and I hope agreeably so; as, instead of finding any occasion of harm to me, they may have found some good to themselves. Nothing else can they have heard here; nothing but what is calculated to confirm the faith of all Christians, and to inculcate those sentiments of the heart, and that conduct in life, which are the proper fruits of that faith." The preacher having said a few words to justify his doctrine, though deemed heretical, defends it briefly from the charge of sedition. "Nothing," says he, "that can by any construction be supposed to have that tendency has ever been delivered from this pulpit, unless it be sedition to teach what the Apostles taught before, viz. that we are to obey God rather than man; and that in what relates to religion and conscience, we disclaim all human authority, even that of king, lords, and commons. In these things we acknowledge only one Father, even God, and one master, even Christ, the messenger or ambassador of God. If any doctrine be really false, being contrary to reason and the Scriptures, it is not an Act of

Parliament that can make it true. Or, if any action be morally wrong, as being contrary to natural justice and equity, it is not an Act of Parliament that can make it be right. But while we thus 'render to God the things that are God's,' we render to Cæsar the things that are Cæsar's. We are subject to every civil 'ordinance of man for the Lord's sake,' though not their ordinances relating to religion. Learn, then, not to give ear to mere calumny. As to us, I trust that we have learned of Christ to bless them that curse us, and to pray for them that despitefully use and persecute us."

The peroration is beautiful and appropriate, and strongly indicates the truly Christian spirit of the venerable fugitive: "Whether, then, you come as friends or as enemies, whether we shall ever see one another's faces again or not, may God, whose providence is over all, bless, preserve, and keep us! Above all, may we be preserved in the paths of virtue and piety, that we may have a happy meeting in that world where error and prejudice will be no more, where all the ground of the party distinctions which subsist here will be taken away; where every misunderstanding will be cleared up, and the reign of truth and of virtue will be for ever established!"

Such was the posture of mind, such the dignity of spirit, of this first of philosphers and of Christians, when taking leave of a country whose reputation he had extended, and to whose intellectual and moral improvement he had devoted his superior energies; but which, too little sensible of his pre-eminent worth, treated him with neglect, and refused redress to his cruel and unmerited injuries; and if she did not absolutely banish from her shores the worthiest of her sons, she at least appeared to withhold from him that protection which he thought essential to his security, and to the peaceable and successful pursuit of his professional duties and his philosophical inquiries. But the spirit of Christianity carried him through all; and Dr. Priestley, in the possession of a good conscience, and in the exercise of the mild, forbearing, forgiving spirit of the gospel, was more truly happy in his mind, and more enviable in his exile, than the most

violent of his enemies and persecutors, on their couches of preferment, or their thrones of state.*

The following Sunday, April 6, Dr. Priestley passed with his
friends in Essex Street, whose faces he was never more to behold
again in this world. Dr. Toulmin that day preached for Dr.
Disney a judicious, seasonable, and affecting discourse, which
made a very deep impression upon a respectable and numerous
audience. The next day Dr. Priestley and his family went to
Gravesend, from which place he addressed the following short
letter to his venerable friend:

"Dear Friend,—We were rather unexpectedly summoned by
the captain to be with him here at two in the afternoon yesterday;
and here we met him and all the company, expecting to sail that
evening. However, we are now actually about to take a boat
and go to the ship, which lies at the Hope, about six miles

---

* After Dr. Priestley had given notice of his intention to leave the country, the
writer of this Memoir had frequent opportunities of accompanying him in his walks to
visit and to take leave of his friends. The conversation upon these occasions usually
turned upon some interesting subjects. Upon one occasion the topic of discussion was
the second advent of Christ : and Dr. Priestley, who had studied the Apocalypse with
great attention, inferred, from the state of the world, compared with the language of
prophecy, that the second personal appearance of Christ was very near at hand.
"You," says he, "may probably live to see it; I shall not. It cannot, I think, be
more than twenty years." Of these twenty years, eighteen are now (1812) elapsed,
and the signs of Christ's appearance are not more perceptible now than they were
twenty years before; and he must be a sturdy believer who now expects the visible
appearance of Christ to restore the Jews to their country, and to assume the government
of the world within two years. Mr. Evanson, who did not in all points coincide with
Dr. Priestley, agreed with him in expecting the early personal appearance and reign
of Christ. But this interpretation, with greater prudence, postponed the event for sixty
years. I have not, however, heard that either of these gentlemen was quite so unreasonable
and inconsistent as the celebrated W. Whiston, who having foretold that the world would
come to an end in twenty years, asked thirty years' purchase for a small estate which he
had to sell. I mention these facts to show how grievously the most enlightened minds
may err when they attempt to apply the language of prophecy to passing events, and to
become prophets themselves, instead of waiting till time unfolds the mysterious volume
of divine dispensations, and points out the true sense of the prophetic vision. Joseph
Mede himself is a memorable instance of the egregious mistakes into which learned
and inquisitive men are liable to fall upon this subject ; who, having supplied the best
key to the mysteries of the Apocalypse, and given the most rational solution of the
symbols which are supposed to refer to events which had long been past, interprets two
of the symbols as relating to the defeat of the Spanish Armada, and to the wars in
Germany against the House of Austria ; events which, however important to the
British nation, make little figure in the history of the world, and are far beneath the
dignity of prophetic notice.

below this place. We spent an agreeable evening, all things considered; Mr. Russell and Mr. Vaughan being of the party. The morning is fine, but the wind still west. When we get to the Downs it is to be determined whether we go north round Scotland or through the Channel. The Pigou sails at the same time; and we hope to keep company.

"Poor Sally (Mrs. Finch, his only daughter) is most affected, as Mr. F. seems more determined than ever not to follow us; but she hopes that circumstances may arise which will change his resolution. However, that resolution will be guided by a will wiser than his or ours; and this is my greatest consolation, especially in parting with you and Mrs. Lindsey.

"Trusting to Mr. J., who said he would take my thermometer to Gravesend himself, I shall be obliged to go without it. I wish, however, you would see him, and desire him to send it by Johnson's package, if it will bear that conveyance. Take also any number you please of any of my publications, and dispose of them as you think proper.

"I will write again from Deal, where the pilot leaves us. Yours and Mrs. Lindsey's most affectionately,   "J. PRIESTLEY."
" Gravesend, April 8, 1794.

The next day, April 9, Dr. Priestley wrote to Mr. Lindsey, as he promised, from Deal.

" Dear Friend,—This, I hope, will be the last time I shall write to you from Old England. Yesterday we had a fair wind to carry us off Margate. We lay-to the greatest part of the night, when a fair wind sprung up, to carry us, they say, within an hour of Deal, by half-past eight, which it now is. Most of the passengers yesterday were ill; my wife most of the day; and I did not wholly escape, though I am better than most of them. To-day we seem to be all pretty well, just ready for breakfast.

" The cabin passengers are only nine, and promise to be sufficiently agreeable, though almost all unknown to each other. I have barely learned their names.

" Mr. Lyon, who had but little time to speak to Mr. Russell on the subject of our purchase of land, desires to have one share with us, if the subscription be not full. He will be a valuable associate, on account of his being an excellent farmer.

"Our captain has just informed us, that if he falls in with the fleet of merchantmen at Portsmouth, he will join them for the sake of the convoy : if so, I will write from that place.

"With my best wishes and prayers for our re-union here, or hereafter, yours and Mrs. Lindsey's, in which my wife joins me, most affectionately,

"J. PRIESTLEY."

The next letter is dated off Falmouth, on Friday evening, April 11.

"Dear Friend,—We came in a very short time opposite to the Start, but then, which was last night, the wind changed, and turned west; so that on this account, and likewise apprehending a storm from that quarter, we have just dropped anchor in Falmouth Road, where we shall stay till to-morrow morning, and then sail or not according as the wind shall be.

"On Wednesday evening we had a strong gale, which continued all night and part of the next day. This made all the passengers very sick, and my wife and myself among them. I could eat nothing till supper. But the next night was calm, and we rose recruited, and all this day have been in very good spirits, but much disappointed at not being able to proceed on our voyage, when we had got further in three days than the captain says he got in three weeks and five days the last voyage. We begin to be acquainted with all our cabin, and many of the steerage passengers, and like them very well. They are all well-behaved, and good company. The only woman cabin passenger is come from France ; knows our friends there, and seems well acquainted with the politics of the country.

"On the whole, I think we shall pass our time pretty well during the voyage. I have much time for reading, and shall be able to write. I am meditating a discourse on the Causes of Infidelity, led to it by reflections on that of Mr. C. and other intelligent men.

"I think I shall nearly read my Greek Testament through before I get to New York; and I think I read it with more satisfaction than ever. Unbelievers, I am confident, do not read it except with a predisposition to cavil. A person waits for our letters, and therefore I am, in haste, yours and Mrs. Lindsey's most affectionately,

"J. Priestley."

Here we see what was uppermost in the mind of this truly apostolic man. An exile from his country, to which he was never more to return, writing in confidence to his most intimate friend, whose face he was never to see again, instead of giving vent to his feelings in effeminate and unavailing lamentations, he thinks of nothing but how he may best fortify his own mind, and confirm the minds of others in the grounds and principles of the Christian faith as the only solid foundation of virtue and peace. Nothing further was heard of Dr. Priestley till his arrival at New York. The following is the first letter addressed to his venerable friend from the shores of the western continent. Its contents are too interesting to require an apology for its length.

"New York, June 6, 1794.

"Dear Friend,—I hope you received the letters I wrote from Gravesend, Deal, and Falmouth. I now write from New York, where we are safely arrived, after a passage of eight weeks and a day, owing to our having had none but westerly winds after we got clear of the Channel till the last fortnight. We also found the coast covered with a thick fog, very unusual at this time of the year, so that we were three days before we could get into the bay after we reached the coast.

"We had an excellent ship; but the captain was not the man he had been represented to me. He swore much, and was given to liquor; and the crew very disorderly. However, he made a point of behaving in his best manner to us; and is naturally very generous and good-natured. Unfortunately the mate and he did not agree; and no care had been taken of the water-casks, so that the steerage passengers suffered much in consequence of it; and we had many complaints : and if the voyage had been much longer, the consequence might have been serious.

" Our society in the cabin was agreeable enough, though the majority were aristocratically inclined ; but all in the steerage were zealous republicans, and persons of good character, and several of good property. In the steerage also was more religion than in the cabin ; but they were universally Calvinists, though the majority very moderate, as you will suppose, from their applying to me to perform divine service to them ; which I did with much satisfaction when the weather and other circumstances would permit, several in the cabin joining us, though some of them were unbelievers—but for want of information. This is the case with Mr. L., a most excellent man, who is now reading my sermons on the Evidences of Revelation,—and I hope to good purpose. He, like thousands of others, told me that he was so much disgusted with the doctrines of the Church of England, especially the Trinity, that he considered the whole business as an imposition, without further inquiry.

" The confinement in the ship would not have been disagreeable if I could have written with convenience, but I could do little more than read. I read the whole of the Greek Testament, and the Hebrew Bible as far as the First Book of Samuel, and I think with more satisfaction than ever. I also read through Hartley's second volume ; and for amusement I had several books of voyages, and Ovid's Metamorphoses, which I read through. I always admired his Latin versification. If I had a Virgil, I should have read him through too. I read a great deal of Buchanan's Poems, and some of Petrarch's and Erasmus's Dialogues. All Peter Pindar's Poems, which Mr. L. had with him, and which pleased me much more than I expected. He is Paine in verse.

" Though it was particularly inconvenient to write long hand, I composed about as much as will make two sermons, on the Causes of Infidelity, which will make a proper addition to the volume of my discourses. If I do not print them here, I will send you a copy. Now that I have access to the first volume of Hartley, in the fine edition Mrs. Lindsey gave me, I think I can improve what

I wrote. The second volume I had in the ship was an odd volume of the set that was destroyed in the riots.

" We had many things to amuse us in the passage, as the sight of some fine mountains of ice, water-spouts, which are very uncommon in those seas, flying fishes, porpoises, whales, and sharks, of which we caught one, luminous sea-water, &c. I also amused myself with trying the heat of the water at different depths, and made other observations which suggest various experiments, which I shall prosecute whenever I get my apparatus at liberty.

" We had some very stormy weather; and one gust of wind as sudden and violent as perhaps ever was known. If it had not been for the passengers, many of the sails had been lost.

" I had not much sea-sickness; but owing to our wretched cookery had no appetite for anything till within a fortnight or three weeks of our landing; but then I was perfectly reconciled to everything. My wife was really very ill a great part of the time; but at last grew very well, and looks better almost than ever. On the whole the voyage has done us no harm, but good.

" J—— and his wife had been waiting for us some time. They and their brothers are well; which is a great satisfaction to us. We shall probably go with them to Philadelphia before we go anywhere else, as I hear there are proposals to be made to me about establishing a new college in some part of Pennsylvania, about which you shall know more when I know more.

" I never saw any place that I liked so well as New York; it far exceeds my expectation, and my reception is too flattering ; no form of respect being omitted. I have received two formal addresses, to which I have given answers. More, I hear, are coming, and almost every person of the least consequence in the place has been or is coming to call upon me. This is rather troublesome, but it shows the difference of the two countries. I am lodged in the house which was the head-quarters of Generals Howe and Clinton, in view of the Bay, which is the finest prospect that I remember ever to have seen.

" This must be a glorious country ; and I doubt not of finding a peaceable and useful establishment in it. When that is accomplished, my only wish will be to have you and a few other Christian friends to come and end their days with us. But we must not promise ourselves too much in this world.

"Say for me everything that a grateful heart can dictate, both from myself, my wife, and my son, to Mrs. Rayner.

"Yours and Mrs. Lindsey's most affectionately,

"J. PRIESTLEY."

Dr. Priestley made but a short stay at New York,* where, not-

---

* It will not perhaps be uninteresting to read the account of Dr. Priestley's reception at New York, by a gentleman who was present at the time, and who soon afterwards returned to England, Mr. Henry Wansey, who wrote the following letter to Mr. Lindsey from Salisbury, August 28, 1794:

"Dear Sir,—A packet was given me by Dr. Priestley to deliver to you, and I fully intended calling upon you with it, but could not get my boxes and baggage passed through the Custom-house, and was obliged to leave London at last without accomplishing it; your parcel, from over care, having been put into it. I lodged at the same house with the Doctor and family at New York, Mrs. Loring's, where you have no doubt heard how well and respectably he was received. All the families of consequence, even some of the clergy, called to pay their respects, though the latter did not carry their civility so far as to offer any pulpit to him during the two Sundays he was there. Dr. Rodgers from his pulpit declared his abhorrence of all those who denied the divinity of Christ, and he hoped none such would come to his administration of the Lord's Supper. Yet Dr. Priestley was not prevented attending divine service there the Sunday after he arrived. The violence of the clergy against this doctrine, particularly on Trinity Sunday last, has been of as great service as a persecution; for many principal families of New York, chiefly English, have stepped forward, and determined to have an Unitarian chapel there. That at Boston, under the care of Mr. Freeman, I observed was well attended, and, Mr. Freeman told me, considerably increased. He (Dr. P.) requests you will get a minister of pleasing address and a good delivery to come to New York immediately. The Doctor, whom I accompanied out of New York across Hudson's River, on his way to Philadelphia, assured me repeatedly he was perfectly satisfied with the change he had made. His reception far exceeded his expectation; his health and spirits were good; but, however, that he should not enter into public life. At Princeton College, I learned from Dr. Smith, the Vice-President, that he would be offered the Presidency of a new College erecting in North Carolina; but he told me he should positively decline it, and, after a very short stay at Philadelphia, go up the Susquehanna to Northumberland, while his sons went on about forty miles further to put forward the new settlement, of which I have so good an opinion that I have taken two shares. Many families of my acquaintance are going to the Loyalsoc, and my only fear is that they do not proceed with clearing and building till next spring, which is certainly losing time. For though the settlement will be rapid after a beginning is made, yet losing this season may induce some of those respectable families now going out to fix elsewhere.

"It is a pleasant country; and the people I found everywhere friendly and hospitable; a great sobriety of manners; equality exemplified in its true sense; nor do I once remember to have seen either a beggar or a ragged person. Adieu, dear Sir, and believe me, &c. &c."

This settlement upon the Loyalsoc did not answer expectation, and upon further in-

withstanding all the respect shown him by the laity, there was not one clergyman who offered him his pulpit, and some thought it

quiry it was given up. The State prosecutions commenced soon after Dr. Priestley left England, and many of his friends were the more reconciled to his emigration, as thinking that he might have been some way or other involved in them. But this was not probable. A man who joined no political society, who attended no public meetings, and who wrote no political books or pamphlets, was not likely to be the object of the vindictive animadversion of an Attorney-General. Even Mr. Lindsey's fears seem to have been needlessly alarmed upon this subject. In a letter to the Rev. William Turner, of Newcastle, dated June 10, 1794, he writes: " Nothing has been known of or from Dr. Priestley since his being off Falmouth, between seven and eight weeks since. But under the protection of a good Providence, we persuade ourselves that he has ere this touched the American shores. And such have been the changes since, that some of his best friends who sought to detain him here are now glad at his departure. For the prejudices against Dissenters, especially of the more liberal sort, as enemies to their country because they are against the present war, are so violent, and would have been so much heightened against him, that it might have made his life unpleasant, though I hope not insecure."

I shall add but one extract more upon this subject from Mr. Lindsey to the same excellent person, the son of his old revered confidential adviser and friend at Wakefield. The letter is dated November 9, 1794, and strongly expresses the affectionate feelings of the venerable writer's heart :

" I rejoice to hear that you have so favourable an opportunity of bearing testimony to such injured worth in exile from our unworthy country, and of recording that intimate friendship and union of studies and pursuits, which subsisted between that excellent person and your most worthy father. To have any place in the niche with two such eminent characters is a real honour. No satisfaction do I know beyond that of recollecting the hours passed and benefit received in friendly communications with both. For some years, particularly when I resigned Catterick, there was no step of importance which I took without consulting both ; and the sketch of the Apology, soon after published, they were so good as to take the trouble of meeting, and passing a day with me at an inn in Knaresborough, when I read it to them.

" I have been made happy by several letters received from Dr. Priestley since his arrival in America. In his last he mentions a very important matter: the large purchase of lands on the Susquehanna was all over. They had been deceived by the proprietors, and by evidence which did not turn out satisfactory, and thus, after much delay and some expense, many will be disappointed.

" In the same letter he says he had an invitation from New York to read lectures philosophical, and to open an Unitarian congregation. But he had declined on account of the distance from the place where his sons would be likely to settle. I am grieved at it, because New York was the place for him, the English American metropolis, the inhabitants more cultivated, of most easy access from Europe, &c. &c. This concern, however, was a little abated by the subsequent paragraph of his letter, relating that the Chemical Professor of the College in Philadelphia was believed to be on his death-bed, and that Dr. Rush had told him that he believed he would be invited to succeed him. This, he adds, will oblige him to four or five months' residence in Philadelphia. And as there is a certain prospect of being able to establish an Unitarian congregation in the place, he shall not hesitate to accept the offer."

This offer was made and declined, much to the regret of many of Dr. Priestley's friends at the time ; but, as there is now reason to believe, not with any eventual detriment to the cause of Christian truth.

their duty to caution their hearers against Unitarian errors. Many persons were, however, much displeased at the bigotry of their ministers; and the venerable exile was given to understand that if he would fix his residence in New York, a chapel and a congregation would not be wanting. But his destination was otherwise. He accompanied his son, who met him at New York, to Philadelphia, where he met with the same flattering attention from the laity, and the same repulsive spirit from the clergy; and after remaining there a few weeks, he went with Mrs. Priestley to Northumberland, a small settlement upon the banks of the Susquehanna, near the western boundary of Pennsylvania; and here, to the great disappointment and extreme regret of all his friends, both in Europe and America, he determined to fix his residence. Nor could the inconvenience of a new settlement, the want of literary and polished society, the many and great obstructions to epistolary intercourse with his philosophical and theological correspondents, the difficulty of obtaining books and philosophical instruments, nor even the offer of the Chemical Professorship, and ultimately of the Presidency of the College of Philadelphia, prevail with him to change his resolution. The reasons upon which a choice so extraordinary and unexpected, and so universally regretted, was founded, were never made known to the public. But whatever these might be, and though Dr. Priestley's resolution to fix his residence at Northumberland was at that time generally disapproved and lamented, the event has shown that it was a most beneficial choice. In no other situation would it have been possible for him to have commanded the leisure which was necessary for drawing up those important, learned, and instructive works which occupied his attention to the last hour of his life, and by which, being dead, he yet speaketh, and will probably continue to speak, and to promote the great cause of Christian truth, and particularly the glorious, long lost doctrine of the Divine Unity, for ages to come. I particularly refer to his excellent Ecclesiastical History, and his judicious and valuable Notes upon the whole Bible, which are the result of much reading and reflection, though he makes no parade of authorities, a species of ostentation which he always despised, and the neglect of which, to a proper extent, may be regarded as a defect in his work much to be regretted.

In this sequestered wilderness the venerable exile maintained a regular correspondence with his reverend and beloved friend the subject of this Memoir, which continued with little or no interruption till within a fortnight of his decease. He numbered his letters: there are one hundred and four; all of them now in the possession of the writer of this work. They are interesting to those who knew and admired and loved the writer, but few of them would be interesting to the public. Dr. Priestley thought little of himself. He seldom touches upon personal concerns; and gives little account of what it would have been particularly interesting to know, the mode of life in a situation so remote from, and so unlike to, that of civilized and polished Europe. His great mind was occupied in greater things. His whole soul was absorbed in the acquisition of knowledge, in the search after truth, and in devising and executing the best means of communicating information to others. And his letters are chiefly occupied in stating what he has done, is doing, and further intends to do, for promoting this great object: they breathe throughout a spirit of ardent zeal, of rational piety, and of active and disinterested benevolence. In the Appendix a few are given, as a specimen of his general manner, and of the style and spirit of his correspondence.* Dr. Priestley, who had originally an excellent constitution, and who generally enjoyed uninterrupted health and an uniform flow of good spirits, naturally and reasonably expected to outlive his aged friend, who was ten years further advanced in life than himself. But Divine Providence ordered otherwise. This great man gradually declined in health, after a severe fever which attacked him in Philadelphia, in the spring of 1801, and from which he was by copious bleeding with much difficulty recovered. He expired in the bosom of his family on the 6th of February, 1804. A most interesting account of his last sickness was written by his son, Mr. Joseph

* Appendix, No. XII.

S

Priestley, in a letter to Mr. Lindsey, which by some means found its way into the public papers, and was, it is believed, copied and circulated in all the periodical publications in Europe, Asia, and America, to testify to the world *how* a well-informed philosophic *Christian can die.*

His aged friend bore the intelligence with the calm dignity and pious resignation of one who placed entire confidence in the hopes and promises of the gospel; and who, feeling the infirmities of age advancing fast upon him, expected soon to rejoin his beloved fellow-labourer in happier circumstances, and in an improved and permanent state of existence, where virtue that has been tried and perfected shall receive its appropriate reward.

CHAPTER XIV.

DR. PRIESTLEY'S REPLY TO PAINE'S AGE OF REASON REPRINTED IN ENGLAND BY MR. LINDSEY, WITH A PREFACE IN VINDICATION OF DR. PRIESTLEY'S CHARACTER. MR. LINDSEY REPUBLISHES ANOTHER WORK OF DR. PRIESTLEY'S, WITH A SHORT PREFACE. DR. PRIESTLEY'S ACKNOWLEDGMENT OF MR. LINDSEY'S KINDNESS. ANALYSIS OF MR. LINDSEY'S LAST PUBLICATION, ENTITLED, CONVERSATIONS ON THE DIVINE GOVERNMENT.

WHEN Dr. Priestley arrived in America, he found that Paine's Age of Reason had been lately imported into that continent, and that by its bold dogmatical spirit, and by its successful attack upon those corruptions of the Christian doctrine which usually pass for Christianity, and which in this treatise were assumed as such, a deep impression had been made upon the minds of the unthinking and the unwary; and that many were seduced by this plausible and popular performance from the Christian faith. No sooner, therefore, was this zealous advocate for revealed truth settled at Northumberland, than he published an answer to Paine's work, in the form of Letters to a Philosophical Unbeliever, in October 1794, a copy of which he sent over to Mr. Lindsey, who reprinted it in England, in the beginning of the year 1795, with a preface, the chief design of which was to vindicate the character of his absent and much-injured friend.

"As every event whatever," says this able advocate of exiled merit, "every circumstance of the life of every man, is ordained and overruled by the infinitely wise and good Creator for the virtuous improvement and present and final happiness of the universe, and of each individual in it, we may be fully persuaded that where man intends evil, God intends and brings forth good, and that the best purposes of the Divine government will be promoted by the means of those unworthy passions which compelled this eminent person to take refuge in America." He adds, that "they have begun to show themselves in the reception which has been given to Dr. Priestley, and in the general estimation in which he is held, notwithstanding the base arts which have been used to poison that people's minds, and to turn them against him."

Mr. Lindsey then states, that it was desired and expected by the friends of divine revelation in America, that he should reply to Paine's Age of Reason, and undertake a cause he was so well able to defend; and he flatters himself that the republication of it in England may contribute to rescue some who are "hastening to the dreary gulf" of infidelity.

He puts the question, "What could raise up such a storm against so respectable a character as to constrain him to retire a voluntary exile from his country, where he was so justly loved and esteemed by some of the most exalted characters?" He instances Dr. Price, Sir George Savile, and Mr. Lee, the late Solicitor-General, who particularly admired his Letters to Mr. Burke, and at whose house "in Lincoln's-Inn-Fields for near twenty years the friends were wont to spend their Sunday evenings together, whenever they were in town, in cheerful pleasantry, and free discussion of all subjects; for two men more

s 2

formed and furnished for social converse than Dr. Priestley and Mr. Lee are rarely found." To the catalogue of Dr. Priestley's friends he also adds the respected names of Dr. Shipley, Bishop of St. Asaph, and Dr. Law, Bishop of Carlisle, "who was in perfect accord with him in his sentiments on most subjects." He concludes with the name of Dr. Jebb, to whom Dr. P. dedicates his Treatise upon Philosophical Necessity. "In that beautiful and luminous composition," says Mr. Lindsey, "proceeding from the fullness of the heart, and conviction of the truth of that glorious principle in which they both agreed, you read the true character of the men, and what all may become who are under the like influences."

It is obvious to remark here how cordially Mr. Lindsey concurs with his learned and virtuous friends in the belief of the truth and importance of what he calls the "g'o.ious principle" of philosophical necessity, and in admitting those grand and consolatory consequences which flow from it, "that every circumstance of the life of every man is ordained and overruled by the infinitely wise and good Creator" for the best purposes. What childish simplicity and ignorance does it betray in some to feign or to feel alarmed at the tendency of those doctrines which are avowed by such men as Lindsey, Priestley, Hartley, and Jebb, and which are represented by them as lying at the foundation of all right views of the Divine government, of all rational piety and virtuous practice, and of all rational and substantial consolation! And yet such persons feel no alarm at the vulgar notion of philosophical liberty, or the power of acting differently in circumstances precisely similar; a notion, the fond persuasion of which encourages men to venture into circumstances of moral danger, and to which thousands of the young and inexperienced, especially, are daily falling victims.

To account for the hostility against Dr. Priestley, which eventually compelled that great and good man to seek an asylum in America, his friendly advocate states most truly, that "Dr. Priestley had an ardent, active zeal for reformation; that, penetrated with the most absolute conviction of the reality of the Divine Unity, and of the connection which the belief of it had with the peace, the virtue, and happiness of mankind, he hesitated not in his immortal writings from the press in the smallest size, and to the level of the lowest capacities, as also in larger and more learned volumes, from the pulpit also on public and proper occasions, to maintain and defend that there was no God but the Father ; and that the worship of Jesus by Protestants was equally idolatrous with the worship of his mother Mary by the Papists." He adds, that "in nothing did Dr. Priestley give more offence, or more excite the ill-will of many against him, than by those freedoms in censuring the interference of the civil power in things of religion, all usurpation upon conscience, wherever lodged, or by whomsoever exercised." And he instances particularly in the Doctor's Familiar Letters to the Inhabitants of Birmingham.

Mr. Lindsey then introduces some just strictures upon the illiberal reflections cast upon the Unitarians by Bishop Hurd, in his Life of his friend and patron, Bishop Warburton. Such obloquy, however, so far as Dr. Priestley was the object of it, he states was abundantly compensated by the grateful and admiring testimony of numbers, both in and out of the Established Church, "to his exalted character and extraordinary merits." As a specimen, he introduces some beautiful lines addressed to Dr. Priestley by Mrs. Barbauld, whom he justly styles "a genius of superior order, and the strains such as Milton himself might have been proud to own." The reader, and I trust the elegant and accomplished writer, will excuse me for inserting them at the bottom of the page. They were written when a panic was for party purposes spread through the country, of a plot to overturn the Government, and when many fulsome addresses were carried up to the throne, and many foul and unfounded calumnies were circulated against the Dissenters, as conspiring to overturn the Government, though they have always shown themselves firm friends to the illustrious family upon the throne.*

* Stirs not thy spirit, Priestley, as the train,
With low obeisance and with servile phrase,
File behind file advance with supple knee,
And lay their necks beneath the foot of power ?

The friendly advocate next animadverts upon the infamous paragraphs circulated in the *Times* and other Ministerial papers, charging Dr. Priestley, who was not present at the dinner, with having given as a toast at the hotel at Birmingham, on the 14th of July, " Destruction to the present Government, and the King's head in a charger ; " which, though it could neither be given nor received by any persons who were not insane, was nevertheless currently believed, and contributed to inflame the frenzy of the day. Another paragraph inserted in the *True Briton* and the *Sun,* replete with falsehood and calumny respecting Dr. Priestley's reception in America, is cited by Mr. Lindsey, who also introduces Mr. Lyon's distinct contradiction and confutation of it.

The generous and spirited advocate then proceeds to notice a cruel attack upon Dr. Priestley, published in America soon after his arrival there, entitled, Observations on the Emigration of Dr. Joseph Priestley, &c., the design of which was to represent Dr. Priestley as a firebrand, an open and avowed enemy to the consti-

> Burns not thy cheek indignant when thy name,
> On which delighted science loved to dwell,
> Becomes the bandied theme of hooting crowds ?
> With timid caution, or with cool reserve,
> When e'en each reverend brother keeps aloof,
> Eyes the struck deer, and leaves thy naked side,
> A mark for power to shoot at ? Let it be,
> " On evil days though fall'n and evil tongues,"
> To thee the slander of a passing age
> Imports not. Scenes like these hold little space
> In his large mind, whose ample stretch of thought
> Grasps future periods. Well can'st thou afford
> To give large credit for that debt of fame
> Thy country owes thee. Calm thou can'st consign it
> To the slow payment of that distant day,
> If distant, when thy name, to Freedom's join'd,
> Shall meet the thanks of a regenerate land.—December, 1792.

It is truly gratifying to all the admirers of taste and genius to find that this lady's muse, though long silent. has not deserted her. The same genius which inspired the strains which immortalized the patriots of Corsica in their struggles with their French and Genoese tyrants shines forth resplendently in the beautiful and sublime poem of ' Eighteen Hundred and Eleven." But as in the former case, the muse, too sanguine in her expectations of success, apologized for having " read the book of destiny amiss," so may it prove with regard to the gloomy forebodings of the latter poem ! And may centuries after centuries elapse, as we trust they will, before the traveller from the western continent shall have occasion to inquire, Where once stood the renowned seats of the Muses, the opulent emporiums of Commerce, or the proud Metropolis of the world ?

tution of his country, &c. It was doubtful whether this scurrilous libel was the production of an author on this or the other side of the Atlantic. Mr. Lindsey justly remarks, that "from whatever quarter it issued, it is the work of a man who showed himself void of truth and of every moral principle, if he were an Englishman; if an American, a gross and ignorant calumniator." This pamphlet, by the falsehood of its assertions and the foulness of its abuse, was rather of use than otherwise to Dr. Priestley in America; and upon this side of the Atlantic it could do him no harm. The *British Critic*, indeed, with its wonted malignity, gave it all the currency it could, by a formal review of this "atrocious attack on the most virtuous of men," in the month of November, 1794. Mr. Lindsey ably exposes the disingenuous and immoral conduct of this band of critics in "deliberately adopting and recommending what they could not but know to be a tissue of abominable calumnies." And it being understood that some persons of literary eminence were then concerned in the conduct of that monthly journal, the author spiritedly expostulates with them upon the baseness of their conduct, so unworthy the estimation in which upon other accounts they were held. "O moral degradation! O shame to Science! when its votaries can lend their rare abilities, Heaven's gift for better purposes, to please the great, and gain their favour, and to lower and depress eminent virtue, and hinder others from reaping advantage from that example and those writings by which they might be formed to goodness, and excellence, and happiness for ever!"

As to the work to which this defence of absent and injured merit is a preface, Mr. Lindsey says that "a copy of it having been put into his hands, he resolved to reprint it immediately." He adds, "It soon occurred that it would be desirable and proper for me, if I could acquit myself in it in any tolerable manner, to take the opportunity that offered, of saying something in behalf of an honoured and beloved friend, that might remove or soften the violent prejudices entertained against him in this country, and in this country only: for in all others his fame is great, and his character revered." And having justly animadverted upon the mean, unmanly conduct of his enemies and slanderers, he adds, with much truth and pertinence, " Dr. Priestley's enemies, however, by their ignorant, malevolent detraction, cannot make him unhappy, but only hurt themselves. Changing his country, he changes not those habits which form the virtuous, the holy, the benevolent, the upright character. These constitute happiness ; these accompany a man wherever he goes, of which no malice or violence can deprive him." *

In the year 1800, Dr. Priestley published in America a treatise upon the Knowledge which the Ancient Hebrews had of a Future State, which Mr. Lindsey republished in England with a short preface, in which he notices with high satisfaction his honoured friend's continued activity as the advocate of true religion ; and augurs that " his writings will continue to promote this great end in his native country and America, and wherever the English language shall prevail, when he shall be no more. A rare privilege of Heaven's chosen favourites and the truly good ! " Dr. Priestley was highly delighted with this kind testimony of his venerable friend, and in a letter dated June 11, 1801, he thus expresses his grateful sense of Mr. Lindsey's friendship :—

* It will not be uninteresting to the reader to see what Dr. Priestley writes to his friend upon the subject of his own work and Mr. Lindsey's preface.

In a letter to Mr. Lindsey, dated Northumberland, October 16, 1794, Dr. Priestley says, " I have nearly printed the Continuation of my Letters to the Philosophers of France, and to a Philosophical Unbeliever; the latter in answer to Mr. Paine's Age of Reason, which is much read, and has made great impression here. Nor will you wonder at it when you consider what kind of Christianity is preached here. I am told that the Quakers read it with great avidity ; and they have no knowledge at all of the proper evidence of Christianity, or the doctrines of it. Many of them, therefore, in this country either actually are, or are easily made, unbelievers. There are great expectations, I am told, from my Answer to Paine, and I hope it will do good."

July 12, 1795, Dr. Priestley writes, " I am exceedingly glad that you have at last got my Answer to Mr. Paine, and that you like it. I wish to see your preface. It cannot give more pleasure to you than it does to me to have our names connected in every possible method. I hope they will be for ever inseparable. One of my greatest mortifications is, that I cannot show you what I write, and be directed by you as usual."

Dr. Priestley's modest and grateful acknowledgment of his venerable friend's kind and zealous vindication of his injured character is thus expressed in a letter dated Northumberland, December 6, 1795 :

" It is not long since I received the copy of your edition of my Answer to Paine. I read the preface with much emotion, from a sense of the friendship to me expressed in it. If I had laboured ten times more than I have, I should not have thought it too much for such a reward."

" I thank you for your very friendly preface. When shall I acknowledge my many obligations to you in person ? Not, I now fear, on this side the grave. I therefore think the more of the state beyond it. But while I remain here, I am thankful that you continue here too. I sometimes think, and not without pain, how I shall feel when you are gone ; though our separation cannot be of long continuance, the difference in our ages not being quite ten years; and I do not expect to survive you so long as that, if indeed at all. Of what unspeakable value is religion in circumstances like mine ! Without this, I think I should hardly have been able to support myself; but with it, all difficulties, troubles, and disappointments are as nothing, being enabled to look beyond them." Such was the Christian spirit which animated the correspondence of these virtuous friends, who were equally distinguished as lovers of truth and examples of piety.

Mr. Lindsey, now declining far into the vale of years, being upon the verge of four-score, but in the enjoyment of perfect health, and the full possession of his intellectual and active powers, seems to have taken up the design of his old friend Dr. Courayer, and to have come to a resolution of laying before the public his last thoughts concerning the doctrines of revelation, and particularly concerning the wisdom and goodness of the Divine administration ; and with this view, in the year 1802, he published a small volume, entitled, " Conversations on the Divine Government; showing that everything is from God, and for Good to all." This volume is dedicated to Mrs. Sophia and Mrs. Frances Chambers, the sisters of the late Dr. Chambers, rector of Achurch, in Northamptonshire, Mr. Lindsey's early friend, of whom mention has been made in a former part of this Memoir. Another brother was an eminent merchant in London, who had a country-house at Morden, where these ladies resided ; and in this house Mr. and Mrs. Lindsey found a quiet and hospitable retreat during the summer season, when they did not take any considerable journey. In the repose and leisure of this delightful mansion, Mr. Lindsey appears to have composed and written this his last present to the public; and he inscribes it to his worthy friends,

" in gratitude for unwearied offices of the most disinterested friendship, for near thirty years, to himself and Mrs. Lindsey, from them and their worthy brother; and in testimony for their enlightened zeal for the worship of the one true God, and a constant unostentatious readiness to do good."

In his preface, he observes that the following work results from the study and experience of a long life; and he apologizes for the introduction of some repetitions by the remark, that " till a full conviction is wrought in the mind that the government of this world is the wisest that could have been adopted, and that the evils and distresses of life are not permitted but for the good of all, the attention of the public cannot be too often solicited for the vindication of our Creator. Under the hope of promoting, in some degree, the interest of his fellow-creatures in so noble a cause, and of leading them to their happiest state, a full confidence and satisfaction in the never-ceasing love of their Maker and God, the following remarks, imperfect as they are, are committed to the candour and serious attention of the benevolent reader."

The conversations are supposed to be held at the same place, and conducted by the same parties, as those upon Christian Idolatry, published ten years before. Victorin, in a letter to his friend Volusian, requests him to give some account of a very curious and interesting question, upon which they had come to an unanimous resolution, viz. " That there is nothing really and ultimately ill in the state of man, but everything ordered for the best for all." Volusian's reply contains an account of each day's conversation; though this incident seems to be lost sight of in the course of the work.

Volusian informs his friend that the company " having fallen into conversation upon the very low repute in which the religion of Christ was everywhere held, at home and abroad," one of the party mentioned that " in Holland and other parts of the continent, a little before the French Revolution, a general persuasion prevailed that the Christian religion would soon be at an end." And he imputes that indisposition to Christianity which appeared to be rapidly increasing, to the corruption of the Christian doctrine.

Photinus, in reply, expresses his confidence that Christianity would maintain its ground; and ascribes the hatred which the philosophers upon the continent bore to revelation, to the interference of the civil power in supporting it by pains and penalties, which led them to conceive that all means, however dishonest, were lawful to overthrow a sanguinary and pernicious superstition. Photinus, however, maintains that the religion of Jesus will remain unshaken, being confirmed by miracles. He affirms the same of the Mosaic revelation, which also rests upon the basis of miracles, and of prophecy which is even now receiving its accomplishment. He makes some just observations on the nature, use, and proveableness of miracles. He then briefly states, what he calls "the plain old argument for a Deity : viz. that otherwise, the world we live in, with all its furniture and inhabitants, must have come into being of itself, without any original designing mind." He adds, that the most serious difficulty with relation to the Divine existence arises from the existence and prevalence of vice and misery in the world; and that if this state of things could by any means be reconciled to perfect goodness, it would provide the best remedy against scepticism. Marcellinus, in the name of the company, requests Photinus to undertake this task; to which he consents, and the conversation is adjourned.

In the process of the preceding conversation, the author, under the character of Photinus, obviates the objection against miracles as inconsistent with the Divine immutability, by the supposition that "those events which we call supernatural may be the result of established laws, and a more comprehensive plan of things, though unperceived by us; so that those operations called miraculous are as much the result of general laws as the most ordinary events." But the learned writer does not seem to have adverted to the fact, that this supposition destroys the very existence of miracles, and subverts the argument founded upon them. The resurrection of Lazarus, upon this hypothesis, is no more miraculous than an eclipse of the sun ; and the prediction of the former, which, according to this theory, would have happened whether foretold or not, no more proves the divine mission of Christ, than foretelling an eclipse proved the inspiration of Thales. This hypothesis is in the highest degree arbitrary and incredible. The essence of a miracle consists in its being a deviation from the established course of nature; and the existence of a miracle proves a divine interposition, because no being but the Author of nature himself could control its laws; and this violation of the law and course of nature in any given case is perfectly consistent with the divine immutability; because, at the instant when the laws of nature were fixed, the Supreme Being foresaw and determined that in this instance he would, for just and sufficient reasons, deviate from that rule of conduct to which it was his pleasure generally to adhere.

The second conversation begins with a vindication by Photinus of the character of Lord Shaftesbury, the author of the Characteristics, as a believer in revelation; though his Lordship speaks lightly of the characters of Abraham, Moses, and others of the Old Testament saints, expresses doubts concerning some of the narratives contained in the Pentateuch, and hesitates to admit the existence of miracles. This is advanced in reply to Volusian, who represents Lord Shaftesbury as one of those infidels who entertain right views of the character and government of God. How far the candid writer, under the character of Photinus, has succeeded in his charitable purpose, is not material to inquire. The remainder of the conversation is employed in a very pleasing dissertation by Photinus upon the great goodness of God, as manifested in the wise and kind provision which he has made for the preservation, support, and enjoyment of animal and rational beings; at the conclusion of which, Marcellinus, after expressing his high approbation of his friend's doctrine, intimates his apprehension that "it would all be regarded merely as a beautiful theory, and these fine capacities of the rational nature to be bestowed in vain, and never likely to be brought to maturity, when we take a survey of the world at large, and scan what mankind have been, and still are, in a moral view;" and he concludes with expressing his hope that

Photinus will continue to give his kind help in "exploring this momentous subject."

In the third conversation, Marcellinus begins with making some remarks upon the account of the Creation and the Fall, in the Book of Genesis, much of which he acknowledges to be "undoubtedly couched in allegory;" while it is "to be taken literally in other parts, which are at the foundation;" the moral instruction intended, is, however, "not difficult to be understood." Photinus, who is the chief speaker in these conversations, having expressed his high satisfaction in the suggestions of his friend, proceeds to inquire what the history of man teaches concerning his attainment of that virtue and happiness for which he is intended. To this end, he enters into a brief detail of the dispensations of God to mankind, as they are related in the Jewish Scriptures, first offering remarks upon the incidents which occur from the Creation to the Deluge, by which "the almighty and merciful Being judged it expedient to destroy the whole race of men from off the earth, all, except one righteous man and his family."

The venerable writer then proceeds to comment upon the divine communications to Noah, to Abraham, and to Moses, and the effect which they produced in restraining the vices of mankind, and in promoting virtue and piety. He contends earnestly for the excellency of the character of the Jewish legislator, the credibility of his history, and the divine authority of his institute, and represents those persons as "true objects of pity who, through some unfortunate bias on their minds, are led to reject a history of facts so well authenticated as those which have Moses for their author." He adds, not altogether in that spirit of candour which was habitual to Mr. Lindsey, that "one is the more concerned for this incredulity, because the rejection of the important truths conveyed in these books, most commonly springs from a fixed determination not to admit any accounts, however well attested, of divine extraordinary communications and revelations to mankind." But, surely, if the venerable writer had for a moment reconsidered the case with his usual calmness and impartiality, he would have seen that a person may be a very firm believer in the divine mission and doctrine of Christ, and be well satisfied with the general evidence of the divine legation of Moses, while he at the same time may entertain very serious doubts whether the books commonly attributed to Moses were really throughout written by him, and whether either the narrative or the institute exist at present exactly in the form in which he delivered them. And these doubts may be so far from springing " from a fixed determination to admit no doctrine as revealed," that they may originate in an anxious concern to extricate revealed truth from those human additions by which it is corrupted and disgraced. The respectable writer, therefore, may perhaps be regarded as not quite correct when he adds, in a tone of sarcasm unwonted with him, that " so long as such a person cannot be brought to see his error by the arguments laid before him, you can only be sorry for him, and wish him a mind more teachable and better informed."

Photinus next goes on to justify the extermination of the Canaanites by the Israelites as an act of obedience to a divine command, and makes light of an argument sometimes offered in defence of this command, as being analogous to events which take place under the natural government of God, where human beings are " destroyed promiscuously by earthquakes and the like: as this is a defence which some are dissatisfied with, not holding the cases to be parallel." And it cannot be doubted, that if a divine command is proved, all objections must give way. If God required this great public execution, it must be consistent with the Divine character to issue this decree ; and if he manifested his displeasure by repeated miraculous interpositions, the conduct of these chosen executioners of the Divine will must be justified to themselves, to the world, and even to the miserable sufferers, by the terrific mandate. So that the history is consistent. God does what he has a right to do, and the Israelites are the innocent, and even meritorious, instruments of executing his sovereign pleasure. The case, however, is attended with difficulty ; and it must be allowed to be a very alleviating circumstance, if it can be shown that the order thus issued is analogous to what happens fre-

quently under the Divine government. He that made has a right
to destroy; and the wise and just Being, who makes use of natural
calamities for the promiscuous extermination of myriads, has an
equal right to use voluntary agents as the instruments of inflicting
similar calamities. But the fact which applies still more closely to
the case in question is, that the righteous Governor of the world
does continually employ voluntary agents as the executioners of
his will in the destruction of their fellow-creatures. Nebuchad-
nezzar is the rod in the Divine hand to execute his vengeance upon
Tyre and Egypt; and a Cæsar, or a Napoleon, are equally the instruments of spreading desolation and destruction among the
human race, as a Joshua or a David, though not equally innocent:
one, if we credit the history, acting under a divine commission;
the other, prompted by bad passions and sanguinary ambition.
The purposes of infinite Wisdom are fulfilled as well by the evil
actions of evil men, as by the good actions of the virtuous. And
this, without any diminution of the responsibility of the agent.
Such is the express doctrine of the Scripture, in perfect harmony
with the true philosophy of the human mind.

The venerable author supports his own assertions and views of
the institutes of Moses and the conduct of the Hebrew nation, by
an appeal to the authority of Dr. Priestley. "See," says he,
"that last and most invaluable work, his Comparison of the Institutions of Moses with those of the Hindoos, of my most
beloved friend Dr. Priestley. Although now far separated during
this transitory life, on the verge of which we both stand, there is
humble hope of meeting again when the sleep of death is over.
His numerous works will continue to enlighten the world till the
only true God will be more universally known, and the pure gospel
of Jesus, his messenger, have its natural influence."

Photinus next proceeds to state the great moral benefit which
the heathen world derived from its enlightened philosophers and
legislators, particularly Socrates and Cicero, the distinguished
moralists and instructors of Greece and Rome in the ages in which
they flourished; at the same time acknowledging that the fairest
characters in heathen story were clouded with many inconsisten-

cies and imperfections, and that their instructions were ineffectual for the reformation of mankind: "nothing was done to recover men to the knowledge of the true God and their obedience to him;" nor "to put men upon attending to the inward principle of their actions, and amending their dispositions."

This naturally introduces the necessity and advantage of the gospel dispensation which was now introduced into the world, and which was to be made known to the whole human race. "This was the new doctrine promulged from heaven, holding forth the supreme love of God, the common Creator and Benefactor, manifesting itself in the love of their fellow-creatures and seeking their good as their own, as the sum and substance of all human duty and of all true religion, and leading to the highest perfection and happiness." This divine religion, however, was soon corrupted; "objects of worship were multiplied, the mother of Christ and other dead persons, male and female, a trinity of three persons in God, instead of the single person of the God and Father of our Lord Jesus Christ and of all mankind." So that, "to preserve the important doctrine of the Divine Unity from being overwhelmed and lost in Christian idolatry, Divine Providence seems to have permitted the impostor Mohammed to succeed in spreading his new religion over a great part of the globe." This religion professed to stand upon the great doctrine of the Divine Unity; in which, as some think, he was at first sincere; but being elated with success, he grew ambitious, insolent, and cruel, and propagated his religion by fire and sword.

Volusian here interposes, and enlarges upon the folly of ascribing to God "a religion, whose first article is a direct violation of the first law of nature, in compelling by force to acknowledge and worship him." He insists upon the absurdity of persecution in every shape; and he observes, that Christians cannot, with any decency, "condemn the Mohammedans for intolerance and cruelty," being themselves equally guilty; and represents it as a very great error, and that which lies at the foundation of all religious bigotry and persecution, to teach that Christians only can be saved, much more "Christians only of this or that particular church or sect;" whereas the truth is, that "all persons will be saved who are made pious and good by their religion, and none else."

Photinus in his reply expresses his approbation of Volusian's principles; and, proceeding in his history of divine dispensations, he takes notice of the increased diffusion of light and knowledge by the dispersion of learned Greeks through Europe, after the taking of Constantinople by the Turks in the fifteenth century, and by the invention of the art of printing. He adds, that much good had been done "by the noble efforts of many excellent Christians, at the hazard, and sometimes the loss, of life, to revive and restore the worship of the true God, and to vindicate the inalienable right of all men to judge for themselves of the things of God." And he expresses himself in terms of high commendation concerning the religious liberty which had lately been established in France. Photinus concludes his long discourse with the general inference that, though the little effect of genuine virtuous principle, and the defective knowledge of God, too much appears in wars and persecutions, yet "it would be unfair and unjust not to admit that knowledge and virtue have been upon the whole progressive, and that very many eminent examples of both have been formed, and are forming, in every age and country."

Photinus, after a pause, expresses his apprehensions, that "the account which had been given of the moral state of the world might not be acceptable to those who look for perfection all at once in everything that comes from God. But as we are convinced that a Being of all goodness has, in fact, appointed otherwise, and as we certainly do not love our fellow-creatures nor desire their improvement and happiness more earnestly than he that made them, and his wisdom can best judge and direct how to attain that happiness, we may probably find that the methods he has actually chosen are fully suited to answer this end, though we may not immediately see it."

He then proceeds to give a brief detail of the discipline by which the moral character is usually formed; the result of which he states to be, that "the bulk of mankind are, and have ever

T

been, employed in useful labours for their families, and in doing good offices to others, their friends, neighbours, and acquaintance, and in giving or procuring relief and assistance where needed, and in a thousand beneficent actions." This favourable view of the human character he confirms by a curious quotation from Archbishop King, on the Origin of Evil.* And Photinus concludes

---

* The sentiments expressed by the learned prelate are so uncommon, and at the same same time so just, and so exactly coincident with those which the writer of this Memoir has offered to the public in a work printed some years ago without any consciousness that they had before met with so able an advocate, that he will take the liberty of transcribing a considerable part of the quotation alluded to above.

The Archbishop is replying to an anonymous opponent who had said, "that the prevalence of wickedness or moral evil is a thing so certain, that he was confident no one could have the least doubt of it, and he durst say the author (the Archbishop) himself believed it."

"The author professes himself to be of a quite different opinion," replies the Archbishop. "He firmly believes, and thinks he very well comprehends, that there is much more moral good in the world than evil. He is sensible there may be more bad men than good, because there are none but do amiss sometimes, and one ill act is sufficient to denominate a man bad. But yet there are ten good acts done by those we call bad men, for one ill one. Even persons of the very worst character may have gotten it by two or three flagrant enormities, which yet bear no proportion to the whole series of their lives. The author must profess, that among such as he is acquainted with, he believes there are hundreds who would do him good for one that would do him hurt, and that he has received a thousand good offices for one ill one. He could never believe the doctrine of Hobbes, that all men are bears, wolves, and tigers, to one another; that they are born enemies to all others, and all others to them; that they are naturally false and perfidious; or that all the good they do is out of fear, not virtue. Nay, the very authors of that calumny, if their own character were called in question, would take all possible pains to remove the suspicion from them, and declare that they were speaking of the vulgar; of the bulk of mankind, and not of themselves. Nor, in reality, do they behave in this manner toward their friends and acquaintance; if they did, few would trust them. Observe some of those who exclaim against all mankind for treachery, dishonesty, deceit, and cruelty, and you will find them diligently cultivating friendship and discharging the several offices due to their friends, their relations, and their country, with labour, pain, loss of goods, and hazard of life itself; even where there is no fear to drive them to it, nor inconvenience attending the neglect of it. This, you will say, proceeds from custom and education. Be it so. However, the world then has not so far degenerated from goodness, but the greater part of mankind exercise benevolence; nor is virtue so far exiled as not to be supported and approved, praised and practised, by common consent and public suffrage, and vice is still disgraceful. Indeed, we can scarce meet with one, unless pressed by necessity or provoked by injuries, who is so barbarous and hardhearted as not to be moved with compassion and delighted with benevolence to others: who is not delighted to show goodwill and kindness to his friends, neighbours, children, relations, and diligence in the discharge of civil duties to all; who does not profess some regard to virtue, and think himself affronted when he is charged with immorality. If any one take notice of his own or another's actions for a day together, he will, perhaps, find one or two blameable, the rest all innocent and inoffensive. Nay, it is doubted whether a Nero or Caligula, a Commodus or Caracalla, though monsters of mankind, and prone to every act

the conversation with observing, " that thus the wisdom and goodness of the Creator are vindicated; that he was not disappointed
in the noblest work of his creation here below; and that the world
has been from the first, and all along, a nursery for virtuous, noble,
and useful characters."

The fourth conversation is short, but by far the most interesting and impressive of the whole. In this, the venerable author
states and argues, with a warmth of feeling which shows how
deeply his own heart was impressed with the magnificent speculation, and with a cogency of argument which can never be refuted,
that all things are from God; that evil as well as good, moral as
well as natural evil, are not only permitted, but appointed by
infinite unsearchable wisdom and benevolence.

The conversation is introduced by Marcellinus, who observes
that if evil be the result of the "untractable nature of matter,"
or of " a powerful evil being whose interference is unavoidable,
we must submit, and make the best of what we cannot avoid or
amend. But all gloom would vanish, if it could be shown that
the great whole of things is in such sort from God, that natural
and moral evil are all of his appointment, and permitted for
good."

Photinus with great solemnity replies, " Be assured, my friends,
that we do not, any of us, deem so highly of the boundless mercy
and goodness of the sovereign Creator and Parent of all things as
his works and dealings with us and with all his creatures call for
and demand, or we should entertain more exalted thoughts of him,
and live under his government with a more uninterrupted joy and
confidence than we seem to do; so as not to admit any the least
doubt or mistrust that his goodness will in the end bear down
every opposition."

After this eloquent exordium, having stated that "we behold
everywhere, and in all things, wise contrivance and intentions of
kindness," also that the rational creation are formed by their

of wickedness and fury, have done more ill than innocent actions through their whole
lives."
    See Bishop Law's Translation of Archbishop King's Origin of Evil, p. 388, fifth
edit. See also Belsham's Elements of the Philos. of Mind, p. 397-403.

great Creator "to be happy with his own happiness," in "supreme love to him and invincible affection to all our fellow-creatures;" he lays it down "as a safe and solid foundation of reasoning, that as the universe and all things in it are made to produce happiness, and as there was nothing to overrule him in his operations, such a discordant revolting mixture as vice and misery would not have been admitted, but because he saw it necessary for the fulfilment of his benevolent purposes, or rather because those purposes could not be obtained without it."

This, which is probable in theory, Photinus proves " to be true in fact;" for, if there had been no moral evil, mankind would have been destitute of those dispositions and affections which are their highest perfection, and the source of their purest happiness. Where would have been patience and forgiveness of injuries; where the godlike disposition of returning good for evil; if there had been no fraud, or cruelties, or oppression? " Had the good and virtuous of mankind been wholly prosperous," says an excellent person; "had goodness never met with opposition, where had been the trial, the victory, the crown of virtue?"   He concludes with the important and sublime inferences, " So that, as it has been justly said of natural evil, pain, diseases, and the like, in vindication of the divine goodness, that there is no useless evil; so must we say of moral evil, sin, and wickedness, that, in the hands of God, every evil of every kind is made an instrument of greater good and higher felicity than would otherwise have been enjoyed."

Here Volusian, in a kind of ecstasy, interrupts Photinus to express his delight in the satisfactory solution which his friend had given of this most difficult of all problems, the introduction of moral evil.   And he laments that the great Frederic and his friend D'Alembert, rather than acquiesce in this easy and probable hypothesis, should have assumed that the Deity, if he exists at all, is an evil and imperfect Being; that Christianity is untrue; and that there is no future life in which the difficulties and obliquities of the present state would be solved and rectified; while he applauds the opposite conduct of M. Turgot, the able and disinterested minister of Louis XVI., who, though, under the influence of invincible and inevitable prejudices, he rejected the Christian revelation, entertained just ideas of the Divine character, and was a believer in a future life.

Photinus, resuming his discourse after Volusian had finished, observes, "that it is matter of the highest exultation and joy, in which we may justly triumph, to be fully assured that mere arbitrary will and sovereignty, from which we could never know what we were to expect, has no sway in the divine government under which we are placed; and that original love and goodness are the beginning and end, the spring and measure, of all the actions of the Deity, and of all his dealings with us. Hence we conclude, that every evil of every kind is ordained for present or ultimate good. All natural and moral evils are from God, and under his sovereign control."

To guard against the abuse of this sublime doctrine, Photinus remarks, that " we frail, ignorant creatures are on no account to transgress the plain rule of moral duty, and to do evil that good may come; because our understandings are weak and limited, and we cannot be sure that the good we intend will happen. But our Maker, out of that limited quantity of evil which he judges fitting to appoint or permit, continually produces virtue and every good." And he offers some observations to obviate the common objection that this doctrine represents God as the author of sin.

" We shall avoid," says Photinus, " some of the perplexity and difficulties in which good minds are wont to be involved, from the idea of the evil actions of men being of divine appointment, as though God himself were the immediate author of sin and wickedness, if we consider that the Almighty Being, if we may so speak, acteth not immediately himself in directing the actions of men and influencing them to good and evil, but by the intervention of second causes; in other words, it is by the different motives which arise in our minds from our situation and circumstances, which are all of divine appointment, that we are led to evil and to good." Upon this supposition he explains the case of Lydia, whose heart the Lord had opened, and that of Pharaoh, whose heart was hardened. He afterwards adds, that "though we cannot but be persuaded that all the actions of men are under the antecedent appointment and direction of God (for how could he otherwise govern the world?), yet mankind are not a mere piece of clock-work, a set of unconscious machines. They acquire voluntary powers, by which they do what they please, choose for themselves, and follow their choice; take blame to, and condemn, themselves when they do what is wicked; and, more than this, think themselves not unrighteously dealt with in being made to suffer for their evil dispositions and actions in order to correct and amend them; nor, if they continue unreformed, to expect to escape punishment in a future state. So that, if God be charged in any way with being the author of men's sins, it is not in any such sense as to acquit the perpetrators, or to excuse them even in their own estimate from being responsible." Photinus sums up his argument by stating that "we are conscious that we are not mere puppets acted upon, but agents responsible for what we do. We are also fully persuaded, that all we do is beforehand known to God, and appointed by him. How this divine knowledge and appointment are to be reconciled to the freedom and responsibility of our actions, is beyond our comprehension; nor need we be at all concerned about it." And he pleads Mr. Locke's declaration and example for giving it up as an inexplicable difficulty.

The venerable writer's solution of this famous difficulty does not appear to be perfectly satisfactory. The question may be considered either popularly or philosophically. As a popular question, it is sufficient to state, that vice and wickedness, arising from the bad passions of men, will and ought to be punished here or hereafter; and, which is indeed true, that the foreknowledge of God makes no difference either in the crime or the punishment. But if the inquisitive mind, pursuing the inquiry in a philosophical way, is brought to the conclusion, which the venerable writer so clearly and forcibly states, that all evil, natural and moral, proceeds from God, and that vice, as well as misery, is of divine appointment, it becomes a serious question, and appears under the shape of a formidable objection to this sublime doctrine, Does it not make God the author of sin ? And is not God unrighteous in punishing sinners ? Nor will such an inquirer be satisfied with being told that God does not act directly upon the will, but through the medium of motives; and that we are conscious that we are not puppets, but responsible agents, and that guilt is deserving of punishment. For in the first case it will immediately occur, that the cause of the cause is the cause of the foreseen effect; and that to leave a child upon a bank, from which it will inevitably roll into the river, is the same as to push him in. And in the second case, it is asked, Where is the justice of punishing what was inevitable ?

The true solution of the first difficulty, whether God be the author of sin ? appears to be this, that God is, strictly speaking, the author of evil; but that, in the first place, he never ordains or permits evil but with a view to the production of a greater good, which could not have existed without it. And, secondly, that though God is the author of evil both natural and moral, he is not the approver of evil; he does not delight in it for its own sake; it must be the object of his aversion, and what he would never permit or endure if the good he intends could have been accomplished without it. As to the second question, concerning the justice of punishment, the best and only philosophical solution of it is, that under the divine government all punishment is remedial. Moral evil is the disease, punishment is the process of cure, of greater or less intensity, and of longer or shorter duration, in proportion to the malignity and inveteracy of the distemper, but ultimately of sovereign efficacy under the divine government to operate a perfect cure; so that those whose vices have been the means of proving, purifying, and exalting the virtues of others, shall, in the end, share with them in their virtue and their triumph; and the impartial justice and infinite benevolence of the Divine Being will be made known, adored, and celebrated to all eternity, through the whole created universe. But to return to the author:

Photinus having finished his discourse, Synesius rose to speak;

but the company agreed to defer the conversation to another opportunity.

In the fifth conversation, Synesius takes the lead. This gentleman, a real character it should seem in the Conversations upon Christian Idolatry, is represented as a blunt man, of sound understanding, zealous for the church, though seldom seen within its walls, and not much attached to its peculiar doctrines. He introduces the conversation with a profession of his conversion, and a recantation of his past errors, particularly in his doubts concerning the Divine character, his scepticism concerning the Mosaic cosmogony, his account of the primitive dispensations of God to the human race, and the destruction of the Canaanites : he expresses his great satisfaction in the "vast care and attention" which the writers of the Old Testament display in " teaching and holding forth" the Unity of God; and wonders that at this time of day Mr. De Luc should take so much pains to " deprive us of the one true God, and introduce in lieu of him a God consisting of three persons," upon the authority of the exploded text of the heavenly witnesses, which the Bishop of Lincoln, " to the credit of his judgment and integrity," gives up as spurious. Synesius further expresses his satisfaction in the solution given to the great difficulty, that " Christianity should have done so little to reform the world : " and he particularly admires Dr. Adams's judicious and temperate reply to the severe and unfounded sarcasms of Mr. Hume upon the Jewish nation, and their sacred writings, citing at length both the objection and the reply. Synesius then notices the character of Abraham, and enters into a defence of the account of his offering up his son Isaac, first in the words of Archbishop Tillotson, and afterwards by some observations of his own.

In conclusion, Synesius observes that his friends, after all, " had left untouched a main difficulty which Christianity puts in their way, by teaching the doctrine of endless punishments." They had indeed shown, that virtue naturally leads to happiness, and vice to misery; and that in the state after death, as we continue under the same laws and divine moral government, those severe

punishments which await evil-doers must, in the progress of infinite ages, produce a return to virtue and goodness." He further
submits to their consideration, that "as the Scriptures teach that
all the dead shall be raised and judged according to their works,
and do thereby implicitly give us hope, may we not rather say,
give us humble assurance, that the gloomy sentence of annihila-
tion will not pass on any of our species; for we cannot entertain a
thought that our benevolent Creator would bring back his
creatures to life to put them on the rack as it were, and make
them suffer for a time and then consign them to their primitive
nothing; we may, therefore, make this inference, that none of the
human race will be consigned to fruitless, unavailing suffering
and misery for ever, but that, by the discipline to which they will
be doomed, all will be brought to repentance and be saved." He
further professes, that "the threatenings of eternal punishment in
the gospel have long since ceased to make any impression upon his
mind, being counterbalanced by contrary declarations that God
loveth all his creatures, and would not that any should perish, but
that all should have everlasting life;" and he cannot be disappointed in his purposes.

Synesius having ended his harangue, Photinus applauds the
observations of his friend, and particularly "what he had done to
relieve the gospel from the imputation of holding forth the
doctrine of eternal torments, a mill-stone which some mistaken
Christians had hung about it, and thereby alienated the minds of
many." He then proceeds to state, that "the words *eternal,
everlasting, for ever*, and the like, generally signify limited periods
of duration: so that our Saviour meant only to express that the
sufferings of a future state would be of an exceeding long duration,
and thereby to enforce the necessity of attending to the divine
laws, and the dreadful danger of violating them;" and he concludes the conversation with a pertinent quotation from Dr.
Hartley's Observations on Man, in which that great philosopher,
with his usual acuteness and strength of argument, establishes
the joyful doctrine of the "ultimate unlimited happiness of all
mankind."

In the sixth and last conversation, Synesius is again almost the only speaker. Having observed to Marcellinus, that after having hinted at the existence of an evil spirit as one of the supposed causes of the "great misery and wickedness complained of in the world, he had afterwards been wholly silent about it;" he represents the vindication of the divine goodness as very "lame and defective," unless they can show the insufficiency of the evidence produced to prove "the existence of such a foul malignant fiend," and "begs permission to state his own thoughts upon the subject, which he had with some diligence put together." The company having expressed high satisfaction, Synesius enters with alacrity upon the interesting argument. He first expresses his surprise that it should be so generally current with the learned as well as the unlearned, that the serpent who tempted Eve was a wicked spirit, when Moses gives no such intimation, and never alludes to the existence of any such evil being in any of the five books ascribed to him.

The word Satan in the Old Testament is only used to signify an adversary, which is its proper meaning. And that the Jewish Scriptures contain no revelation of the existence and agency of an evil spirit is evident, because "we perceive not in them any religious exhortations or cautions to beware of the wiles and power of such an evil being from first to last."

Synesius further argues, that "as the Christian Scriptures certainly contain no new revelation of an evil being, and as the Jewish Scriptures did not teach it, the Jews must have acquired this notion during the captivity, and probably from the Chaldeans among whom they dwelt." This doctrine was incorporated into their theology, and their language framed and accommodated to it; and this would remain in common use even after the doctrine itself was given up. "And to this language our Saviour and his apostles would conform themselves, though there be no good reason to think that either the one or the other gave credit to the reality of this evil being."

The speaker having remarked that no evil being had any concern in Christ's temptation, proceeds to state our Lord's own sentiments concerning Satan ; and shows—1. "That Christ very commonly uses the word in its primary sense, as signifying an adversary, as when he said to Peter, Get thee behind me, Satan." 2. "There is no reason to believe that he ever means to imply that there was in reality any such being ;" for example, by the expression, " I saw Satan as lightning fall from heaven," he means nothing more than selfish worldly desires, hatred of God and goodness, &c.* He then adduces many passages in which the word Satan, devil, &c., are used figuratively to express the principle of evil in general, or evil habits and affections in particular. And from various citations from the Acts and the Epistles he draws the conclusion, that "the apostles of Christ, like their great Master, seem not to have understood that there was any devil or evil being without them whom men need to be afraid of."

"The sum of all is this : There is no evil in the world but what takes its rise from men themselves; nor any devils, but so far as men extremely wicked and abandoned may deserve the name. And to uphold such evil beings is to engraft heathenism on Christianity."†

" To these conclusions of Synesius the whole company gave their

* Satan, i.e. the enemy, the principle of hostility, the opposing persecuting power ; Christ, by the spirit of prophecy, foresaw that his gospel should make a rapid progress in the world, and triumph over all opposition. This interpretation seems better to suit the primary sense of the word and the connection in which it is introduced, than that of the venerable writer in the character of Synesius. See the Improved Version on Luke x. 17, 18.

† The venerable author in a note, highly gratifying, though too partial to the writer of this Memoir, has referred to a passage upon the subject of this conversation in his review of Mr. Wilberforce's Treatise. A more complete and accurate view of the subject may be found in the Rev. John Simpson's Dissertations on the Language of Scripture. The writer of this Memoir has also treated the subject much more at large in a series of Discourses delivered from the pulpit, which may perhaps at some future time be offered to the public. In the mean time, may he be permitted to express the high gratification he feels at the recollection that when his venerable friend, bending under the weight of years, was taking his final leave of the public, almost the last sentence that he penned should be a public testimony of affection and friendship to the writer of this Memoir, which that writer esteems as the highest honour and happiness of his life, and an ample compensation for all his exertions and sacrifices, whatever they may have been, in the cause of truth and undefiled Christianity, even (as Dr. Priestley expresses it on another occasion) had they been ten times more and greater than they were.

hearty concurrence; and after these friendly conferences, they returned to their respective homes and duties, more fully impressed with their obligation as Christians to study the word and works of God, to add practice to knowledge, and to communicate to others that light and truth which lead to eternal life."

The "Conversations upon the Divine Government" are not, perhaps, equal, as a composition, to those upon Christian Idolatry, which were published ten years before. The speeches are rather too long and too formal; and the sentiments of the speakers are not sufficiently contrasted to keep up the spirit of the dialogue. Also, the arguments and criticisms are such as will not in every case satisfy the critical reader. And the venerable writer has needlessly encumbered his work, and in some degree weakened his argument, by assuming, and that in rather too lofty a tone, the credibility of the whole, or at least of too great a proportion, of what is commonly called the Mosaic history. But the work is curious and interesting, as containing the last thoughts of an eminently pious, benevolent, and inquisitive mind upon a variety of subjects of great practical importance. Much of the philosophical part of the work is admirable, and the arguments are irresistible. In his conclusions he sometimes falters by adopting popular rather than philosophical language. But in the grand conclusion of all, the assertion of the great and sublime doctrine of the ultimate unlimited virtue and happiness of all mankind as the glorious consummation of the divine government, and the illustrious and magnificent display of infinite and impartial goodness overruling, absorbing, and extinguishing all vice and misery in the creation, the venerable author is explicit and decided. The work exhibits a most interesting view of the aged patriarch's pious, candid, benevolent, and cheerful mind, of his humble and devotional spirit, and of the happy influence of that rare combination of the principles of a sublime philosophy with the doctrines of a pure and unsophisticated Christianity, which, when they become the ruling principles of conduct, elevate the human character to its highest dignity, and ensure the most substantial, exalted, and permanent felicity. Thus gently, thus usefully, did this eminent

servant and minister of Christ pursue his way to that quiet abode
which is the house appointed for all the living.

CHAPTER XV.

MR. LINDSEY SUFFERS A PARALYTIC SEIZURE, BUT RECOVERS.
DR. PRIESTLEY'S REFLECTIONS UPON THE SITUATION OF HIS
FRIEND, AND UPON MR. LINDSEY'S LAST WORK. MR. LINDSEY
INTERESTS HIMSELF IN THE APPOINTMENT OF THE AUTHOR
TO THE CHAPEL IN ESSEX STREET. ENCOURAGES AND ASSISTS
THE IMPROVED VERSION. HIS GRADUAL DECLINE AND DEATH.
CONCLUSION OF THE WORK.

MR. LINDSEY, after the resignation of his office in 1793, continued for some years to enjoy an uncommon portion of health,
vigour, and activity, and that uniform flow of cheerfulness which
is the natural result of a good constitution, and the recollections
of a well-spent life. His retrospects were most gratifying, his
anticipations delightful, his principles most rational and consolatory, his circumstances easy. He was happy in the affection and
attention of the best of women, in the society of chosen and virtuous friends of principles and spirit similar to his own, in frequent correspondence with the man after his own heart, in an
ardent but unostentatious piety and confidence in God, in unlimited
resignation to the Divine will, and in the growing success of the
great cause which was nearest to his heart, the cause of Christian
truth and Christian virtue, to the revival of which he could not
but know that his own exertions and example had in a considerable
degree contributed; he possessed his faculties entire, bodily and
mental, and seemed to be in a degree privileged with exemption
from the infirmities of age. The first alarm was excited in the

spring of 1801, when Mr. and Mrs. Lindsey were upon a visit for a few days at Reigate, the residence of their learned and estimable friend, Francis Maseres, Esq., Cursitor Baron of the Exchequer.* The weather being uncommonly warm for the season, Mr. Lindsey experienced a slight paralytic affection on one side, which however disappeared in a few days. But in the latter end of December of the same year, he suffered a severe stroke, which at first excited the greatest apprehension. From this indeed he soon recovered surprisingly, so as to be able in the beginning of January following to finish his last interesting work, the Conversations upon the Divine Government. After this seizure he gradually declined in bodily strength and vigour, though he was generally free from pain, and his faculties for a considerable time were not sensibly impaired.

The writer of this Memoir first announced the painful tidings to the venerable exile at Northumberland. Soon afterwards Mrs. Lindsey wrote, and at that time Mr. Lindsey was so far recovered as to be able to add a postscript. The feelings of Dr. Priestley's affectionate heart, upon the sad intelligence of his friend's illness, are expressed with so much simplicity, and in a strain of such exalted piety, founded upon such just and philosophic views of the Christian revelation, in the following letters, that they cannot fail to be exquisitely gratifying to the serious reader.

(*To Mrs. Lindsey.*)

" Northumberland, May 8, 1802.

" Dear Madam,

" I cannot express how much I was affected on reading your letter; though I was apprized of the situation of my best friend

---

* To Mr. Baron Maseres, Mr. Lindsey acknowledges himself indebted for many favours for near thirty years, and describes his friend as " one whose liberal, benevolent, and generous labours are constantly exerted in various ways to benefit mankind, and promote the cause of true religion and virtue." And he adds that to this gentleman's "suggestions, jointly with those of John Lee, Esq., was owing the variation made in the last edition of the Reformed Liturgy in 1793, after the model of the excellent Dr. Samuel Clarke, by changing the threefold address retained in the liturgy to one solemn and appropriate one ; they justly observing, that a threefold address would keep up the old impression of a threefold nature in the Deity, so contrary to the Scriptures." Conversations on the Divine Government, p. 140, note.

by the letters of Mr. B., so that I had no reason to expect any different account. But the few lines he added with his own hand quite overcame me; and if I read them, as I shall do, a hundred times, I shall have the same emotions. Such friendship as his and yours has been to me can never be exceeded on this side the grave: and, independent of the real emolument, has been a source of such satisfaction to me as I have not derived from any other quarter. And yet what I feel is not properly grief. For, considering how near we both must be to the close of life, in which we could not promise ourselves much more enjoyment, or be of much more use, what remains cannot, according to the common course of nature, be of much value, and therefore the privation of it is no great loss. And considering how soon we may expect, and I hope without much presumption, to meet again in more favourable circumstances, the causes of joy may almost be allowed to balance those of grief. The loss to you will be much greater than to any other person, as that of such a constant companion and Christian friend necessarily must be. How few couples are there so suited to one another in dispositions and views, and those of the best and noblest kind, as you are! I have never known the like. You have therefore every reason to expect a renewal of your union, though in some other way, hereafter.

" If you saw me now, you would not flatter me with the prospect of long surviving my excellent friend. Judging from my illnesses last year, and my present feelings, I am far from expecting it myself. And indeed, as it will be the will of God, whatever the event be, and therefore no doubt for the best, I cannot say that I greatly wish it. My labours, of whatever kind and whatever be their value, are nearly over; and I have now hardly any wish but to see the printing of my Church History and Notes on the Scriptures.

" I beg, dear Madam, you would not fail to continue the correspondence of your excellent husband, and write as you say upon all sorts of subjects. Whatever interests you will interest me, and I hope Mr. Lindsey, whenever he is able, will add his signature.

"Yours and Mr. Lindsey's most affectionately,

"J. P."

(*Rev. T. Lindsey.*)

"Northumberland, June 26, 1802.

"Dear Friend,

"Whether it be you or Mrs. Lindsey that is my correspondent, I consider it as the same thing. You are alike my friends, and my best friends; and whoever survives, this correspondence will not, I hope, cease, while it is possible to continue it, on this side the grave. This great change to which we are making near approaches, I regard, I hope I may say, with more curiosity than anxiety. It is the wise order of Providence that death should intervene between the two different modes of existence, and what engages my thoughts is the change itself, more than the mere manner of making it. I look at your portrait, and that of Dr. Price and Mr. Lee, which are always before me, and think of my deceased friends whose portraits I have not, with peculiar satisfaction, under the idea that I shall at no great distance of time see them again, and I hope with pleasure. But *how* we shall meet again, and *how* we shall be employed, we have little or no ground even for conjecture. It should satisfy us, however, that we shall be at the disposal, and under the government, of the same wise and good Being who has superintended us here, and who knows what place and employment will best suit all of us. The more I think of the wonderful system of which we are a part, the less I think of any difficulties about the reality or the circumstances of a future state. The resurrection is really nothing compared to the wonders of every day in the regular course of nature: and the only reason why we do not wonder is, because the appearances are common. Whether it be because I converse less with *men* in this remote situation, I contemplate the scenes of nature, as the production of its great Author, more, and with more satisfaction, than I ever did before ; and the new discoveries that are now making in every branch of science, interest me more than ever in this connection. I see before us a boundless field of the noblest investigation, and all we yet know appears to me as nothing, compared to what we are wholly ignorant of, and do not as yet perceive any means of access to it. I now take great pleasure in my garden, and plants as well as other objects engage more of my attention than they ever did before; and I see those things in a more pleasing light than ever. I wish I knew a little more of botany, but old as I am I learn something new continually. I admire Dr. Darwin's Phytologia, and am reading it a second time. But this work, which I believe contains all that we yet know of this part of nature, shows me how little that *all* is. Before he died, I am informed he was about to publish another work, in which he maintained the doctrine of equivocal generation; and of all absurdities this appears to me to be the greatest, if by it they mean to exclude intelligence from the system of nature. And I cannot see any other reason why unbelievers in revelation should lean, as many now do, to that doctrine. Their faith has certainly less evidence than ours.

" I have written a dedication of the second part of my History to Mr. Jefferson, and have sent him a copy of it for his approbation. The preface is the longest I ever wrote; but I hope you will not dislike it. It consists chiefly of reflections on the middle and dark ages. As soon as a copy can be made up, one shall be sent to you. In the Monthly Magazine I see an account of your late publication. How I long to see it ! and surely it might have been here as soon as that magazine.

" I have not heard from Mr. Johnson for near two years. My time is short and uncertain, and consequently my wants, though not many, are urgent.

" Yours and Mrs. Lindsey's most affectionately,

" J. P.

" I have just received yours of March 23. I need not say how happy it makes me."

U

Dr. Priestley's next letter is an answer to this of Mr. Lindsey's ; the insertion of it will need no apology ; the sentiments contained in it must be acceptable to every friend of the Christian religion who has a head to think, or a heart to feel.

" Northumberland, July 3, 1802.

" Dear Friend,

" How rejoiced I was to receive your letter *written wholly with your own hand,* after your late alarming attack ! I now hope I shall have more of them ; and nothing on this side the grave gives me more satisfaction.   And yet, considering how soon we may hope to meet again, the separation by death should not give us much concern.   While we live we ought to value life and friendship, especially Christian friendship, as the balm of it.   But we have a better life in prospect, and therefore should not regret the parting with the worse, provided we have enjoyed it properly, and improved it so as to have ensured the better.   Absolute confidence does not become any man, conscious, as we all must be, of many imperfections, of omissions, if not of commissions.   But surely, a general sincere endeavour to do what we apprehend to be our duty, will authorize so much hope as will be the reasonable foundation of joy, with respect to a future state, without being chargeable with arrogance or presumption.

" You could not have made choice of a more pleasing or interesting subject than that of the work which you have happily completed, and which, as I believe it is in Philadelphia, I expect very soon to receive.   It occupies my own thoughts, I may say almost constantly, and is the greatest source of satisfaction that in my present situation, and under my late trials, I enjoy.   Indeed the reflection that we are under the government of the wisest and best of Beings, and that nothing can befall us without his permission, is sufficient to balance the very idea of evil, and make us regard everything as a good, for which we ought to be thankful.   At the moment, none who have the hearts and feelings of men but must grieve for many things that he sees and feels.   But Christian principles soon bring relief, and are capable of converting all sorrow into joy.   But this will be in proportion to the strength of our faith, in consequence of the exercise of it; when, according to Hartley, speculative faith is converted into practical.

"We have printed one volume of the History, and, as I told you, I have dedicated it to Mr Jefferson. I enclose his letter on receiving a manuscript copy of it. I have since altered it, I hope, to his mind, and shall very soon send it, together with the volume. I do not mean to dispose of any of the copies till all the three volumes be completed, which, if I do not take a journey in October, will be done about Christmas. I now hope you will see this work, and even the Notes on the Scriptures, which I hope you will like still better. As I wish you particularly to see the Preface and Dedication, I shall send a copy by the next post. The latter will not please you, as not calculated for England. But I have done with that country, and am indifferent to what my enemies may think of me. I shall always appear, as I am, a sincere friend to the country, and shall not with intention say anything offensive of its constitution, or the administration of it. I rejoice that its situation is much better than I feared such a war would leave it.

"Yours and Mrs. Lindsey's most affectionately,

"J. PRIESTLEY."

How great must be the excellence of those principles which, in circumstances that to a common mind would be most depressing, could produce this habitual consolation, peace and hope, and could convert evil itself into good, and sorrow into joy! How infinitely superior to that sad and cheerless scepticism which can meet the troubles of life, the evils of oppression and persecution, and the separation or death of friends, with nothing better than a stern and stoical apathy, and is destitute of every pleasing and consolatory hope of a life to come! It was a just observation of Lord Rochester, that if Christianity be a delusion, it is a pleasing delusion. And strictly true is the remark of Dr. Price, that the worst which can happen to the Christian is the best which can be expected by the unbeliever. On the other hand, how much more dignified that equal tenor of mind, that tranquil and sublime satisfaction, which is the result of enlarged and comprehensive views, and of a sober

U 2

and rational faith, than those ecstatic raptures of which some make their boast, which result from a fancied arbitrary election of themselves to happiness, and the unintelligible imputation of another's righteousness as a substitute for their own, while millions are left to perish, and even doomed to eternal torments, for the sin of a remote ancestor !　One marks the fond credulity of a child; the other, the cultivated intellect of the man.　How much to be desired, how pleasing to look forward to, that new and happy era which the word of prophecy authorizes us to anticipate, when all those puerile conceits, those anti-Christian doctrines, which are the crude offspring of ages of ignorance and superstition, which obscure and disgrace the fair form of true religion, shall be dispelled as mists before the rising sun, and genuine, uncorrupted Christianity, with its beautiful and animating ray, shall enlighten every understanding, and enliven every heart !

Mr. Jefferson's answer to Dr. Priestley's letter, enclosing a copy of it for the President's perusal, previous to its publication, is given in the notes as an interesting document, highly creditable to the character of that eminent person.*　The original letter, with Mr. Jefferson's signature, is in the author's possession.

(*To the Rev. Dr. Priestley.*)

" Dear Sir,　　　　　　　　　　　" Washington, June 19, 1802.
" Your favour of the 12th has been duly received, and with that pleasure which the approbation of the good and the wise must ever give.　The sentiments it expresses are far beyond my merits or pretensions.　They are precious testimonies to me, however, that my sincere desire to do what is right and just is received with candour.　That it should be handed to the world under the authority of your name is securing its credit with posterity.

" In the great work which has been effected in America, no individual has a right to take a great share to himself.　Our people, in a body, are wise, because they are under the unrestrained and unperverted operation of their own understandings.　Those whom they have assigned to the direction of their affairs have stood with a pretty even front. If any one of them was withdrawn, many others, entirely equal, have been ready to fill his place with as good abilities.　A nation composed of such materials, and free in all its members from distressing wants, furnishes hopeful implements for the interesting experiment of self-government, and we feel that we are acting under obligations not confined to the limits of our own society.　It is impossible not to be sensible that we are acting for all mankind : that circumstances, denied to others but indulged to us, have imposed on us the duty of proving what is the degree of freedom and self-government in which a society may venture to leave its individual members.

" One passage in the paper you enclosed me must be corrected ; it is the following : ' And all say that it was yourself more than any other individual that planned and established the Constitution.'　I was in Europe when the Constitution was planned and established,

In the letter enclosing this from Mr. Jefferson, dated August 28, 1802, and addressed to Mr. Lindsey, Dr. Priestley tells his friend that he had just been very happy by the receipt of a letter from him, dated May 5, and expresses his great satisfaction at hearing of a scheme which had been formed and adopted for defraying the expense of printing his two great works. In noticing Mr. Jefferson's letter, he adds, " Such things as these give us a better idea of a man's principles and character than more public documents. I shall not be able to visit him as he wishes. Indeed the state of my health is such as warns me that I have no time to lose; and I am desirous of doing all I can in what remains of life. If well spent, longer or shorter makes no difference; but mine has been a long life, though not so long as yours. Whenever we die, we shall start together at the same time hereafter. May it be in the same place, and our happy connection be resumed !"

In the next letter, dated September 25, after expressing his anxiety to hear about his friend's state of health, Dr. Priestley adds, " It would be extreme folly for either of us to flatter our-

and never saw it till after it was established. On receiving it, I wrote strongly to Mr. Madison, urging the want of provision for the freedom of religion, freedom of the press, trial by jury, habeas corpus, the substitution of militia for a standing army, and an express reservation to the States of all the rights not specifically granted to the Union. He accordingly moved, in the first session of Congress, for these amendments, which were agreed to and ratified by the States as they now stand. This is all the hand I had in what related to the Constitution. Our predecessors made it doubtful how far even these were of any value. For the very law which endangered your personal safety, the Alien Act, as well as that which restrained the freedom of the press, were gross violations of them. However, it is still certain, that though written Constitutions may be violated in moments of passion or delusion, yet they furnish a text to which those who are watchful may again rally, and recall the people. They fix too for the people principles for their practical creed.

" We shall all absent ourselves from this place during the sickly season, say, from the 22nd of July to the last of September. Should your curiosity lead you hither either before or after that interval, I shall be very happy to receive you, and shall claim you as my guest. I wish the advantages of a mild over a winter climate had been tried for you, before you were located where you are. I have ever considered this as a public as well as personal misfortune. The choice you made of our country as your asylum, was honourable to it; and I lament that, for the sake of your happiness and health, its most benign climates were not selected. Certainly it is a truth that climate is one of the sources of the greatest sensual enjoyment. I received in due time the letter referred to in your last with the pamphlet it enclosed, which I read with the pleasure I do everything from you. Accept assurances of my highest veneration and respect.

" THOS. JEFFERSON."

selves with the prospect of many years to come; nor at our time of life is it in general desirable. Before this time, the business of life, whatever it has been, must be over, and nothing can remain but retrospect; and with respect to neither of us, I trust, is this very painful; though no man ever lived who might not have done more good in the world (and for that end we came into it) than he actually did. Of late, but not more than a fortnight, I have had a better prospect of health than I have had for a considerable time, having no ague or indisposition of any kind, and I feel nothing of the languor which I did for some time past, but as much ardour in my pursuits as I generally have had, though I find I am not capable of doing as much. I now hope, that with care, I may see through the printing of both my works, and I have hardly a wish to live longer, especially as I shall hardly be capable of undertaking anything more of much importance."

I shall insert the next letter almost entire; not only because it contains Dr. Priestley's opinion of Mr. Lindsey's last work, and expresses many fine sentiments concerning the wisdom and goodness of the divine government, but because of the strong testimony which, after a friendship of thirty years, the venerable writer bears to the excellence of Mrs. Lindsey's character, and her vigorous and successful exertions in doing good, which can hardly be conceived by those who only saw that extraordinary woman in the last year or two of her active and useful life, when her health and faculties were in a rapid decline. The letter is dated October 16, 1802, and is addressed to Mrs. Lindsey:

"Dear Madam,—What do I not owe to you and Mr. Lindsey, and at present more particularly to yourself? If I have been of any use in the world since my acquaintance with you, one half of it at least must be placed to your account. I have, I hope, endeavoured to improve my opportunities and means, but these have been in a great measure furnished by you. Without your active assistance I find that the works which I have now in hand would hardly have been printed in my lifetime, unless I should live longer than I have any reason to expect.* Dr. Doddridge used to say, he was confident there would be more women in heaven. than men; and certainly you excel in the milder, and, what are more peculiarly called, the Christian virtues of patience, meekness, sympathy, and kindness; and I think that the history of persecutions proves you have your full share of the more heroic virtues,

* Dr. Priestley here alludes to the exertions which were made by his friends in England to raise a sum of money to defray the expense of printing his two great works. The writer of this Memoir learning, from his own and Mr. Lindsey's correspondence with Dr. Priestley, the difficulties which had occurred upon this subject, and apprehensive lest, after all, the Christian world might be deprived of the benefit of his most valuable labours for want of a sufficient fund to enable him to publish the work, it occurred to him that if a hundred persons could be found to subscribe five pounds each for a copy of the whole of both the works, and to pay their subscriptions in advance, every difficulty would be surmounted. No sooner was the proposal made than it was adopted with great ardour and zeal by Dr. Priestley's numerous friends, and the friends of freedom of inquiry in general; so that the sum wanted was very soon far exceeded, and the venerable exile's mind was made perfectly easy. Mrs. Lindsey exerted her usual energies in the cause, and his friends at Birmingham and Hackney were not deficient; and among these no one was more indefatigable or successful than Benjamin Travers, Esq., then resident at Clapton. The list of subscribers was numerous and respectable. The Duke of Grafton, with his accustomed liberality, subscribed fifty pounds, and his noble friend Lord Clarendon twenty, Mr. Lindsey twenty, and Robert Slaney, Esq., of Tong Lodge, the generous friend of all that is liberal and good, thirty guineas, with a promise of more if more should be wanted. And now that he is at rest beyond the reach of envy and of calumny, from which neither exalted station nor exalted merit could have protected him here, it may be permitted to mention, that by far the most liberal subscriber to this object was the late Right Reverend Dr. John Law, Bishop of Elphin, one of the numerous able and prosperous family of the late learned and liberal prelate of Carlisle, and brother to the late Lord Chief Justice of England, and to the Bishop of Chester. An extract from the Bishop of Elphin's interesting letter shall close this note. It is addressed to Mr. Lindsey, who had sent him a copy of his last publication, dated Elphin, October 7, 1802.

"My dear Sir,—Want of health, and indisposition, have prevented me from thanking you for your letter and obliging present sooner. I have read your valuable work with as much attention as pains in the head and stomach, arising from a flying gout, would let me; and think it is calculated to do a great deal of good.

"Enclosed is a draft for one hundred pounds, which you will apply in aid of Dr. Priestley's publication, in any way he chooses; but my name must on no account be mentioned to him, or any one else, as it would involve me with some acquaintance here, and do me more mischief than you can imagine, and which I am sure you would not wish. Our religion hereabouts is evidenced chiefly in hating and abusing those that differ from us; and excepting this zeal, we scarce show in other things that we have any. You will be surprised at it, but neither Popery nor Methodism are losing any ground.

"Reprint my father's Life of Christ whenever you please, and believe me to be, with the sincerest esteem,

"Your very faithful and obedient servant,
"J. ELPHIN."

Mr. Lindsey availed himself of the Bishop's permission to reprint the Life of Christ, and this small but valuable tract is now upon the catalogue of books circulated by the Unitarian Society.

and have shown as much true courage as men. When I reflect, as I often do, on the character of my good aunt, that of Mrs. Rayner, and to those let me add yours, I do not think that I can find many of my acquaintances to compare with them among men; and yet I have known many of great excellence. Of these, the foremost in my list are Dr. Price, Mr. Tayleur of Shrewsbury, and Mr. Lindsey. Those in a lower class, however, are numerous; and I doubt not but that hereafter we shall find there has always been more virtue than vice in the world, and that the vice has had its use in producing virtue. The more I contemplate the great system, the more satisfaction I find in it; and the structure being so perfect, there cannot be a doubt but that the end and use of it in promoting happiness will correspond to it. These views, as I take more pleasure than ever in Natural History, contribute much to brighten the evening of my days. But my great resource is the Scriptures, which I have not of a long time passed a single day without reading a portion of, and I am more interested in it continually. I seem now to see it with other eyes, and all other reading is comparatively insipid.

" But I shall tire you with my moralizing. You are very kind to interest yourself about my health. On this day se'nnight I wrote to Dr. Disney, and told him I was much recruited. But this week I have relapsed again, but without fever. The least thing disorders my power of digestion: and when I have anything amiss there, it is a long time before I get right again. At present, a long continued indigestion seems to have affected the liver. I feel in several respects as I did when I was subject to the gall-stones; and being further advanced in life, I am less able to struggle with disease of any kind. My flesh and muscular strength are greatly impaired. I hope, however, that with care I may live to print the two works, and then my mind will be entirely at ease. Whatever may be thought of them, I have spared no pains to make them as perfect as I could, and both the works are of a kind that I am sure are much wanted.

" I find by Mr. Lindsey that my tract on Baptism has arrived: and his two words of approbation are a sufficient reward for my labour. I hope he will live to see what I am now printing, as the History will probably be printed before the winter be out, and another year will be sufficient for the Notes on the Scriptures. I no more expect fame than I do profit from either of these works, but neither of them is any object with me at present. I have had enough of every thing that this world can give me, and consider my lot as having been a *singularly happy one.* But I flatter myself that my writings, which are overlooked at present, will be found useful some time hence.

" Mr. Lindsey's last work I read with peculiar satisfaction ; it is excellently adapted to gain its object, and discovers a happy and most desirable state of mind with which to take leave of the world : praising the great and benevolent Author of it, and looking forward to the same excellent disposition of things hereafter.

" Give my best respects to the ladies at Morden. I shall never forget their excellent characters, or their kindness to myself. Remember me also to Dr. Blackburne.* I often wish I was under his care.

" Yours and Mr. Lindsey's most affectionately,

" J. PRIESTLEY."

Many letters of thanks and testimonies of approbation were sent to Mr. Lindsey upon the publication of his last excellent work : of these I shall take the liberty of inserting an extract from one by the Rev. Christopher Wyvill, of Burton Hall, near Bedale, in Yorkshire, a name that will be ever dear to the friends of civil and religious liberty, the celebrated Chairman of the Yorkshire Association for the Reform of the Commons House of Parliament, and who is terminating his long career of patriotic exertion by a series of vigorous and benevolent efforts in the cause of universal religious liberty, to which few would be equal even in the meridian of life. Nor is it to be despaired of, considering the changes which have lately taken place in the political world, that the

* An eminent physician in London; the Archdeacon's youngest son, and half-brother to Mrs. Lindsey, now resident near Wells, in Somersetshire.

veteran champion of the rights of conscience may live to see the complete success of his generous exertions, at a time when success was the least expected. In a letter dated from Burton Hall, March 31, 1802, he thus addresses his aged friend, whose views and principles upon almost every subject were congenial with his own:

" My dear Sir,—Last night I finished the perusal of your Conversations on the Divine Benevolence, and other subjects connected with it, and I hasten to return you my cordial thanks for the pleasure and benefit I have derived from it. I think your last work, if it is to be your last work, closes your labours with great honour to yourself and utility to the world, by presenting such an amiable picture of religion, as must, one would hope, win the affections of many who are at present disinclined. I saw nothing in which I could not agree with you; as I have long been accustomed, like yourself, to consider the goodness of God as the true foundation of religion. It is the principle of St. John; for God, he says, is love. It is the principle of our Lord; for God so loved the world that he gave his only-begotten Son, that whosoever believeth in him shall not perish, but have everlasting life. For God sent not his Son into the world to condemn the world, but that the world through him might be saved. That is the gracious design of Providence we see: and what Providence designs, as you justly argue in your book, must come to pass. On this principle, therefore, of Divine love, I have raised a structure nearly similar to that which you have built upon the same ground. I have found it the consolation of my mind, and it will be still more so from having read what you have so well drawn together to illustrate that great truth. I will only add, that the temper of your mind in the whole course of your composition well accords with the amiable principle you are recommending."

In the beginning of the year 1804, Mr. Lindsey lost his admired and beloved friend and correspondent Dr. Priestley; an event which he felt as deeply as any calamity which could have happened to him in his declining state of health and vigour, but the tidings of which he bore, as has been already observed, with the Christian fortitude and resignation of one who was hastening apace to the same quiet and undisturbed abode, and who hoped for a speedy and happy re-union in a better state, and in more auspicious circumstances.

Two events occurred after the decease of Dr. Priestley, which, from the-light in which they were viewed by the venerable patriarch, contributed greatly to cheer and enliven his closing day. The first was the very lively interest which he took in the appointment of the writer of this Memoir to be the officiating minister at the chapel in Essex Street, in succession to Dr. Disney, whose infirm state of health obliged him to resign his charge in the spring of 1805. This event, the idea of which first occurred to Mr. Lindsey, and to the accomplishment of which both he and Mrs. Lindsey contributed their utmost and united efforts, seemed for a time at least to infuse fresh vigour into his debilitated frame; and upon this occasion he resumed his seat in the chapel, from which he had for some time withdrawn on account of his declining health. This attendance upon public worship Mr. Lindsey continued with exemplary regularity for upwards of two years and a half: he often expressed himself as particularly gratified with the attendance of the young persons upon those Lectures on the Evidences and Doctrines of Revealed Religion, which were introduced by the preacher after the morning service; and he augured the best consequences to the interests of truth and goodness from that spirit of inquiry which discovered itself in the rising generation. May those favourable prognostications be happily verified in the event! After the first Sunday in November, 1807, Mr. Lindsey's feeble state of health and his growing infirmities compelled him finally, but reluctantly, to withdraw from the chapel worship.

The other event alluded to was the publication of the Improved Version of the New Testament by the Unitarian Society, of which it will be proper to give a brief account.

In the spring of the year 1789, Dr. Priestley, whose active and benevolent mind was always engaged in some scheme for the instruction and improvement of mankind, formed a project, which he communicated to Mr. Lindsey, for a continually improving translation of the Scriptures of the Old and New Testament. This plan was matured at the annual interview which he had with his friend in the month of April; and it was determined immediately to engage a competent number of coadjutors, and to complete the work within the year. The general idea was, that the whole Scripture should be distributed among a certain number of translators; that the translators should adhere to certain rules which were laid down for the purpose; the principal of which was, not to deviate from the public version without an evident necessity: and superintendents were appointed to revise and correct the translation previously to its being sent to the press.* Dr.

* The following is the plan, accompanied with the rules of translating, which was printed, and circulated among those whose assistance was solicited, or to whom it was thought expedient to communicate the design :—

A Plan to procure a continually improving Translation of the Scriptures.

I. Let three persons, of similar principles and views, procure the assistance of a number of their learned friends, and let each of them undertake the translation of a portion of the whole Bible, engaging to produce it in the space of a year.

II. Let each of the translations be carefully perused by some other person than the translator himself; and especially let each of the three principals peruse the whole, and communicate their remarks to the translators.

III. Let the three principals have the power of making what alterations they please; but if the proper translator prefer his own version, let the three principals, when they print the work, insert his version in the notes or margin, distinguished by his signature.

IV. If any one of the three differ in opinion from the other two, let his version be also annexed with his signature.

V. Let the whole be printed in one volume without any notes, except as few as possible relating to the version, or the phraseology.

VI. Let the translators, and especially the three principals, give constant attention to all other new translations of the Scriptures, and all other sources of information, that they may avail themselves of them in all subsequent editions, so that this version may always be in a state of improvement.

VII. Let the three principals agree upon certain *rules of translating*, to be observed by all the rest.

VIII. On the death of any of the three principals, let the survivors make choice of another to supply his place.

IX. Let all the profits of the publication be disposed of by the three principals to some public institution in England, or any other part of the world, or in any other manner that they shall think most subservient to the causes of truth.

————

RULES OF TRANSLATING.

I. Let the translators insert in the text whatever they think it was most probable that the authors really wrote, if it has the authority of any ancient version or MS.; but if it differ from the present Hebrew or Greek copies, let the version of the present copies be inserted in the margin.

. II. If the translators give the preference to any emendation of the text not autho-

Priestley undertook to translate the Hagiographa, and engaged the writer of this Memoir to assist him in the book of Job. Mr. Frend, whose abilities and learning are well known, and who had lately seceded from the Established Church, and resigned all his well-founded hopes of preferment in it for the sake of truth and a good conscience, undertook to translate the Pentateuch, or the historical books. Mr. Dodson was applied to for translating the prophetical writings; but that gentleman not having leisure sufficient, Dr. Priestley undertook the whole. Mr. Garner, a learned, liberal, and respectable clergyman at Bury St. Edmund's, in Suffolk, engaged for, and executed, the translation of the whole New Testament. Mr. Lindsey and Mr. Dodson were to revise the work. The task, however, was found to be too great even for Dr. Priestley's energies to accomplish within the year; and it having been postponed till the summer of 1791, the riots of Birmingham unfortunately intervened, and the ruffians who broke into Dr. Priestley's house, among other valuable papers, demolished his translation of the New Testament, and in their demoniac fury they left not a wreck behind.*

This disastrous event put an entire termination to the promising

rized by any MS. or ancient version, let such conjectural emendation be inserted in the margin only.

III. Let the additions in the Samaritan copy of the Pentateuch be inserted in the text, but distinguished from the rest.

IV. Let not the present English version be changed, except for the sake of some improvement.

V. In the Old Testament, let the word Jehovah be rendered by Jehovah, and also the word *κυριος* in the New, in passages in which there is an allusion to the Old, or where it may be proper to distinguish *God* from *Christ*.

VI. Let the present division of chapters be adhered to with as little variation as possible, and the whole be divided into *paragraphs*, not exceeding about twenty of the present verses; but let all the present divisions of chapters and verses be noted in the margin.

VII. To each chapter let there be prefixed a summary of the contents, as in the common version.

* For a complete account of the irreparable loss which the theological, the philosophical, and the learned world sustained from this unparalleled outrage, see Dr. Priestley's Appeal to the Public on the Riots in Birmingham, p. 36. Of these losses, if the writer of this Memoir may presume to judge, the greatest and the most irreparable is a manuscript volume containing Illustrations of Hartley's Doctrine of the Association of Ideas, and further Observations on the Human Mind. No one ever understood Dr. Hartley's theory better than Dr. Priestley, and no writer ever exceeded him in simplicity and clearness of exposition, or in appositeness of illustration.

project of a new and continually improving translation. But the
design was never lost sight of for a moment; and when the
Unitarian Society was instituted in 1791, and especially after the
destruction of Dr. Priestley's manuscripts, the translation of the
Scriptures, and particularly of the New Testament, was a main
object of their attention.

With this view, application was first made by a deputation from
the Society, consisting of Mr. Lindsey, Mr. Dodson, and the
writer of this Memoir, to the late celebrated and learned Gilbert
Wakefield for leave to introduce his valuable translation into the
Society's catalogue; to which request Mr. Wakefield not only
gave his cordial consent, but promised to revise his translation
with the utmost care, and to render it as perfect as he was able
for the Society's use. In this generous purpose he was defeated
by the contract which he had made with his bookseller, who had
not then disposed of all the copies of the second edition. Afterwards, the Unitarian Society in the West of England formed a
project for a new translation of the New Testament, which was
soon abandoned in consequence of the sudden and unexpected
decease of the Reverend Timothy Kenrick, who took the lead in
that and every other scheme for promoting learning, truth, and
genuine Christianity in principle and practice in that district of
the united kingdom.

Here the matter rested till the General Meeting of the London
Unitarian Society in April, 1806, when it was unanimously resolved, that this important undertaking should be no longer
deferred; and a committee, consisting of all the ministers who
were members of the Society, and of a certain proportion of lay
gentlemen, was nominated to carry the resolution into effect. It
was also unanimously agreed, that instead of a translation entirely new, some respectable version already in existence should be
adopted as the basis of the new publication, into which might be
inserted the alterations which were judged necessary. The principal reasons for this decision were, that a new translation would
require a considerable length of time; that few persons had
leisure sufficient for the purpose, or were willing to incur the

responsibility; and that such a version, however impartially conducted, would be exposed to the vulgar cavil of an intentional warping of the Scripture to support an unscriptural hypothesis. As Mr. Wakefield's Version could not be obtained, Archbishop Newcome's Translation was selected, with the full consent of the late Mr. Johnson, to whom it was understood that the copyright belonged. And the reasons for selecting this Version were, that, though not faultless, it was in the main excellent; that the style in general was simple and unaffected; that the translation was fair and impartial; that it rectified many errors in the public Version; but chiefly, because the learned prelate had, in his translation, followed the corrected text of Griesbach. And though it was taken from Griesbach's first edition, the variations in the second, though numerous, are in general very inconsiderable; that learned and laborious critic having himself remarked, that his later inquiries had in general served only to confirm the critical principles and to justify the variations which he had introduced into the first edition. Another inducement for adopting the Primate's Version was, that it was out of print, without the least probability of its ever being printed again.* In order to preserve the uniformity of style, it was resolved that no alterations should be made in the Primate's language but those which were judged to be absolutely necessary. And, to preclude every possibility of misleading the reader, wherever it was thought proper to give a different translation of any passage, or to deviate even in a single expression from the Primate's text, his own words, with the initials of his name, were required to be set down at the foot of the page. So that the editors of the Improved Version, far from desiring to cast a slur upon the Primate's orthodoxy, or to avail themselves improperly and dishonourably of

---

* It is very well known that the Translation was printed while the Primate was living, but that it was withheld from the public at the request, and by the influence, of some in high station, who thought it not expedient for an Archbishop to let the public into the secret, that the common Version is capable of improvement, and that the received text, formed by the meritorious but not infallible labours of Erasmus, Stephens, Beza, and Elzevir, is not inspired. Unfortunately, the impression of the Primate's Works was much damaged in crossing the water, in consequence of being carelessly packed. So that the copies which were left for sale were comparatively very few.

his truly respectable name, to give currency to opinions contrary to his avowed sentiments, really considered themselves as entitled to thanks for having rescued a meritorious work from oblivion, and having given a wider extent to its circulation; and they conscientiously believed that the pious and venerable prelate himselt, had he been living, would not have condemned the liberty which they have taken with it.*

* The only person, excepting the possessor of the copyright, who had a right to be offended at the liberty taken by the editors in adopting the Primate's Version as the basis of their own, was Dr. Stock, the late venerable Bishop of Killala, and afterwards of Waterford, who published an interesting account of the invasion of Ireland by the French, who seized the Episcopal palace at Killala, and made it their head-quarters, detaining the Bishop and his family prisoners. This worthy and learned prelate also distinguished himself by his new Version of the books of Job and Isaiah; and being a near relative by affinity of the venerable Primate, he may be regarded as the proper guardian of his reputation. From this learned and respectable prelate the author of this Memoir received the following mild and polite expostulation, very different from the gross language in which the Improved Version is commonly attacked :—

" Reverend Sir,   "Bath, Aug. 7, 1809.

" I shall with pleasure avail myself, when occasion offers, of your kind invitation to call on you at Hackney. I may then, perhaps, be allowed to expostulate with you, not on the religious opinions you maintain, for these I leave to every man's own conscience, but on the covert, I had almost said the unfair, manner in which your Society have endeavoured, by the means of the New Translation, to instil those opinions into the minds of the common people. Two things I mainly object to you ; the name your Society has assumed, which is calculated to deceive by its resemblance in sound to that of another and more ancient Society in London, whose labours have been confined to the spreading of gospel truths without any mixture of opinions disputed among Christians. And, secondly, your adopting through the greater part of your work the Version of Archbishop Newcome, while, by alterations of your own, and by your comments, you endeavour to lead the reader into opinions which that respected Father of our Church entertained no more than I do. It is true you have sought to obviate this charge, by marking in your notes the difference between your interpretation and our Primate's ; but common readers will not be ready to advert to such distinctions; neither can the friends to Primate Newcome's reputation be pleased to see his name coupled, as it was sometimes most untruly in his lifetime, with those of the Unitarians and Socinians. I have the honour to be, with respect, Reverend Sir, your most obedient humble servant.

" JOSEPH KILLALA."

The author of this Memoir wrote an answer to the venerable and liberal prelate, which, he trusts, satisfied his Lordship that the editors, even if they erred in their judgment, intended nothing disingenuous or unfair. He hoped to have had an opportunity by personal intercourse to have effaced every remaining unfavourable impression. But his Lordship's infirm health, and his professional avocations, did not admit of his return to the metropolis.

The reader will judge how far the Bartlett's Buildings Society, who do not venture to circulate the Bible itself but in connection with the Common Prayer Book, are entitled to the worthy prelate's encomium, of " confining themselves to spreading gospel truths without any mixture of disputed opinions." And as to the rumour that the late learned Primate favoured the Unitarian principles, it is a certain fact that the Primate's own

It was an object of primary consideration with the society, that the Version published under their sanction should contain notes explanatory of those passages which are commonly understood as giving the greatest countenance to popular errors, and especially of those which bear upon the Unitarian controversy. And it was judged expedient that these notes should commonly be extracted from the works of authors who are esteemed by Unitarians as the most judicious expositors of the Scriptures, and, as far as might be, should be expressed in their own words; and, at any rate, without any asperity of censure upon Christians of different sentiments who interpret the Scriptures in a different manner. ' By the introduction of these notes, in which brevity was to be consulted as far as was consistent with perspicuity, it was intended that Unitarian Christians who might be in possession of the Improved Version, might at all times be able to recur to the most approved interpretations of difficult and disputed texts, especially those which are of the greatest importance for establishing the doctrine of the Unity and unrivalled supremacy of God, and of the proper humanity of God, and of the proper humanity of Jesus Christ; and others who wished to know what the real sentiments of the Unitarians are, and how they explain those texts which are commonly understood as contradicting their opinions, might gain the information which they desire.

It was determined to publish two large editions at the same time; one in royal octavo, the other for common use in royal duodecimo. And as some expressed a wish for the Version without the explanatory Notes, a numerous edition in a smaller form was printed for their satisfaction. It was also resolved that a

brother, who was a worthy tradesman in London, not perhaps deeply versed in theological lore, did assure Dr. Priestley that his brother's opinions coincided with Dr. Priestley's, and that he had heard the Primate say it. The Primate's Works, and Dr. Stock's testimony, prove that this respectable gentleman was mistaken. Perhaps, however, the learned Primate, who was certainly a profound theologian, and mighty in the Scriptures, might satisfy his mind, as Mr. Lindsey once did, with Dr. Wallis's hypothesis, sanctioned by the University of Oxford, and the three names in the Trinity, of Father, Son, and Holy Spirit, were nothing more than three different titles of the same individual person; like the God of Abraham, the God of Isaac, and the God of Jacob; which is, in fact, the purest Unitarianism.

x

-subscription should be opened to defray the expense of the under-taking, and that the money should be paid in advance; that the Committee, who were appointed to superintend the publication, might be in possession of ready money to enable them to go to the best market.

This plan of an Improved Version with explanatory Notes was adopted by the Unitarians and their friends with the greatest ardour. The subscription was filled rapidly. The venerable patriarch, who is the subject of this Memoir, delighted and grate-ful to Divine Providence that he had lived to see the accomplish-ment of the fervent and favourite wish of his heart, approving most heartily, in concurrence with his intelligent and zealous consort, of every part of the plan, was eager to open the sub-scription with a liberal donation of fifty pounds; the Duke of Grafton gave fifty guineas, and a second donation of fifty pounds. Samuel Prime, Esq., in whom every scheme for the improvement and happiness of mankind found an enlightened and munificent patron, gave fifty guineas to the first and twenty to the second subscription.* The example of liberality set by these eminent

---

* The laudable example of William Smith, Esq. (whose manly, independent, and persevering exertions in the cause of civil and religious liberty, in that honourable house of which he is now a veteran member, are universally acknowledged and admired,) ought not to be passed over in silence; who, in addition to his own liberal subscription to the Improved Version, purchased a considerable number of copies, which he sent down to the tutors of the colleges at York and Wymondely, to be distributed as presents among the candidates for the ministry in those respectable institutions; to which copies were prefixed the following judicious remarks:

" Search the Scriptures; for in them ye think that ye have everlasting life; and they bear witness of me."

It having been thought expedient to attempt an Improved Version of the New Testa-ment for the reason stated in the Introduction to the following work, this copy of it is presented to the student, not with any view or wish unduly to influence his opinion by authority, or to entrap him by the charm of novelty into any change; but merely to afford him additional motives and facilities for the careful and anxious study of the Sacred writings.—This, in proportion to his opportunities, is allowed to be the duty of every Christian; but more especially of those dedicated to the ministry, who, before they commence teachers of others, should themselves be diligent to learn; and should resolve not to rest satisfied with any system which, from education, connection, example, or authority, may have been their early creed, unless by serious, and, as far as is permitted to human frailty, impartial inquiry, they shall have acquired for themselves a conviction of its truth.

The writer of this notice may be supposed himself to have settled opinions; but he has ever been adverse to the practice, too prevalent among all sects, of usurping to

characters was followed by many others equally willing, if not
equally able to contribute ; and in a short time the sum requisite
for the commencement of the undertaking was raised, and the
press was not delayed for an hour by the want of necessary funds.
In two years the work was complete ; and the several parts, as
they were printed, were placed in Mr. Lindsey's hands, who was
pleased to express his high approbation both of the plan and of
the execution ; and it may truly be said that the perusal of the
Improved Version, reading it himself or hearing it read by others,
constituted the principal part of Mr. Lindsey's enjoyment during
the remainder of his life.

Of a work in which many are so deeply interested, and of which
every one thinks himself competent to judge, it is impossible that
there should not be a great diversity of opinion, both as to the
design and execution. Accordingly, when the Improved Version
made its appearance it soon became an object of rigid criticism
and severe animadversion.

The " Title " was objected to as arrogant and assuming. The
editors, however, are not conscious of being influenced by an
improper spirit. They called it an Improved Version, because
they regarded Archbishop Newcome's translation as a very great
improvement upon the public Version, and they conceived their
own alterations to be an improvement upon the Version of the
learned prelate. Nor did they see that there was greater arrogance
in calling their work, or rather that of the Primate, an Improved

themselves epithets, in their very terms decisive of all controversy. Who but the infallible shall presume to arrogate to himself alone the title of orthodox or evangelical ?—
who, duly conscious of the weakness of his reason and the strength of his prejudices,
shall claim to be exclusively rational and liberal ?—The question still remains, as in our
Saviour's time, " What is *the* truth ?" *i.e.* the true doctrine of the Gospel. That which
is not such cannot be either orthodox or evangelical. Nor is it possible that this truth
of God as it is in Jesus, when ascertained, should not be found sufficiently rational and
liberal for his creature man :—rational,—for, " He that giveth understanding, shall not
he know ?"—and liberal, — (if indeed in such a connection the word be at all allowable)
for it is of the essence of that truth to " make us free,"—free from error—free from
prejudice—free from uncharitableness.—While then to the Gospel all Christians equally
appeal, it is surely equally incumbent on all to scrutinize its contents, with patience
and reverence indeed, but without that servile fear which, as it paralyses man's
intellect, can surely never be pleasing to God who gave it, commanding us therewith
to " search the Scriptures " " that we may know Him and Jesus Christ whom he hath
sent."

x 2

Version, than in calling Dr. Clarke's Liturgy, a Reformed Liturgy, or the Protestant Church, a Reformed Church.

The editors are also blamed for stating that their Version is "upon the basis of Archbishop Newcome's," as though they intended to impose upon their readers, and to make the Archbishop responsible for their opinions. But the reasons which induced them to adopt the learned Primate's Version have been assigned already: and not to have acknowledged the obligation would have justly exposed them to the charge of fraud and plagiarism.—That they intended to shelter their own peculiar opinions under the authority of the Primate's name cannot be believed for a moment by any person of common understanding who reads beyond the title page.*

It has even been surmised that the editors, professing that the Improved Version is "published by a society for promoting Christian knowledge and the practice of virtue by the distribution of books," intended to insinuate that they published under the patronage of the society at Bartlett's Buildings for distributing Bibles and Common Prayer Books. But the venerable society may rest assured that it was an object the most remote from the thoughts of the editors to take shelter under their fostering wing. They did not even know that the title of the society, under whose direction they acted, so nearly accorded with that of any other society. In fact, they thought it needless to insert the word Unitarian in the title page, which would deter some ignorant and prejudiced people from looking into a work from which they might

---

* The enemies of the Improved Version may well be angry with the editors for having assumed the Archbishop's Translation as the basis of their own, for it has been the means of leading unwary critics into some egregious mistakes. Grievous have been the wounds which the unfortunate Primate has received from the hands of his undiscerning friends through the sides of his heretical editors. One accomplished critic wonders, forsooth, that a Unitarian Version should not be more elegant and classical : not adverting to the fact that the Version, in the main, is not theirs, but the Primate's. Another learned and sagacious opponent cites the Archbishop's own words, as a proof how the Unitarians pervert the Scriptures to support their own unscriptural tenets. Some future opportunity may perhaps be taken to animadvert upon these and other misrepresentations. In the mean time it may be sufficient to remark, that these pitiable and ludicrous blunders cannot fail foreibly to remind the reader of the wisdom of those discriminating judges in the fable, who hissed the pig itself.

otherwise derive instruction. The learned and the honest Whitby did not think it necessary to write Armenian in his title page; nor Guyse, nor Doddridge, Calvinist in theirs; but each of those pious and laborious expositors explained the sacred text to the best of his own judgement: so do the editors of the Improved Version.

It has been alleged as a great offence, that these editors have "given up the authenticity of the prefaces of Matthew and Luke." But they have assigned their reasons for this conclusion, and let their adversaries refute them if they can.

It is further objected, that "they appeal to Lardner as favourable to their hypothesis," though he decides directly against them. But all which they appeal to Lardner for, is to prove, which he has done most abundantly, that Herod died at least seventeen years before Augustus; but Luke himself informs us, that Jesus was but lately turned of thirty in the fifteenth year of Tiberius :* and consequently he must have been born two years after Herod's death. And as to the idle fiction of the double date of Tiberius's reign, it is well known to all who are conversant with Roman history, that this is a distinction which never existed till the time of the Lower Empire.

It is further charged upon these daring editors, that they have presumed to "print the suspected chapters in a different type." Had they, indeed, left out a passage that is found in all manuscripts which are now extant, however suspicious in itself, there might have been some reason for charging them with indiscretion. But it was their fixed rule not to remove from the text any passage which was supported by the consent of manuscripts, however doubtful upon other grounds, and whatever proof there might be of its omission in copies of greater antiquity. But being convinced by the evidence alleged that these chapters are a palpable forgery, they considered themselves as fully justified in fixing the mark of reprobation upon them, though they would not wholly omit them.

Some have objected to the introduction of any "theological Notes" whatever, as savouring too much of a sectarian spirit, and of

* See Grotius in Luc. iii. 23.

dogmatism. But it has been already observed, that the main object of the society in publishing the Improved Version, was to represent what they believed to be the genuine sense of the sacred writings, and to guard against popular delusions. And of course the editors, being from inquiry and conviction Unitarians, would interpret the text in the Unitarian sense. And what should hinder them from doing so? It is a practice in use among all parties, and laudably so. Had they, indeed, distorted the Scriptures, or forged texts to support their doctrines, they would have been justly liable to censure; but of this they are either not accused, or not convicted.

The editors of the Improved Version are further accused of not having "strictly adhered to Griesbach's text, and of not adopting all the improvements of his second edition." But everyone who is acquainted with Griesbach knows that more than nine tenths of his various readings are of the most trivial kind, and make not the least alteration in the sense. But to have introduced every trifling variation into the text, and to have supported it by notes and references in the margin, would have wasted much time; would have answered no one valuable end; and would either have swelled the work to too large a size, or would have occupied the space of more useful exegetical Notes. The design of the editors was to introduce the variations of Griesbach's interior margin; and if they have omitted even one which would make a difference in the sense of the text, it was on their part wholly unintentional, and they will feel obliged to any friendly critic who will point out the error that it may be corrected in succeeding editions. As to various readings by which the sense is not affected, a very minute attention to these was not within the scope of their design. Yet they do not deny that where gentlemen have leisure and inclination to undertake the task, a translation including all Griesbach's preferable readings, supported by his authorities, would be a gratification to the curious.*

* In the fourth edition of the Improved Version a very minute attention has been paid to all the various readings of Griesbach's second edition, by the late reverend and much to be lamented T. B. Broadbent.

The exertions, however feeble, which Mr. Lindsey made, in concurrence with the more active energies of Mrs. Lindsey, to encourage the progress and to extend the circulation of the Improved
Version, may be regarded as the last public act of Mr. Lindsey's
life ; as the perusal of that work, when it was complete, was his
last and greatest delight. To its composition it was too late for
him personally to contribute. But to his valuable writings and
comments upon the Scriptures, the Notes of the Improved Version,
are deeply indebted. And to the aged saint it was an exquisite
gratification to see, that though he was now about to obtain his
dismission from the world, his writings, and particularly his
accurate and learned observations upon the Scriptures, would continue to support Christian truth after he was gone. This bright
star, which had so long diffused its mild and benignant influence,
was now rapidly hastening to its horizon. Mr. Lindsey's health
declined apace, and his infirmities visibly increased. But though
at times he suffered much ; yet through the constant attention and
great professional skill of Dr. Blackburne (who had thoroughly
studied his case, and who watched and prescribed for his revered
relative with filial solicitude), and by the tender, judicious, and unwearied care of Mrs. Lindsey, his sufferings were greatly mitigated,
so that he continued upon the whole in a comfortable state ; and
to the last week of his life he enjoyed the company of his friends,
though he was not able to support much conversation with them.
Mr. Lindsey's strength declined so fast through the summer of
1808, as to allow little hope that he would be able to struggle
through the severity of the winter. But no symptom of immediate
danger appeared till the latter end of October, when he was attacked
with a complaint which was judged to be a pressure upon the
brain : and though the disorder appeared to yield in part to the
usual applications, it was nevertheless attended with a very considerable degree of fever, which made it necessary for him to
take to his bed on Thursday the twenty-seventh. The fever now
increased rapidly, and it soon became evident how it would terminate. After Monday he lay in a state approaching to stupor and
insensibility ; he took little notice of anything, and spoke little or

nothing. Thus he was prevented from bearing that testimony to
the truth and power of Christian principles in his last hours, which
his friend Dr. Priestley had done, and which Mr. Lindsey himself,
notwithstanding his great natural reserve, and his abhorrence of a
loquacious and ostentatious piety, would no doubt have been glad
to do. It is, however, said that some of the last rational expressions which he was heard to utter were, " God's will is best ; " but
whether he spoke these words or not, we are sure that the principle
was uppermost in his thoughts as long as reason and thought remained; for a mind more resigned and more devoted to the will of
God, more desirous and disposed to sacrifice all its fondest wishes
and views to the decrees of all-governing wisdom and goodness,
never existed.* He appeared to suffer little bodily pain; but his
respiration grew gradually shorter, till at six o'clock in the evening
of Thursday the third of November he ceased to breathe; and left
the world destitute of one of the most upright, consistent, and eminently virtuous characters which ever adorned human nature.
Mr. Lindsey died in the eighty-sixth year of his age. He
was buried in Bunhill Fields on Friday the eleventh of November,
agreeably to his own request, in the most private manner, in a
vault the property of which he had purchased twenty years before,
and where the remains of his kind and generous friends Mrs.
Rayner had, by her express desire, been already deposited ; and in
the vicinity of which reposed his learned and venerable associate in
labours and in self-denial, Dr. John Jebb. A sermon upon the
occasion was preached at Essex Street on the following Sunday to a
crowded audience of attentive and deeply-affected mourners, which
was afterwards published.†

* When Mr. Lindsey was a little recovered after his severe paralytic seizure in the
beginning of the year 1802, Mrs. Lindsey thus expresses herself in a letter to the
author, who was then upon a visit to a friend in the country : " He said this morning,
after reading family prayer in his usual good manner, " I wish, if it is the will of God,
to be enabled to finish my little work ; but should be sorry any moment that the will of
God should not take place of mine, either by incapacity or by death. "

† Discourses were delivered upon the same mournful occasion by many other ministers,
friends and admirers of Mr. Lindsey, some of which were published ; particularly by the
Rev. Robert Aspland, at Hackney ; the Rev. Dr. Toulmin, and Rev. John Kentish, at
Birmingham ; and the Rev. J. H. Bransby, at Dudley : and Memoirs of Mr. Lindsey
were published by Mrs. Cappe in The Monthly Repository, Mr. Joyce in The Monthly
Magazine, and by Mr. Frend.

Of the character of Mr. Lindsey, if the writer of this memoir has succeeded in giving a faithful exhibition of his mind and of his works, no large recapitulation is necessary. Disinterested glowing benevolence, springing from rational, ardent, and deeply-rooted piety; supreme solicitude to discover truth; unwearied pains in searching after it; and inflexible firmness in what, after due inquiry, he believed to be right; just views of revealed religion, combined with earnest but not obtrusive zeal for their promulgation, and blended with the most unaffected humility, and a singular courteousness of manners, formed by early and familiar intercourse with the great; finally and eminently, a commanding sense of God and duty, constituted the principal lineaments in the character of this excellent and truly venerable man. To have been his coadjutor in the cause of divine truth, his friend, his successor, and his biographer, is a privilege of no common value : and to be admitted hereafter into the society of such men as Lindsey, Priestley, Price, and Jebb, and of other eminent lovers of truth, and confessors in the glorious cause, and to share in their lot, whatever it be, is the highest felicity of which the writer of this memoir can form a conception, or to which he presumes to aspire. And happy will he think himself, and amply rewarded for all his labour, if this imperfect delineation of the character of his venerable friend shall excite the ambition of any of his readers, and especially among the rising generation of ministers, to emulate the spirit of the departed prophet, and like him to be ready, when duty calls, to sacrifice every secular consideration upon the altar of truth and integrity, leaving consequences without dismay in the hands of governing wisdom and goodness; which, if their future services be needful, will open a different and perhaps a more extensive sphere of usefulness ; or, if that should be denied, will not forget in the day of final remuneration the generous self-denial, the dutiful submission, nor the virtuous purpose, of the pious and upright heart.

Mrs. Lindsey survived her venerable husband three years and two months. The health of this excellent lady was completely broken up by her close and anxious attendance upon Mr. Lindsey during his long illness and growing infirmities: so that had he lived a few months longer he would probably have been the survivor. And though her constitution seemed for a time to recover itself, and gave reason to hope for continued life, yet the stamina appear to have been worn out; and a gradual decay both of corporeal and mental vigour soon began to take place, till after a short illness she expired January 18, 1812, in the seventy-second year of her age, and was buried the week following in the same vault with Mr. Lindsey and Mrs. Rayner. A funeral discourse bearing testimony to the uncommon merits of this admirable woman, was delivered to a numerous and sympathizing audience on the Sunday after the funeral, and has since been published. It may be added that Mrs. Lindsey's intimate friend, Mrs. Jebb, the relict of the celebrated Dr. John Jebb, a lady of the highest intellectual attainments and accomplishments, a fellow labourer and fellow sufferer in the same righteous cause, died two or three days after Mrs. Lindsey, and was buried with her husband in the contiguous grave.

THE END.

APPENDIX.

No I. p. 5.

The following letters exhibit a specimen of the terms upon which Mr. Lindsey stood with his noble patronesses, and of the high estimation in which he was held by them:—they also contain no mean illustration of the piety and virtue of the illustrious writers.

FROM THE DUTCHESS OF SOMERSET.

Percy Lodge, July the 9th, O.S. 1751.

Sir,

I received your letter last week, and intended writing on Sunday as usual, but when that day came I found it impracticable ; Mr. Saunders having found it more employment than I chose, by sending a long letter of business which I was obliged to answer. I hope your little pupil is well, though you did not name him in your last. Mrs. Pearse* dined here yesterday, in her way to the Forest, she looks thin, but otherwise well, and in pretty good spirits. She owns that Mrs. Scott has done more for her than she could have expected from the best daughter, and has taken the whole trouble and business off her hands. I find she thinks her circumstances will be easy, though not great ; the house in the Forest is to be sold ; she is not yet resolved about that in London. As things generally happen crossly, Lord Bateman and Mr. Bateman came in a little before three, and old Saunders just at twelve, but we left him to himself: however, he chose to stay din-

* This is the lady referred to in p. 6, who bequeathed to Mr. Lindsey the next presentation to the rectory of Chew Magna.

ner. Mr. Cowslad says you write to us because you think it civil, when you are not a bit inclined to it : he is a good deal better, and so am I, but we can neither of us yet boast of our activity.

My domesticks go on pretty peaceably, though Edward met with a trial of his patience last Saturday, which would have staggered yours or mine. He was almost mad with the pain of a hollow tooth, and went to Colebrook to get it drawn; but the cruel operator, instead of it, drew the only sound one in his head. I do not know what you will think of me when I tell you I am going to try the Glastonbury water here, and own to you that I am induced to it by a persuasion that the discovery of it is in some degree miraculous; and if one may believe affidavits, witnessed by ministers of parishes and churchwardens, the cures it has performed are so too, in scorbutic cases, king's evil, and asthmas of many years standing, as it is witnessed by their nearest neighbours. I have had no letter from Lady Huntingdon, but I hear she is at Cheltenham, and pretty well. Clavering has done plaguing me, but I have sent his son ten guineas this morning. I have heard but twice from Lady Northumberland since she left London, by which I conclude, she finds diversions and company are not confined to the town. You judge very rightly that a little spirit and resolution would contribute greatly to my tranquillity; and I often lament the want of it, not only as a misfortune, but as a fault, since it is often necessary, to enable one to support one's integrity through a wayward and designing world, where few are what they appear to be: yet even that would be of little consequence, was one perfectly assured of being in the right one's self.

My gentlemen send you their compliments; and I desire my compliments to little H. who, I hope, improves in more things than his French; for, though that is a very proper accomplishment of a gentleman, there are yet higher titles to be aimed at, those of an humble Christian, and lover of all mankind. I am glad you find the air you are in agrees with your health. Lord Albemarle is made groom of the stole, and Lord Rockingham lord of the bedchamber.

I am, Sir,

Your affectionate friend and humble servant,

F. SOMERSET.

A. Monsieur
Monsieur Lindsey, chez Monsieur Pillard,
à Blois.

Sir,

We were all very sorry to find by your last letter that you have
had so violent a cold; but if your weather has been (as I think
by your letter it has) like ours in England, it is no wonder that
you have suffered from it, for I never remember so cold and wet
a summer. You may depend upon my silence, in regard to your
observations on Lord W——'s constitution, as I know the
ticklishness of treating some subjects without giving offence,
which I am sure neither you nor I intend to do. I am so far
from thinking you oddly employed, when you were contemplating
the storm of thunder and lightning, that I rather envy you for
the fortitude which is necessary to be a calm spectator of so awful
and noble a scene. My own want of that virtue often makes me
apprehensive that I am in the number of the wicked, who flee
when no man pursueth, while the righteous are bold as a lion;
yet I do not despair of becoming better, and consequently more
courageous, as I can with truth affirm it is the only point I have
in view; and my most earnest desire to keep God in all my
thoughts. Yet how apt are the cares, and even the amusements
of life, to displace his image, and obtrude their own vexatious impertinence in his room! Poor Lady Thanet is dead. I am told
that when Lady Huntingdon heard of her illness, she sent to
offer her to come and prepare her for that solemn hour: but
Lady Thanet sent her word it was in vain, for she could neither
be prepared to live or die. Her great care upon her death-bed
was the fear of being buried alive; to prevent which, she ordered
herself not to be taken out of her bed for twelve days. She has
left her daughters ten thousand pounds a-piece. The last we
heard of the Dutchess of Richmond was, that her doctors had
little or no hopes of her. The mortality which within two years
and a half has been so remarkable amongst men of the first rank,
seems beginning amongst the ladies, but still the same eternal
round of dissipation is pursued; cards and gay parties are the
great business of the modish world. The Duke of St. Alban's
died last Saturday se'nnight, and I am afraid has left his family
in very indifferent circumstances. If going abroad is a preserva-
tive for health, I may expect to be very well; for within these last
three weeks I have been at London, twice at Sion, dined with
Mrs. Mordaunt, been at Thorpe with Mrs. Foley, visited at Bul-

strode, and, in short, tired myself and my horses sufficiently. To-morrow Lord and Lady Brooke, Lady Archibald and Miss Hamilton, Mrs. Mordaunt, and Mr. Hamilton, are all to dine here; and on Thursday Lord Guernsey and Lady Charlotte. I dined last week at Isleworth with the Dutchess of Somerset, and saw my little nephew, who is a fine child. Mr. Bernard spoke of you in a very friendly manner; I think he appears a modest pretty kind of man. A sermon of his is much talked of at Islesworth for the singularity of the text, which was "Remember Lot's wife;" and his discourse greatly admired for the piety and good sense of it. I am with very sincere friendship,

Sir,

Your most faithful humble servant,

F. SOMERSET.

To the Reverend Mr. Lindsey.

FROM THE SAME.

Michaelmas Day, O.S. Sunday, 1751.

Sir,

I fully intended writing to you, either by Sunday or Tuesday's post, but was prevented by a swelled face and pain in my head, which put me extremely out of order: it is not yet quite gone; but as it is something better, I would no longer defer tell-ing you that I am very glad to see Lord and Lady Northumberland lay hold of the first opportunity in their power of showing their regard for you. I only wish that the living of Chatton were of greater value, or that in Yorkshire were entirely free, which-ever you choose; they have had the kindness to tell me they will not think of your leaving my family; but I know your thoughts in relation to the duty of a parish too well to reckon upon keeping you in it; for which reason I must apply to you whenever it becomes necessary for you to change your situation, that you will be so good as to choose a successor who will conduct himself as nearly like you as possible, for I am as little fond of a pretty gentleman in a gown as out of one. I opened Mr. Comber's letter because you desired me; it did not contain above eight lines, complaining of not hearing from you, begging to do it soon to relieve his fears for your health; and telling you he had met with many mortifications, that he feared he had lost Almira's correspondence, by no fault of his, but her over delicacy. The huge paper enclosed was two or three hundred lines, on the immensity of the Divine Being, which appeared to me unequal to a much humbler subject.

I had a very agreeable letter last week from Dr. Oliver, who tells me that Lady Huntington is pretty well, and much employed in attending Dr. Doddridge, who is in a deep consumption at Bath, but is to set out in a few days in order to embark at Falmouth for Lisbon, from whence, it is Dr. Oliver's opinion, he will never return. Lady F. Shirley was with me two days ago; she told me that Mr. Hervey is quite recovered: but Lady Pembroke's marriage with a man of no birth or money (though, it is said, a very sensible agreeable man,) pinned us down to mere worldly conversation; and to tell you the truth in a whisper only for your own ear, her ladyship seemed to think, that as Lady Pembroke could not be easy to live without him, she had acted more prudently if she had taken him on any other terms! You will easily believe this doctrine amazed me in the mouth of so pious a person, and that I have not thought fit to mention it to one of my company, as he needs no new motives to censure whatever he fancies aims at being more serious than the fine world in general. Mr. Wilkins writes me word that Mrs. Wilkins is almost well, and proposes being here himself a few days after Michaelmas.

A. C. is ill at Oxford, and his wise father has wrote to desire he may come hither to be taken care of and drink asses milk, and desires me to send for Dr. Hayes as often as is necessary. This I must beg to be excused from, as Lord and Lady N. will be here this week, and I expect Mrs. Pearse and Mr. Scot very soon. I have only one milch ass, of which my poor gardener is drinking the milk, though I doubt to very little purpose, for he appears quite spent in a consumption, though James's powder did cure his fever. I thank you for the epigram, which I read without blushing. I should have been glad to see the young nun take the veil, but at the same time have felt some concern lest, in so tender an age, she might have been influenced or awed into it by her friends; or supposing it were her inclination at present, how little it could be depended upon to last fifty or sixty years, which she may probably live. I saw Lady Pomfret last Saturday, and said all I could think of to express your gratitude and my own, both to her and the Bishop of Blois, for his civility to you and your little charge, to whom I desire my blessing. I think the King of France disposes of his money in giving portions to young women much better than if it were to procure fire-works, masquerades, &c.

I had left all the space betwixt these two lines to direct my letter, that it might not be a double one; but Lord and Lady N. came in just as I was finishing it on Thursday, and staid till eleven o'clock this day; they bid me make their compliments to you, and send Lord W. their blessing. Lady Pomfret sent us a letter in English, which she has received from the Bishop of Blois, where he expresses himself so kindly on Lord W.'s account, that his father and mother as well as myself are extremely obliged by the notice he takes in it both of him and you.

The Duke of Bolton I fancy will find a stronger restorative in his Dutchess's death than from all the air in France; she died last Monday was se'nnight. How widely do the great and little folks differ in sentiments! Poor Obadiah is in the deepest affliction for the loss of his wife. They tell me you will be obliged to come over, if you accept either of the livings, in which case I hope you will find a few hours, if not days, to let us see you at Percy Lodge, where you may always be assured of a most friendly and sincere welcome from,

Sir, Your most faithful humble servant,

F. SOMERSET.

FROM THE SAME.

Downing Street, March 14th, O.S. 1752.

Sir,

I heartily wish my constitution would as readily enable me to comply with the desires of my friends as my inclination submits to what they prescribe, but I am afraid I have little reason to indulge so flattering a hope; I have hardly enjoyed an hour's health since I came hither, and though I have been out four or five times I am now confined again with great pain and lameness; a great inflammation upon my leg cannot be produced by fancy! and sitting continually in one place has brought an almost constant pain in my stomach, attended with great oppression and shortness of breath; these are not good ingredients to give me spirits for mixing with the beau monde; and indeed were I in better health, I believe I should as easily enter into the manners of the fine folks in the moon, as into the present fashionable way of life in London, so different it is from what it was when I left it three years ago. I have had a letter from Lady Huntingdon, who seems very much pleased with Lady Rawdon's marriage, and says that Lady Selina is much better. Lord Coventry was married to Miss Gunning this day se'nnight, and Lady Charlotte Capel is to be so very soon to Mr. Villiers, Lord Jersey's brother, and Lady Di. Egerton to Mr. Seymour's son by Lady Hinchinbrooke. The Chapter is to be held on Friday for giving away the garters, the new knights are declared, and they are not all those who were first talked of; they are Prince Edward the little Stadtholder, Lord Lincoln, Lord Winchelsea, and Lord Cardigan.

The constant good accounts you send us of Lord W. are very encouraging; pray assure him of my blessing, and tell him his papa has won the service of Dresden china, which was raffled for at White's, and valued at £400. I see by the advertisement that Mr. Mason is going to publish a poem called Elfrida, which I shall certainly buy if I am alive at the time it comes out. Miss Blandy is condemned for the barbarous murder of her father, and you will wonder at me for being discontented that she is only to be hanged. H. is marched off at last, though I could not get her out of my house till the new housekeeper had been two days in it. I hope she will prove more peaceable. It signifies little what outward appearances and ceremonies are observed, if the heart and intentions remain inflexible; and yet some shadow of regard to the mere observances of religion, may serve to renew the remembrance that there is the reality of such a thing in nature, though laid aside for the present; but here the names of times or seasons are never thought of, unless when the fine ladies are expressing their gratitude to Lady Cobham for comforting them in the Dutchess of Dorset's absence by having an assembly on Sundays.

The Dutchess of Somerset, my mother-in-law, did me the honour of a visit yesterday morning; she is not well, and is to go to Bristol as soon as Lady Charlotte is brought to bed, which is expected about the beginning of May.

I am with sincere friendship,
Sir,
Your most faithful humble servant,
F. SOMERSET.

A Monsieur
Monsieur Lindsey, à Orleans.

Y

Downing Street, March 19, 1752.

Sir,

As I do not love to have any of my bright actions pass unobserved by my friends, and as I am afraid they may be neglected
by the foreign news-writers, I had a mind to let you know under
my own hand, that I was last night at a ball at Northumberland
House, where all the people who are famed for beauty, youth,
gaiety, and grandeur, were assembled; the house and suppers in
three rooms were truly magnificent, and the owners did the
honours with a politeness and cheerfulness which I think could
not fail to please, at least it ought not, for it must have given them
infinite trouble as well as great expense, and poor Lady Northumberland had a violent cold. I saw Lady Coventry there, who is
certainly very handsome, but appears rather too tall to be genteel,
and her face rather smaller than one would wish, considering the
height it is placed, and her dress appeared more in the style of an
opera dancer than an English lady of quality. Lady Di. Egerton
and Mrs. Selwyn's granddaughter, Miss Townsend, appeared either
of the full as pretty in my eyes with the addition of great
modesty.

The pure and eloquent blood spoke in their cheeks:

which it would do in very few there, for they cannot paint more
in France than our ladies do here; and as we always run into
extremes, white is as liberally laid on as rouge: poor Lady Mary
Capel had, I believe, only the latter, but that in such abundance
that it made her look older and plainer than ever I saw her. Now
I must tell you under the seal of confession, that from some
civilities I had received from Lady Lincoln, I thought it proper to
make her some compliment; but when I came near her with that
design, she was so very immodestly stripped that I was ashamed
to look toward her and forced to drop my speech. The wind last
Sunday alarmed me extremely here, but did me much greater
injury at Percy Lodge, where it blew down the high elm behind
King Edward's bench, turned the bench itself topsy-turvy and
broke it all to pieces, blew down several rod of paling, and some
of the best trees in my fields; it broke a very tall fir-tree near the
Gothic bench, above fourteen feet above the ground, and carried it
over the wood into the Abbey walk, where it set it upright. Here

some bricks were blown off Payne's chimney, who was dressing me, and rolled along the room over our heads; and at that instant we heard the most dreadful yell below stairs that you can conceive : but what was our amaze when, upon running out, we found the staircase so filled with smoke and soot that we could scarce see one another or breath ! and Lady C. Petersham, with her hair about her ears, four children, and five or six maids with another woman whom I did not know, all screaming as if they were bewitched ! A stack of chimneys had fallen there, and the fire catched in two or three places; but by the mercy of God nobody was hurt, and the fire soon stopped.   The woman I did not know was Mrs. Cibber, who was reading a new farce to Lady C. when this accident happened.   I meant to have dined alone that day, so my meal was slender; but I could not help asking Lord Petersham and Lady Caroline to partake of it, as they could have nothing dressed at home, and none of their acquaintance (though Lady Lincoln lives but two doors off and was alarmed at the noise) had the humanity to invite them, which Lady C. seemed to resent, and I thought with reason.   As I have now wrote sooner than my usual time, perhaps I shall exceed it before I write again ; and if the date of my next should not happen to please you, I hope you will not tear the letter before you read it.   Pray assure your little charge of my blessing, and Mr. Thierchen of my remembrance.

I am, Sir,

Your very sincere and faithful humble servant,

F. SOMERSET.

A Monsieur
Monsieur Lindsey, à Orleans.

FROM THE SAME.

Percy Lodge, March 5th, 1754.

Sir,

I feel myself extremely obliged to you for both your last letters, and would have told you so sooner if I could have resolved to send you a half a side of paper with nothing but formal thanks, which I think is not an obliging way of corresponding with one's friends.

I was surprised to meet Lady Huntingdon upon the road last Saturday was fortnight; she was on her way to London, but her coach drove by so fast that I had only time to send Lomas after

Y 2

her with my compliments; she seemed to me to look as well as
ever I saw her.

Poor Mr. Thierchen has been laid up with the gout almost
these three weeks, but insists it is the effect of having worn too
short a stocking, in spite of the apothecary. A. has passed a
month with me since Christmas: if he is not quite so droll as he
was, he makes amends by displaying the seeds of every virtuous
and generous disposition, with the most docile temper I ever
knew: he would not tell a lye to avoid the severest punishment
that he can have a notion of, and has no peace if he thinks he has
offended the lowest person about the house. Poor Lord G. is the
melancholy reverse of all these amiable qualities: with the face of
a cherub, he is one of the most perverse, obstinate, ill-disposed,
children that ever was born. He is severely and constantly
whipped, at least once a week, but discovers no fear of punishment, and (what is much worse) no sense of shame when he is
detected in lies that he has stood in for a week together, or for
taking other people's things unknown to them; and this last week
he even ventured to sell a reading-glass for two shillings and there
is no making him confess how he came by it.

I am yet far from being in a good state of health, though I
bless God, in a much less painful one than I was some months
ago; I have now no remains of lameness, but I am, from the
shortness of my breath, obliged to be always carried up stairs
and often down; yet this is not to excuse me from a London
journey. I have promised to make my appearance there next
Friday se'nnight, if no unforeseen accident happens; but hope
not to make a longer stay than I did last year, unless I am
detained in Westminster Abbey.

I was much obliged to you for sending that fragment of Milton,
which pleased me much, and I took the liberty to copy and convey it to Miss Talbot, who was delighted with it, but made the
same objection with yours, that he was wrong in regard to that
part of the Bible account of David's misfortunes and their source!
I must now, under the seal of confession, own to you, that after
reading the Bible every day of my life for forty years together, · I
always understood it as Milton seems to have done. But since I
received your letter I have read the history of David in Samuel,
with all the attention I am mistress of, to find some other cause,
and rummaged the library to find some commentator who would
explain it—but they all seem to be in Milton's error—and even

consulted the only divine in my reach (Clavering), who stared, and said he had always thought as Milton did. I hope you have some neighbours that you can converse with; for, as partial as I am to retirement, I think absolute solitude is too melancholy a way of life for creatures intended by the wise ruler of all things for society. Our excellent friend Dr. Courayer has been very ill, but is got quite well again, and I had a very good and cheerful letter from him on Sunday morning. Indeed he has the only true cause for cheerfulness, the reflection on a well spent life, and having prepared himself to leave it whenever its great Author shall call him from hence. This preparation I hope I have been seriously endeavouring after for many months and some years past; but we are so apt to flatter and deceive ourselves, that I dare not trust myself too far, and find such continual defects in my best meant actions, as would take away all hopes of their efficacy if I did not trust in the merits and sufferings of our ever blessed Lord and Saviour Jesus Christ.

I have told you I am better, and to outward appearances I am so; yet I should not be surprised myself, nor would have my friends be so, if I should be dead before this letter reaches you. Dr. Hayes calls my disease a nervous asthma, in which case I may possibly suffer on some years longer; but by my own feelings, especially the violent beating of my heart and jugular veins, I should suppose it some great obstruction in my blood. I have hardly left room to subscribe myself,

Sir,

Your very sincere friend, &c.,

F. SOMERSET.

No. II., p. 7.

FROM THE COUNTESS OF NORTHUMBERLAND.

Stanwick, June 27.

Dear Sir,

I know your friendship for me will prevent your thinking a letter troublesome, though it comes fraught with no other news but that of my safe arrival at this place, which happened on Wednesday last, after I cannot say a pleasant (for the first day we were choaked with dust, and the second deluged with rain) journey of three days, one of which we spent at York with Mrs. Smithson, where we have deposited Elizabeth. I find the whole country here in an uproar, as they say their former Archbishop (the late Metropolitan) Hutton died an Arian; they own they do not know what that is, but are sure it is something that is not the right religion. We are impatient to hear of the taking of St. Malo's; which good news I hope a few more days will bring us. We leave this place for Newcastle to-morrow, where we shall stay a week, and then proceed to Alnwick. I had the ill luck to sprain my knee in such a manner at York, that I am not able to stir a step without a stick, which confines me from walking; which, however, I the less regret, as the weather is thoroughly disagreeable, being both damp and cold. As I am in some doubt about your direction, I shall send this to Northumberland House, and order them to carry it to Lord Huntington, where, I conclude, they will be able to learn how to convey it safely to you. My Lord desires his compliments to you, and I beg to trouble you with mine to Lady Huntingdon, Lady Selina, and Mrs. Hastings. I am, with the truest friendship,

Dear Sir,
Your most affectionate humble servant,
E. NORTHUMBERLAND.

To the Rev. Mr. Lindsey.

FROM THE SAME.

Alnwick Castle, July 25th.

Dear Sir,

I am very much mortified to find that you have entirely forgot me, for I verily think that if you had not, you would have let me have had the pleasure of hearing from you before now; to no other cause can I assign it but your being in love, and to that account will I place it, as I think love the only justifiable excuse for forgetting one's friends; and where that passion is divested of some of its sensual attributes, I think such an oblivion far from blameable, highly praiseworthy, as I am convinced no passion exalts the soul so much as it does, nay, even in great measure, spiritualizes it; but this being a subject I am much more versed in the theory than the practice of, I am liable, like other theoretical and aerial castle-builders, to have no foundation for my sparkling edifices; but as they in beauty resemble the bubbles blown by children, they probably do the same in fragility and short duration. Thus far had I talked wisely without meaning (as many wise people do), when I received the favour of your letter, for which I heartily thank you, and assure you, your letters are always truly welcome to me, come they often or seldom; and though I am always glad to hear from you when you have nothing else to do, yet I am far from wishing you to write when you have either business, company, or what you allow me to guess at to prevent you. I was, as you observe, at Stanwick for two nights only; but notwithstanding the shortness of the stay, I had time enough to hear a most admirable character of Mrs. Lindsey elect, which gave me extreme great pleasure; and I also heard of a chance for a certain four thousand pounds, which (though I assure you, in an inferior degree) gave me great pleasure also. We set out for Scotland the sixth day of next month, but of how long a duration our stay there will be I know not. We go from Berwick by Haddingtoun to Edinburgh, and from thence by Stirling and Glasgow to Air, so that we shall entirely cross that part of the island from east to west; but as we do not proceed to the Isle of Skey, I fear I shall return without the gift of second-sight. Something of after-sight I believe I have mentioned to you that I really think I have of a night when I go to bed, a very odd instance of which I had lately; but the story is not interesting, and is besides too long for a letter. The last accounts we had of Lord Warkworth were from Minden, where he arrived July 16th, after a most tedious march of twenty-five days (through miserable roads, in wretched weather), in perfect good health and spirits, and hoped to join the army the 18th or 19th. You may believe I am under the greatest anxiety for a son so deservedly dear to me; but to the care of the Almighty I commit him, who, I hope, will cover his head in the day of battle, and afford me the unspeakable pleasure of receiving him again after the campaign safe and with honor. I am sure he has not only my daily but hourly prayers, and I also beg to recommend him to yours. You are very good to have wrote to him; I have sent him your letter, the receipt of which I am sure will make him very happy. I am very sorry any company I had deprived me of the satisfaction of seeing you, or wishing you a good journey, before you left London. Lord Ilchester's estate is a noble one, and I hope he bestows it nobly; otherwise I am sure he does not deserve

it. You have no notion how glad I was to hear of Sir Harry
Heron; I was very desirous to know if any of that family (one of
the most ancient in this county) were yet in being. If ever you,
Sir Harry, and myself are in London at the same time, I desire
you will present me to him. I have often heard Mr. Delaval (the
member for this county) say, that his mother frequently told him
that in her memory nothing but trenchers were in use in Northumberland, and that his grandfather had seventeen dozen of them ;
and that in all the gentlemen's families an officer called a trencher-
scraper (for they were not to be washed) was kept for that purpose
only; and that Seaton Delaval (the seat of Long Delaval) and
Chipchase (the seat of the Herons) were the only houses where
they had pewter (and theirs was only dishes, and but few of them),
which was only used on high days and holidays, and was admired
by the whole country as an unusual piece of magnificence. This
anecdote of his ancestors' grandeur I daresay Sir Harry never
heard. Supper bell rings; so I have only time to add my lord's
compliments, and that I am ever,

Dear Sir,
Your faithful friend and humble servant,
ELIZABETH NORTHUMBERLAND.

No. III., p. 11.

FROM ARCHDEACON BLACKBURNE.

March 1, 1756.

My Dear Friend,

I am much obliged to you for your last kind remembrance of
me from Bristol; and if you had not made me a sort of promise
that it would be followed presently by another, you would probably have had this acknowledgment a post or two sooner. A
gentleman, whose correspondence does me honour, lately transmitted to me a most curious case of a British dissenting clergyman, who went to Geneva to be ordained, that he might avoid
subscription to the Westminster Confession, *or any such tests of
human orthodoxy.* He was chaplain to the Scots Greys (being yet

unordained), travelled as tutor to two young gentlemen of the first
rank, was himself a fine gentleman and excellent scholar, and yet,
when, after having made the tour of Europe, and displayed his
ministerial talents in Holland with the greatest applause, he came
to settle in a congregation in Ireland, he met with rather worse
treatment than Mr. Emlyn, being, as I understand him, persecuted and put to flight for opinions which he really held not,
merely because he would not subscribe to those he did hold. By
the way, this account (if 1 mistake not) was sent me upon a
chimerical suspicion which my friend, himself a dissenter of eminence, has entertained that I am secretly pushing for a settlement
among his brethren; among whom he finds himself as uneasy
as we find ourselves in the church of England. And lest you
should think I have any such aim, it may not be amiss to inform
you, that all these surmises have arose from a letter I wrote to a
loquacious man, to enquire after the character of a dissenting
academy in his neighbourhood, with a view of furnishing a young
man for whom I am concerned, with a little mathematical learning. You must not expect long letters from me from hence to
the other side of Easter, as I have not only additional sermons
weekly, during Lent, and catechising, &c., but am pressed on all
hands to dispatch the Confessional, the plan after much debate,
ab intus et extra, being now settled, and all occasions cut of squib-
bing at the fungose Doctor, otherwise than as his solutions are
considered in form among those of other men.

March 2. No letter but one from Watson, announcing his safe
arrival, and transmitting a curious MS. (wrote by a lady) and
tending to prove an indispensable obligation upon Christians to
keep two Sabbaths in a week. When one sees what different
opinions are founded upon the Scriptures, by different heads, and
none of them void of plausibility, I am strongly tempted to parody
a striking passage in the Gospel thus: Except your charity
exceeds the charity of the Athanasians, methodists, mystics, and
zealots of every sect, ye shall in nowise enter into the kingdom of
heaven. O my friend, what shall we do to unlade our hearts of
the world, and to fill them with God, so as to do, think, and say
all to his glory? I am so far a mystic as to think this attainable,
and am miserable, wretchedly miserable, in finding myself so far
behind those who have already attained hitherto. Pray for me,
dear Mr. Lindsey, as I do daily for you, that we may be really
instrumental in doing some of that good which is well-pleasing to

God ; and, at least, that this ευδοκια may receive no let, either from our indolence, or the incongruity of our doctrine or manners. O, what a glory to carry with us one soul to heaven for seraphs to rejoice over, and to raise the exultations of the heavenly host ! What are all the cares, riches, pleasures, or anxieties in the world, compared to this ? Teach me, for I know you can, how that frame of mind is to be put on which must carry us to our utmost perfection in Christ.

I am, with unabated love for you, the unworthiest of all your fellow servants, F. B.

FROM THE SAME.

Richmond, Nov. 15th, 1757.

The choicest blessings of heaven on your noble and thrice worthy patroness for espousing, and on my dear good friend for recommending, the cause of the fatherless. If any thing farther remains to be done on our part towards forwarding the relief of these orphans you will let me know, and in the meantime I beg you would, with all humility, tender my sincerest acknowledgements to her good ladyship, to whose humanity and christian charity I hold myself the more obliged, as some other *would-be-good* ladies were applied to without success. Lady Northumberland indeed would have delivered our petition, but that was to the *other* court, which we thought not so expedient as at Leicester House. My lord, too, has done an act of humanity and gratitude to a poor shoe-maker of this town, who was his schoolfellow, and often assisted him in his exercises at Richmond school, which will make me love him as long as I live. How shall I express the sense I have of the parental feelings of the good lady for her afflicted son ! Would to God my poor intercessions might take place, either towards removing, or alleviating what cannot be removed ! I was lately in company with a physician who told me he had been so fortunate as to prevent guttæ serenæ in two ladies (one of them his own wife) by gentle and seasonable mercurial purges, at proper intervals. He says the sight of *both* is weak in general, and they have returns of the visual obstructions ; but the cinnabar pills have as yet never failed to remove them, and they pass their time very comfortably, so comfortably, that if he had not told me this circumstance I should never have suspected his lady (whom I see very often) of any such infirmity. He added, that in some other cases he had known this malady attended with a defluxion, in which case a solution of camphire in French brandy, softened with an emulsion of almonds, has done service by way of outward application. He adds, that he knew an infirmity of this kind brought upon a young lady by over-bathing in Harrowgate waters. If any farther information I can get about these cases will be of use, let me know, and depend upon my utmost endeavours.

Be ingenuous, my good friend: were any of the noble family with which you are connected, to be opposed in a borough, where your situation were the same as mine, could you be an indifferent spectator? I wish I had time to tell you the beginning and whole progress of my engagements; but Heaven has heard my prayers, and I trust the disagreeable contest is now at an end for this time. For such has been the firmness and unanimity of Mr. Yorke's friends, that Sir Conyers Darcy thought proper the other day to send a message to the corporation, that, "in consideration of *the peace of the town*, he would acquiesce in any person the burgesses should make choice of." This has amazed some people, who knew not our preparations, of which the old knight had some intimations from London. Though, indeed, as he had secured the returning officer, I for my part expected he would have put us to our petition. Yesterday it was reported that the borough was sold to a young baronet, who has made some purchases of that sort in his own county. But this is so very dishonourable to a certain principal officer of state, that I cannot tell how to believe it, though apart from the circumstance of *honour*, it might not perhaps be improbable. My good friend will be cautious of mentioning these matters *as from me*. However, take notice, all I have been concerned in has been fair and upright, and void of all corruption, which our worthy candidate abhors so much that he could not be brought into some measures recommended to him by some very honest friends as merely *prudential*, which if he had taken, he might have secured his seat beyond all dispute; but his answer was, "That he had lived to the seventy-first year of his life without one reproach from his heart of contributing to the public corruption, and he would not sow the seeds of those thorns at this time of life." You will now collect perhaps an apology for me, without taking in my particular obligations and alliance to this family. But after all, alas! I find too feelingly, that all this is but to busy ourselves about *burying the dead*, when we should

be preaching the kingdom of God; and it is impossible to tell you
the impressions of my heart under a load of trash, which my soul
abhors, and from which it shall ever be my study for the future
to escape, if possible.

I have not time to collect all the scraps I have of David Hartley's meditations, which are chiefly dispersed in M. P. H.'s letters
to me. But you may expect a summary of them from me within
a very few posts. What good may be done in our parishes, and
by whom the most, is a problem that I cannot undertake to solve
for myself, much less for you. Pray God direct you in every
thing; your present avocation is not to be found fault with, and
if Heaven had given me talents such as yours for consolation, I
should surely have dispensed with my public province (at least for
a time) when the occasion called me to the relief of such sufferers.
For the rest, you know I put the whole upon a prior obligation to
him who called me; an obligation I mean prior to all engagements, to church-modes and church nonsense in support of them.
My principle of attachment to the Scriptures would make me
uneasy in any other church l know of. If I can be of any service
in this, God have the praise, it is a reason why I should press
forward. He will reform all in his good time, and will not im-
pute a failure in duty to those who would but cannot. In the
mean time, I trust as to sincerity we have a good conscience. We
fail not on all proper occasions to bear our testimony. We scruple
not to acknowledge our own weakness in being drawn in to subscribe, especially the last time, when we fear the good opinion we
had of a dear friend, and the regard we paid to his judgment,
prevailed more with us than any conviction from the weight of his
arguments, which we have since found to be feeble and insufficient.
In the mean time, this we know, if we know any thing of ourselves, that though we labour under manifold difficulties, arising
from a large family, and a scanty income, and the necessity upon
us of spending every shilling of it to answer the expectations of
the world in our station, and to avoid the least suspicions of
avarice, yet would we not repeat our subscription, to gain the
wealth of the Indies, or the honour and power of a popedom.
Some people, my dear friend, would be much mortified that they
could not give their children that polish of education which is
necessary to recommend to respectable connexions with the world.
I do not boast when I say I am got above all this. My endeavours shall not be wanting to create them the most important

connexions with God : if I succeed there, I and they are happy; happy in our obscurity and disengagements from many temptations; happy in seeing our own infirmities, and ten times happy in the protection of a wise and gracious Providence, who will never leave us nor forsake us. Here comes three of them to call me to dinner.

Grace and peace from the fountain of both be with you. ·

The following letter from Thomas Hollis, Esq. under the fictitious name of Pierce Delver, throws some light upon the reported invitation of the Archdeacon to succeed Dr. Chandler at the Old Jewry.

Saturday morning, Oct. 18, 1766.

Dear Sir,

It gives me great pleasure to hear of the perfect recovery of the excellent A.D. (Archdeacon.) I fear he studies, labours too intensely, though to such noble purposes and great effects ; and the human machine though a very fine is yet a *very delicate* one. Let us applaud his magnanimity, however, and wish him every good !

At my visit to worthy Mr. Fleming, he told me, that he had been assured the people of the Old Jewry were inclined to invite the excellent A. D. B. to their chair, in the room of the late Dr. C. if they thought he would accept it. The same was told me more generally afterwards in mixt company.

September 27. Worthy Dr. H. (Dr. W. Harris) wrote me as follows: " What think you of A. D. B.'s succeeding the late Dr. C. at the Old Jewry ? I saw Mr. Amory at Taunton, and he tells me it is talked of by that society. The Confessional is much read and admired." To this I replied generally, as I remember, for I cannot copy everything, as follows :

That I had avoided writing to you on the subject.

That I knew the incomparable A.D. had a real and high esteem for the body of Protestant Dissenters.

That whatever his resolution might be, I was confident the proposition, if made, would be treated by him with perfect civility and respect.

That for my own part, I should be *sorry* the A. D. should accept the proposition, however handsomely tendered, for his own sake and the public; as I was persuaded it would render uncomfortable, and shorten his *valuable* life by town air and customs; and lesson his power of doing *great* public good, by taking him out of the alone, *precise* situation in which, with his powers and magnanimity to effect it, he

> " Rides in the whirlwind and *directs* the storm."

From Dr. H. I have not since heard.

For the rest. The Dissenters are, it may be, best seen in their principles and not individually; though the people of the Old Jewry rank, not only in point of wealth, but of sense and politeness, among the first of them.

I am, with highest respect to two gentlemen, Dear Sir,

Your affectionate friend and most obedient servant,

PIERCE DELVER.

To the Rev. T. Lindsey, Catterick.

No. IV., p. 35.

A LETTER FROM HANS STANLEY, ESQ., TO MR. LINDSEY, ASSIGNING HIS REASONS FOR DECLINING TO SUPPORT THE CLERICAL PETITION.

Paultons, Nov. 12, 1771.

Dear Sir,

You certainly need no apology for addressing yourself to me upon any subject; your own merit and our long acquaintance entitle you to my attention, and give you a right to expect that answer, which you are pleased to ask as a favour.

You will give me leave to follow your introduction of this matter, by assuring you on my part, that if your request related to any private interest of your own within my small power, I should heartily wish to serve you; but in the present case it cannot weigh with me to promote innovations in the law, which I think not only unnecessary, but extremely mischievous.

The peace of mankind is a fortieth article of my religion, which I hold to be much more important than any of the thirty-nine objected to by those who, with a very blameable indiscretion (and some, I believe, from worse motives), are willing to disturb it. I shall not easily concede that any alteration either in these or the Liturgy is necessary, unless they contain doctrines contrary to sound morality and civil obedience, but even then I should by no means concur in the prayer of your petition; I should rather be led to a conclusion totally different, for I should think that the specific article ought to be amended, and not the whole set aside; but this is a work in the first instance for synods and convocations: many preparatory steps, which I have not wisdom enough to indicate, ought to precede the parliamentary consideration.

I deny that any of the Reformers whose names are transmitted to posterity with respect, ever adopted so wild an idea as that of a Christian society without an established church holding certain defined tenets. The liberty of judging for yourselves of the sense of Scripture is a possession, which, you say, all men have a right to enjoy; I not only agree with you in this proposition, but I will add, that you have a right to teach and inform others according to your own sense of Scripture, provided your lessons are conducive, or at least indifferent, to the happiness of mankind and the tranquillity of the state; but these concessions do not exclude every government from giving the preference to such forms, or to such doctrines, which appear most eligible in their united public sense, which constitutes the law. Therefore the ministers of Separatists are maintained at the expense of their congregations; dignities and preferment belong exclusively to the Established Church alone; this has been, is, and ever must be the rule in the most tolerant states, and even in the freest republics.

The wisdom of Providence seems in its dispensations to have reserved this authority for the future succession of Christian churches; it never could be supposed that the poor, and the ignorant, who compose the greater number of the laity, could give up their labour for, and pass their lives in, the investigation of this divine system. It may perhaps be asserted, that the Scripture is so clear, and so full, that it wants no interpretation, nor any supplementary addition. If this be true, how happens it, that we are hitherto not better agreed? Why has the world been disturbed by so many leaders of sects and heresiarchs, who (if they were all now alive upon the face of the earth) might compose as large an army as that with which Alexander the Great conquered the Persian empire? Yet, all these men were convinced and maintained that their opinions were founded in, or derived from, Holy Writ.

If the Scripture needs no explanation, I will turn Quaker, and join in any measure which tends to set aside your whole order as an useless expense. But if it does require explanation, I chuse to trust that task rather to the well digested and mature studies of our venerable Hierarchy, than to the crude transient notions which caprice, vanity, self-conceit, and folly may suggest to every idle coxcomb, who wants to be taken notice of for his singularity. I am therefore (within the bounds of toleration which I have laid down) an advocate not only for strict subordination, to overawe and coerce such dangerous impertinences, but for written canons, creeds, and articles to warn rash unthinking men of the future censure and punishment they may incur; for it is essential to justice to mark out plainly offences of every kind, and it is an arbitrary exertion of power to inflict penalties without such notice. I should at the same time strenuously oppose the compelling any individual to sign any article of faith whatever. But nothing of this kind is at present done; every man is left to his own free choice, and every honest man will therein follow the dictates of his own opinion; nor will there arise the slightest inconvenience if (from peculiar objections to the Liturgy, or the Thirty-Nine Articles) some few persons more should chuse in the various professions of laymen to follow an active life of virtuous industry: I thank God we live neither in a desart country, nor an illiterate age, and I hope we are not likely soon to want a decent and worthy succession in our priesthood.

If (as you are pleased to inform me) bishops and others have in their writings, preachings, &c. receded from what they have signed, and what the law has enjoined, I do not think the precedent so good as to wish the practice general; nor does the example of a College in Cambridge weigh greatly with me: I have quite accidentally heard somewhat of the secret history which has passed within those wall; if I am not deceived, that signature has been chiefly promoted by a factious abetter of those senseless seditious disputes which have divided us upon political subjects, and which are already enough envenomed without your throwing in the fresh corrosive of religious controversy.

How total a fermentation such a mixture may produce is well known to all those who have read the history of this country for the last century. As no church is so purely of divine institution as not to smell a little of humanity, our Establishment may be liable to some errors; yet does it leave you sufficient scope to be, as you actually are, a very good man, and to contribute greatly to render your parishioners such. The wisdom of government, ever since the house of Hanover ascended the throne, has maintained your order in the possession of sufficient respect, and has kept you perfectly quiet; neither the good treatment you have enjoyed nor your want of power have been founded of the plan of any particular administration, they have arisen from the general sense and temper of this age. The reign of the Angelick and Seraphick Doctors is past and gone; were they now to appear again, the world would busy itself very little about their subtilities; nay, I am sanguine enough to believe that Prynne, Burton, and Bastwick would at present have few partizans unless they were persecuted, which I think very unlikely to happen to any man. The vice of the present times is rather too much indifference about religious matters, and opinions: if I might, therefore, as a real friend, presume to advise the clergy, they ought not, while total infidelity is gaining ground upon them, to expose any partial weaknesses of their system, and thus by trivial and frivolous disagreements among themselves perhaps endanger the whole fabrick. I have sometimes in my more serious hours regretted that the poor Apocrypha found no better advocate, because by rejecting those books the rest of the Bible was perhaps brought under some degree of doubt; and if the Liturgy or the Thirty-Nine Articles were now deserted, who knows where the growing incredulity of mankind would stop?

Upon the whole, my dear sir, I heartily wish it was possible for you to desist from a design which I so highly disapprove and must so entirely discountenance; but I well know the warmth with which these speculations are pursued by those who have once adopted them. I trust, however, there will be found sobriety and understanding enough in the House of Commons to reject your petition without any more debate than what every single member has a right to command upon every question however improper to be moved. I beg you will believe that though we differ so widely upon this public point, which I have endeavoured to treat with all

z

possible candour and frankness, I shall ever be ready to receive
your commands with regard to all matters which regard yourself,
or in which I can prove to you the affection and esteem with
which I am, dear sir,

Your most obedient and most humble servant,

H. STANLEY.

Correspondence of Dr. Markham, Bishop of Chester, afterwards
Archbishop of York, with Mr. Lindsey, upon his Resignation of
the Vicarage of Catterick.

FROM THE REV. T. LINDSEY TO THE BISHOP OF CHESTER.

Catterick, Nov. 12, 1773.

My Lord,

It is my duty, and full time that I should acquaint your Lordship with my intention of resigning the vicarage of Catterick, in
your diocese of Chester, the latter end of this month.

If your place of residence had been within any convenient distance, as it would have been more respectful, I should have been
desirous to have waited on your Lordship, and made my resignation
into your own hands.

I am obliged to take this step after long deliberation, for the
relief of my own mind, not being able in any way to satisfy myself
with officiating according to the present forms of our church, and
not thinking myself at liberty to make those very material alterations that would satisfy me : I mean in changing the *object of
worship*, which to me appears to be sadly mistaken in many parts
of the service.

I have the honour to be,
My Lord,
Your Lordship's most humble and obedient servant,

T. LINDSEY.

FROM THE BISHOP OF CHESTER TO THE REV. T. LINDSEY.

Sion End, near Brentford, Nov. 16, 1773.

Reverend Sir,

I received this morning the favour of your letter, acquainting
me with your intention to resign your vicarage, and at the same

time signifying your motives. The business is so important, and the time you mention so very short, that I am using the first moment to give you my sentiments, in hopes that I may possibly put the question in such a light as may at least procure a suspension of your design. For, to say the truth, my heart has taken a very serious and sad concern in this transaction, not only from the charity which I owe to you, as my brother, and because I seek the truth, as I believe you do, but from the impressions which I have received of your character from two very good men, Mr. Cooper and Mr. Smelt. I have heard from them that you are a sincere believer of the Holy Scriptures : upon that ground I speak to you : the question is not be tried at the bar of human reason, but depends entirely upon a true explanation of the divine writings, which those who have supported the opinions which you seem to hold are used to interpret in such a manner as the original languages can no wise suffer, and without it they could never have contrived to get over a number of texts which are as strong and explicit as any in the Bible. But carnal wisdom is followed. Philosophy will know everything, and has as yet discovered nothing ; it is still a stranger to the essence of the meanest thing about us, and yet will know the essence of the Deity, and will say this and this is contrary to it. Our religion is supported by the fullest and clearest testimonies, and yet the whole of it is truly incomprehensible from the creation of man to his final resurrection ; but the filiation of our Saviour is not only a great mystery, but though explained to us as far as is useful in our present state is from the nature of the subject particularly involved. We are prepared for this difficulty by the Prophet Isaiah ; his words are, as quoted in the Acts, τηνδε γενεαν αυτου τις διηγησεται ? But the embarrassment has chiefly risen from the number of texts that seem to militate against his divine nature ; which must necessarily happen, as he is most commonly spoken of in his inferior capacity, the man Jesus, the visible Agent on earth, the Teacher, the Redeemer, in which characters he has a more immediate relation to the human race ; and in which his office and ministration were exemplified. But there are other texts which are very express. I will mention a few of such as occur to me, and which I think least liable to disputation, because they appear in both the Old and New Testament, in the first applied to God, in the second to our Saviour.

When Moses asks the name of God, he is told in those words

z 2

which denote eternal existence that his name is *I am*. Our Saviour answers the Jews, Verily before Abraham was, *I am*.

Isaiah says of God, At his name every knee shall bow, of things in heaven, &c., which very words are by St. Paul used directly of our Saviour.

God is continually spoken of in the Old Testament, by the names of *the just one, the holy one*, &c. The same are applied to our Saviour. The appellation of *the Lord* is given to God throughout the Old Testament, by which Christ is constantly named in the New.

Indeed I do not know what they would make of that person who is so often declared to be far above all angels, and whose shoes St. John Baptist (who had been declared greater than a prophet) was not worthy to unloose.

I cannot flatter myself that this slight discussion of a great subject should have so much weight, as at once to determine you against your former deliberate reasonings ; but it may call to your memory how often we are told μη ὑπερφρονειν παρ ὁ δει φρονειν, that without humbleness of mind our faith is always in danger. It may prevent your taking a hasty step, by which, if I do not misconceive your character, you of all men may be made most miserable, if you should see occasion to change your opinion, and then reflect that you had not only deserted your station, but had encouraged schism and heresy. Indeed, if you reflect that the words In the name of the Father, the Son, and the Holy Ghost were given by our Saviour to the Apostles, and that St. Stephen called upon Christ to receive his soul, you cannot think yourself unauthorised in the use of our forms, and may satisfy your conscience in acquiescing, at least, till all that is said in support of them can be disproved. I write this for your own use, and confidentially. I detest the wrangle of controversy. Ει τις δοκει ειναι φιλονεικος, ἡμεις ουκ εχομεν τοιαυτην συνηθειαν. I quote by memory, probably incorrectly. Pray, consider this, and give me your answer.

I am, with a true regard,

Your affectionate brother,

W. Chester.

EXTRACT FROM MR. LINDSEY'S REPLY.

I am surely obliged to the friends your Lordship mentions for giving your Lordship such a favourable representation of my character, and feel the serious concern and kindness which dictated the letter I have the honour to receive from you this morning.

It was natural for your Lordship with these dispositions towards me to bid me beware of precipitation in a matter of such moment. But though suddenly and so lately communicated to your Lordship, this resolution is no hasty step, but the result of many years' anxious enquiry and deliberation, and trying every expedient that might give me ease.

And my faith is built not on a system of philosophy, but on an impartial examination of the mind and will of God, as discovered in the Old and New Testament. And I am constrained on this occasion to tell your Lordship, that I am so persuaded of the strict unity of God, taught by Moses and the prophets, and last of all by our Saviour Christ, that though no one is further from condemning others that differ; I should hold it impiety in me to continue to worship Christ, or any other being or person. I cannot, therefore, continue to lead the devotions of a congregation in the Church of England, who esteem it sinful in myself constantly to use that worship and abet it.

Your Lordship will believe, all those texts which you point out to me have fallen under consideration, and which if I note, it is not in the spirit of dispute, which ill becomes me towards you on such an occasion, but out of respectful attention to what you are pleased to select.

[Mr. Lindsey having suggested the usual explanations of the texts alleged by the worthy prelate, proceeds as follow s :

Whatever be the distressing consequences of this determination with regard to worldly things, I can never repent of it, as led to it by no motive but a desire to approve myself to God, and what my duty to him required.

No. V..

Letters to Mr. Lindsey upon his resignation.

FROM THE RIGHT HONOURABLE GREY COOPER.

Kew Lane, Nov. 6, 1773..

My Dear Sir,

I have received your letter, which filled my heart with grief, and made my eyes glisten with tears; I have not a word to say or an argument to offer against your resolution to quit your preferment; I must, however, lament the cruel necessity that forces you out of a situation in which you and your good wife might have continued blessings to your parish and neighbourhood; I will add only this short but sincere assurance, that it would give me the utmost satisfaction to have it in my power to assist you in any new course of life which you may think proper to follow. Lord North has seen your letter, and was affected by reading it; he has an excellent heart, and a just feeling for every act of honour and conscience. It is not yet decided who is to have Catterick; Mr. Chayter has applied for it, and his brother-in-law, Mr. Robinson, my colleague;—will you allow me to ask what is the annual income of it, and on what account it is as you say eligible? Perhaps it may be better than my brother's at Mansfield, and in that case I would try to manage an exchange between Mr. Chayter and my brother. I beg pardon for troubling you with such things at this time; but as soon as I receive your answer I shall be able to inform you with certainty who will be your successor; at present I am rather inclined to think it will be Mr. Chayter. My wife sends her best compliments to you; she was much moved with the contents of your letter.

I am, my dear sir,
Your affectionate friend and servant,
GREY COOPER.

FROM EARL PERCY, LATE DUKE OF NORTHUMBERLAND.
Nov. 1773.

Stanwick, Wednesday morning.

Dear Sir,

I am sorry to find by your letter which I received just now, that I have been deprived of the pleasure of seeing you by a cold. When my mother was so good as to show me her answer to your letter, I told her I thought she had said all that could be said on that subject, but that I knew your way of thinking on that affair much too well, to suppose anything on earth could prevent you from resigning a living, which your conscience told you, you could no longer hold as a honest man, void of time-serving hypocrisy. I hope, however, I shall have the pleasure of seeing you here before you leave the country, as I do not think of going to town till after Christmas. At any rate I shall wish much to see your *Reasons*, when they are published; and have not the least doubt but they will give me great satisfaction. I beg my respects to Mrs. Lindsey, and be assured I am and ever will be

Your sincere friend,

PERCY.

York, Nov. 1, 1773.

Dear Sir,

Your truly christian and heroical determination is above my praise, and will afford you such hope and joy in God as will render human praise unnecessary to you, and human censure insignificant. I thank God from my heart, that there are men in the world who will buy the truth and sell it not. Your example, I think, cannot fail to increase the number of them. Sure, it must impress some hearts with a conviction that there is something serious in religious truth and liberty, and something real that is not of this world. The comfort and reward of confessing Christ you must have, and your name I trust will be held in everlasting remembrance by the friends of truth and virtue, and will continue to do good when your personal services are over. Those who esteem you as they ought, cannot be unaffected with the inconveniences you may suffer, and that not in your own person only, from your integrity. It is an afflicting thought; but the utility of your example is connected with this circumstance, and I hope in God that the righteous will not be forsaken. As to the business you mentioned, Mr. Hotham (who presents to you his most respectful compliments and the sincerest tenders of his service) will join with me to do the best we can for you. If you will send either the books or a list of them, we will treat with a bookseller about them. If his proposal comes not up to your idea of their value, and the books are numerous enough, it may be worth while to sell them by a marked catalogue, and this, if you approve of it, we will do. I am greatly obliged to you for the tender regard you express toward me and my little family, and I remain, with the highest esteem, and all manner of good wishes for you and every one that is dear to you,

Your affectionate humble Servant,

N. CAPPE.

To the Rev. Mr. Lindsey, at Catterick.

June 11, 1774.

Rev. Sir,

Having read your Apology with peculiar pleasure, I cannot resist the impulse of writing to you. There was a time when, shackled by the bonds of intellectual slavery, I should have shuddered at your freedom, and have forgot your honesty amidst your heterodoxy. But now I measure mankind on a larger scale, and if I see the former I forget the latter. My travels in the theologic region have been variously conducted: but amidst every intricacy I never lost sight of sincerity. When reason was hoodwinked, that, like a faithful companion, attended even my wanderings; and I hope I shall never forfeit the protection of such a friend. I enter into your feelings with a sympathy which I cannot express. I insensibly catch your spirit as it shines forth in the mild lustre of primitive simplicity; and pray that I may be a follower of those who through faith and patience pursue the promises.

Most heartily do I congratulate you on that exalted superiority of mind which, abstracting you from the world, must inspire you with such joys as the world cannot give nor take away. They flow from that noble independence which is the first gift of heaven. Go on and prosper. May the influence of your example be as diffusive as corruption hath been! Truth, like the sun, may be clouded, but cannot be extinguished—No: it will, when it begins to dawn, pursue its course till it gains the perfect day. Then will the sons of ignorance and bigotry fly with dismay, when the Lord shall scatter the one with the breath of his mouth, and eclipse the other in the brightness of his coming.

Fox's letter at the end of your Apology is really an excellent one. I have translated it, to gratify a friend; and have been urged to publish it for general entertainment in some paper or magazine.

I beg leave to ask you one question,—Was you the author of a paper in the Theological Repository, signed *Socrates Scholasticus?* I think I trace *Mr. Lindsey* in it. *Barnuensis* is the very person who is now writing to you; and it would not in the least lessen my esteem and love of you, if I was sure that you had opposed me. In one respect I merited correction; though in another respect it was doing me too much honour. Let this plead for my pertness. 1 was scarcely two-and-twenty when I writ that paper, and did it in a hurry, urged on by the warm solicitations of bigotry.

I suppose you are acquainted with that worthy man Dr. Priestley. I am happy in his friendship, and owe much to his writings. I love every good man with the most sincere affection; and in proportion as he is distinguished for the noble qualities of disinterested zeal and sincerity, so proportionably do I value and esteem him, as the highest character that earth can be blessed with. On these principles,

I am, dear Sir,
Your most affectionate brother and friend,
S. BADCOCK.

To the Rev. Theoph. Lindsey.

No. VI.

Extracts of Letters from the late Thomas Hollis, Esq., under the title of Pierce Delver, to the Rev. T. Lindsey.

As I think to be well informed, Mrs. Macaulay has lately sold to Messrs. Dilly, booksellers, in the Poultry, the power of making an octavo edition of her works, she reserving her right afterward in those works for 900l. ! Also, the right of every future volume which she shall write, for one thousand pounds each volume ! It seems this lady thinks there will be three more volumes to the elevation of the House of Hanover. When those are written, she purposes to write the History of the Tudors. And then, to place a large Introduction before her History, which shall begin with the earliest account of Britain, and stride down to her History of the Tudors.

The bargain seems to be a good one on her part. But, to me, it would be a sad case to write of liberty, magnanimity, at a price, and against a reason, at any price !

It seems for some time past, when only three volumes of her History were published, Mrs. M. wanted Mr. Cadell to buy the copyright of them, &c.; but he chose not to meddle with her History in so imperfect, uncertain a state.

On the present occasion she has not said one word to him, though always in every shape most respectful toward her and vigilant to promote her interests. Mr. C. is rather concerned at her behaviour;

and tells me that he should have been glad to have taken share in the octavo edition, but not in the agreement for the future un-begotten volumes at any rate.

The other day I paid her a visit at her house in Berners Street, Oxford Road, on a particular occasion, by desire. That house, a new one, she has bought, and furnished handsomely. She had the air of a princess, out-Cornelised the Cornelisians, and had the frank Bath air upon her countenance.

It seems she keeps two servants in laced liveries, treats cleverly and elegantly, and in short, author or fine lady, surpasses all her sex.

All this *in confidence*, for I respect her exceedingly, and she is to be maintained in much just commendation for her many extra-ordinary qualities and the cause sake.

I am, with great esteem, dear Sir,
Your affectionate friend and most obedient servant,
PIERCE DELVER.

FROM THE SAME.

The writer, considering the uncertainty and accidents of life, is desirous of sending a copy of a curious letter written to him by a worthy person, August 3, 1767.

" THOMAS SECKER was born about the year 1693 or 4, son of a reputable shopkeeper in Chesterfield, in Derbyshire. His sister married Sam. Wildbore, of Brewhouse-yard, near Nottingham, a Protestant Dissenter, and by trade a dyer. His brother George was put to the Coventry business, where he lived many years, a professed Protestant Dissenter; and, for aught I know, may yet live; though the ABP has one of his sons in the church.

"Thomas Secker, after he left the Grammar-school, I think went to the Academy at Attercliff, and, however this, he finished at Sam. Jones's Academy in Tewksbury. There it was he wrote some letters in the controversy between Dr. S. Clarke and Leibnitz, on *Liberty and Necessity*, which gained him the Doctor's favour.

After this, he was some time with his sister aforesaid, in Brew-house-yard, where he constantly attended the worship of the Pro-testant Dissenting church, under the pastoral care of the Rev. Mr. Bateson, with whom he was very familiar.

"He then went to study physic at Leyden; and then took the degree of M.D.

"Becoming acquainted with one of the sons of Dr. Talbot, Bishop of Durham, he travelled with him; when great affection for T.S. led the son to recommend him so strongly to the patronage of the Bishop, that he gave him expectation of providing for him in the church: whereupon he went to Oxford, studied there some time, and would have exchanged his diploma of M.D. for that of D.D., but could not obtain any higher than LL.D., which is his signature to this day.

"Bishop Talbot gave him a rich prebend in the Durham cathedral, and also soon a great living. He married a lady in the Talbot family, as was thought by some in gratitude. Chancellor Talbot was his friend; and he thus had the ladder of preferment made easy to him."

No. VII.

Letters from the Rev. W. Hopkins.

Cuckfield, March 29, 1784.

Dear Sir,

I have lately perused your Historical View of the State of the Unitarian Doctrine and Worship, and take an early opportunity to express my grateful thanks for this useful and entertaining history But before I proceed to take any notice of the contents of it, I cannot help sending my sincere congratulation upon the victory you and Mrs. Lindsey have gained over one of the greatest temptations of human life, and have set a noble example of Christian fortitude, even in these times. You have laid a glorious foundation for the establishment of genuine Christianity amongst all Protestants, which of course will prove an excellent means to demolish the gross corruptions of Popery, which derive some support from the flagrant errors yet remaining in Protestant churches. In your Historical View I meet with many curious anecdotes with which I was unacquainted; though, several years ago, I was engaged in a scheme something resembling the Historical View, but was interrupted after some little progress made in it. I was very much surprised to find that the eminent Dr. Doddridge should contend for that very absurd notion of Christ's being possessed of two natures ; but the vast convenience of being provided with a solution, well accommodated to reconcile the most palpable contradictions, had too much influence upon his mind. Philpot's case affords a striking instance of a cruel persecuting temper, at the very time he was suffering himself for his religious principles. The cause of Christianity was at first supported and propagated by fair and open professions, though frequently attended with terrible evils. But it is to be lamented that, during the corrupt state of the apostate church, many nice arts have been employed to palliate established forms, and hinder the progress of the plain simplicity of the gospel of Christ. Your strictures upon those great and good men, Sir Isaac Newton, Dr. Clarke, and Bishop Hoadly, are, I think, very just. What persecution could the bigots have inflicted upon such persons, since this family came to the throne, if they had taken very bold steps in maintaining the cause they certainly had at heart? It may perhaps appear not impertinent to take notice of a conversation that passed many years ago, when I was very young, at a worthy clergyman's house, who had been preferred by Bishop Hoadly, and likewise was intimate with Dr. Clarke. The clergyman was speaking in a soft and cautious way of his friend Dr. Clarke, and observed *that he could not make it do very well :* in other plainer terms, it was difficult to make the Athanasian Creed consistent with subscription. But the Doctor, he said, *could say as much for a bad cause as any one.* This declaration made a strong and lasting impression upon my mind. It only shows that the Doctor was an able pleader, and at the same time the cause was bad : and indeed I found, by dear-bought experience, that it proved a bad cause to me. The learned Mr. Wasse, of whom you make mention, gave a noble example to the members of Oxford and Cambridge, by his open professions and declaration of holding a debate with Dr. Potter, late Archbishop of Canterbury, at that time Regius Professor of Divinity at Oxford. I have been always of opinion that the method proposed by Mr. Wasse was an excellent one, and am really concerned that this plan has never been imitated and reduced to practice. Of what use are theological debates, as commonly held by the Professors of Oxford and Cambridge, when the disputants are tied down to determine the questions proposed by established standards of orthodoxy ? I cannot help my hearty approbation of your inserting Archbishop Herring's letter to Dr. Jortin : I am of opinion that this letter will be of service to the cause. I have the satisfaction to find in the list of your worthies, names which I never heard of before : viz. Mr. Maty, Mr. Harries, and Mr. Ross of Scotland. May the number of such worthy persons perpetually increase? My own story relative to the cause is not worth relating, and I pass it off in silence. But I would just remind you, that you have omitted some Unitarians worthy of notice, viz. Gilbert Clerke, fellow of a college in Cambridge before the Restoration. As the statutes obliged him to go into orders by a particular time, he made it his choice to resign his fellowship, and all pretensions to church preferment. The great Mr. Locke, the Rev. Mr. Tomkins, the Rev. Mr. Gibbs, two dissenting ministers who were ejected from their congregations upon account of their Unitarian principles.

Unitarians, as they are uniformly agreed in the grand points of the question, should carefully avoid disagreeable altercations upon their lesser differences. Upon a review, the whole of what I now maintain is no more than this, that the direct invocation of Christ is lawful upon some occasions, and that I cannot protest against the lawfulness of it, as I have openly done against the third and seventh petitions of the Litany, and all passages of a similar nature. It is now high time that I should make my sincere acknowledgements to you and Dr. Disney for the trouble you have given yourselves about my translation, which I find is done in an handsome manner. I heartily wish all possible success to your ministry at the chapel in Essex Street, and likewise to the Society ; and am, dear Sir, with my respectful compliments to Dr. and Mrs. Disney, to Dr. and Mrs. Jebb, and Mrs. Lindsey,

Your much obliged friend,

W. HOPKINS.

P.S. Unless my memory deceive me, for I am not in possession of the tracts, Dr. Price and Dr. Priestley had a friendly debate upon liberty and necessity. I profess myself strongly attached to the cause of moral liberty in the strictest sense, in opposition to necessity of every kind, whether arising from external or internal causes. If I remember right, Dr. Price maintained his point, viz., liberty, in an able and rational way ; but when he came to the grand difficulty, which has perplexed the best writers upon the subject, viz., how to reconcile prescience with liberty, he seemed distressed. It has generally been taken for granted on both sides, that divine prescience must be admitted as a truth. But really I entertain very great doubts, occasioned by a careful

perusal of a chapter in Crellius's *De Sapientia Dei,* which does not
seem to have engaged the attention of the learned so much as it
deserves. A rational and sensible person was going to write upon
this subject, to whom I recommended this chapter of Crellius;
but as he was unacquainted with the learned languages, I engaged
to translate part of the chapter. If Dr. Price has never seen
this chapter, and Crellius's works have not fallen in his way, I
should esteem it as a favour if you would present my respects to
him, and beg of him to accept of this translation, if not disagreeable, which possibly may tend to illustrate a subject he has frequently considered. The person for whom it was originally intended has been dead some time. If the Doctor be in possession
of Crellius's works, I must ask his pardon for this impertinence,
as I am sensible he understands the language much better than
the translator. 'Tis proper to add that I did not translate the
whole chapter.

FROM THE SAME.

Cuckfield, April 29, 1784.

Dear Sir,
  Last week your extraordinary favour came to hand, and I think
myself obliged to take an early opportunity to acknowledge with
gratitude the kind and friendly manner with which you treat me.
I thought it not improper to take notice of some names omitted
in your very useful work, and am really surprised that the learned
Mr. Peirce should escape my observation, of whom I had conceived
an high opinion, and some of whose excellent works I have in my
possession. With respect to Mr. Gilbert Clerke, I can communicate no other particulars than what you may find in Mr. Nelson's
Life of Bishop Bull (pag. 497, 499, 502, 508—513). He seems
to have given an impartial account of the Life and Character of
Mr. Gilbert Clerke; but what was naturally to be expected, he
speaks slightingly of his performances, in part of which he presumed to differ from the celebrated Defender of the Nicene Faith.
The Bishop, as you rightly observe, treats poor Mr. Clerke in an
indecent manner, more especially as Mr. Nelson himself has given
him a good character; I call him poor, for in one part of his life
he ran the hazard, for the sake of conscience, of wanting the
common necessaries of life. As I have the tract of Mr. Clerke,
upon which Bishop Bull made animadversions, I compared them
together many years ago, and I find this observation in a vacant

space before the title page, " The famous Bull wrote animadversions upon this treatise, but he has left many arguments without the least appearance of an answer, which strongly support the Unitarian cause; this cause indeed is founded upon such powerful evidence as cannot be overthrown by the wit of man." I am inclined to judge that Bull saw something which he could not answer, and this raised his indignation. I entirely agree with Mr. Clerke, that Bull, in the last section of his Defence, relative to the subordination, had yielded great part of the question up to the Unitarians, or, rather, had given it quite up. Subordination, in any sense, absolutely demolishes the Athanasian system. All that appears of Mr. Philip Gibbs is, that as he had been bred up in the Calvinistic plan, upon a more exact examination of Scripture, and the study of the best authors, he became an Unitarian, and gave up predestination, original sin, &c. In consequence of his conviction, he addressed a letter to his congregation, wherein he openly and fairly delivered his sentiments : upon which they desired him to withdraw peaceably from their communion. He was afterward taken into partnership with a considerable trades-man, and died within a few years in that station.

Be pleased to return my best respects to Dr. Price, for taking in good part what I thought might prove useful to his design. But I find a disinclination in many learned persons to give up the divine prescience. Crellius, I really think, has argued the point with sagacity and deep penetration, and has stated the case in such a guarded manner as not to break in upon omniscience itself, when understood in a perfectly rational sense ; and has likewise made it consistent with prophecies delivered in the Old and New Testament. I did not translate the whole chapter, but am of opinion that the whole deserves the careful perusal of curious Beræans. I perused several years ago with peculiar satisfaction Dr. Price's Review of the principal Questions and Difficulties of Morals, and likewise his four Dissertations. I objected only to one sentence in his dissertation on Providence, which it is not necessary to mention, as it has been taken notice of by others; and the Doctor, I dare say, can guess at my meaning. I gave my hearty assent to his Political Treatise, published at a season-able time, well calculated to answer those purposes the worthy author had in view, and which, I believe, have been eventually answered. I sincerely wish him joy of his success. Upon the whole I ought to acknowledge with gratitude that I have received considerable improvement and much rational pleasure from the excellent writings of Dr. Price, which have engaged my attention, but am not qualified to form a proper judgment of that part of them which are taken up in curious and nice calculations, as being deficient in that branch of science. I must beg the favour of you to express my particular satisfaction to Dr. Priestley for the very candid observations he has made on our difference of sentiments, which shews a disposition to promote peace and harmony among Christians, and possibly an uniform agreement in some grand and essential points through the whole Christian world. If Dr. Priestley judges that there is no real difference betwixt him and Dr. Price, the same thing may be said of myself, as, unless I am mistaken, we are very nearly of the same sentiments. I certainly have expressed myself in a way different from that of Dr. Priestley, with regard to some opinions he has published, and at the same time have esteemed him for several of his practical treatises, which have fallen in my way. I sincerely believe that he is well disposed to promote the cause of natural and revealed religion, which plainly appears from his tracts on that subject, and which I had an opportunity of reading some time ago with satisfaction. I am a stranger to his philosophical discoveries and disquisitions, as having never acquired anything farther than a superficial knowledge of that science, which he has so happily cultivated and improved. I heartily wish him success in all his commendable undertakings : philosophy, when in the hands of a truly religious and ingenious person, has a natural tendency to display the glory of the One Supreme God and Father of all. You guess right about the book relative to the controversy of necessity betwixt Dr. Price and Dr. Priestley, it not being in my possession, and so should be glad to accept of your kind offer. With respect to Dr. Priestley's present undertaking, by that little acquaintance I had formerly with the primitive fathers, I am induced to believe that the Doctor will be able to prove his point to the satisfaction of unprejudiced inquirers.

It gives me peculiar satisfaction, that anything I have done relating to the book of Exodus has your approbation ; only I would observe that your candid opinion of the author has prevailed upon you to pass a too favourable sentence. I thought it right to speak my mind freely of Dr. Kennicott's short attempt to please the reputed orthodox, and presume he could not have taken it amiss, if he had been alive. You are so very obliging as to think of mentioning my name among the worthies, if your very useful work should come to a second edition, which I heartily wish it may for the public good; but I make this request, that, if upon a review you should judge it improper in any respect to mention my name, you would suppress it. I am very much concerned to hear of Dr. Jebb's precarious state of health; but you express some hopes that he may get the better of it, which I sincerely wish may prove the case. You tell me great news concerning the Bishops: surely a review will be attempted at last, and possibly I may have the pleasure of seeing something actually done in the glorious cause before I die, though far advanced in years.

I am, dear Sir, with my kind respects to Mrs. Lindsey, Dr. and Mrs. Disney, Dr. and Mrs. Jebb,

Your very affectionate friend, and deeply obliged humble servant,

W. HOPKINS.

FROM THE SAME, AND MARKED BY MR. LINDSEY, "THE EXCEL-
LENT MR. HOPKINS'S LAST LETTER."

Cuckfield, December 17, 1785.

Dear good Sir,

I hope to be able to send you some sort of answer to your very kind and Christian letter, which I received the last post.

With respect to my scruples relating to church matters, they are entirely removed by your determination. Your solicitous concern for my welfare is very engaging, and which you have plainly shown by procuring for me a very handsome present from a worthy member of the Society. I accept of it with grateful thanks, as my imprudent son has very much wasted my substance by his vicious extravagance; but still I am provided with a decent support by proper management. I will take care to employ a person some day next week to call at your house for the generous gift. And as you think my name may be something in the Society book, though a poor something, I revoke my design of having it struck out, and refer the time of my little payment to you and the Society.

I cannot conclude without taking notice that your charity in-duces you to entertain a more favourable opinion than I really deserve; neither ought I to put myself upon a footing with such worthy persons as yourself, who have maintained an unblemished

A A

character all their lives ; that of a poor humble penitent is all that I can justly claim.

May the One Supreme God and Father of all give a blessing and success to all your sincere endeavours to promote the cause of his true. religion, and likewise those of your worthy associates ! and may all possible success attend the Christian Society which you have formed for the ·same excellent purpose ! which is the earnest prayer of, good Sir,

Your highly obliged friend, and humble servant,

W. HOPKINS.

No. IX.

P. Courayer to the Rev. T. Lindsey.

A Percy Lodge, ce 29 Septembre, 1875.

Dear Mr. Lindsey,*

Je suis charmé que votre progrès dans la langue Françoise vous rende ma recommandation inutile. Car par vous même vous saurez assez vous recommander à ceux avec qui vous ferez connoissance. La science et la bonne conduite sont un excellent passe-par-tout auprès de tous les honnêtes gens.

Quoi que je ne puisse convenir avec Mr. de St. Perne que ma retraite ait été une perte pour personne, je suis persuadé, comme lui, que si j'étois resté en France je n'y aurois pu demeurer sans m'exposer à de grandes difficultez et à quelques dangers ; et quelque mortification que j'aye eu à souffrir en quittant une societié et un pais où je vivois avec agrément et satisfaction, je ne me repens point de cette démarche, qui m'a dedommagé de ce que j'ai perdu par les avantages que j'ai retrouvez ici, et qui a mis ma conscience à couvert des troubles et des tentations aux quelles elle auroit été exposée en demeurant dans ma patrie.

Rien n'est plus triste, comme vous l'observez, que de voir les hommes se persécuter pour des opinions sur des points obscurs, dont la décision est aussi incertaine que le sont les points mêmes en question, et qui d'ailleurs n'ont que très peu d'influence sur les mœurs et la conduite des hommes. Mais on veut

* So in the original.

dominer sur la foi des autres ; et la même ambition qui porte les princes à étendre leurs domaines, engage les théologiens à vouloir faire régner leurs opinions. C'est un mal aussi ancien que le monde, et il y a long tems que, comme l'a dit un ancien, l'homme se comporte en bête féroce à l'égard des autres : *homo homini lupus.* Que faire pour remédier à ce mal ? En gémir devant Dieu lui demander la grace de changer le cœur des hommes, et de les ramener à des sentimens plus éclairez, censurer cet esprit de domination quand l'occasion se présente de le faire avec utilité, et si on ne peut reformer les autres, s'éloigner soi même d'une pareille disposition, et laisser la liberté à chacun de suivre ses propres lumières en conservant l'esprit d'union et de charité qui fait proprement l'essence de la religion.

La demande que vous me faites est si vague que je ne saurois pour cette fois y répondre. Vous me priez de vous faire connoître quelques petits traitez que vous puissiez vous procurer. Je ne sais ce que vous entendez par la. Sont-ce des traités de pieté, ou de controverse, ou de belles lettres ? Sont-ce ou des ouvrages de morale ou des sermons, ou simplement des ouvrages d'esprit ? Pardonnez moi de ne rien répondre à une demande qui est trop générale pour que je puisse y satisfaire.

J'ai pris part comme toute la France à la naissance du Duc de Bourgogne. Je crois même que c'est un bien pour toute l'Europe, qu'un défaut de succession pourroit rengager dans une guerre générale. Mon exil ne me rend point insensible aux avantages de ma patrie. Mais comme ce n'est pas tout d'avoir un prince à moins qu'il ne soit bon, mes vœux présentement se bornent à en souhaiter un qui fasse le bonheur de son royaume, et qui rende ses peuples aussi heureux que sa naissance leur donne de satisfaction.

Après quatre mois de séjour à Percy Lodge, je m'en retourne cette semaine à Londres. J'ai la satisfaction de laisser la Duchesse en assez bonne santé. Je lui en souhaite la continuation, d'autant plus que d'elle, dépend le support et la subsistance de bien des pauvres aux besoins desquels sa charité fournit.

Je ne sais si je dois vous faire mes complimens sur les bénéfices que My Lord Northumberland vous offre. Le plus considérable n'est qu'un dépôt, que je ne regarde pas trop comme légitime, et que nous regardons en France comme une sorte de simonie. L'autre ne vous donne qu'une simple subsistance, et vous m'avez souvent avoué que vous ne vous conteuteriez pas d'une cure qui

A A 2

ne vous donnât pas de quoi fournir aux pauvres dont vous seriez chargé. Ainsi j'attens que vous ayez pris votres résolution pour savoir si je dois vous en féliciter.

Mr. Cowslad vous fait ses complimens, quoi qu'il soit en colère que vous ne lui ayez pas envoyé la recette de la crême de Blois qu'il vous avoit demandée. Mes tendres amitiés à Mr. de St. Perne, et mes complimens à My Lord Warkworth, à qui je souhaite la continuation de sa santé.

Comme je suppose que la Duchesse vous mande les nouvelles courantes, je ne me charge point de ce détail. Il n'est question pour moi que de m'entretenir dans votre souvenir, et de vous demander la continuation de votre amitié. Personne ne la mérite mieux, s'il suffit pour la mériter d'avoir pour vous autant d'estime et d'attachement que j'en ai. Il ne tiendra qu'à vous de me fournir quelque occasion de vous en donner pes preuves; et de vous convaincre que personne n'est plus sincèrement,

Mon cher ami,

Votre très humble et très obéissant serviteur,

P. fr. LE COURAYER.

A Monsieur Lindsey.

No. X.

From William Wells, Esq., of Boston, in New England, to the Author.

Boston, March 21, 1812.

My dear Sir,

I am glad to hear you received the sermons safe. About six weeks ago I forwarded to Mr. Freme a parcel for you, containing the first No. of "The General Repository and Review." For this you are indebted to Mr. B. I think a letter from him accompanied the Review, but am not sure, as I took no memorandum of the contents of the parcel. A second number will shortly appear, which shall be forwarded by the earliest opportunity. I believe I mentioned in my last the name of the editor, Mr. Norton, an excellent young man. Of his abilities you will be able to judge. I think the first article, and the review of the Horsleian and Priestleian controversy display a soundness of judgment which at his age is rare. A number of young men who have taken their bachelor's degree now reside at Cambridge as theological students. Several of them are the sons of men of fortune, some, as far as I can judge, of superior talents; and all are pursuing their professional studies with a zeal which is well directed by the very worthy and learned Dr. Ware, professor of divinity, and Dr. Kirkland, the president, and an honesty which is entirely unfettered and unbiassed by any system whatever. We have to contend here, as you in England, for the first principles of Protestantism, but I see no reason to fear that the ensuing generation will be destitute of able champions for the right of private judgment.

With regard to the progress of Unitarianism, I have but little to say. Its tenets have spread very extensively in New England, but I believe there is only one church *professedly* Unitarian. The churches at Portland and Saco, of which you speak, hardly ever saw the light, and exist no longer. The Mr. Thacher who was formerly a member of Congress, and the Judge T: whom Mr. Merrick mentions, are the same. He is one of the Judges of our Supreme Court, an excellent man and most zealous Unitarian. He is now on the circuit in this town, and tells me he is obliged on Sunday to stay at home or to hear a Calvinistic minister. He is no relation to our friend.

Most of our Boston clergy and respectable laymen (of whom we have many enlightened theologians) are Unitarian. Nor do they think it at all necessary to conceal their sentiments upon these subjects, but express them without the least hesitation when they judge it proper. I may safely say, the general habit of thinking and speaking upon this question in Boston is Unitarian. At the same time the controversy is seldom or never introduced into the pulpit. I except the Chapel church. If publications make their appearance attacking Unitarian sentiments, they are commonly answered with spirit and ability; but the majority of those who are Unitarian are perhaps of these sentiments, without any distinct consciousness of being so. Like the first Christians, finding no sentiments but those in the N. T., and not accustomed to hear the language of the N. T. strained and warped by theological system-makers, they adopt naturally a just mode of thinking.

This state of things appears to me so favourable to the dissemination of correct sentiments, that I should perhaps regret a great degree of excitement in the public mind upon these subjects. The majority would eventually be against us. The ignorant, the violent, the ambitious, and the cunning, would carry the multitude with them in religion as they do in politics. One Dr. M., in a contest for spreading his own sentiments among the *great body* of the people, would, at least for a time, beat ten Priestleys. Not to dwell upon the consideration that Unitarianism consists rather in *not* believing; and that it is more easy to gain proselytes to absurd opinions, than to make men zealous *in refusing* to believe. With what arms, when the οἱ πολλοι are the judges, can virtue and learning contend with craft and cunning and equivocation and falsehood and intolerant zeal? Learning is worse than useless, virtue is often diffident of her own conclusions, and, at any rate, more anxious to render men good Christians than to . make them Christians of her own denomination; and that self-respect, which is the companion of virtue, disdains to meet the low cunning of her adversaries, or to flatter the low prejudices of her judges. I think then it must be assumed as an axiom, that a persevering controversy upon this question would render the multitude bigoted and persecuting Calvinists. Then come systems and catechisms in abundance. Every conceited deacon, every parishioner who has, or thinks he has, a smattering in theology, becomes the inquisitor of his pastor. In such circumstances learning and good sense have no chance. They cannot even be heard.

The violent party here have chosen to meet their opponents upon very unfavourable ground. Instead of making it a cause of orthodoxy against heresy, they have very unwisely preferred to insist upon a subscription to articles of faith. This has given great offence to many who are disposed to be in favour of their creed, and thrown them into the opposite scale. Dr. Osgood is really orthodox in sentiment, but a noble and determined supporter of the right of private judgement, and on the best possible terms with our Boston friends. This is also the case with the venerable Dr. Lathrop, of West Springfield, Mr. Palmer's friend, and many others. In short, we are now contending for the liberty of being Protestants. If we can persuade the people (and we stand upon advantageous ground) that we have a right to think upon religious subjects as our consciences and the Scriptures direct, things will go on very well. Learning, good sense, and virtue will then produce their natural effects; and just modes of thinking upon subjects of this nature, as upon all others, will necessarily prevail. Will you, my dear Sir, excuse my unintentional prolixity? I do not know that you will approve my sentiments, nor am I very confident of their justness; but I have seen the contest between truth and falsehood, *before the multitude;* between everything which is respectable and everything which is detestable, so unequal in politics, that I dread the event in matters of religion. Still I would be no advocate for timidity, much less for anything like equivocation or evasion; and it must be confessed that prudence often degenerates into these vices.

I remain, dear Sir, with the greatest esteem,
Yours affectionately,
W. WELLS, JUN.

To the Rev. Thomas Belsham.

No. XI.

From the Rev. Thomas Fyshe Palmer to Mr. Lindsey, giving some account of his treatment on board the Surprise transport.

N. S. Wales, Sydney, Sept. 15, 1795.

My dear Sir,

It was with inexpressible pleasure that I again saw your hand-writing; receiving your letter and parcel of books safe, for which I am much obliged to you. I long to read with attention the Commentary on the Revelation, which I believe will nearly (from a hasty glimpse of it) meet my own ideas. I am happy to find that my edition of Elwall is in the hands of a person who will give them away; it was printed for that very purpose, nor must I allow your kind partiality to frustrate it.

I must begin with telling you that we have all enjoyed uninterrupted health, excepting that, landing with weak eyes and using them very much at the time, the common malady of the climate has ever since grievously affected them, so that I have been obliged to give over reading and writing. But they are now considerably better.

By this time you will, I imagine, have received the dismal nar-

rative of my sufferings on board the Surprise; the master of which
accused me and Mr. Skirving of hiring people to murder him and
the principal officers. He pitched on some unhappy people as
our associates, and what he made them and us endure is hardly
to be credited. It must have been more than human help which
supported me. One week of it at any other time would have despatched me. In the torrid zone when I could not bear the cover-
ing of my shirt, Mr. Skirving and I were shut up in a box six
feet square, and not suffered to pass the threshold. At night, as
a vast indulgence, we were separated, and I laid in a bed not merely
wet but soaked through with salt water and rain, which my tyrant
would not permit me or my friends to dry. The pretended associates were much worse treated; every cruelty and every artifice
were employed to make them accuse us. They were flogged, and
illegally reduced to half allowance. They were loaded with sixty
pounds' weight of irons, and all chained to an iron bar and exposed
on the poop all weather, in that dreadful temperature. When I
landed, six or seven people went voluntarily to a magistrate, and
swore that C. offered them great rewards if they would swear that
I and Mr. Skirving hired them to murder him and the principal
officers, that he held a pistol in his hand and threatened to shoot
some if they did not, and to treat them as we traitors were. The
whole of this I have entrusted to Mr. White, principal surgeon of
the settlement, who went home in the Dædalus in December last.
I believe I should have fallen before my inhuman tyrant, had it
not been for the courageous and active friendship of James Ellis
and Mr. Boston, the young man I wrote to you about, and his
wife. They were threatened with irons, even Mrs. Boston; and
when Mr. Boston landed, C. blasted all his prospects by accusing
him of Jacobinism and drinking destruction to the K——. This
last was proved to be an infamous falsehood. They gave another
signal proof of their friendship. Somehow or other their knowledge of the arts was spread abroad at Rio de Janeiro, and the
Viceroy paid them every attention, kept a splendid table for them,
had a man of rank to attend them, set them to work, and, when
convinced of their ability, offered them any sum to set up in business, and £300 per annum each to settle at Rio. They firmly
rejected the offer (though both were without a shilling), and every
solicitation made use of for their compliance, as it was their firm
belief that C. would have murdered me in their absence. After
such kindness it followed of course that we lived together, and

that they shared what I had. It was fortunate for them that I had something left from the plunder of C. and his crew. The destructive and oppressive monopoly of the military officers forbad every one to purchase of the ships that came to this harbour. The military officers alone bought, and resold to all the colony at 1,000 per cent. profit, and often more. They firmly, but in guarded language, insisted on the rights of British subjects to carry on any trade, not prohibited, in one of His Majesty's harbours. This irritated the whole governing despotic power of the settlement against them. They were refused a grant, servants, and never employed, though, by making salt and curing fish, they could have saved the colony from a famine. Where everything is so immensely dear, you may guess that it has laid heavy on me; but my money could not have been so well employed. The worst is over. They manufacture beer, vinegar, salt, soap, &c., for sale. I have a farm. But, above all, Governor Hunter, who is, I hear from all hands, a good man, and their friend, has arrived, and the despotism and infamous monopolies of the last government are no more.

The clergyman here, Mr. Johnson, is a most dutiful son of the Church of England, thinking it to be the best constituted church in the world. He is a Moravian Methodist, and was bred, I believe, at Magdalen, Cambridge. I believe him to be a very good, pious, inoffensive man. None of our household ever have heard him, though I confess I could have heard him yesterday with pleasure. It was the first Sunday after Governor Hunter's arrival. He exposed the last government, their extortion, their despotism, their debauchery and ruin of the colony, driving it almost to famine by the sale of liquors at 1,200 per cent. profit. He congratulated the colony at the abolition of a military government, and the restoration of a civil one, and of the laws. Orders are this day, Tuesday, given out that no officer shall sell any more liquor.

I rejoice to hear of the safety, the care, and the reception of Dr. Priestley, and the door of usefulness opened to him in America.

I have sealed up my letter to Mr. Rutt. I must therefore desire you to get our mutual friend Dyer to tell him that I have received his letter of June 23rd, and the parcel of newspapers and pamphlets, and especially the highly interesting (to us) Reports of the Secret Committee, sent to the care of Mr. Johnson. He must tell him that I am overwhelmed with his goodness, and only fear that I shall not show myself sufficiently deserving of it. He must know that Mr. Muir lives with me, and that he, Skirving, and I live in great cordiality; our houses at Sydney are contiguous, as also our farms in the country.

I have written by every conveyance, and by the last to Dr. Disney, to whom and Mrs. Disney I must beg to be particularly remembered. Mrs. Lindsey will accept of my best regard; her spectacles often recall her to my mind.

Farewell, dear Sir. I hope it is reserved for me to see you again in this state; and I earnestly pray never to be separated from you in the next.

I am your affectionate and obliged
Thos. Fyshe Palmer.

To the Rev. Mr. Lindsey,
  Essex Street, London.

No. XII.

Select Extracts from the Letters of Dr. Priestley to Mr. Lindsey, and from Thomas Jefferson, Esq., President of the United States, to Dr. Priestley.

FROM DR. PRIESTLEY.

Birmingham, Aug. 26, 1789.

The Archdeacon had indeed an euthanasia, and I find his friend the Bishop of Carlisle died about the same time, and at about the same age. They have been useful men in their day, and you justly observe none are without their failings, and least of all great minds. This I see confirmed, and I am sorry to see it so much so, in Beausobre's History of the Reformation, which I have read through with peculiar satisfaction. Luther had great defects indeed, and of a very disagreeable kind; especially envy, and dislike of other reformers. He wished all to follow him, and was angry if they went one step farther. His behaviour to Carlostadt and Zuinglius, &c., is inexcusable. But he had great and good qualities notwithstanding, and would, I doubt not, have been an intrepid martyr. Beausobre is far more satisfactory than Sleidan, but I am sorry that he goes no farther than the year 1530. He certainly meant to have written more. The last volume is particularly interesting.

. . . . . .

In a letter from Mr. Palmer in Scotland, you will see that he corresponds with Mr. Robinson, of Cambridge, as an avowed Unitarian. But he ought to make a public declaration after what he has written. . . . .

FROM THE SAME.

Birmingham, Oct. 3, 1789.

At my return I found a letter from Mr. Tayleur, with a bill of 150 pounds for the expenses of my Ecclesiastical History. I told him I apprehended it would be considerably too much, and that I should consult with you, and did not doubt we should dispose of the overplus to his satisfaction. I send you the letter and bill, which I wish you would put into the hands of Mr. Chambers, who, as usual, will give a receipt, and allow interest for it. How unboundedly generous Mr. Tayleur is! I may well afford to give my books, when they are paid for beforehand. Before I took my journey, I ordered 25 copies of my History of Early Opinions to be sent to you. I am told they were immediately sent by a waggon that goes to the Castle and Falcon, Aldersgate Street. You say nothing about the parcel, and therefore it has not been delivered. I am really desirous of giving a great part of the impression. I cannot consider them as my property, and only wish to place them where they may be of the most use.

You will be pleased to be informed that at Manchester I met with two Unitarian street-preachers, men of good sense and great zeal, who had read hardly anything besides the Bible, nothing of mine or yours. They are Baptists, and 14 in number; not more than two months' standing. One of them had been in Mr. Wesley's connection. As they had hired a building for their meetings in the winter, and were at expense in travelling to preach in the neighbouring towns, &c., I gave them five guineas. They are all working men. I was exceedingly pleased with their conversation. They told me of another society of the same kind in York of 60 members; and others are forming in different places. Young Mr. Toulmin was with me, and gave them some of my small pieces; and I promised to send them other books. The name of one of them was John Laycock, and the other —— Burton. Two others of their friends were also preachers. They spake with great fluency and propriety. . . . .

Birmingham, May 24, 1790.

I greatly admire Mr. ——'s spirit and zeal, but I cannot approve of his plan. Neither Christianity nor the Reformation was carried on in that way, but more silently and naturally, like the growth of corn, to which our Saviour compared the former. So ostentatious a method of proceeding would engage our opponents in similar measures, and excite a spirit of party, which is hostile to free inquiry. Besides, the relief of sufferers, publicly held out, would draw endless claimants, to whom no satisfaction could be given. Assistance in particular and well-known cases may still be given, books may be distributed, and lay preachers, who want but little money, may be encouraged, without making much noise. The very apparatus and correspondence necessary for such a scheme as Mr. ——'s would alone be very expensive, and the same money may be much better employed. . . . .

Birmingham, June 11, 1790.

Dear Friend,

We have had a melancholy scene here since I wrote last. Mr. Robinson, who preached our charity sermon on Sunday last, was found dead in his bed on Wednesday morning at Mr. Russell's. He was much enfeebled in body and mind, but had been bent on taking the journey, and exerting himself to the utmost. His disorder the physicians call *angina pectoris.* Two nights he was with me, and on Monday evening he had a fit, from which I thought he would hardly have recovered. However, he was much better the next day, when he dined with Mr. Hawkes, and after dinner was in remarkably good spirits, and entertained us with many stories and anecdotes. He ate a hearty supper, and went to bed seemingly in good health; but it was evident that he had another fit soon after he went to bed, and that he expired in it, for he was almost cold at nine o'clock the next morning.

He was by no means fit to preach; and though he was not at a loss for words, he rambled into many things quite foreign to the subject, dwelling much on Unitarianism at both meetings, though they were different sermons. He used no notes. I have composed a sermon on the occasion of his death, which I shall preach next

Sunday. We expect letters or messengers from Cambridge, but expect to bury him here.

I am very glad that you propose to omit the Creed, and to make a discourse on the occasion. Your example will give a sanction to the-measure everywhere else. Mr. Robinson said he never felt so sensible a relief to his mind as when he read what I published on the Miraculous Conception. He had always doubted the story, but never ventured to mention his suspicion to anybody.

He was correcting some of the last sheets of his History of Baptism, which I dare say will be a curious and valuable work.

Yours and Mrs. Lindsey's most affectionately,

J. Priestley.

FROM THE SAME.

Birmingham, June 24, 1790.

Dear Friend,

You will see by the enclosed that I will not publish the Sermon till I hear from the family. I beg therefore that you would take back those I sent you, or take the trouble to deliver the alterations I may have occasion to make in it.

It is evident that Mr. Robinson, though an Unitarian, did not wish to incur the *odium* of it with all his old friends.

I want to know how Mr. Dodson goes on with his translation of the Prophets. I stick close to my part, and hope to have finished all that is essential before you come, at the end of the next month, or the middle of it. I do a certain quantity per day. We must make a point of despatching the whole this year. I shall see Mr. B., and talk to him about his part. I shall also write to Mr. F., and give him any help that he may want. My method is to paste paper to the margin of a quarto Bible, and make the alterations there. This I think better, on every account, than to write the whole, and especially much easier to those who examine it.

Yours and Mrs. Lindsey's most affectionately,

J. Priestley.

FROM THE SAME.

Birmingham, June 26, 1790.

I send you with this a few copies of my Sermon for Mr. Robinson, to be disposed of as presents to whom you please. Do not forget Mr. Radcliffe. None will be sold in London or

Cambridge till it has been seen by the family, and they allow the account given of Mr. Robinson. There can be no doubt of his change of sentiment, whether it should appear in his writings or not. He had been a cautious man, and forbore to announce his change of opinion to his congregation; but I hope he never deceived them. The letter in the preface is Mr. C.'s, his son-in-law, the same that called upon you. There was, however, something I cannot account for with respect to his former opinion of the divinity of Christ, unless he held the indwelling scheme. For he said in my hearing, he always thought the doctrine of the Trinity an absurdity. On this supposition, however, I cannot vindicate his writing that book. I hear he was uncommonly eager to read your reply. It was brought by Mr. C. before your present of it arrived, and he sat up all night to read it, and was much agitated by it. He was also more affected than he ought to have been by the reception he met with among his old friends after his change of opinion was known. When Mr. Hobson, who was an old acquaintance of his, first saw him, he said, "They have killed me;" and he complained to me, that among all his former friends in London he had only two subscribers to his book. He had no doubt been too fond of popularity, which is too often the case with those who have the power of being so. However, his well-known change of sentiment cannot fail to have a considerable effect.

FROM THE SAME.

Birmingham, July 6, 1790.

Mr. Robinson certainly died a natural death, but not so I believe Mr. Silas Deane. Mr. W. Wilkinson says he always talked of taking laudanum in extremity, and doubts not but he did it. He had the greatest aversion to going to America with less honour than he left it; and though he had nothing to fear, he was poor, and would have been overlooked. He had lived a very licentious life at Paris: but Mr. Wilkinson says he spent almost all he was worth to purchase arms for the Americans, and was never repaid.

FROM THE SAME.

Birmingham, July 22, 1790.

If you see Mr. Dodson, tell him it will by no means do to reprint either Blayney or Bishop Newcome, as we must keep much nearer to the phraseology of the present version than they do. We must content ourselves with departing from it only for the sake of some real improvement. I have now gone once through the Psalms and Proverbs, and I will undertake Daniel and the Minor Prophets, if he will do Jeremiah and Ezekiel. Or, as I have more than six months before me, and I am determined to make this my principal business, I can very well do the whole; and if you think so, you need not say anything to him; or tell him that I shall undertake it if he has not leisure, or that he may take what he pleases, and leave me the rest. I fear some quaintness in his style, and we must avoid everything of the kind, as we shall be laughed at.

LETTERS FROM DR. PRIESTLEY TO MR. LINDSEY SOON AFTER HIS ARRIVAL IN AMERICA.

No. 1.

New York, June 15, 1794.

Dear Friend,

We have now been here near a fortnight, and I begin to expect to hear from you, which is the greatest satisfaction that I expect in this country. But I sometimes think that everything here is so promising, and everything with you so threatening, that perhaps even you and Mrs. Lindsey may be induced to end your days with us. To accomplish this, I should at any time come over and fetch you. Indeed, the difference between the aspect of things here and with you is not to be expressed. I feel as if I were in another world. I never before could conceive how satisfactory it is to have the feeling I now have from a sense of perfect security and liberty, all men having equal rights and privileges, and speaking and acting as if they were sensible of it. Here are no beggars to be seen, and families are easily maintained by any kind of labour; and whether it be the effect of general liberty, or some other cause, I find many more clever men, men capable of conversing with propriety and fluency on all subjects relating to government, than I have met with anywhere in England. I have seen many of the members of Congress on their return from it, and, without exception, they seem to be men of first-rate ability, though some of them plain in their manners. With respect to myself, the difference is great indeed. In England I was an object of the greatest aversion to every person connected with government; whereas here they are those who show me the most respect. With you the Episcopal Church is above everything. In this city it makes a decent figure, but the Presbyterians are much above them, and the Governor (Clinton), who is particularly attentive to me, goes to the meeting-house.

But the preachers, though all civil to me, look upon me with dread, and none of them have asked me to preach in their pulpits. This, however, does them no good. Several persons express a wish to hear me, and are ashamed of the illiberality of the preachers, and some are avowed Unitarians; so that I am fully persuaded an Unitarian minister, of prudence and good sense, might do very well here. If I were here a Sunday or two more I would make a beginning, and I intend to return for this purpose. The greatest difficulty arises from the indifference of liberal-minded men as to religion in general; they are so much occupied with commerce and politics. One man of proper spirit would be sufficient to establish a solid Unitarian interest; and I am persuaded it will soon be done. As I am much attended to, and my writings, which are in a manner unknown here, begin to be inquired after, I will get my small pamphlets immediately printed here; and wherever I can get an invitation to preach I will go. With this view I shall carefully avoid all the party politics of the country, and have no other object besides religion and philosophy. Philadelphia will be a more favourable situation than this, and there I shall make a beginning. It will be better, however, to wait a little time, and not show much zeal at the first; and as my coming here is much talked of, I shall reprint my Fast and Farewell Sermons.

As it may serve to amuse you and Mrs. Lindsey, I will enclose copies of some Addresses, and my answers; and also some letters from persons who are of a party opposite to the addressers, but equally friendly to me; and I find I have given as much satisfaction to them by the caution I have observed in my answers, as to the addressers, who, however, I believe, are now well satisfied that I do not openly join any of their societies, though at first I am informed they were very desirous of it. The parties are the Federalists and Anti-federalists: the former meaning the friends of the present system, with a leaning to that of England, and friendship with her.; the latter wishing for some improvements, leaning to the French system, and rather wishing for war. With a little more irritation the latter will certainly prevail. They are now, I believe, by far the most numerous, especially in the country, though the other prevail in the towns, especially here. The people of Vermont on the one hand, and those of Kentucky on the other, can hardly be restrained from falling on the English and Spanish settlements, and the latter particularly seem disposed to break off from the Union rather than not have their way.

The exchange is so greatly in favour of the drawer (near nine per cent.) that I am drawing for most of my money in England. On Mr. Chambers I have drawn for £300, which is very nearly what I have in his hands, and I have told him that the small difference on either side he may settle with you. On Mr. Johnson I have drawn for £50. I wish you would mention this to them, lest the letters miscarry.

As Dr. Disney desired me to write to him, and I had a parcel to deliver for him to Bishop Prevost, I inclose the letter for him in this packet to you. I have also written to Mr. Belsham, whom I hope, some time or other, to draw hither. He will tell you my scheme. But as I am going to Philadelphia, I shall soon know more on the subject.

I was never more mortified than I now am at not having with me any of my small tracts in defence of the divine unity, as my being here leads many persons to wish to read what I have written on the subject. If Mr. Johnson has not sent the box of books (chiefly my own publications) that he was to forward to Philadelphia, desire him to do it the first opportunity. I shall reprint them, and I flatter myself they will produce a considerable effect. Indeed my coming hither promises to be of much more service to our cause than I had imagined. But time is necessary, and I am apt to be too precipitate. I want your cool judgment. You waited patiently a long time in London; but what an abundant harvest have you had there!

Nothing can be more delightful than the weather is here at present, and I do not think the climate will be at all too hot for

B B

me. I have only two days more to stay here : to-day I dine with
Mr. Bridges, a friend of Mr. Kemble's, and to-morrow with
General Gates, whom I have seen often, and like very much. I
have met him frequently, and he is particularly attentive to me,
and was so to my son before I came.

With my best respects to Mrs. Rayner and all friends, in
which my wife joins,

I am, dear friend,

Yours and Mrs. Lindsey's most affectionately,

J. PRIESTLEY.

P.S. When you have done with the Addresses, &c. please to
forward them to Mr. J. Wilkinson by his banker, Sir B. Hammet

No. 2.

Philadelphia, June 24, 1794.

Dear Friend,

This is my third letter to you. The last was by the Hope,
from New York. On Thursday last I arrived at this place. Our
journey was very pleasant, and the aspect of the country better
than I expected. This city is by no means so agreeable as New
York ; but, upon the whole, more eligible than any other for my
residence till our settlement be ready for me. With respect to
religion, things are exactly in the same state here as in New York.
Nobody asks me to preach, and I hear there is much jealousy and
dread of me ; and on the whole I am not sorry for the circumstance, as it offends many who have, on this account, the greater
desire to hear me ; so that I have little doubt but that I shall
form a respectable Unitarian society in this place. The alarm of
the danger of Unitarianism has been sounded so long that it has
ceased to be terrific to many; and I stand so well with the country
in other respects that I dare say I shall have a fair and candid
hearing; and at my return from the Susquehannah, where I propose to go the next week, I believe some place will be prepared for
me. In the meantime I am printing an edition of my Appeal
and Trial of Elwall, which will be ready, I am told, by the next
Monday. Part of the impression will be sent to New York, where
things are in as great forwardness as here. If I do not greatly
deceive myself, I see a great harvest opening upon me ; and there
is room for many labourers, but it will require great prudence and
judgment at first. Also, those that come must not be discouraged

at first appearances, and be able to support themselves, and at a greater expense than would be necessary in England; and in New York or here, greater than in London itself. This unexpected expense makes a great proportion of the emigrants repent of their coming, the women especially, who do not easily find any society. Notwithstanding the flattering attention that is paid to me, I cannot help sometimes regretting the society I had in England. But I am fully satisfied that I did right to leave it, and I firmly believe that much good will be done here by my removal, and in this I rejoice.

My wife will find much more difficulty than myself. All people complain of the difficulty of getting tolerable servants, and we find we acted unwisely in bringing any. The woman, for whose passage we paid twelve guineas, behaved in such a manner that my wife dismissed her the first week; and the boy, for whose passage we paid the same, and at least ten pounds in fitting out, is run away, and for anything that we yet know, may have carried many things with him. We shall know more before night, when we shall examine the things that came from New York.

The boy is since found; he had taken nothing; but as he was bent on going to sea we have let him go.

I have seen Mr. P., who made a genteel appearance, and gave good reasons for his wife not having heard from him. He had written: his passage was uncommonly long and unfortunate; and then an embargo was laid here on all shipping for England.

I fear, too, that when this was heard of with you, an embargo would also be laid on ships going from England to America, and that this may be the reason why we have not yet heard from any body, and indeed have had no news of any kind from England. We must have patience; but we are very anxious to hear what passes on the continent of Europe. Here, both the Indians and the English are making encroachments; and if orders from England do not stop these proceedings, a war will be inevitable; and people in the back settlements are so eager for it that they can hardly be restrained even now.

Since I wrote the former part of this letter I have almost determined to make my residence in Northumberland, and spend a few months of the winter in this city. This will on many accounts be better than living chiefly here. The expense will be prodigiously less; I shall have more leisure for all my pursuits, and I shall be, on the whole, of as much use in propagating Unitarianism as if I resided constantly in the town. I see so great a certainty of planting Unitarianism on this continent, that I wish you and Mr. Belsham would be looking out for proper persons to establish in New York and Philadelphia, and also to supply the College, which you may take for granted will be established at the place of my residence. A place of worship is building here by a society who call themselves Universalists : they propose to leave it open to any sect of Christians three days in the week, but they want money to finish it. My friends think to furnish them with money, and engage the use of it for Sunday mornings. The society itself, I hear, intend to apply to me to open it; which I shall gladly do. A person with a proper spirit and prudence may do great things here. Mr. H. was the most imprudent of men, and did apparently much harm here; but eventually even that may be for the best. I find I have great advantages, and I hope to make a good use of them.

I shall enclose an address to me from the Philosophical Society in this place, which is the only one that I have received; and also the Preface to the American edition of my Appeal. Thompson is here, and superintends the office where it is printed. He will soon set up for himself.

With all our respects,

Yours and Mr. Lindsey's most affectionately,

J. PRIESTLEY.

A LETTER FROM THOMAS JEFFERSON, ESQ., PRESIDENT OF THE UNITED STATES, TO DR. PRIESTLEY, SOON AFTER HIS ELEC-TION TO THAT HIGH OFFICE.

Washington, March 21, 1801.

Dear Sir,

I learnt some time ago that you were in Philadelphia, but that it was only for a fortnight, and supposed you were gone. It was not till yesterday I received information that you were still there; had been very ill, but were on the recovery. I sincerely rejoice that you are so. Yours is one of the few lives precious to mankind, and for the continuance of which every thinking man must be solicitous; bigots may be an exception. What an effort, my dear sir, of bigotry in politics and religion have we gone through ! The barbarians really flattered themselves they should be able to bring back the times of Vandalism, when ignorance put everything into the hands of power and priestcraft. All advances in science were proscribed as innovations; they pretended to praise and encourage education, but it was to be the education of our ancestors; we were to look backwards, not forwards, for improvement; the President himself declaring in one of his answers to addresses, that we were never to expect to go beyond them in real science. This was the real ground of all the attacks upon you; those who live by mystery and charlatanerie, fearing you would render them useless by simplifying the Christian philosophy, the most sublime and benevolent, but the most perverted system that ever shone on man, endeavoured to crush your well-earned and well-deserved fame; but it was the Lilliputians upon Gulliver. Our countrymen have recovered from the alarm into which art and industry had thrown them; science and honesty are replaced on their high ground; and you, my dear sir, as their great apostle, are on its pinnacle. It is with heartfelt satisfaction, that in the first moments of my public action I can hail you with welcome to our land, tender you the homage of its respect and esteem, cover you under the protection of those laws which were made for the wise and the good, like you, and disclaim the legitimacy of that libel on legislation, which, under the form of a law, was for some time placed among them. As the storm is now subsiding, and the horizon becoming serene, it is pleasant to consider the phenomenon with attention. We can no longer say there is nothing new under the sun; for this whole chapter in the history of man is new; the great extent of our Republic is new; its sparse habitation is new; the mighty wave of public opinion, whic hhas rolled over it, is new; but the most pleasing novelty is its so quickly subsiding, over such an extent of surface, to its true level again. The order and good sense displayed in this recovery from delusion, and in the momentous crisis which lately arose, really bespeak a strength of character in our nation which augurs well for the duration of our Republic. And I am much better satisfied now of its stability, than I was before it was tried. I have been, above all things, solaced by the prospect which opened on us in the event of a non-election of a President;* in which case the federal government would have been in the situation of a clock or watch run down: there was no idea of force, nor of any occasion for it. A Convention,

* The votes of the Senate were for some time equally divided between Mr. Jefferson and Mr. Burr.

invited by the Republican members of Congress, with the virtual President and Vice-President, would have been on the ground in eight weeks, would have repaired the constitution where it was defective, and wound it up again. This peaceable and legitimate resource to which we are in the habit of implicit obedience, super-seding all appeal to force, and being always within our reach, shews a precious principle of self-preservation in our composition, till a change of circumstances shall take place, which is not within prospect at any definite period. But I have got into a long disquisition on politics, when I only meant to express my sympathy in the state of your health, and to tender you all the affections of public and private hospitality. I should be very happy indeed to see you here. I leave this about the 30th instant, to return about the 25th of April; if you do not leave Philadelphia before that, a little excursion hither would help your health. I should be much gratified with the possession of a guest I so much esteem, and should claim a right to lodge you, should you make such an excursion. Accept the homage of my high consideration and respect, and assurances of affectionate attachment.

THOMAS JEFFERSON.

FROM DR. PRIESTLEY TO MR. LINDSEY.

Northumberland, April 15, 1803.

Dear Friend,

I am happy to hear by Mr. B. that your health is still good; and as his letter is dated the 1st of February, I hope you have got well over the winter. There is hardly anything that I wish for, or think of, more than the continuance of your life and health, that you may see the last of my labours, and I may hear your opinion of them. On this I have always laid more stress than on that of all the world besides; and if you die before me, I shall lose one of my most powerful stimuluses to exertion. As to philosophy, I do not now give much attention to it, though I do not wholly neglect it. With the good Dr. Heberden, Sir John Pringle, and many others, who in early life engaged in philosophical pursuits, but were real Christians, I think it natural as we draw nearer to a future and better world to think more of it, and to have our reading and pursuits directed more than ever towards it.

For the same reason I think more of my departed friends, Mrs. Rayner, Dr. Price, Dr. Jebb, and others who have been my chief friends and benefactors, than before; forming conjectures (wild ones no doubt) concerning our meeting and employment hereafter. Such speculations as these have at least the effect to make the thoughts of leaving the world, and our friends in it, less unpleasant, indeed sometimes almost desirable. If the disciples of Jesus rejoiced so much at his resurrection, what will they do at his second coming, in his proper kingdom, and when all their friends will rise again, never to be separated any more? And the firm faith that you and I have that even the wicked, after a state of wholesome discipline (and that not more severe than will be necessary) will be raised, in due time, to a state of happiness, greatly diminishes our concern on their account.

Such reflections as these occur to me more particularly when I am not well, and my thoughts are less occupied with my pursuits. But though I had a pretty long relapse of bad health after my last to you, when I thought myself quite well, and to have recovered my usual good state of health, I am now again, I thank God, pretty well, and nearly as busy as formerly.

Since I wrote the above I have received a letter from Mr. Jefferson, on the subject of my pamphlet about Socrates, which I will copy, and send it you the next post. I wish I could send you all his letters; but they are rather too long to copy, and a specimen or two may be sufficient.

Yours and Mrs. Lindsey's most affectionately,

J. PRIESTLEY.

FROM THOMAS JEFFERSON, ESQ., PRESIDENT OF THE UNITED STATES, TO DR. PRIESTLEY, UPON HIS "COMPARATIVE VIEW OF SOCRATES AND JESUS."

Washington, April 9, 1803.

Dear Sir,

While on a short visit lately to Monticello, I received from you a copy of your Comparative View of Socrates and Jesus, and I avail myself of the first moment of leisure after my return to acknowledge the pleasure I had in the perusal, and the desire it excited to see you take up the subject on a more extensive scale. In consequence of some conversations with Dr. Rush in the years

1798-99, I had promised some day to write him a letter, giving him my view of the Christian system. I have reflected often on it since, and even sketched the outlines in my own mind. I should first take a general view of the moral doctrines of the most remarkable of the ancient philosophers, of whose ethics we have sufficient information to make an estimate: say, of Pythagoras, Epicurus, Epictetus, Socrates, Cicero, Seneca, Antoninus. I should do justice to the branches of morality they have treated well, but point out the importance of those in which they are deficient. I should then take a view of the Deism and ethics of the Jews, and show in what a degraded state they were, and the necessity they presented of a reformation. I should proceed to a view of the life, character, and doctrines of Jesus, who, sensible of the incorrectness of their ideas of the Deity, and of morality, endeavoured to bring them to the principles of a pure Deism, and juster notions of the attributes of God; to reform their moral doctrines to the standard of reason, justice, and philanthropy, and to inculcate the belief of a future state. This view would purposely omit the question of his divinity, and even of his inspiration. To do him justice, it would be necessary to remark the disadvantages his doctrines have to encounter, not having been committed to writing by himself, but by the most unlettered of men, by memory, long after they had heard them from him, when much was forgotten, much misunderstood, and presented in very paradoxical shapes. Yet such are the fragments remaining, as to show a master-workman, and that his system of morality was the most benevolent and sublime probably that has been ever taught, and more perfect than those of any of the ancient philosophers. His character and doctrines have received still greater injury from those who pretend to be his special disciples, and who have disfigured and sophisticated his actions and precepts from views of personal interest, so as to induce the unthinking part of mankind to throw off the whole system in disgust, and to pass sentence as an impostor on the most innocent, the most benevolent, the most eloquent and sublime character that has ever been exhibited to man. This is the outline; but I have not the time, and still less the information, which the subject needs. It will therefore rest with me in contemplation only. You are the person who of all others would do it best, and most promptly: you have all the materials at hand; and you put together with ease. I wish you could be induced to extend your late work to the whole subject. I have not heard particularly what is the state of your health ; but as it has been equal to the journey to Philadelphia, perhaps it might encourage the curiosity you must feel to see, for once, this place, which nature has formed on a beautiful scale, and circumstances destined for a great one : as yet we are but a cluster of villages. We cannot offer you the learned society of Philadelphia, but you will have that of a few characters whom you esteem, and a bed and hearty welcome with one who will rejoice in every opportunity of testifying to you his high veneration and affectionate attachment.

Th. Jefferson.

Dr. Joseph Priestley.

FROM DR. PRIESTLEY TO MR. LINDSEY, CONTAINING REMARKS UPON MR. JEFFERSON'S LETTER.

Northumberland, April 23, 1803.

Dear Friend,

In my last I promised to send you a copy of Mr. Jefferson's letter on reading my pamphlet entitled " Socrates and Jesus compared." The above is that copy. He is generally considered as an unbeliever : if so, however, he cannot be far from us, and I hope in the way to be not only almost, but altogether what we are. He now attends public worship very regularly, and his moral conduct was never impeached. I should, on several accounts, be glad to make the visit he proposes, but my business will not admit of it. If I leave this place, either the printing of my works must be intermitted, or I must request the aid of Mr. C., which I am not fond of doing; and though he does his best, I find he has not been sufficiently used to the work.

DR. PRIESTLEY'S LAST LETTERS TO MR. LINDSEY, WRITTEN A FEW WEEKS BEFORE HIS DECEASE.

No. 1.

Northumberland, Nov. 4, 1803.

Dear Friend,

I cannot now expect to hear often from you, but I shall write as usual, as long as you or Mrs. Lindsey are living, provided I be living myself. But my health is such that I really do not expect to survive you. I have now, of several mouths, the same feelings that I had when I formerly had gall-stones; but at the same time I had a difficulty in swallowing, which, as it varied, and sometimes disappeared, I hoped was nothing but a spasm in the œsophagus, near the entrance into the stomach; but it is now constant, and it is painful to me to swallow anything; and if I do not eat very slow, all that is in the œsophagus comes up; and not only that, but it fills again from the stomach, and this operation continues until the stomach is entirely empty. My guard against this is eating very slowly. For the last three months I have not been able to eat any flesh meat. I live on broth and vegetables, besides milk and mild cheese; but I take even these with difficulty. I am thankful, however, that excepting while I eat, I have but little pain, though while I had gall-stones I had a good deal of pain, and sometimes very acute. The first symptom of this disorder I had about a year ago, but sometimes I had nothing of it. Of late, however, it has increased very much. But I have abundant reasons to be satisfied with life, and the goodness of God in it. Few have had so happy a lot as I have had, and I now see reason to be thankful for events which at the time were the most afflicting.

As to my daughter, I cannot grieve on her account. She had nothing before her in this life but a prospect of increasing trouble, and I hope soon to meet her in more favourable circumstances. I am only concerned about the children, and I do not know what can be done for them. My only source of satisfaction, and it is a never-failing one, is my firm persuasion that every thing, and our oversights and mistakes among the rest, are parts of the great plan, in which every thing in time will appear to have been ordered and conducted in the best manner. When I hear my son's children crying, I consider that we who are advanced in life are but children ourselves, and as little judges of what is good for ourselves or others.

As you were pleased with my comparison of Socrates and Jesus, I have begun to carry the same comparison to all the heathen moralists, and I have all the books that I want for the purpose, except Simplicius and Arrian on Epictetus, and them I hope to get from a library in Philadelphia : lest, however, I should fail there, I wish you or Mr. Belsham would procure and send them from London. While I am capable of any thing I cannot

be idle, and I do not know that I can do anything better. This, too, is an undertaking that Mr. Jefferson recommends to me.
With every good wish, I am
Yours and Mrs. Lindsey's most affectionately,
J. PRIESTLEY.

No. 2.

Northumberland, Dec. 19, 1803.

Dear Sir,

I am once more made happy by the receipt of yours of the 9th of September. I value your letters more than gold, but I am sensible it is unreasonable to expect them from you, difficult as it must now be to you to write. But a single line will suffice.

I thank God I begin to recover from an illness which has been very near carrying me off. It was ill understood by our physicians at first, and their prescriptions did me harm; but now I hope I am in a good way, though exceedingly weak, and my feet and ancles much swelled from that cause. I live now almost altogether on animal food, which I was used to think would never agree with me; but still I cannot eat any fibrous flesh meat, only the gelatinous parts, such as calves' feet; and for some days past I have eat nothing but oysters, which agree with me better than anything else. On this, or soup or broth, with a dish of tea, I live altogether. But by this means I am so much recovered, that I hope soon to be able to eat as I used to do. I should not, however tire you with my complaints; but this encourages me to hope that I may live a few years longer, so as to finish the work I am printing and composing, which is my utmost wish.

With the work that I am now composing I go on much faster and better than I expected; so that in two or three months, if my health continue as it now is, I hope to have it ready for the press; though I shall hardly proceed to print it till we have dispatched the Notes. It is upon the same plan with that of "Socrates and Jesus compared," considering all the more distinguished of the Grecian sects of philosophy, till the establishment of Christianity in the Roman empire. If you liked that pamphlet, I flatter myself you will like this. I hope it is calculated to show, in a peculiarly striking light, the great advantage of revelation, and that it will make an impression on candid unbelievers, if they will read.

But I find few that will trouble themselves to read anything on the subject; which, considering the great magnitude and interesting nature of the subject, is a proof of a very improper state of mind, unworthy of a rational being.

The next thing I wish to do is to assist in the publication of a whole Bible from the several new translations of particular books, smoothing and correcting them where I can. I shall propose it to some of our booksellers, cheerfully giving my own labour to so useful a work. If anything remain of the subscription to my present publication, I shall spend it on others, particularly on the Alphabetical Index to the Bible, which has been some time completely ready for the press.

I wish this may come safely to your hands; but I dread the approaching contest, which may throw every thing into confusion. It has probably taken place before this time. But there is a sovereign ruler, and he, we cannot doubt, will bring good out of all evil.

The excellent character and behaviour of my daughter is a great consolation to me in the thoughts of her death.

Hoping still to have the great satisfaction of hearing from you a few times more, I am

Yours and Mrs. Lindsey's most affectionately,

J. PRIESTLEY.

No. 3.

Northumberland, Jan. 16, 1804.

Dear Friend,

Having just received a box of books from Mr. Johnson, after I had given up all expectation of them, I beg you would make an apology for the impatience I expressed about them, and my dissatisfaction with respect to his conduct. In my situation such books are invaluable, especially as my deafness confines me in a manner at home, and my extreme weakness prevents my making any excursions. Winter also keeps me from my laboratory, so that reading and composing are my sole occupation and amusement. Here, too, I have not the convenience of borrowing books.

This situation, however, is not without its advantages. I have abundant leisure, and I have endeavoured to make the most of it. I have now finished and transcribed for the press my Comparison of the Principles of the Grecian Philosophers with those of Revelation, and with more ease, and more to my own satisfaction, than I expected. They who liked my pamphlet entitled " Socrates and Jesus compared" will not, I flatter myself, dislike this work. It has the same object, and completes the scheme. It has increased my own sense of the unspeakable value of revelation, and must, I think, that of every person who will give due attention to the subject.

We are all anxious to hear the result of the threatened invasion. I have some faint hopes that it will not be undertaken, at least upon England. What confusion and distress would it not occasion in the most favourable issue! God preserve you, my friend, from the general calamity! How enviable is our situation compared to yours! Our only consolation must arise from regarding the hand of God in all events, confident that the final issue will be right and good.

> Yours and Mrs. Lindsey's most affectionately,
>
> J. PRIESTLEY.

N.B. This is the last letter which Dr. Priestley wrote to his venerated and beloved friend. That truly great and excellent man, whose active spirit was incessantly engaged in devising or performing something for the interest of truth and virtue, was released from his labours and sufferings on the 4th of February following, a little more than a fortnight after writing this letter.

No. XIII.

The following is a Catalogue of Mr. Lindsey's Publications:—

1. A Farewell Address to the Parishioners of Catterick.
2. An Apology on resigning the Vicarage of Catterick.
3. A Sequel to the Apology.
4. A Sermon preached at the Opening of the Chapel in Essex Street, April 17, 1774.
5. The Book of Common Prayer Reformed for the Use of the Chapel in Essex Street, with Hymns.
6. A Sermon preached in Essex Street on Opening the New Chapel, March 29, 1778.

7. Two Dissertations. First, On the Preface to St. John's Gospel :—Secondly, On Praying to Christ.

8. The Catechist, or An Inquiry concerning the only true God, and Object of Worship.

9. An Historical View of the State of the Unitarian Doctrine and Worship.

10. *Vindiciæ Priestleianæ.* An Address to the Students of Oxford and Cambridge.

11. A Second Address to the same.

12. An Examination of Mr. Robinson's Plea for the Divinity of Christ.

13. A List of false Readings and Mistranslations of the Scriptures.

14. Conversations on Christian Idolatry.

15. A Sermon on Forms of Prayer.

16. A Sermon addressed to the Congregation in Essex Street on resigning the Pastoral Office among them.

17. Conversations on the Divine Government, showing that every thing is from God and for Good to all. 1802.

18. Sermons with appropriate Prayers annexed, 2 vols. Printed for J. Johnson and Co., St. Paul's Churchyard.

Woodfall and Kinder, Printers, Milford Lane, Strand, London, W.C.